G.A. Hen

The Lost Heir

G.A. Henty

The Lost Heir

1st Edition | ISBN: 978-3-75232-916-2

Place of Publication: Frankfurt am Main, Germany

Year of Publication: 2020

Outlook Verlag GmbH, Germany.

THE LOST HEIR

BY G. A. HENTY

CHAPTER I.

A BRAVE ACTION.

A number of soldiers were standing in the road near the bungalow of Brigadier-General Mathieson, the officer in command of the force in the cantonments of Benares and the surrounding district.

"They are coming now, I think," one sergeant said to another. "It is a bad business. They say the General is terribly hurt, and it was thought better to bring him and the other fellow who was mixed up in it down in doolies. I heard Captain Harvey say in the orderly-room that they have arranged relays of bearers every five miles all the way down. He is a good fellow is the General, and we should all miss him. He is not one of the sort who has everything comfortable himself and don't care a rap how the soldiers get on: he sees to the comfort of everyone and spends his money freely, too. He don't seem to care what he lays out in making the quarters of the married men comfortable, and in getting any amount of ice for the hospital, and extra punkawallahs in the barrack rooms during the hot season. He goes out and sees to everything himself. Why, on the march I have known him, when all the doolies were full, give up his own horse to a man who had fallen out. He has had bad luck too; lost his wife years ago by cholera, and he has got no one to care for but his girl. She was only a few months old when her mother died. Of course she was sent off to England, and has been there ever since. He must be a rich man, besides his pay and allowances; but it aint every rich man who spends his money as he does. There won't be a dry eye in the cantonment if he goes under."

"How was it the other man got hurt?"

"Well, I hear that the tiger sprang on to the General's elephant and seized him by the leg. They both went off together, and the brute shifted its hold to the shoulder, and carried him into the jungle; then the other fellow slipped off his elephant and ran after the tiger. He got badly mauled too; but he killed the brute and saved the General's life."

"By Jove! that was a plucky thing. Who was he?"

"Why, he was the chap who was walking backwards and forwards with the General when the band was playing yesterday evening. Several of the men remarked how like he was to you, Sanderson. I noticed it, too. There certainly was a strong likeness."

"Yes, some of the fellows were saying so," Sanderson replied. "He passed close to me, and I saw that he was about my height and build, but of course I did not notice the likeness; a man does not know his own face much. Anyhow, he only sees his full face, and doesn't know how he looks sideways. He is a civilian, isn't he?"

"Yes, I believe so; I know that the General is putting him up at his quarters. He has been here about a week. I think he is some man from England, traveling, I suppose, to see the world. I heard the Adjutant speak of him as Mr. Simcoe when he was talking about the affair."

"Of course they will take him to the General's bungalow?"

"No; he is going to the next. Major Walker is away on leave, and the doctor says that it is better that they should be in different bungalows, because then if one gets delirious and noisy he won't disturb the other. Dr. Hunter is going to take up his quarters there to look after him, with his own servants and a couple of hospital orderlies."

By this time several officers were gathered at the entrance to the General's bungalow, two mounted troopers having brought in the news a few minutes before that the doolies were within a mile.

They came along now, each carried by four men, maintaining a swift but smooth and steady pace, and abstaining from the monotonous chant usually kept up. A doctor was riding by the side of the doolies, and two mounted orderlies with baskets containing ice and surgical dressings rode fifty paces in the rear. The curtains of the doolies had been removed to allow of a free passage of air, and mosquito curtains hung round to prevent insects annoying the sufferers.

There was a low murmur of sympathy from the soldiers as the doolies passed them, and many a muttered "God bless you, sir, and bring you through it all right." Then, as the injured men were carried into the two bungalows, most of the soldiers strolled off, some, however, remaining near in hopes of getting a favorable report from an orderly or servant. A group of officers remained under the shade of a tree near until the surgeon who had ridden in with the doolies came out.

"What is the report, McManus?" one of them asked, as he approached.

"There is no change since I sent off my report last night," he said. "The General is very badly hurt; I certainly should not like to give an opinion at present whether he will get over it or not. If he does it will be a very narrow shave. He was insensible till we lifted him into the doolie at eight o'clock yesterday evening, when the motion seemed to rouse him a little, and he just opened his eyes; and each time we changed bearers he has had a little ice between his lips, and a drink of lime juice and water with a dash of brandy in it. He has known me each time, and whispered a word or two, asking after the other."

"And how is he?"

"I have no doubt that he will do; that is, of course, if fever does not set in badly. His wounds are not so severe as the General's, and he is a much younger man, and, as I should say, with a good constitution. If there is no complication he ought to be about again in a month's time. He is perfectly sensible. Let him lie quiet for a day or two; after that it would be as well if some of you who have met him at the General's would drop in occasionally for a short chat with him; but of course we must wait to see if there is going to be much fever."

"And did it happen as they say, doctor? The dispatch told us very little beyond the fact that the General was thrown from his elephant, just as the tiger sprang, and that it seized him and carried him into the jungle; that Simcoe slipped off his pad and ran in and attacked the tiger; that he saved the General's life and killed the animal, but is sadly hurt himself."

"That is about it, except that he did not kill the tiger. Metcalf, Colvin, and Smith all ran in, and firing together knocked it over stone dead. It was an extraordinarily plucky action of Simcoe, for he had emptied his rifle, and had nothing but it and a knife when he ran in."

"You don't say so! By Jove! that was an extraordinary act of pluck; one would almost say of madness, if he hadn't succeeded in drawing the brute off Mathieson, and so gaining time for the others to come up. It was a miracle that he wasn't killed. Well, we shall not have quite so easy a time of it for a bit. Of course Murdock, as senior officer, will take command of the brigade, but he won't be half as considerate for our comfort as Mathieson has been. He is rather a scoffer at what he calls new-fangled ways, and he will be as likely to march the men out in the heat of the day as at five in the morning."

The two sergeants who had been talking walked back together to their quarters. Both of them were on the brigade staff. Sanderson was the Paymaster's clerk, Nichol worked in the orderly-room. At the sergeants' mess the conversation naturally turned on the tiger hunt and its consequences.

"I have been in some tough fights," one of the older men said, "and I don't know that I ever felt badly scared—one hasn't time to think of that when one is at work—but to rush in against a wounded tiger with nothing but an empty gun and a hunting-knife is not the sort of job that I should like to tackle. It makes one's blood run cold to think of it. I consider that everyone in the brigade ought to subscribe a day's pay to get something to give that man, as a token of our admiration for his pluck and of our gratitude for his having saved General Mathieson's life."

There was a general expression of approval at the idea. Then Sanderson said:

"I think it is a thing that ought to be done, but it is not for us to begin it. If we hear of anything of that sort done by the officers, two or three of us might go up and say that it was the general wish among the non-coms. and men to take a share in it; but it would never do for us to begin."

"That is right enough; the officers certainly would not like such a thing to begin from below. We had better wait and see whether there is any movement that way. I dare say that it will depend a great deal on whether the General gets over it or not."

The opportunity did not come. At the end of five weeks Mr. Simcoe was well enough to travel by easy stages down to the coast, acting upon the advice that he should, for the present, give up all idea of making a tour through India, and had better take a sea voyage to Australia or the Cape, or, better still, take his passage home at once. Had the day and hour of his leaving been known, there was not a white soldier in the cantonments who would not have turned out to give him a hearty cheer, but although going on well the doctor said that all excitement should be avoided. It would be quite enough for him to have to say good-by to the friends who had been in the habit of coming in to talk with him daily, but anything like a public greeting by the men would be likely to upset him. It was not, therefore, until Simcoe was some way down the river that his departure became known to the troops.

Six weeks later there was a sensation in the cantonments. General Mathieson had so far recovered that he was able to be carried up to the hills, and the camp was still growling at the irritating orders and regulations of his temporary successor in command, when the news spread that Staff Pay-Sergeant Sanderson had deserted. He had obtained a fortnight's furlough, saying that he wanted to pay a visit to some old comrades at Allahabad; at the end of the fortnight he had not returned, and the Staff Paymaster had gone strictly into his accounts and found that there was a deficiency of over £300, which he himself would of course be called upon to make good. He had, indeed, helped to bring about the deficiency by placing entire confidence in the sergeant and by neglecting to check his accounts regularly.

Letters were at once written to the heads of the police at Calcutta and Bombay, and to all the principal places on the roads to those ports; but it was felt that, with such a start as he had got, the chances were all in his favor.

It was soon ascertained at Allahabad that he had not been there. Inquiries at the various dak-bungalows satisfied the authorities that he had not traveled by land. If he had gone down to Calcutta he had gone by boat; but he might have started on the long land journey across to Bombay, or have even made for Madras. No distinct clew, however, could be obtained.

The Paymaster obtained leave and went down to Calcutta and inspected all the lists of passengers and made inquiries as to them; but there were then but few white men in the country, save those holding civil or military positions and the merchants at the large ports, therefore there was not much difficulty in ascertaining the identity of everyone who had left Calcutta during the past month, unless, indeed, he had taken a passage in some native craft to Rangoon or possibly Singapore.

On his arrival at Calcutta he heard of an event which caused deep and general regret when known at Benares, and for a time threw even the desertion of Sergeant Sanderson into the shade. The *Nepaul*, in which John Simcoe had sailed, had been lost in a typhoon in the Bay of Bengal when but six days out. There was no possible doubt as to his fate, for a vessel half a mile distant had seen her founder, but could render no assistance, being herself dismasted and unmanageable and the sea so tremendous that no boat could have lived in it for a moment. As both ships belonged to the East India Company, and were well known to each other, the captain and officials of the *Ceylon* had no doubt whatever as to her identity, and, indeed, the remains of a boat bearing the *Nepaul's* name were picked up a few days later near the spot where she had gone down.

"It's hard luck, that is what I call it," Sergeant Nichol said with great emphasis when the matter was talked over in the sergeants' mess. "Here is a man who faces a wounded tiger with nothing but a hunting-knife, and recovers from his wounds; here is the General, whose life he saved, going on first-rate, and yet he loses his life himself, drowned at sea. I call that about as hard luck as anything I have heard of."

"Hard luck indeed!" another said. "If he had died of his wounds it would have been only what might have been expected; but to get over them and then to get drowned almost as soon as he had started is, as you say, Nichol, very hard luck. I am sure the General will be terribly cut up about it. I heard Major Butler tell Captain Thompson that he had heard from Dr. Hunter that when the General began to get round and heard that Simcoe had gone, while he was lying there too ill to know anything about it, he regularly broke down and cried like a child; and I am sure the fact that he will never have the chance of thanking him now will hurt him as bad as those tiger's claws."

"And so there is no news of Sanderson?"

"Not that I have heard. Maybe he has got clean away; but I should say it's more likely that he is lying low in some sailors' haunt until the matter blows over. Then, like enough, he will put on sea-togs and ship under another name before the mast in some trader knocking about among the islands, and by the time she comes back he could take a passage home without questions being asked. He is a sharp fellow is Sanderson. I never quite liked him myself, but I never thought he was a rogue. It will teach Captain Smalley to be more careful in future. I heard that he was going home on his long leave in the spring, but I suppose he will not be able to do so now for a year or so; three hundred pounds is a big sum to have to fork out."

The news of the loss of the *Nepaul*, with all hands, did indeed hit General Mathieson very heavily, and for a time seriously delayed the progress that he was making towards recovery.

"It's bad enough to think," he said, "that I shall never have an opportunity of thanking that gallant fellow for my life; but it is even worse to know that my rescue has brought about his death, for had it not been for that he would have by this time been up at Delhi or in Oude instead of lying at the bottom of the sea. I would give half my fortune to grasp his hand again and tell him what I feel."

General Mathieson's ill luck stuck to him. He gained strength so slowly that he was ordered home, and it was three years before he rejoined. Four years later his daughter came out to him, and for a time his home in Delhi, where he was now stationed, was a happy one. The girl showed no desire to marry, and refused several very favorable offers; but after she had been out four years she married a rising young civilian who was also stationed at Delhi. The union was a happy one, except that the first two children born to them died in infancy. They were girls. The third was a boy, who at the age of eight months was sent home under the charge of an officer's wife returning with her children to England. When they arrived there he was placed in charge of Mrs. Covington, a niece of the General's. But before he reached the shores of England he was an orphan. An epidemic of cholera broke out at the station at which his father, who was now a deputy collector, was living, and he and his wife were among the first victims of the scourge.

General Mathieson was now a major-general, and in command of the troops in the Calcutta district. This blow decided him to resign his command and return to England. He was now sixty; the climate of India had suited him, and he was still a hale, active man. Being generally popular he was soon at home in London, where he took a house in Hyde Park Gardens and became a regular frequenter of the Oriental and East Indian United Service Clubs, of which he had been for years a member, went a good deal into society, and when at home took a lively interest in his grandson, often running down to his niece's place, near Warwick, to see how he was getting on.

The ayah who had come with the child from India had been sent back a few months after they arrived, for his mother had written to Mrs. Covington requesting that he should have a white nurse. "The native servants," she wrote, "spoil the children dreadfully, and let them have entirely their own way, and the consequence is that they grow up domineering, bad-tempered, and irritable. I have seen so many cases of it here that Herbert and I have quite decided that our child shall not be spoilt in this way, but shall be brought up in England as English children are, to obey their nurses and to do as they are ordered."

As Mrs. Covington's was a large country house the child was no trouble; an excellent nurse was obtained, and the boy throve under her care.

The General now much regretted having remained so many years in India, and if an old comrade remarked, "I never could make out why you stuck to it so long, Mathieson; it was ridiculous for a man with a large private fortune, such as you have," he would reply, "I can only suppose it was because I was an old fool. But, you see, I had no particular reason for coming home. I lost my only sister three years after I went out, and had never seen her only daughter, my niece Mary Covington. Of course I hoped for another bout of active service, and when the chance came at last up in the north, there was I stuck down in Calcutta. If it hadn't been for Jane I should certainly have given it up in disgust when I found I was practically shelved. But she always used to come down and stay with me for a month or two in the cool season, and as she was the only person in the world I cared for, I held on from year to year, grumbling of course, as pretty well every Anglo-Indian does, but without having sufficient resolution to throw it up. I ought to have stayed at home for good after that mauling I got from the tiger; but, you see, I was never really myself while I was at home. I did not feel up to going to clubs, and could not enter into London life at all, but spent most of my time at my own place, which was within a drive of Mary Covington's, who had then just married.

"Well, you see, I got deucedly tired of life down there. I knew nothing whatever of farming, and though I tried to get up an interest in it I failed altogether. Of course there was a certain amount of society of a sort, and everyone called, and one had to go out to dinner-parties. But such dinner-parties! Why, a dinner in India was worth a score of them. Most of them were very stiff and formal, and after the women had gone upstairs, the men talked of nothing but hunting and shooting and crops and cattle; so at last I could stand it no longer, but threw up six months of my furlough and went out again. Yes, of course I had Jane, but at that time she was but fourteen, and was a girl at school; and when I talked of bringing her home and having a governess, everyone seemed to think that it would be the worst thing possible for her, and no doubt they were right, for the life would have been as dull for her as it was for me.

"Of course now it is different. I feel as young and as well as I did twenty years ago, and can thoroughly enjoy my life in London, though I still fight very shy of the country. It is a satisfaction to me to know that things are pretty quiet in India at present, so that I am losing nothing that way, and if I were out there I should be only holding inspections at Barrakpoor, Dumdum, or on the Maidan at Calcutta. Of course it was pleasant enough in its way, for I never felt the heat; but as a man gets on in life he doesn't have quite so much enjoyment out of it as he used to do. The men around him are a good deal younger than himself. He knows all the old messroom jokes, and one bit of scandal is like scores of others he has heard in his time.

"I am heartily glad that I have come home. Many of you here are about my own standing, and there is plenty to talk about of old friends and old days. You were a young ensign when I was a captain, but Bulstrode and I got our companies within a few days of each other. Of course he is only a lieutenant-colonel, while I am a major-general, but that is because he had the good sense to quit the service years ago. There are scores of others in the club just about my own standing, and one gets one's rubber of whist in the afternoon, and we dine together and run down the cooking and wines, although every one of us knows at heart that they are both infinitely better than we got in India, except at the clubs in the Presidency towns.

"Then, of course, we all agree that the service is going to the dogs, that the Sepoys are over-indulged and will some day give us a lot of trouble. I keep my liver all right by taking a long ride every morning, and altogether I think I can say that I thoroughly enjoy myself."

The General, on his first visit to England, had endeavored, but in vain, to find out the family of John Simcoe. He had advertised largely, but without effect.

"I want to find them out," he said to his niece; "I owe that man a debt of gratitude I can never repay, but doubtless there are some of his family who may be in circumstances where I could give them a helping hand. There may be young brothers—of course I could get them cadetships in the Indian army—maybe portionless sisters."

"But if he was traveling in India for pleasure he must have been a well-to-do young fellow. Men cannot wander about in the East without having a pretty full purse."

"Yes, no doubt; but I don't fancy it was so in his case, and he said casually that he had come in for some money, and, as he had always had a great desire to travel, he thought that he could do nothing better than spend a year or two in the East, but that he hoped before it was gone he should fall on his legs and obtain some sort of employment. He did not care much what it was, so that it was not quill-driving. He thought that he could turn his hands to most things. I laughed at the time, for I was by no means sure that he was in earnest, but I have felt since that he must have been. If it had not been so, my advertisements would surely have caught the eye of someone who knew his family. A family wealthy enough for one of the sons to start on two years' travel must be in a fair position, whether in town or country. Had it been so I should have heard of it, and therefore I think that what he said must have had some foundation in fact. He was certainly a gentleman in manner, and my idea now is that he belonged to a middle-class family, probably in some provincial town, and that, having come into some money at the death of his father or some other relative, he followed his natural bent and started on a sort of roving expedition, thinking, as many people do think, that India is a land where you have only to stretch out your hands and shake the pagoda tree.

"He would have found out his mistake, poor fellow, if he had lived. The days are long past when any dashing young adventurer can obtain a post of honor in the pay of an Indian Rajah. Still, of course, after what he did for me, had he remained in India, and I found that he really wanted a berth, I might have done something for him. I know numbers of these Indian princes, some of them intimately, and to some I have been of very considerable service; and I fancy that I might have got him a berth of some kind or other without much difficulty. Or had he made up his mind to return to England I would have set him up in any business he had a fancy for. He has gone now, and I wish I could pay someone he cared for a little of the debt of gratitude I owe him. Well, I have done my best and have failed, from no fault of my own; but remember that if ever you hear of a family of the name of Simcoe, I want you to make inquiries about them, and to give me full particulars concerning them."

But no news ever reached the General on this head, and it was a frequent cause of lamentation to him, when he finally settled in town, that although he had again advertised he had heard nothing whatever of the family of which he was in search.

CHAPTER II.

IN THE SOUTH SEAS.

An island in the Pacific. The sun was shining down from a cloudless sky, the sea was breaking on the white beach, there was just sufficient breeze to move the leaves of the cocoanut trees that formed a dark band behind the sands. A small brig of about a hundred tons' burden lay anchored a short distance from the shore. The paint was off in many places, and everywhere blistered by the sun. Her sails hung loosely in the gaskets, and the slackness of her ropes and her general air of untidiness alike showed the absence of any sort of discipline on board.

In front of a rough shanty, built just within the line of shade of the cocoanuts, sat three men. Two drunken sailors lay asleep some fifty yards away. On the stump of a tree in front of the bench on which the three men were sitting were placed several black bottles and three tin pannikins, while two gourds filled with water and covered with broad banana leaves stood erect in holes dug in the sand.

"I tell you what it is, Atkins, your men are carrying it on too far. Bill here, and I, were good friends with the natives; the chief gave us wives, and we got on well enough with them. What with the cocoanuts, which are free to us all, and the patches of ground to cultivate, we had all we wanted, and with the store of beads and bright cotton we brought here with us we paid the natives to fish for pearls for us, and have collected enough copra to trade for rum and whatever else we want. You have got all our copra on board, and a good stock of native trumperies, and I should recommend you to be off, both for your own sake and ours. Your men have been more or less drunk ever since they came here. I don't mind a drinking bout myself now and again, but it does not do to keep it up. However, it would be no odds to us whether your men were drunk all the time or not if they would but get drunk on board, but they will bring the liquor on shore, and then they get quarrelsome, use their fists on the natives, and meddle with the women. Now, these fellows are quiet and gentle enough if they are left alone and treated fairly, but I don't blame them for getting riled up when they are ill-treated, and I tell you they are riled up pretty badly now. My woman has spoken to me more than once, and from what she says there is likely to be trouble, not only for you but for us."

"Well, Sim," the man that he was addressing said, "there is reason enough in what you say. I don't care myself a snap for these black fellows; a couple of musket-shots would send them all flying. But, you see, though I am skipper, the men all have shares and do pretty much as they like. At present they like to stay here, and I suppose they will stay here till they are tired of it."

"Well, Atkins, if I were in your place I should very soon make a change, and if you like, Bill and I will help you. You have got six men; well, if you shot three of them the other three would think better of it; and if they didn't I would settle them too."

"It is all very well talking like that, Sim. How could I sail the brig without hands? If I only kept three of them I should be very short-handed, and if I ever did manage to get to port they would lay a complaint against me for shooting the others. It is all very well for you to talk; you have lived here long enough to know that one can only get the very worst class of fellows to sail with one in craft like this and for this sort of trade. It pays well if one gets back safely, but what with the risk of being cast ashore or being killed by the natives, who are savage enough in some of the islands, it stands to reason that a man who can get a berth in any other sort of craft won't sail with us. But it is just the sort of life to suit chaps like these; it means easy work, plenty of loafing about, and if things turn out well a good lump of money at the end of the voyage. However, they ought to have had enough of it this job; the rum is nearly gone, and if you will come off to-morrow I will let you have what remains, though if they are sober I doubt if they will let you take it away."

"We will risk that," the third man said. "We are not nice about using our pistols, if you are. I was saying to Simcoe here, things are going a lot too far. Enough mischief has been done already, and I am by no means sure that when you have gone they won't make it hot for us. We are very comfortable here, and we are not doing badly, and I don't care about being turned out of it."

"The pearl fishing is turning out well?" Atkins asked quietly.

"It might be worse and it might be better. Anyhow, we are content to remain here for a bit.

"I don't like it, Jack," he said, as the skipper, having in vain tried to rouse the two drunken men, rowed himself off to the brig. "My woman told me this morning that there had been a big talk among the natives, and that though they did not tell her anything, she thought that they had made up their minds to wipe the whites out altogether. They said that if we hadn't been here, the brig would not have come; which is like enough, for Atkins only put in because he was an old chum of ours, and thought that we should have got copra enough to make it worth his while to come round. Well, if the niggers only wiped out the crew, and burned the ship, I should say nothing against it, as long as they let Atkins alone. He has stood by me in more than one rough-and-tumble business, and I am bound to stand by him. But there aint no discrimination among the niggers. Besides, I am not saying but that he has been pretty rough with them himself.

"It makes all the difference whether you settle down and go in for making a pile, or if you only stop to water and take in fruit; we agreed as to that when we landed here. When we stopped here before and found them friendly and pleasant, and we says to each other, 'If we can but get on smooth with them and set them fishing for us we might make a good thing out of it.' You see, we had bought some oysters one of them brought up after a dive, and had found two or three pearls in them.

"Well, we have been here nine months, and I don't say I am not getting tired of it; but it is worth stopping for. You know we reckoned last week that the pearls we have got ought to be worth two or three thousand pounds, and we agreed that we would stay here till we have two bags the size of the one we have got; but unless Atkins gets those fellows off, I doubt if we shan't have to go before that. There is no reasoning with these niggers; if they had any sense they would see that we can't help these things."

"Perhaps what the women tell us is untrue," the other suggested.

"Don't you think that," Simcoe said; "these black women are always true to their white men when they are decently treated. Besides, none of the natives have been near us to-day. That, of course, might be because they are afraid of these chaps; but from this shanty we can see the canoes, and not one has gone out to-day. Who is to blame them, when one of their chiefs was shot yesterday without a shadow of excuse? I don't say that I think so much of a nigger's life one way or another; and having been in some stiff fights together, as you know, I have always taken my share. But I am dead against shooting without some reason; it spoils trade, and makes it unsafe even to land for water. I have half a mind, Bill, to go on board and ask Atkins to take us away with him; we could mighty soon settle matters with the crew, and if there was a fight and we had to shoot them all, we could take the brig into port well enough."

"No, no," said Bill, "it has not come to that yet. Don't let us give up a good thing until we are sure that the game is up."

"Well, just as you like; I am ready to run the risk if you are. It would be hard, if the worst came to the worst, if we couldn't fight our way down to our canoe, and once on board that we could laugh at them; for as we have proved over and over again, they have not one that can touch her."

"Well, I will be off to my hut; the sun is just setting and my supper will be ready for me." He strolled off to his shanty, which lay back some distance in the wood. Simcoe entered the hut, where a native woman was cooking.

"Nothing fresh, I suppose?" he asked in her language.

She shook her head. "None of our people have been near us to-day."

"Well, Polly,"—for so her white master had christened her, her native appellation being too long for ordinary conversation,—"it is a bad business, and I am sorry for it; but when these fellows have sailed away it will soon come all right again."

"Polly hopes so," she said. "Polly very much afraid."

"Well, you had better go to-morrow and see them, and tell them, as I have told them already, we are very sorry for the goings on of these people, but it is not our fault. You have no fear that they will hurt you, have you? Because if so, don't you go."

"They no hurt Polly now," she said; "they know that if I do not come back you be on guard."

"Well, I don't think there is any danger at present, but it is as well to be ready. Do you take down to the canoe three or four dozen cocoanuts and four or five big bunches of plantains, and you may as well take three or four gourds of water. If we have to take to the boat, will you go with me or stay here?"

"Polly will go with her master," the woman said; "if she stay here they will kill her."

"I am glad enough for you to go with me, Polly," he said. "You have been a good little woman, and I don't know how I should get on without you now; though why they should kill you I don't know, seeing that your head chief gave you to me himself."

"Kill everything belonging to white man," she said quietly; and the man knew in his heart that it would probably be so. She put his supper on the table and then made several journeys backwards and forwards to the canoe, which lay afloat in a little cove a couple of hundred yards away. When she had done she stood at the table and ate the remains of the supper.

An hour later the man was sitting on the bench outside smoking his pipe, when he heard the sound of heavy footsteps among the trees. He knew this was no native tread.

"What is it, Bill?" he asked, as the man came up.

"Well, I came to tell you that there is a big row going on among the natives. I can hear their tom-tom things beating furiously, and occasionally they set up a tremendous yell. I tell you I don't like it, Simcoe; I don't like it a bit. I sent my woman to see what it was all about, but though she had been away three hours, she hadn't come back when I started out to talk it over with you."

"There has been a biggish row going on on board the brig too," the other said. "I have heard Atkins storming, and a good deal of shouting among the men. I suppose you have got your pearls all right in your belt? Things begin to have an awkward look, and we may have to bolt at short notice."

"You trust me for that, Simcoe; I have had them on me ever since the brig came in. I had no fear of the natives stealing them out of my hut, but if one of those fellows were to drop in and see them he would think nothing of knifing the woman and carrying them off."

"I see you have brought your gun with you."

"Yes, and my pistols too. I suppose you are loaded, and ready to catch up at a moment's notice?"

"Yes; my girl has been carrying down cocoanuts and plantains to the canoe, so, if we have to make a bolt, we can hold on comfortably enough until we get to the next island, which is not above three days' sail, and lies dead to leeward, as the wind is at present. Still, Bill, I hope it is not coming to that. I think it is likely enough they may attack the brig in their canoes, but they have always been so friendly with us that I really don't think they can turn against us now; they must know that we cannot help these people's doings."

"That is all very well," the other said, "but you and I know half a dozen cases in which the niggers have attacked a ship, and in every case beachcombers were killed too."

Simcoe made no answer; he knew that it was so, and could hardly hope that there would be an exception in their case. After thinking for a minute he said, "Well, Bill, in that case I think the safest plan will be to take to the canoe at once. We can stay away a few weeks and then come back here and see how matters stand."

"But how about Atkins?"

"Well, we will shout and get him ashore and tell him what we think of it, and give him the choice of either stopping or going with us. Nothing can be fairer than that. If he chooses to stop and harm comes of it we cannot blame ourselves. If we come back in a few weeks of course we should not land until we had overhauled one of their canoes and found out what the feeling of the people was. They will have got over their fit of rage, and like enough they will have said to each other, 'We were better off when the two white men were here. They paid us for our fishing and our copra, and never did us any harm. I wish they were back again.'"

"That is reasonable enough," the other agreed. "What about the trade things?"

“Well, we have only got some beads and small knick-knacks left. Polly shall carry them down to the canoe; we shall want them for trading till we come back here again.”

He said a few words to the woman, who at once began to carry the things down to the canoe. Then he went down to the beach and shouted, “Atkins!”

“Hullo!” came back from the brig.

“Come ashore; we want to talk to you about something particular.” They saw the dinghy pulled up to the ship’s side, then Atkins rowed ashore.

“I have been having a row with the crew,” he said. “I thought it was coming to fighting. Two or three of them took up handspikes, but I drew my pistols and things calmed down. What do you want me for?”

“Bill here has brought news that there is a row among the natives. They are beating their drums and yelling like fiends, and we expect it means mischief. At any rate it comes to this: we are so convinced that there is going to be trouble that we mean to cut and run at once. We have got enough grub put on board our canoe to take us to the next island, but we did not want to leave you in the lurch, to be speared by the niggers, so we have called you to offer you a seat in the canoe.”

“That is friendly,” Atkins said, “but I should lose the ship and cargo; and pretty near all that I have got is in her. Why should not you two bring your canoe off alongside and hoist her up? Then we could get up anchor and be off. Three of the fellows are dead-drunk and the other three half stupid. I would give you each a share in the profits of the voyage.”

“Well, what do you think of that, Simcoe?” Bill said.

“I tell you straight I don’t care for it. You and I are both good paddlers, and the canoe sails like a witch in a light wind. Once afloat in her and we are safe, but you can’t say as much for the brig. I have sailed in her before now, and I know that she is slow, unless it is blowing half a gale. It is like enough that the natives may be watching her now, and if they saw us get under way they would be after her, and would go six feet to her one. As to fighting, what could we three do? The others would be of no use whatever. No, I like our plan best by far.”

“Well, I don’t know what to say,” Atkins said. “It is hard to make a choice. Of course if I were sure that the natives really meant mischief I would go with you, but we cannot be sure of that.”

“I feel pretty sure of it anyhow,” Bill said. “My girl would be safe to follow me here when she got back and found the hut empty, but I am mightily afraid that some harm has come to her, or she would have been back long before this. It wasn't half a mile to go, and she might have been there and back in half an hour, and she has been gone now over three hours, and I feel nasty about it, I can tell you. I wish your crew were all sober, Atkins, and that we had a score of men that I could put my hand on among the islands. I should not be talking about taking to a canoe then, but I would just go in and give it them so hot that they would never try their pranks on again."

"Have you got all the things in, Polly?" Simcoe asked the woman, as she crouched down by the door of the hut.

"Got all in," she said. "Why not go? Very bad wait here."

"Well, I think you are about right. At any rate, we will go and get on board and wait a spear's-throw off the shore for an hour or so. If Bill's Susan comes here and finds we have gone she is pretty safe to guess that we shall be on board the canoe and waiting for her. What do you say to that, Bill?"

"That suits me; nothing can be fairer. If she comes we can take her on board, if she doesn't I shall know that they have killed her, and I will jot it down against them and come back here some day before long and take it out of them. And you, Atkins?"

"I will go straight on board. Like enough it is all a false alarm, and I aint going to lose the brig and all that she has got on board till I am downright certain that they——"

He stopped suddenly, and the others leaped to their feet as a burst of savage yells broke out across the water.

"By Heavens, they are attacking the ship!" Simcoe cried; "they will be here in a moment. Come on, Polly! come on, Atkins! we have no choice now." Taking up his arms, he started to run. "Quick, quick!" he cried; "I can hear them."

They had gone but some thirty yards when a number of natives burst from the wood. Had they arrived a minute sooner at the hut none of its occupants would have lived to tell the tale, but the impatience of those in the canoes lying round the brig had caused the alarm to be given before they had placed themselves in readiness for a simultaneous rush on the hut. There was no further occasion for silence; a wild yell burst out as they caught sight of the flying figures, and a dozen spears flew through the air.

"Don't stop to fire!" Simcoe shouted; "we shall have to make a stand at the boat and shall want every barrel."

They were three-quarters of the way to the boat and the natives were still some twenty yards behind them. Suddenly Bill stumbled; then with a savage oath he turned and emptied both barrels of his fowling-piece into the natives, and the two leading men fell forward on their faces, and some shouts and yells told that some of the shots had taken effect on those behind.

"Are you wounded, Bill?" Simcoe asked.

"Yes, I am hit hard. Run on, man; I think I am done for."

"Nonsense!" Simcoe exclaimed. "Catch hold of my arm; I will help you along."

One native was in advance of the rest. He raised his arm to hurl his spear, but the native woman, who had all along been running behind Simcoe, threw herself forward, and the spear pierced her through the body. With an exclamation of fury Simcoe leveled his musket and shot the native through the head.

"Throw your arms round my neck, Bill; the poor girl is done for, curse them. Can you hold on?"

"Yes, I think so," he replied.

Simcoe was a very powerful man, and with his comrade on his back he ran on almost as swiftly as before.

"Now, Atkins, give them every barrel that you have got, then lift Bill into the boat, and I will keep them back. I am not going until I have paid some of them out for poor Polly."

Atkins fired his pistols, and with so steady an aim that each shot brought down a savage; then he lifted Bill from Simcoe's shoulders and laid him in the canoe.

"Get up the sail!" Simcoe shouted. "They will riddle us with spears if we paddle." He shot down four of the natives with his double-barreled pistols, and then clubbing his gun threw himself with a hoarse shout upon them. The loss of seven of their leaders had caused their followers to hesitate, and the fury of Simcoe's attack and the tremendous blows he dealt completed their discomfiture, and they turned and fled in dismay.

"Now is your time!" Atkins shouted; "I have cut the cord and got the sail up." Turning, Simcoe was in a moment knee-deep in the water; pushing the boat off, he threw himself into it.

"Lie down, man, lie down!" he shouted to Atkins. But the warning was too late; the moment Simcoe turned the natives had turned also, and as they reached the water's edge half a dozen spears were flung. Two of them struck Atkins full in the body, and with a cry he threw up his arms and fell over the side of the canoe. Then came several splashes in the water. Simcoe drew the pistols from his companion's belt, and, raising himself high enough to look over the stern, shot two of the savages who were wading out waist deep, and were but a few paces behind.

The sail was now doing its work, and the boat was beginning to glide through the water at a rate that even the best swimmers could not hope to emulate. As soon as he was out of reach of the spears Simcoe threw the boat up into the wind, reloaded his pistols and those of his comrade, and opened fire upon the group of natives clustered at the water's edge. Like most men of his class, he was a first-rate shot. Three of the natives fell and the rest fled. Then with a stroke of the paddle he put the boat before the wind again, and soon left the island far behind.

"This has been a pretty night's work," he muttered. "Poor little Polly killed! She gave her life to save me, and there is no doubt she did save me too, for that fellow's spear must have gone right through me. I am afraid that they have done for Bill too." He stooped over his comrade. The shaft of the spear had broken off, but the jagged piece with the head attached stuck out just over the hip. "I am afraid it is all up with him; however, I must take it out and bandage him as well as I can."

A groan burst from the wounded man as Simcoe with some effort drew the jagged spear from the wound. Then he took off his own shirt and tore some strips off it and tightly bandaged the wound.

"I can do nothing else until the morning," he said. "Well, Polly, I have paid them out for you. I have shot seven or eight and smashed the skulls of as many more. Of course they have done for those drunkards on board the brig. I did not hear a single pistol fired, and I expect that they knocked them on the head in their drunken sleep. The brutes! if they had had their senses about them we might have made a fair fight; though I expect that they would have been too many for us."

Just as daylight was breaking Bill opened his eyes.

"How do you feel, old man?"

"I am going, Simcoe. You stood by me like a man; I heard it all till Atkins laid me in the boat. Where is he?"

"He is gone, Bill. Instead of throwing himself down in the boat, as I shouted to him directly he got up the sail, he stood there watching, I suppose, until I was in. He got two spears in his body and fell overboard dead, I have no doubt."

"Look here, Sim!" The latter had to bend down his ear to listen. The words came faintly and slowly. "If you ever go back home again, you look up my brother. He is no more on the square than I was, but he is a clever fellow. He lives respectable—Rose Cottage, Pentonville Hill. Don't forget it. He goes by the name of Harrison. I wrote to him every two or three years, and got an answer about the same. Tell him how his brother Bill died, and how you carried him off when the blacks were yelling round. We were fond of each other, Tom and I. You keep the pearls, Sim; he don't want them. He is a top-sawyer in his way, he is, and has offered again and again that if I would come home he would set me up in any line I liked. I thought perhaps I should go home some day. Tom and I were great friends. I remember——" His eyelids drooped, his lips moved, and in another minute no sounds came from them. He gave one deep sigh, and then all was over.

"A good partner and a good chum," Simcoe muttered as he looked down into the man's face. "Well, well, I have lost a good many chums in the last ten years, but not one I missed as I shall miss Bill. It is hard, he and Polly going at the same time. There are not many fellows that I would have lain down to sleep with, with fifteen hundred pounds' or so worth of pearls in my belt, not out in these islands. But I never had any fear with him. Well, well," he went on, as he took the bag of pearls from his comrade's belt and placed it in his own, "There is a consolation everywhere, though we might have doubled and trebled this lot if we had stopped three months longer, which we should have done if Atkins had not brought that brig of his in. I can't think why he did it. He might have been sure that with that drunken lot of villains trouble would come of it sooner or later. He wasn't a bad fellow either, but too fond of liquor."

CHAPTER III.

A DEAF GIRL.

"Yes, Lady Moulton, I will undertake the gypsy tent business at your fête; that is to say, I will see to the getting up of the tent, provide a gypsy for you, and someone to stand at the door and let in one visitor at a time and receive the money. Do you mean to make it a fixed charge, or leave it to each to pay the gypsy?"

"Which do you think will be best, Hilda? Of course the great thing is to get as much money for the decayed ladies as possible."

"I should say that it would be best to let them give what they like to the gypsy, Lady Moulton."

"But she might keep some of it herself."

"I think I can guarantee that she won't do that; I will get a dependable gypsy. You see, you could not charge above a shilling entrance, and very likely she would get a good deal more than that given to her."

"Well, my dear, I leave it all to you. Spare no expense about the tent and its fitting up. I have set my heart upon the affair being a success, and I think everything else has been most satisfactorily arranged. It is a very happy thought of yours about the gypsy; I hope that you will find a clever one. But you must mind and impress upon her that we don't want any evil predictions. Nothing could be in worse taste. It is all very well when a girl is promised a rich husband and everything to match, but if she were told that she would never get married, or would die young, or something of that sort, it would be a most unpleasant business."

"I quite agree with you, and will see that everything shall be 'couleur de rose' as to the future, and that she shall confine herself as much as possible to the past and present."

"I leave it in your hands, and I am sure that it will be done nicely."

Lady Moulton was a leading member of society, a charming woman with a rich and indulgent husband. Her home was a pleasant one, and her balls were among the most popular of the season. She had, as her friends said, but one failing, namely, her ardor for "The Society for Affording Aid to Decayed Ladies." It was on behalf of this institution that she was now organizing a fête in the grounds of her residence at Richmond. Hilda Covington was an orphan and an heiress, and was the ward of her uncle, an old Indian officer, who had been a great friend of Lady Moulton's father. She had been ushered into society under her ladyship's auspices. She had, however, rather forfeited that lady's favorable opinion by refusing two or three unexceptionable offers.

"My dear," she remonstrated, "no girl can afford to throw away such chances, even if she is, as you are, well endowed, pretty, and clever."

The girl laughed.

"I am not aware that I am clever at all, Lady Moulton. I speak German and French perfectly, because I have been four or five years in Hanover; but beyond that I am not aware of possessing any special accomplishments."

"But you are clever, my dear," the other said decidedly. "The way you seem to understand people's characters astonishes me. Sometimes it seems to me that you are almost a witch."

"You are arguing against yourself," the girl laughed. "If I am such a good judge of character I am not likely to make a mistake in such an important matter as choosing a husband for myself."

Lady Moulton was silenced, but not convinced; however, she had good sense enough to drop the subject. General Mathieson had already told her that although he should not interfere in any way with any choice Hilda might make, he should make it an absolute condition that she should not marry until she came of age; and as she was at present but eighteen, many things might occur in the three years' interval.

On her return home, after arranging to provide a gypsy for Lady Moulton's fête, Hilda related what had occurred to a girl friend who was staying with her.

"Of course, Netta, I mean to be the gypsy myself; but you must help me. It would never do for me to be suspected of being the sorceress, and so you must be my double, so that I can, from time to time, go out and mix with the crowd. A few minutes at a time will do."

The other laughed. "But what should I say to them, Hilda?"

"Oh, it is as easy as A B C. All that you will have to do is to speak ambiguously, hint at coming changes, foresee a few troubles in the way, and prophesy a happy solution of the difficulties. I will take upon myself the business of surprising them, and I fancy that I shall be able to astonish a few of them so much that even if some do get only commonplaces we shall make a general sensation. Of course, we must get two disguises. I shall have a small tent behind the other where I can change. It won't take a moment—a skirt, and a shawl to go over my head and partly hide my face, can be slipped on and off in an instant. Of course I shall have a black wig and some sort of yellow wash that can be taken off with a damp towel. I shall place the tent so that I can leave from behind without being noticed. As we shall have the tent a good deal darkened there will be no fear of the differences between the two gypsies being discovered, and, indeed, people are not likely to compare notes very closely."

"Well, I suppose you will have your way as usual, Hilda."

"I like that!" the other said, with a laugh. "You were my guide and counselor for five years, and now you pretend that I always have my own way. Why, I cannot even get my own way in persuading you to come and settle over here. I am quite sure that you would get lots of pupils, when people understand the system and its advantages."

"That is all very well, Hilda, but, you see, in the first place I have no friends here except yourself, and in the second it requires a good deal of money to get up an establishment and to wait until one gets pupils. My aunt would, I know, put in the money she saved when you were with us if I were to ask her, but I wouldn't do so. To begin with, she regards that as my fortune at her death. She has said over and over again how happy the knowledge makes her that I shall not be left absolutely penniless, except, of course, what I can get for the house and furniture, and I would do anything rather than sell that. She admits that I might keep myself by teaching deaf children, but, as she says, no one can answer for their health. I might have a long illness that would throw me out. I might suddenly lose a situation, say, from the death of a pupil, and might be a long time before I could hear of another. She said to me once, 'I do hope, Netta, you will never embark one penny of the little money that will come to you in any sort of enterprise or speculation, however promising it may look.' We had been talking of exactly the plan that you are now speaking of. 'The mere furnishing of a house in England large enough to take a dozen children would swallow up a considerable sum. At first you might have to wait some time till you could obtain more than two or three children, and there would be the rent and expenses going on, and you might find yourself without money and in debt before it began to pay its way; therefore I do hope that you will keep the money untouched except to meet your expenses in times of illness or of necessity of some kind. If you can save up money sufficient to start an establishment, it will, I think, be a good thing, especially if you could secure the promise of four or five pupils to come to you at once. If in a few years you should see your way to insure starting with enough pupils to pay your way, and I am alive at the time, I would draw out enough to furnish the house and will look after it for you.' That was a great concession on her part, but I certainly would not let her do it, for she is so happy in her home now, and I know that she would worry herself to death."

"Well, Netta, you know I am still ready to become the capitalist."

Both girls laughed merrily.

"Why not, Netta?" the speaker went on. "I know you said that you would not accept money as a loan even from me, which, as I told you, was very stupid and very disagreeable, but there is no reason why we should not do it in a business way. Other women go into business, why shouldn't I? As you know, I can't absolutely touch my money until I come of age, and it is nearly three years before that; still, I feel sure that the General would let me have some money, and we could start the Institute. It would be great fun. Of course, in the first place, you would be principal, or lady superintendent, or whatever you like to call yourself, and you would draw, say, five hundred pounds a year. After that we could divide the profits."

Again both girls laughed.

"And that is what you call a business transaction?" the other said. "I know that your guardian is very kind, and indeed spoils you altogether, but I don't think that you would get him to advance you money for such a scheme."

"I am really in earnest, Netta."

"Oh, I don't say that you would not do it, if you could. However, I think, anyhow, we had better wait until you come of age. There is plenty of time. I am only twenty yet, and even in three years' time I doubt whether I should quite look the character of professor or lady superintendent."

"Well, directly I get of age I shall carry out my part of the plan," Hilda said positively, "and if you are disagreeable and won't do as I want you, I shall write to the professor and ask him to recommend a superintendent."

The other laughed again.

"You would have a difficulty, Hilda. You and I are, so far, the only two English girls who have learned the system, and either your superintendent would have to learn English or all her pupils would have to learn German."

"We will not discuss it further at present, Miss Purcell," Hilda said with dignity. "Oh, dear, those were happy days we had in that dear old house, with its pretty garden, when you were thirteen and I was eleven. I have got a great deal of fun from it since. One gets such curious little scraps of conversation."

"Then the people do not know what you learned over with us?"

"No, indeed; as you know, it was not for a year after I came back that I became altogether the General's ward, and my dear mother said to me just before she died, 'It would be better for you, dear, not to say anything about that curious accomplishment of yours. I know that you would never use it to any harm, but if people knew it they would be rather afraid of you.' Uncle said the same thing directly I got here. So of course I have kept it to myself, and indeed if they had not said so I should never have mentioned it, for it gives me a great deal of amusement."

When Hilda Covington was ten years old, she had, after a severe attack of scarlet fever, lost her hearing, and though her parents consulted the best specialists of the time, their remedies proved of no avail, and at last they could only express a hope, rather than an opinion, that in time, with added health and strength, nature might repair the damage. A year after her illness Mr. Covington heard of an aurist in Germany who had a European reputation, and he and Mrs. Covington took Hilda over to him. After examining her he said, "The mischief is serious, but not, I think, irreparable. It is a case requiring great care both as to dieting, exercise, and clothing. If it could be managed I should like to examine her ears once a fortnight, or once a month at the least. I have a house here where my patients live when under treatment, but I should not for a moment advise her being placed there. A child, to keep in good health, requires cheerful companions. If you will call again to-morrow I will think the matter over and let you know what I recommend."

Mr. and Mrs. Covington retired much depressed. His opinion was, perhaps, a little more favorable than any that they had received, but the thought that their only child must either make this considerable journey once a month or live there altogether was very painful to them. However, on talking it over, they agreed that it was far better that she should reside in Hanover for a time, with the hope of coming back cured, than that she should grow up hopelessly deaf.

"It will only be as if she were at school here," Mr. Covington said. "She will no doubt be taught to talk German and French, and even if she is never able to converse in these languages, it will add to her pleasures if she can read them."

The next day when they called upon the doctor he said, "If you can bring yourself to part with the child, I have, I think, found the very thing to suit her. In the first place you must know that there is in the town an establishment, conducted by a Professor Menzel, for the instruction of deaf mutes. It is quite a new system, and consists in teaching them to read from the lips of persons speaking to them the words that they are saying. The system is by no means difficult for those who have still, like your daughter, the power of speech, and who have lost only their hearing. But even those born deaf and dumb have learned to be able to converse to a certain degree, though their voices are never quite natural, for in nine cases out of ten deaf mutes are mutes only because they have never learned to use their tongue. However, happily that is beside the question in your daughter's case. I hope that she will regain her hearing; but should this unfortunately not be the case, it will at least be a great mitigation to her position to be able to read from the lips of those who address her what is said, and therefore to converse like an ordinary person. I can assure you that many of Herr Menzel's pupils can converse so easily and rapidly that no one would have the least idea of the misfortune from which they suffer, as in fact they feel no inconvenience beyond the fact that they are not aware of being addressed by anyone standing behind them, or whose face they do not happen to be watching."

"That would indeed be a blessing!" Mrs. Covington exclaimed. "I never heard of such a system."

"No, it is quite new, but as to its success there can be no question. I called upon Professor Menzel last evening. He said that as your daughter did not understand German the difficulties of her tuition would be very great. He has, however, among his pupils a young English girl two years older than your daughter. She lives with a maiden aunt, who has established herself here in order that her niece might have the benefit of learning the new system. Here is her name and address. The professor has reason to believe that her income is a small one, and imagines that she would gladly receive your daughter as a boarder. Her niece, who is a bright girl, would be a pleasant companion, and, moreover, having in the two years that she has been here made very great progress, she would be able to commence your daughter's education by conversing with her in English, and could act as her teacher in German also; and so soon as the language was fairly mastered your daughter could then become a pupil of the professor himself."

"That would be an excellent plan indeed," Mrs. Covington said, and her husband fully agreed with her. The doctor handed her a slip of paper with the name, "Miss Purcell, 2nd Etage, 5 Koenigstrasse."

Hilda had already been informed by the finger alphabet, which had been her means of communication since her illness, of the result of the conversation with the doctor on the previous day, and although she had cried at the thought of being separated from her father and mother, she had said that she would willingly bear anything if there was a hope of her regaining her hearing. She had watched earnestly the conversation between the doctor and her parents, and when the former had left and they explained what was proposed, her face brightened up.

"That will be very nice," she exclaimed, "and if I could but learn to understand in that way what people say, instead of watching their fingers (and some of them don't know the alphabet, and some who do are so slow that one loses all patience), it would be delightful."

Before going to see Miss Purcell, Mr. and Mrs. Covington talked the matter over together, and they agreed that, if Miss Purcell were the sort of person with whom Hilda could be happy, no plan could be better than that proposed.

"It certainly would not be nice for her," Mrs. Covington said, "to be living on a second floor in a street; she has always been accustomed to be so much in the open air, and as the doctors all agree that much depends upon her general health, I am sure it will be quite essential that she should be so now. I think that we should arrange to take some pretty little house with a good garden, just outside the town, and furnish it, and that Miss Purcell and her niece should move in there. Of course we should pay a liberal sum for board, and if she would agree, I should say that it would be best that we should treat the house as ours and should pay the expenses of keeping it up altogether. I don't suppose she keeps a servant at present, and there are many little luxuries that Hilda has been accustomed to. Then, of course, we would pay so much to the niece for teaching Hilda German and beginning to teach her this system. I don't suppose the whole thing would cost more than three hundred pounds a year."

"The expense is nothing," Mr. Covington said. "We could afford it if it were five times the amount. I think your idea is a very good one, and we could arrange for her to have the use of a pony-carriage for two or three hours a day whenever she was disposed. The great thing is for her to be healthy and happy."

Ten minutes after they started with Hilda to see Miss Purcell, after having explained to her the plan they proposed. At this she was greatly pleased. The thought of a little house all to themselves and a girl friend was a great relief to her, and she looked brighter and happier than she had done since she had lost her hearing. When they knocked at the door of the apartment on the second floor, it was opened by a bright-faced girl of thirteen.

"This is Miss Purcell's, is it not?" Mrs. Covington asked.

"Yes, ma'am," the girl replied, with a slight expression of surprise which showed that visitors were very rare.

"Will you give my card to her and say that we shall be glad if she will allow us a few minutes' conversation with her?"

The girl went into the room and returned in a minute or two. "Will you come in?" she said. "My aunt will be glad to see you."

Miss Purcell was a woman of some fifty years old, with a pleasant, kindly face. The room was somewhat poorly furnished, but everything was scrupulously neat and tidy, and there was an air of comfort pervading it.

"We have called, Miss Purcell," Mrs. Covington began, "in consequence of what we have learned from Dr. Hartwig, whom we have come over to consult, and who has been good enough to see Professor Menzel. He has learned from him that your niece here is acquiring the system of learning to understand what is said by watching the lips of speakers. The doctor is of opinion that our daughter may in time outgrow the deafness that came on a year ago, after scarlet fever, but he wishes her to remain under his eye, and he suggested that it would be well that she should learn the new system, so that in case she does not recover her hearing she would still be able to mingle with other people. Hilda is delicate, and it is necessary that she should have a cheerful home; besides which she could not begin to learn the system until she had become familiar with German. The doctor suggested that if we could persuade you to do us the great kindness of taking her under your charge it would be the best possible arrangement."

"I should be glad to do so, madam, but I fear that I could not accommodate her, for it is a mere closet that my niece sleeps in, and the other apartments on this floor are all occupied. Were it not for that I should certainly be glad to consider the matter. It would be pleasant to Netta to have a companion, for it is but dull work for her alone with me. We have few acquaintances. I do not mind saying frankly that my means are straitened, and that I cannot indulge her with many pleasures. She is a grandniece of mine; her father died some years ago, her mother three years since, and naturally she came to me. Shortly after, she lost her hearing through measles. Just at that time I happened to hear from a German workman of the institution which had been started in this town, of which he was a native. I had no ties in England, and as I heard that living was cheap there, and that the fees were not large, I decided to come over and have her taught this new system, which would not only add greatly to her own happiness, but would give her the means of earning her livelihood when she grew up; for although I have a small pension, as my father was an Excise officer, this, of course, will expire at my death."

"Happily, Miss Purcell, we are in a position to say that money is no object to us. Hilda is our only child. We have talked it over, of course, and will tell you exactly what we propose, and I hope that you will fall in with the arrangement."

She then stated the plan that she and her husband had discussed.

"You see," she went on, "you would, in fact, be mistress of the house, and would have the entire management of everything as if it was your own. We are entirely ignorant of the cost of living here, or we might have proposed a fixed monthly payment for the expenses of servants and outgoings, and would still do that if you would prefer it, though we thought that it would be better that you should, at the end of each month, send us a line saying what the disbursements had been. We would wish everything done on a liberal scale. Hilda has little appetite, and it will, for a time, want tempting. However, that matter we could leave to you. We propose to pay a hundred a year to you for your personal services as mistress of the house, and fifty pounds to your niece as Hilda's companion and instructor in German and in the system, until she understands the language well enough to attend Professor Menzel's classes. If the house we take has a stable we should keep a pony and a light carriage, and a big lad or young man to look after it and drive, and to keep the garden in order in his spare time. I do hope, Miss Purcell, that you will oblige us by falling in with our plans. If you like we can give you a day to consider them."

"I do not require a minute," she replied; "my only hesitation is because the terms that you offer are altogether too liberal."

"That is our affair," Mrs. Covington said. "We want a comfortable, happy home for our child, and shall always feel under a deep obligation to you if you will consent."

"I do consent most willingly and gratefully. The arrangement will be a delightful one for me, and I am sure for Netta."

Netta, who had been standing where she could watch the lips of both speakers, clapped her hands joyously. "Oh, auntie, it will be splendid! Fancy having a house, and a garden, and a pony-chaise!"

"You understand all we have been saying then, Netta?"

"I understand it all," the girl replied. "I did not catch every word, but quite enough to know all that you were saying."

"That certainly is a proof of the goodness of the system," Mr. Covington said, speaking for the first time. "How long have you been learning?"

"Eighteen months, sir. We have been here two years, but I was six months learning German before I knew enough to begin, and for the next six months I could not get on very fast, as there were so many words that I did not know, so that really I have only been a year at it. The professor says that in another year I shall be nearly perfect and fit to begin to teach; and he has no doubt that he will be able to find me a situation where I can teach in the daytime and still live with my aunt."

In a week the necessary arrangements were all made. A pretty, furnished house, a quarter of a mile out of town, with a large garden and stables, had been taken, and Netta and Hilda had already become friends, for as the former had learned to talk with her fingers before she came out she was able to keep up her share of the conversation by that means while Hilda talked in reply.

"The fingers are useful as a help at first," Netta said, "but Professor Menzel will not allow any of his pupils to use their fingers, because they come to rely upon them instead of watching the lips."

CHAPTER IV.

THE GYPSY.

Mr. and Mrs. Covington remained for a week after Hilda was installed with the Purcells in their new home. To her the house with its garden and pretty pony-carriage and pony were nothing remarkable, but Netta's enjoyment in all these things amused her, and the thought that she, too, would some day be able to talk and enjoy life as her companion did, greatly raised her spirits. Her father and mother were delighted at hearing her merry laugh mingled with that of Netta as they walked together in the garden, and they went home with lighter hearts and more hopeful spirits than they had felt since the child's illness began.

Every three or four months—for a journey to Hanover was a longer and more serious business in 1843 than it is at present—they went over to spend a week there. There could be no doubt from the first that the change was most beneficial to Hilda. Her cheeks regained their color and her limbs their firmness. She lost the dull look and the apathy to whatever was going on around her that had before distressed them. She progressed very rapidly in her study of German, and at the end of six months her conversations with Netta were entirely carried on in that language. She had made some little progress in reading from her companion's lips and had just entered at Herr Menzel's academy. She could now take long walks with Netta, and every afternoon, or, as summer came on, every evening, they drove together in the pony-chaise. With renewed health and strength there had been some slight improvement in her hearing. She could now faintly distinguish any loud sounds, such as those of the band of a regiment marching past her or a sudden peal ofbells.

"I think that we shall make an eventual cure," Dr. Hartwig said. "It will be slow, and possibly her hearing may never be absolutely good; but at least we may hope that she may be able to eventually hear as well as nine people out of ten."

In another year she could, indeed, though with difficulty, hear voices, and when she had been at Hanover three years her cure was almost complete, and she now went every morning to school to learn French and music. She herself was quite content to remain there. She was very happy in her life and surroundings, and could now read with the greatest facility from the lips, and indeed preferred watching a speaker's mouth to listening to the voice. It was a source of endless amusement to her that she could, as she and Netta walked through the streets, read scraps of conversation between persons on the other side of the street or passing in carriages.

Another six months and both the doctor and Professor Menzel said that they could do nothing more for her. She was still somewhat hard of hearing; but not enough so to be noticeable; while she could with her eyes follow the most rapid speaker, and the Professor expressed his regret that so excellent an example of the benefit of his system should not be in circumstances that would compel her to make a living by becoming a teacher in it. Netta was now a paid assistant at the institution.

The end of what had been a very happy time to Hilda came abruptly and sadly, for three weeks before the date when her parents were to come over to take her home, Miss Purcell, on opening a letter that came just as they had finished breakfast, said, after sitting silent for a few minutes, "You need not put on your things, Hilda; you cannot go to school this morning; I have some bad news, dear—very bad news."

The tone of voice in which she spoke, even more than the words, sent a chill into the girl's heart.

"What is it, aunt?" she said, for she had from the first used the same term as Netta in addressing her.

"Your father has had a serious illness, my dear—a very, very serious and sudden illness, and your mother wishes you to go home at once."

Hilda looked at her with frightened, questioning eyes, while every vestige of color left her cheeks. "Is he—is he——" she asked.

"Here is an inclosure for you," Miss Purcell said, as she got up, and taking Hilda's hand in one of hers drew her with the other arm close to her; "your mother wrote to me that I might prepare you a little before giving it to you. A terrible misfortune has happened. Your dear father is dead. He died suddenly of an affection of the heart."

"Oh, no, no; it cannot be!" Hilda cried.

"It is true, my dear. God has taken him. You must be strong and brave, dear, for your mother's sake."

"Oh, my poor mother, my poor mother!" Hilda cried, bursting into a sudden flood of tears, "what will she do!"

It was not until some time afterwards that she was sufficiently composed to read her mother's letter, which caused her tears to flow afresh. After giving the details of her father's death, it went on:

"I have written to your uncle, General Mathieson, who is, I know, appointed one of the trustees, and is joined with me as your guardian. I have asked him to find and send over a courier to fetch you home, and no doubt he will arrive a day or two after you receive this letter. So please get everything ready to start at once, when he comes."

Two days later General Mathieson himself arrived, accompanied by a courier. It was a great comfort to Hilda that her uncle had come for her instead of a stranger.

"It is very kind of you to come yourself, uncle," she said as she threw herself crying into his arms.

"Of course I should come, dear," he said. "Who should fetch you except your uncle? I had to bring a courier with me, for I don't understand any of their languages, and he will take all trouble off my hands. Now let me look at your face." It was a pale, sad little face that was lifted up, but two days of sorrow had not obliterated the signs of health and well-being.

"Whiter than it ought to be," he said, "but clear and healthy, and very different from what it was when I saw you before you came out. You have grown wonderfully, child. Really, I should hardly have known you again."

And so he kept on for two or three minutes, to allow her to recover herself.

"Now, dear, you must take me in and introduce me to your kind friends here."

Hilda led the way into the sitting room.

"I have heard so much of you and your niece, Miss Purcell," he said as he shook hands with her, "that I do do not feel that you are a stranger. You certainly seem to have worked wonders between you for my niece, and I must own that in the first place I thought it a mistake her being here by herself, for I had no belief that either her hearing would be restored or that she would ever be able to follow what people were saying by only staring at their lips."

"Yes, indeed, Hanover has agreed with her, sir, and it is only a small part of the credit that is due to us."

"I must differ from you entirely, madam. If she had not been perfectly happy here with you, she would never have got on as she has done."

"Have you any luggage, sir? Of course you will stay with us to-night."

"No, thank you, Miss Purcell. We have already been to the Kaiserhof, and long before this my courier will have taken rooms and made every preparation for me. You see, I am accustomed to smoke at all times, and could not think of scenting a house, solely inhabited by ladies, with tobacco. Now, if you will excuse me, I will ask Hilda to put on her bonnet and take a stroll with me."

"I shall be very glad for her to do so. It is just getting cool and pleasant for walking, and half an hour in the fresh air will do her good."

It was an hour before they returned. General Mathieson had gently told her all there was to tell of her father's death, and turning from that he spoke of her mother, and how nobly she was bearing her troubles, and erelong her tears, which had burst out anew, flowed more quietly, and she felt comforted. Presently she said suddenly:

"What is going to be done here, uncle? I have been thinking over that ever since it was settled that I was to come home next month, and I am sure that, although she has said nothing about it, Miss Purcell has felt the change that is coming. She said the other day, 'I shall not go back to the apartments where you found us, Hilda. You see, we are a great deal better off than we were before. In the first place I have had nothing whatever to spend, and during the four years the ridiculously liberal sum paid to Netta and myself has been all laid aside and has mounted up to six hundred pounds. My pension of eighty pounds a year has also accumulated, with the exception of a small sum required for our clothes, so that in fact I have nearly a thousand pounds laid by. Netta is earning thirty pounds a year at the Institute; with that and my pension and the interest on money saved we shall get on very comfortably.' I should not like, uncle, to think of them in a little stuffy place in the town. Having a nice garden and everything comfortable has done a great deal for Miss Purcell. Netta told me that she was very delicate before, and that she is quite a different woman since she came out here from the town. You cannot tell how kind she has always been. If I had been her own child, she could not have been more loving. In fact, no one could have told by her manner that she was not my mother and Netta my sister."

"Yes, dear, I ran down to your mother before starting to fetch you to help in the arrangements, and she spoke about Miss Purcell. Under ordinary circumstances, of course, at the end of the four years that you have been here the house would be given up and she would, as you say, go into a much smaller place; but your mother does not consider that these are ordinary circumstances, and thinks that her care and kindness have had quite as much to do with the improvement in your health as has the doctor. Of course we had no time to come to any definite plan, but she has settled that things are to go on here exactly as at present, except that your friend Netta will not be paid for acting as companion to you. I am to tell Miss Purcell that with that exception everything is to go on as before, and that your mother will need a change, and will probably come out here in a month or so for some time."

"Does she really mean that, uncle?"

"Certainly, and the idea is an excellent one. After such a shock as she has had an entire change of scene will be most valuable; and as she knows Miss Purcell well, and you like the place very much, I don't think that any better plan could be hit upon. I dare say she will stay here two or three months, and you can continue your studies. At the end of that time I have no doubt some plan that will give satisfaction to all parties will be hit upon."

Hilda returned to Hanover with her mother a month later. At the end of three months Mrs. Covington bought the house and presented the deeds to Miss Purcell, who had known nothing whatever of her intentions.

"I could not think of accepting it," she exclaimed.

"But you cannot help accepting it, dear Miss Purcell; here are the deeds in your name. The house will be rather large for you at present, but in a few years, indeed in two or three years, Netta could begin to take a few pupils. As soon as she is ready to do so I shall, of course, mention it among my friends, and be able to send a few children, whose parents would be ready to pay well to have them taught this wonderful method of brightening their lives, which is at present quite unknown in England."

So it was arranged; but a few months after her return to England Mrs. Covington, who had never altogether recovered from the shock of her husband's death, died after a short illness, and Hilda became an inmate of her uncle's house. Since that time three years had elapsed, and Hilda was now eighteen, and Netta was over for a two months' visit.

The scene in the grounds of Lady Moulton's charming villa at Richmond, a fortnight after the conversation between that lady and Hilda, was a gay one. Everyone in society had been invited and there were but few refusals; the weather was lovely, and all agreed that even at Ascot the costumes were not brighter or more varied.

Although the fête was especially on behalf of a charity, no admission fees were charged to guests, but everyone understood that it would be his duty to lay out money at the various picturesque tents scattered about under the trees. In these were all the most popular entertainers of the day. In one pavilion John Parry gave a short entertainment every half-hour. In a larger one Mario, Grisi, Jenny Lind, and Alboni gave short concerts, and high as were the prices of admission, there was never a seat vacant. Conjurers had a tent, electro-biologists—then the latest rage from the United States—held their séances, and at some distance from the others Richardson's booth was in full swing. The Grenadiers' band and a string band played alternately.

Not the least attraction to many was the gypsy tent erected at the edge of a thick shrubbery, for it soon became rumored that the old gypsy woman there was no ordinary impostor, but really possessed of extraordinary powers of palmistry. Everything had been done to add to the air of mystery pervading the place. Externally it was but a long, narrow marquee. On entering, the inquirer was shown by an attendant to a seat in an apartment carpeted in red, with black hangings and black cloth lining the roof. From this hung a lamp, all other light being excluded. As each visitor came out from the inner apartment the next in order was shown in, and the heavy curtains shut off all sound of what was passing. Here sat an apparently aged gypsy on an old stump of a tree. A fire burned on the ground and a pot was suspended by a tripod over it; a hood above this carried the smoke out of the tent. The curtains here were red; the roof, as in the other compartment, black, but sprinkled with gold and silver stars. A stool was placed for the visitor close enough to the gypsy for the latter to examine her hand by the light of two torches, which were fastened to a rough sapling stuck in the ground.

Hilda possessed every advantage for making the most of the situation. Owing to her intimacy with Lady Moulton, and her experience for a year in the best London society, she knew all its gossip, while she had gathered much more than others knew from the conversations both of the dancers and the lookers-on.

The first to enter was a young man who had been laughingly challenged by the lady he was walking with to go in and have his fortune told.

"Be seated, my son," the old woman said; "give me your hand and a piece of money."

With a smile he handed her half a sovereign. She crossed his palm with it and then proceeded attentively to examine the lines.

"A fair beginning," she said, "and then troubles and difficulties. Here I see that, some three years back, there is the mark of blood; you won distinction in war. Then there is a cross-mark which would show a change. Some good fortune befell you. Then the lines darken. Things go from bad to worse as they proceed. You took to a vice—cards or horse-racing. Here are evil associates, but there is a white line that runs through them. There is a girl somewhere, with fair hair and blue eyes, who loves you, and whom you love, and whose happiness is imperiled by this vice and these associates. Beyond, there is another cross-line and signs of a conflict. What happens after will depend upon yourself. Either the white line and the true love will prove too powerful for the bad influences or these will end in ruin and—ah! sudden and violent death. Your future, therefore, depends upon yourself, and it is for you to say which influence must triumph. That is all."

Without a word he went out.

"You look pale, Mr. Desmond," the lady said when he rejoined her. "What has she told you?"

"I would rather not tell you, Mrs. Markham," he said seriously. "I thought it was going to be a joke, but it is very far from being one. Either the woman is a witch or she knew all about me personally, which is barely within the limits of possibility. At any rate she has given me something to think of."

"I will try myself," the lady said; "it is very interesting."

"I should advise you not to," he said earnestly.

"Nonsense!" she laughed; "I have no superstitions. I will go in and hear what she has to say." And leaving him, she entered the tent.

The gypsy examined her hand in silence. "I would rather not tell you what I see," she said as she dropped the hand. "Oh, ridiculous!" the lady exclaimed. "I have crossed your palm with gold, and I expect to get my money's worth," and she held out her hand again.

The gypsy again examined it.

"You stand at the crossing of the ways. There are two men—one dark, quiet, and earnest, who loves you. You love him, but not as he loves you; but your line of life runs smoothly until the other line, that of a brown man, becomes mixed up in it. He loves you too, with a hot, passionate love that would soon fade. You had a letter from him a day or two back. Last night, as he passed you in a dance, he whispered, 'I have not had an answer,' and the next time he passed you, you replied, 'You must give me another day or two.' Upon the answer you give the future of your life will depend. Here is a broad, fair line, and here is a short, jagged one, telling of terrible troubles and misery. It is for you to decide which course is to be yours."

As she released her hold of the hand it dropped nerveless. The gypsy poured out a glass of water from a jug by her side, but her visitor waved it aside, and with a great effort rose to her feet, her face as pale as death.

"My God!" she murmured to herself, "this woman is really a witch."

"They do not burn witches now," the gypsy said; "I only read what I see on the palm. You cannot deny that what I have said is true. Stay a moment and drink a glass of wine; you need it before you go out."

She took a bottle of wine from behind her seat, emptied the water on to the earth, half filled a tumbler, and held it out. The frightened woman felt that indeed she needed it before going out into the gay scene, and tossed it off.

"Thank you!" she said. "Whoever you are, I thank you. You have read my fate truly, and have helped me to decide it."

Desmond was waiting for her when she came out, but she passed him with a gesture.

"You are right!" she said. "She is a witch indeed!"

Few other stories told were as tragic, but in nearly every case the visitors retired puzzled at the knowledge the gypsy possessed of their life and surroundings, and it soon became rumored that the old woman's powers were something extraordinary, and the little ante-room was kept filled with visitors waiting their turn for an audience. No one noticed the long and frequent absences of Hilda Covington from the grounds. The tent had been placed with its back hiding a small path through the shrubbery. Through a peep-hole arranged in the curtain she was able to see who was waiting, and each time before leaving said a few words as to their lives which enabled Netta to support the character fairly. When the last guest had departed and she joined Lady Moulton, she handed over a bag containing nearly a hundred pounds.

"I have deducted five pounds for the gypsy," she said, "and eight pounds for the hire of the tent and its fittings."

"That is at least five times as much as I expected, Hilda. I have heard all sorts of marvelous stories of the power of your old woman. Several people told me that she seemed to know all about them, and told them things that they believed were only known to themselves. But how did she get so much money?"

Hilda laughed. "I hear that they began with half-sovereigns, but as soon as they heard of her real powers, they did not venture to present her with anything less than a sovereign, and in a good many cases they gave more—no doubt to propitiate her into giving them good fortunes. You see, each visitor only had two or three minutes' interview, so that she got through from twenty to thirty an hour; and as it lasted four hours she did exceedingly well."

"But who is the gypsy, and where did you find her?"

"The gypsy has gone, and is doubtless by this time in some caravan or gypsy tent. I do not think that you will ever find her again."

"I should have suspected that you played the gypsy yourself, Hilda, were it not that I saw you half a dozen times."

"I have no skill in palmistry," the girl laughed, "and certainly have not been in two places at once. I did my duty and heard Jenny Lind sing and Parry play, though I own that I did not patronize Richardson's booth."

"Well, it is extraordinary that this old woman should know the history of such a number of people as went into her tent, few of whom she could ever have heard of even by name, to say nothing of knowing them by sight."

Several ladies called within the next few days, specially to inquire from Lady Moulton about the gypsy.

"Everyone is talking about her," one said. "Certainly she told me several things about the past that it was hardly possible that a woman in her position could know. I have often heard that gypsies pick up information from servants, or in the country from village gossip; but at least a hundred people visited this woman's tent, and from what I hear everyone was as astonished as I was myself at her knowledge of their family matters. It is said that in some cases she went farther than this, and told them things about the present known only to themselves and two or three intimate friends. Some of them seemed to have been quite seriously affected. I saw Mrs. Markham just after she had left the tent, and she was as white as a sheet, and I know she drove away a few minutes afterwards."

To all inquiries Lady Moulton simply replied:

"I know no more about the gypsy than you do. Miss Covington took the entire management of the gypsy tent off my hands, saw to the tent being erected, and engaged the gypsy. Where she picked her up I have no idea, but I fancy that she must have got her from their encampment on Ham Common. She turned the matter off when I asked her point-blank, and I imagine that she must have given the old crone a promise not to let it be known who she was. They are curious people, the gypsies, and for aught I know may have an objection to any of the tribe going to a gathering like ours to tell fortunes."

Some appeals were made to Hilda personally; but Lady Moulton had told her the answer she had given, and taking her cue from it she was able to so shape her replies that her questioners left her convinced that she had really, while carrying out Lady Moulton's instructions, lighted on a gypsy possessing some of the secrets of the almost forgotten science of palmistry.

CHAPTER V.

A GAMBLING DEN.

In a corner of one of the winding courts that lie behind Fleet Street stood a dingy-looking house, the lamp over the door bearing the words, "Billiards and Pool." During the daytime no one would be seen to enter save between the hours of twelve and two, when perhaps a dozen young fellows, after eating a frugal lunch, would resort there to pass their hour out of office in smoking and a game of billiards. Of an evening, however, there were lights in every window, and the click of balls could be heard from the ground floor and that above it. In each of these there were two tables, and the play continued uninterruptedly from seven until eleven or half-past.

The lights on the second floor, however, often burned until two or three o'clock in the morning, and it was here that the proprietor reaped by far the larger proportion of his profits. While the billiard-room windows generally stood open, those of the large room on the second floor were never raised, and when the lights below were extinguished, heavy curtains were dropped across the windows to keep both the light and the sounds within from being seen or heard in the court below. Here was a large roulette table, while along the sides of the room were smaller tables for those who preferred other games. Here almost every evening some thirty or forty men assembled. Of these, perhaps a third were clerks or shop assistants, the remainder foreigners of almost every nationality. Betting lists were exposed at one end of the room. Underneath these a bookmaker had a small table, and carried on his trade.

In 1851 there were a score of such places in the neighborhood of the Strand and Fleet Street, but few did a larger business than this. It was generally understood that Wilkinson, the proprietor, had been a soldier; but the belief originated rather from his upright carriage and a certain soldierly walk than from anything he had himself said, and he was not the sort of man whom even the most regular of the frequenters of his establishment cared to question. He was a tall man, some five-and-forty years of age, taciturn in speech, but firm in manner while business was going on. He kept admirable order in the place. He was generally to be found in the room on the second floor, but when a whistle blew, and one of the markers whispered up a speaking-tube that there was a dispute going on between the players or lookers-on, he was at once upon the spot.

"Now, gentlemen," he would say, interposing between them, "you know the rules of this establishment; the marker's decision on all points connected with the game is final, and must be accepted by both parties. I will have no quarrels or disputes here, and anyone making a row goes straight out into the street, and never comes in here again."

In the vast majority of cases this settled the matter; but when the men were flushed with liquor, and inclined to continue the dispute, they were seized by the collar by Wilkinson's strong arm and were summarily ejected from the house. In the inner room he preserved order as strictly, but had much more difficulty in doing so among the foreign element. Here quarrels were not uncommon, and knives occasionally drawn; but Wilkinson was a powerful man and a good boxer, and a flush hit from the shoulder always settled the business.

But though stern in the management of his establishment, Wilkinson was popular among its frequenters. He was acquainted with most of their callings and business. Indeed, none were admitted to the upper room unless well introduced by *habitués*, or until he had made private inquiries concerning them. Thus he knew among the foreigners whom he could trust, and how far, when, after a run of ill luck, they came to him and asked him for a loan, he could venture to go.

With the English portion of his customers he was still more liberal. He knew that he should not be a loser from transactions with them; they must repay him, for were it known to their employers that they were in the habit of gambling, it would mean instant dismissal. There were among them several lawyers' clerks, some of whom were, in comparison with their means, deeply in debt to him. One or other of those he would often invite up to his private room on the floor above, where a bottle of good wine would be on the table, a box of excellent cigars beside it, and here they would chat more or less comfortably until the roulette room opened.

Mr. Wilkinson made no pretense that these meetings were simply for the purpose of drinking his wine and smoking his cigars. "I am a straightforward man," he would say, "and business is business. I oblige you, and I expect you to oblige me. I have always had a fancy that there is money to be made in connection with lawyers' businesses. There are missing heirs to be huntedup; there are provisos in deeds, of whose existence some one or other would give a good deal to know. Now, I am sure that you are not in a position to pay me the amount I have lent you, and for which I hold your I. O. U.'s. I have no idea of pressing you for the money, and shall be content to let it run on so long as you will let me know what is being done at your office. The arrangement is that you will tell me anything that you think can be used to advantage, and if money is made out of any information you may give me, I will engage to pay you a third of what it brings in. Now, I call that a fair bargain. What do you say?"

In some cases the offer was closed with at once; in others it was only agreed to after threats that the debt must be at once paid or an application would be made forthwith. So far the gambling-house keeper's expectations had not met with the success he had looked for. He had spent a good deal of time in endeavoring to find the descendants of persons who stood in the direct line of succession to properties, but of whom all clew had been lost. He had indeed obtained an insight into various family differences that had enabled him to successfully extort blackmail, but his gains in this way had not, so far, recouped him for the sums he had, as he considered, invested in the speculation.

He was, however, a patient man, and felt, no doubt, that sooner or later he should be able to make a coup that would set him up for life. Still he was disappointed; his idea had been the one held by many ignorant persons, that lawyers are as a class ready to resort to tricks of all kinds, in the interests of their clients or themselves. He had found that he had been altogether wrong, and that although there were a few firms which, working in connection with money-lenders, financial agents, and the lowest class of bill discounters, were mixed up in transactions of a more or less shady character, these were the black sheep of the profession, and that in the vast majority of cases the business transacted was purely technical and connected with the property of their clients. Nevertheless, he took copious notes of all he learned, contending that there was no saying what might come in useful some day.

"Well, Dawkins," he said one day to a dark-haired young fellow with a handsome face that already showed traces of the effect of late hours and dissipation, "I suppose it is the usual thing; the lawsuit as to the right of way at Brownsgrove is still going on, the settlements in Mr. Cochrane's marriage to Lady Gertrude Ivory are being drawn up, and other business of the same sort. You never give me a scrap of information that is of the slightest use. I am afraid that your firm is altogether too eminently respectable to have anything to do with doubtful transactions."

"I told you so from the first, Wilkinson; that whatever your game might be, there would be nothing in our office that could be of the least use to you, even if you had copies of every deed drawn up in it. Ours is what you might call a family business. Our clients have for the most part dealt with the firm for the last hundred years; that is to say, their families have. We have drawn their wills, their marriage settlements, their leases, and done everything relating to their property for years and years. My own work for the last two or three days has been drafting and engrossing the will of a General Mathieson, whose father and grandfather were our clients before him."

"Mathieson—he is an old Indian officer, isn't he, if it is the man I mean? He was in command at Benares twenty years ago. He was a handsome man, then, about my height and build."

"Yes, I have no doubt that is the man—John Le Marchand Mathieson."

"That is him. He was very popular with the troops. He used to spend a good deal of money in improving their rations and making them comfortable. Had a first-rate stable, and they used to say he was a rich man. Anyhow, he spent a good deal more than his pay."

"Yes, he was a second son, but his elder brother died, and he came into the property; but instead of coming home to enjoy it he stopped out in India for years after he came into it."

"He had a daughter, quite a little girl, in those days; her mother died out there. I suppose she inherits his property?"

"Well, no; she married some time back; she and her husband are both dead, and their son, a boy, six or seven years old, lives with the old man."

"How much does he leave?"

"Something over a hundred thousand pounds. At least I know that that is about the value of the estates, for we have always acted as his agents, collected the rents, and so on."

"I should like to see a copy of his will," Wilkinson said, after sitting for some time silent. "I don't want all the legal jargon, but just the list of the legacies."

"I can easily jot those down for you. The property goes to the grandson, and if he dies before coming of age, to a niece, Hilda Covington, who is his ward and lives with him. He leaves her beside only five hundred pounds, because she is herself an heiress. There are a score of small legacies, to old servants, soldiers, widows, and people of that sort."

"Well, you may as well give me the list entire."

Dawkins shrugged his shoulders.

"Just as you like," he said; "the will was signed yesterday, but I have the note of instructions still by me, and will bring round the list to-morrow evening; though, upon my word, I don't see what interest it can possibly have for you."

"I don't know myself," the other said shortly, "but there is never any saying."

After talking for a few minutes on other subjects he said, "The room is open downstairs now, Dawkins, and as we have finished the bottle I will not keep you any longer. In fact, the name of that old General has called up some queer memories of old times, and I should like to think them over."

When the clerk had left, Wilkinson sat for a long time in thought.

"It is a great idea," he murmured to himself at last; "it will want a tremendous lot of planning to arrange it all, and of course it is tremendously risky. Still, it can be done, and the stake is worth trying for, even if it would be seven years' transportation if anything went wrong. In the first place I have to get some proofs of my identity. I own that I have neglected my family scandalously," and his face, which had been stern and hard, softened into a smile. "Then, of course, I must establish myself in chambers in the West End, and as I have three or four thousand pounds in hand I can carry on for two or three years, if necessary. At the worst the General is likely to add me to his list of legatees, but of course that would scarcely be worth playing for alone. The will is the thing. I don't see my way to that, but it is hard if it can't be managed somehow. The child is, of course, an obstacle, but that can certainly be got over, and as I don't suppose the old man is going to die at present I have time to make my plans. When I see how matters go I can put my hand on a man who could be relied on to help me carry out anything I might put in his way. Well, I always thought that I should hit on something good through these young scamps who come here, but this is a bigger thing than I ever dreamed of. It will certainly be a difficult game to play, but, knocking about all over the world as I have been for fifteen years before I came back and set up this show, I think that I have learned enough to pass muster anywhere."

Somewhat to the surprise of the *habitués* of the room below it was nearly eleven o'clock before the proprietor made his appearance there, and even when he did so he took little interest in what was going on, but moved restlessly from one room to another, smoking cigar after cigar without intermission, and acknowledging but briefly the greetings of those who were the most regular frequenters of his establishment.

Two days later the following advertisement appeared, not only in the London papers, but in a large number of country journals:

> "JOHN SIMCOE: Any relatives of John Simcoe, who left England about the year 1830 or 1831, and is supposed to have been lost at sea in the Bay of Bengal, in the ship *Nepaul*, in December, 1832, are requested to communicate with J. W. Thompson & Co., Newspaper Agents, Fleet Street, when they will hear of something to their advantage."

Only one reply was received. It was dated "Myrtle Cottage, Stowmarket," and was as follows:

> "SIR: A friend has shown me the advertisement in the Ipswich paper, which must, I think, refer to my nephew, who left here twenty years ago.

I received a letter from him dated December 2, 1832, from Calcutta, saying that he was about to sail for China in the *Nepaul*. I never heard from him again, but the Rector here kindly made some inquiries for me some months afterwards, and learned that the vessel had never been heard of after sailing, but was believed to have foundered with all hands in a great gale that took place a few days after she sailed. So far as I know I am his only relative. Awaiting a further communication from you,

"I remain,
"Your obedient servant,
"MARTHA SIMCOE."

Great was the excitement caused by the advertisement at Myrtle Cottage. Miss Simcoe, who with a tiny servant was the sole inmate of the cottage, had called together all her female acquaintances, and consulted them as to what the advertisement could mean, and as to the way in which she should answer it.

"Do you think it would be safe to reply at all?" she inquired anxiously. "You see, my nephew John was a very wild young fellow. I do not mean as to his conduct here; no one could say anything against that. He was a clerk in the bank, you know, and, I believe, was very well thought of; but when his father died, and he came into two thousand pounds, it seemed to turn his head. I know that he never liked the bank; he had always wanted to be either a soldier or a sailor, and directly he got the money he gave up his situation at the bank, and nothing would do but that he must travel. Everyone told him that it was madness; his Aunt Maria—poor soul, you all knew her—and I cried over it, but nothing would move him. A fine-looking fellow he was, as some of you will remember, standing six feet high, and, as everyone said, looking more like a soldier officer than a clerk at a bank.

"We asked him what he would do when his money was gone, but he laughed it off, and said that there were plenty of things for a man to do with a pair of strong arms. He said that he might enter the service of some Indian prince, or marry the daughter of a black king, or discover a diamond mine, and all sorts of nonsense of that sort. He bought such an outfit as you never did see—guns and pistols and all sorts of things; and as for clothes, why, a prince could not have wanted more. Shirts by the dozen, my dear; and I should say eight or ten suits of white clothes, which I told him would make him look like a cricketer or a baker. Why, it took three big trunks to hold all his things. But I will say for him that he wrote regular, either to me or to my sister Maria. Last time he wrote he said that he had been attacked by a tiger, but had got well again and was going to China, though what he wanted to go there for I am sure I don't know. He could not want to buy teacups and saucers; they would only get broken sending home. Well, his death was a great blow to us."

"I don't know whether I should answer the advertisement, Miss Simcoe," one of her friends said. "There is no saying what it might mean. Perhaps he got into debt in India, and the people think that they might get paid if they can find out his relations here."

The idea came like a douche of cold water upon the little gathering.

"But the advertisement says, 'will hear of something to their advantage,' Mrs. Maberley," Miss Simcoe urged timidly.

"Oh, that is nothing, my dear. That may be only a lawyer's trick; they are capable of anything, I have heard."

"But they could not make Miss Simcoe pay," another urged; "it seems to me much more likely that her nephew may have left some of his money in the hands of a banker at Calcutta, and now that it has been so many years unclaimed they are making inquiries to see who is his heir. That seems much more likely."

A murmur of assent ran round the circle, and after much discussion the answer was drafted, and Miss Simcoe, in a fever of anxiety, awaited the reply.

Two days later a tall, well-dressed man knocked at the door of Myrtle Cottage. It was a loud, authoritative knock, such as none of Miss Simcoe's usual visitors gave.

"It must be about the advertisement," she exclaimed.

The little servant had been enjoined to wear her Sunday clothes in case a visitor should come, and after a hasty glance to see if she was tidy, Miss Simcoe sat down in her little parlor, and tried to assume an appearance of calmness. The front door opened, and a man's voice inquired, "Is Miss Simcoe in?" Then the parlor door opened and the visitor entered, pushing past the girl, who had been instructed how to announce him in proper form, and exclaiming, "My dear Aunt Martha," fairly lifted the astonished old lady from her seat and kissed her.

"Dear me! Dear me!" she gasped, as he put her on her feet again, "can it be that you are my nephew John?"

"Why, don't you know me, aunt? Twenty years of knocking about have changed me sadly, I am afraid, but surely you must remember me."

"Ye—es," she said doubtfully, "yes, I think that I remember you. But, you see, we all thought that you were dead; and I have only got that likeness of you that was cut out in black paper by a man who came round when you were only eighteen, and somehow I have always thought of you as like that."

"Yes, I remember," he laughed. "Well, aunt, I have changed since then, there is no doubt. So you see I was not drowned, after all. I was picked up by a passing ship, clinging to a spar, but I lost all my money in the wreck of the *Nepaul*. I shipped before the mast. We traded among the islands for some months, then I had a row with the captain and ran away, and threw in my lot with the natives, and I have been knocking about in the East ever since, and have come back with enough to live on comfortably, and to help you, if you need it."

"Poor Maria died four years ago," she said tearfully. "It would have been a happiness to her indeed, poor creature, if you had come back before."

"I am sorry indeed to hear that," he replied. "Then you are living here all alone, aunt?"

"Yes, except for my little maid. You see, John, Maria and I laid out the money our father left us in life annuities, and as long as we lived together we did very comfortably. Since then, of course, I have had to draw in a little, but I manage very nicely."

"Well, well, aunt, there will be no occasion for you to stint yourself any more. As I said, I have come home with my purse warmly lined, and I shall make you an allowance of fifty pounds a year. You were always very kind to me as a boy, and I can very well afford it, and I dare say it will make all the difference to you."

"My dear John, I could not think of taking such a sum from you."

"Pooh, pooh, aunt! What is the use of money if one cannot use it to make one's friends comfortable? So that is settled, and I won't have anything more said about it."

The old lady wiped her eyes. "It is good of you, John, and it will indeed make all the difference to me. It will almost double my income, and I shan't have to look at every halfpenny before I spend it."

"That is all right, aunt; now let us sit down comfortably to chat about old times. You don't mind my smoking, I hope?"

Miss Simcoe, for almost the first time in her life, told a lie. "Not at all, John; not at all. Now, how was it that you did not come down yourself instead of putting in an advertisement, which I should never have seen if my friend Mrs. Maberley had not happened to notice it in the paper which she takes in regularly, and brought it in to show me?"

"Well, I could not bring myself to come down, aunt. Twenty years make great changes, and it would have been horrible to have come down here and found that you had all gone, and that I was friendless in the place where I had been brought up as a boy. I thought that, by my putting it into a local paper, someone who had known me would be sure to see it. Now let me hear about all the people that I knew."

John Simcoe stayed for three days quietly at the cottage. The news of his return spread rapidly, and soon many of the friends that had known him came to welcome him. His aunt had told her own circle of her nephew's wealth and liberality, and through them the news that John Simcoe had returned home a wealthy man was imparted to all their acquaintances. Some of his old friends declared that they should have known him anywhere; others said frankly that now they knew who he was they saw the likeness, but that if they had met him anywhere else they did not think they should have recognized him.

John Simcoe's memory had been greatly refreshed by his aunt's incessant talk about his early days and doings, and as his visitors were more anxious to hear of his adventures abroad than to talk of the days long past, he had no difficulty whatever in satisfying all as to his identity, even had not the question been settled by his liberality to his aunt, from whom no return whatever could possibly be expected. When he left he handed her fifty pounds in gold.

"I may as well give you a year's money at once," he said; "I am a careless man, and might forget to send it quarterly."

"Where can I write to you, John?" she asked.

"I cannot give you an address at present," he said; "I have only been stopping at a hotel until I could find chambers to suit me. Directly I do so I will drop you a line. I shall always be glad to hear of you, and will run down occasionally to see you and have a chat again with some of my old friends."

The return of John Simcoe served Stowmarket as a subject for conversation for some time. He had spent his money generously while there, and had given a dinner at the principal hotel to a score of those with whom he had been most intimate when a boy. Champagne had flowed in unstinted abundance, and it was generally voted that he was a capital fellow, and well deserved the good fortune that had attended him. In the quiet Suffolk town the tales of the adventures that he had gone through created quite a sensation, and when repeated by their fathers set half the boys of the place wild with a desire to imitate his example, and to embark in a life which was at once delightful, and ended in acquiring untold wealth. On leaving he pressed several of them, especially one who had been a fellow-clerk with him at the bank, and was now its manager, to pay him a visit whenever they came to town.

"I expect to be in diggings of my own in a week or two," he said, "and shall make a point of having a spare bed, to put up a friend at any time."

"YOU DON'T REMEMBER ME, GENERAL?"

CHAPTER VI.

JOHN SIMCOE.

General Mathieson was on the point of going out for a drive with his niece, who was buttoning her glove, when a servant entered the drawing room and said that a gentleman wished to speak to him.

"Who is he? Did he give you his name or say what was his business?"

"No, sir. I have not seen him before. He merely asked me to give you his message."

"I suppose I had better see him, Hilda."

"Well, uncle, I will get out of the way and go downstairs when he has come in. Don't let him keep you, for you know that when I have put you down at your club I have an engagement to take Lina Crossley to do some shopping first, and then for a drive in the park."

"I don't suppose that he will be five minutes, whoever he is."

Hilda slipped away just in time to avoid the visitor. As the manservant opened the door the General looked with some interest at the stranger, for such it seemed to him his visitor was. He was a tall man, well dressed, and yet without the precision that would mark him as being a member of a good club or an *habitué* of the Row.

"You don't remember me, General?" he said, with a slight smile.

"I cannot say that I do," the General replied. "Your face does not seem unfamiliar to me, though I cannot at the present moment place it."

"It is rather an uncommon name," the visitor said; "but I am not surprised that you do not remember it or me, for it is some twenty years since we met. My name is Simcoe."

"Twenty years!" the General repeated. "Then it must have been in India, for twenty years ago I was in command of the Benares district. Simcoe!" he broke off excitedly. "Of course I knew a gentleman of that name who did me an inestimable service; in fact, he saved my life."

"I don't know that it was as much as that, but at least I saved you from being mauled by a tiger."

"Bless me!" the General exclaimed, taking a step forward, "and you are the man. I recognize you now, and had I not believed that you had been lost at sea within a month after you had saved my life I should have known you at once, though, of course, twenty years have changed you a good deal. My dear sir, I am happy indeed to know that the report was a false one, and to meet you again." And he shook hands with his visitor with the greatest warmth.

"I am not surprised that you did not recognize me," the latter said; "I was but twenty-five then, and have been knocking about the world ever since, and have gone through some very rough times and done some very hard work. Of course you saw my name among the list of the passengers on board the *Nepaul*, which went down with, as was supposed, all hands in that tremendous storm in the Bay of Bengal. Happily, I escaped. I was washed overboard just as the wreck of the mainmast had been cut away. A wave carried me close to it; I climbed upon it and lashed myself to leeward of the top, which sheltered me a good deal. Five days later I was picked up insensible and was carried to Singapore. I was in hospital there for some weeks. When I quite recovered, being penniless, without references or friends, I shipped on board a vessel that was going on a trading voyage among the islands. I had come out to see the world, and thought that I might as well see it that way as another. It would take a long time to relate my after-adventures; suffice it that at last, after numerous wanderings, I became chief adviser of a powerful chief in Burmah, and finally have returned home, not exactly a rich man, but with enough to live upon in more than comfort for the rest of my life."

"How long have you been in London?"

"I have been here but a fortnight; I ran down home to see if I had relatives living, but found that an old lady was the sole survivor of my family. I need scarcely say that my first business on reaching London was to rig myself out in a presentable sort of way, and I may say that at present I feel very uncomfortable in these garments after being twenty years without putting on a black coat. I happened the other day to see your name among those who attended the *levée*, and I said to myself at once, 'I will call upon the General and see if he has any remembrances of me.'"

At this moment a servant entered the room with a little note.

> "My Dear Uncle: It is very naughty of you to be so long. I am taking the carriage, and have told them to put the other horse into the brougham and bring it round for you at once."

For more than an hour the two men sat talking together, and Simcoe, on leaving, accepted a cordial invitation from the General to dinner on the following day.

"Well, uncle, who was it?" Hilda asked, when they met in the drawing room a few minutes before the dinner hour. "You said you would not be five minutes, and I waited for a quarter of an hour and then lost patience. I asked when I came in how long he had stayed, and heard that he did not leave until five o'clock."

"He was a man who had saved my life in India, child."

"Dear me! And have you never heard of him since, uncle?"

"No, dear. I did my best to find out his family, but had no idea of ever seeing the man himself, for the simple reason that I believed that he died twenty years ago. He had sailed in a vessel that was reported as lost with all hands, so you may well imagine my surprise when he told me who he was."

"Did you recognize him at once, uncle?"

"Not at first. Twenty years is a long time; and he was only about five-and-twenty when I knew him, and of course he has changed greatly. However, even before he told me who he was I was able to recall his face. He was a tall, active young fellow then, and I could certainly trace the likeness."

"I suppose he was in the army, uncle?"

"No; he was a young Englishman who was making a tour through India. I was in command at Benares at the time, and he brought me letters of introduction from a man who had come out in the same ship with him, and also from a friend of mine in Calcutta. A few days after he arrived I was on the point of going up with a party to do some tiger-shooting in the Terai, and I invited him to come with us. He was a pleasant fellow and soon made himself popular. He never said much about himself, but as far as I understood him he was not a rich man, but he was spending his money in seeing the world, with a sort of happy confidence that something would turn up when his money was gone.

"We were out a week and had fair sport. As you have often heard me say, I was passionately fond of big-game shooting, and I had had many narrow escapes in the course of my life, but I never had so narrow a one as happened to me on that occasion. We had wounded a tiger and had lost him. We had spent a couple of hours in beating the jungle, but without success, and had agreed that the brute could not have been hit as hard as we had believed, but must have made off altogether. We were within fifty yards of the edge of the jungle, when there was a sudden roar, and before I could use my rifle the tiger sprang. I was not in a howdah, but on a pad; and the tiger struck one of its forepaws on my knee. With the other he clung for a moment to the pad, and then we went down together. The brute seized me by the shoulder and sprang into the jungle again, carried me a dozen yards or so, and then lay down, still holding me by the shoulder.

"I was perfectly sensible, but felt somewhat dazed and stupid; I found myself vaguely thinking that he must, after all, have been very badly hit, and, instead of making off, had hid up within a short distance of the spot where we saw him. I was unable to move hand or foot, for he was lying on me, and his weight was pressing the life out of me. I know that I vaguely hoped I should die before he took a bite at my shoulder. I suppose that the whole thing did not last a minute, though to me it seemed an interminable time. Suddenly there was a rustling in the bush. With a deep growl the tiger loosed his hold of my shoulder, and, rising to his feet, faced half round. What happened after that I only know from hearsay.

"Simcoe, it seems, was riding in the howdah on an elephant behind mine. As the tiger sprang at my elephant he fired and hit the beast on the shoulder. It was that, no doubt, that caused its hold to relax, and brought us to the ground together. As the tiger sprang with me into the jungle Simcoe leaped down from the howdah and followed. He had only his empty rifle and a large hunting-knife. It was no easy work pushing his way through the jungle, but in a minute he came upon us. Clubbing his gun, he brought it down on the left side of the tiger's head before the brute, who was hampered by his broken shoulder, and weak from his previous wound, could spring. Had it not been that it was the right shoulder that was broken, the blow, heavy as it was, would have had little effect upon the brute; as it was, having no support on that side, it reeled half over and then, with a snarling growl, sprang upon its assailant. Simcoe partly leaped aside, and striking again with the barrel of his gun,—the butt had splintered with the first blow,—so far turned it aside that instead of receiving the blow direct, which would certainly have broken in his skull, it fell in a slanting direction on his left shoulder.

"The force was sufficient to knock him down, but, as he fell, he drew his knife. The tiger had leaped partly beyond him, so that he lay under its stomach, and it could not for the moment use either its teeth or claws. The pressure was terrible, but with his last remaining strength he drove the knife to the full length of its blade twice into the tiger's body. The animal rolled over for a moment, but there was still life in it, and it again sprang to its feet, when a couple of balls struck it in the head, and it fell dead. Three officers had slipped down from their howdahs when they saw Simcoe rushing into the jungle, and coming up just in time, they fired, and so finished the conflict.

"There was not much to choose between Simcoe and myself, though I had certainly got the worst of it. The flesh of his arm had been pretty well stripped off from the shoulder to the elbow; my shoulder had been broken, and the flesh torn by the brute's teeth, but as it had not shifted its hold from the time it first grasped me till it let go to face Simcoe, it was not so bad as it might have been. But the wound on the leg was more serious; its claws had struck just above the knee-cap and had completely torn it off. We were both insensible when we were lifted up and carried down to the camp. In a fortnight Simcoe was about; but it was some months before I could walk again, and, as you know, my right leg is still stiff. I had a very narrow escape of my life; fever set in, and when Simcoe went down country, a month after the affair, I was still lying between life and death, and never had an opportunity of thanking him for the manner in which, practically unarmed, he went in to face a wounded tiger in order to save my life. You may imagine, then, my regret when a month later we got the news that the *Nepaul*, in which he had sailed, had been lost with all hands."

"It was a gallant action indeed, uncle. You told me something about it soon after I came here, when I happened to ask you how it was that you walked so stiffly, but you did not tell it so fully. And what is he going to do now?"

"He is going to settle in London. He has been, as he says, knocking about in the East ever since, being engaged in all sorts of adventures; he has been for some time in the service of a native chief some way up near the borders of Burmah, Siam, and China, and somehow got possession of a large number of rubies and other precious stones, which he has turned into money, and now intends to take chambers and settle down to a quiet life, join a club, and so on. Of course I promised to do all in my power to further his object, and to introduce him into as much society as he cared for."

"What is he like, uncle?"

"He is about my height, and I suppose about five-and-forty—though he looks rather older. No wonder, after such a life as he has led. He carries himself well, and he is altogether much more presentable than you would expect under the circumstances. Indeed, had I not known that he had never served, I should unhesitatingly have put him down as having been in the army. There is something about the way he carries his shoulders that you seldom see except among men who have been drilled. He is coming here to dine to-morrow, so you will see him."

"That relieves me of anxiety, uncle; for you know you had a letter this morning from Colonel Fitzhugh, saying that he had been unexpectedly called out of town, and you said that you would ask somebody at the club to fill his place, but you know you very often forget things that you ought to remember."

“I certainly had forgotten that when I asked him to come, and as I came home I blamed myself for not having asked someone else, so as to make up an even number.”

A month later Mr. Simcoe had become an intimate of General Mathieson’s house. It had always been a matter of deep regret to the General that he had been unable to thank the man who at terrible risk to his life had saved him from death, and that feeling was heightened when the news came that his preserver had been drowned, and that the opportunity of doing so was forever lost. He now spared no pains to further his wishes. He constantly invited him to lunch or dinner at his club, introduced him to all his friends in terms of the highest eulogium, and repeated over and over again the story of his heroic action. As his own club was a military one he could not propose him there, but he had no difficulty in getting friends to propose and support him for two other clubs of good standing.

Several of the officers to whom he introduced Simcoe had been at Benares at the time he was hurt. These he recognized at once, and was able to chat with them of their mutual acquaintances, and indeed surprised them by his knowledge of matters at the station that they would hardly have thought would be known to one who had made but a short stay there. One of them said as much, but Simcoe said, laughing, “You forget that I was laid up for a month. Everyone was very good to me, and I had generally one or two men sitting with me, and the amount of gossip I picked up about the station was wonderful. Of course there was nothing else to talk about; and as I have a good memory, I think I could tell you something about the private affairs of pretty nearly every civilian and military man on the station.”

Everyone agreed that Simcoe was a very pleasant and amusing companion. He was full of anecdotes of the wild people that he had lived among and of the adventures and escapes he had gone through. Although none of the Benares friends of the General recognized Simcoe when they first met him, they speedily recalled his features. His instant recognition of them, his acquaintance with persons and scenes at and around Benares was such that they never for a moment doubted his identity, and as their remembrance of the General’s visitor returned they even wondered that their recognition of him had not been as instant as his of them. As to his means, not even to the General had Simcoe explained his exact position. He had taken good apartments in Jermyn Street, gave excellent little dinners there, kept undeniably good wine and equally excellent cigars, dressed well, and was regarded as being a thoroughly good fellow.

The General was not a close observer. Had he been so, he would speedily have noticed that his niece, although always polite and courteous to Mr.

Simcoe, did not receive him with the warmth and pleasure with which she greeted those who were her favorites. On his part the visitor spared no pains to make himself agreeable to her; he would at once volunteer to execute any commission for her if she happened to mention in his presence anything that she wanted. One evening when she was going to a ball he sent her an expensive bouquet of flowers. The next day when she saw him she said:

"I am very much obliged to you for those lovely flowers, and I carried the bouquet last night, but please do not send any more. I don't think that it is quite nice to accept presents from anyone except very near relations. It was very kind of you to think of it, but I would really rather that you did not do it again. Uncle gives me carte blanche in the way of flowers, but I do not avail myself of it very largely, for the scent is apt to make me feel faint, and beyond the smallest spray I seldom carry any. I made an exception last night, for those you sent me were most lovely. You don't mind my saying that, do you?"

"Not at all, Miss Covington; and I quite understand what you mean. It seemed natural to me to send you some flowers. Out in the Pacific Islands, especially at Samoa and Tahiti, and, indeed, more or less everywhere, women wear a profusion of flowers in their hair, and no present is so acceptable to them."

"I fancy flowers do not cost so much there as they do here, Mr. Simcoe?"

"No," the latter laughed; "for half a dollar one can get enough to render a girl the envy of all others."

"I think you were right to ask Mr. Simcoe not to repeat his present, Hilda," the General said. "I particularly noticed the bouquet that you carried last night."

"Yes, uncle, there was nothing equal to it in the room; it must have cost three or four guineas."

"I don't think that you quite like him; do you, Hilda?"

"I like him, uncle, because he saved your life; but in other respects I do not know that I do like him particularly. He is very pleasant and very amusing, but I don't feel that I quite understand him."

"How do you mean that you don't understand him?"

"I cannot quite explain, uncle. To begin with, I don't seem to get any nearer to him—I mean to what he really is. I know more of his adventures and his life than I did, but I know no more of him himself than I did three months ago when I first met him at dinner."

"At any rate you know that he is brave," the General said, somewhat gravely.

"Yes, I know that, of course; but a man can be brave, exceptionally brave, and yet not possess all other good qualities. He did behave like a hero in your case, and I need not say that I feel deeply grateful to him for the service that he rendered you; still, that is the only side of his nature that I feel certain about."

"Pooh! pooh! Hilda," the General said, with some irritation. "What do you know about nine-tenths of the men you meet? You cannot even tell that they are brave."

"No, uncle; I know only the side they choose to present to me, which is a pleasant side, and I do not care to know more. But it is different in this case. Mr. Simcoe is here nearly every day; he has become one of our inner circle; you are naturally deeply interested in him, and I am, therefore, interested in him also, and want to know more of him than I have got to know. He is brave and pleasant; is he also honest and honorable? Is he a man of thoroughly good principles? We know what he tells us of his life and his adventures, but he only tells us what he chooses."

The General shrugged his shoulders.

"My dear child, you may say the same thing of pretty nearly every unmarried man you meet. When a man marries and sets up a household one does get to know something about him. There are his wife's relations, who, as a rule, speak with much frankness concerning a man who has married their daughter, sister, or cousin. But as to bachelors, as a rule one has to take them at their own valuation. Of course, I know no more than you do as to whether Simcoe is in all respects an honorable gentleman. It is quite sufficient that he saved my life, almost at the sacrifice of his own, and whatever the life he may have led since is no business of mine. He is distinctly popular among those I have introduced him to, and is not likely in any way to discredit that introduction."

That Hilda was not entirely satisfied was evident by the letter she wrote when her uncle had, as usual, gone up one afternoon to his club.

> "My Dear Netta: I have told you several times about the Mr. Simcoe who saved uncle's life out in India, and who is so intimate at the house. I can't say that either my acquaintance with or my liking for him increases. He does not stand the test of the system, and the more I watch his lips the less I understand him. He talks fluently and quickly, and yet somehow I feel that there is a hesitation in his speech, and that his lips are repeating what they have learned, and not speaking spontaneously.

You know that we have noticed the same thing among those who have learned to speak by the system but are not yet perfect in it, so I need not explain further what I mean, as you will understand it. For example, I can always tell at a public meeting, or when listening to a preacher, whether he is speaking absolutely extemporarily or whether he has learned his speech by heart beforehand.

"I really strongly misdoubt the man. Of course I know that he saved my uncle's life; beyond that I know nothing of him, and it is this very feeling that I do know nothing that disquiets me. I can no more see into him than I can into a stone wall. I can quite understand that it is of very great importance to him to stand well with the General. He came here a stranger with a queer history. He knew no one; he had money and wanted to get into society. Through my uncle he has done so; he has been elected to two clubs, has made a great number of acquaintances, goes to the Row, the Royal Academy, the theaters, and so on, and is, at any rate, on nodding terms with a very large number of people. All this he owes to my uncle, and I fail to see what else he can wish for. It would be natural with so many other engagements that he should not come to us so often as he used to do, but there is no falling off in that respect. He is the tame cat of the establishment. I dare say you think me silly to worry over such a thing, but I can't help worrying. I hate things I don't understand, and I don't understand this man.

"Another thing is, Walter does not like him. He constantly brings the child toys, but Walter does not take to him, refuses absolutely to sit upon his knee, or to be petted by him in any way. I always think that it is a bad sign when a child won't take to a man. However, I will not bother you more about it now; I will keep him out of my letters as much as I can. I wish I could keep him out of my mind also. As I tell myself over and over again, he is nothing to me, and whether he possesses all the virtues or none of them is, or at any rate should be, a matter of indifference to me. I can't help wishing that you had come over here two months later, then I should have had the benefit of your advice and opinion, for you know, Netta, how accustomed I was for years to consider you almost, if not quite, infallible."

CHAPTER VII.

JOHN SIMCOE'S FRIEND.

There was a great sensation among the frequenters of the house in Elephant Court when they were told that Wilkinson had sold the business, and the new proprietor would come in at once. The feeling among those who were in his debt was one of absolute dismay, for it seemed to them certain the amounts would be at once called in. To their surprise and relief Wilkinson went round among the foreigners, whose debts in no case exceeded five pounds, and handed to them their notes of hand.

"I am going out of the business," he said, "and shall be leaving for abroad in a day or so. I might, of course, have arranged with the new man for him to take over these papers, but he might not be as easy as I have been, and I should not like any of you to get into trouble. I have never pressed anyone since I have been here, still less taken anyone into court, and I should like to leave on friendly terms with all. So here are your papers; tear them up, and don't be fools enough to borrow again."

Towards his English clients, whose debts were generally from ten to twenty pounds, he took the same course, adding a little good advice as to dropping billiards and play altogether and making a fresh start.

"You have had a sharp lesson," he said, "and I know that you have been on thorns for the last year. I wanted to show you what folly it was to place yourself in the power of anyone to ruin you, and I fancy I have succeeded very well. There is no harm in a game of billiards now and then, but if you cannot play without betting you had better cut it altogether. As for the tables, it is simply madness. You must lose in the long run, and I am quite sure that I have got out of you several times the amount of the I. O. U.'s that I hold."

Never were men more surprised and more relieved. They could hardly believe that they were once more free men, and until a fresh set of players had succeeded them the billiard rooms were frequently almost deserted. To Dawkins Wilkinson was somewhat more explicit.

"You know," he said, "the interest I took in that will of General Mathieson. It was not the will so much as the man that I was so interested in. It showed me that he was most liberally disposed to those who had done him a service. Now, it happens that years ago, when he was at Benares, I saved his life from a tiger, and got mauled myself in doing so. I had not thought of the matter for many years, but your mention of his name recalled it to me. I had another name in those days—men often change their names when they knock about in queer places, as I have done. However, I called upon him, and he expressed himself most grateful. I need not say that I did not mention the billiard room to him. He naturally supposed that I had just arrived from abroad, and he has offered to introduce me to many of his friends; and I think that I have a good chance of being put down in his will for a decent sum. I brought money home with me from abroad and have made a goodish sum here, so I shall resume my proper name and go West, and drop this affair altogether. I am not likely to come against any of the crew here, and, as you see," and he removed a false beard and whiskers from his face, "I have shaved, though I got this hair to wear until I had finally cut the court. So you see you have unintentionally done me a considerable service, and in return I shall say nothing about that fifty pounds you owe me. Now, lad, try and keep yourself straight in future. You may not get out of another scrape as you have out of this. All I ask is that you will not mention what I have told you to anyone else. There is no fear of my being recognized, with a clean-shaven face and different toggery altogether, but at any rate it is as well that everyone but yourself should believe that, as I have given out, I have gone abroad again. I shall keep your I. O. U.'s, but I promise you that you shall hear no more of them as long as you hold your tongue as to what I have just told you. Possibly I may some day need your assistance, and in that case shall know where to write to you."

It was not until after a great deal of thought that John Simcoe had determined thus far to take Dawkins into his confidence, but he concluded at last that it was the safest thing to do. He was, as he knew, often sent by the firm with any communications that they might have to make to their clients, and should he meet him at the General's he might recognize him and give him some trouble. He had made no secret that he had turned his hand to many callings, and that his doings in the southern seas would not always bear close investigation, and the fact that he had once kept a billiard room could do him no special harm. As to the will, Dawkins certainly would not venture to own that he had repeated outside what had been done in the office. The man might be useful to him in the future. It was more than probable he would again involve himself in debt, and was just the weak and empty-headed young fellow who might be made a convenient tool should he require one.

So Elephant Court knew Mr. Wilkinson no more, and certainly none of the *habitués* could have recognized him in the smooth-shaven and faultlessly dressed man whom they might meet coming out of a West End club. Dawkins often turned the matter over in his mind, after his first relief had passed at finding the debt that had weighed so heavily upon him perfectly wiped out.

"There ought to be money in it," he said to himself, "but I don't see where it comes in. In the first place I could not say he had kept a gambling place without acknowledging that I had often been there, and I could not say that it was a conversation of mine about the General's will that put it into his head to call upon him, and lastly, he has me on the hip with those I. O. U.'s. Possibly if the General does leave him money, I may manage to get some out of him, though I am by no means sure of that. He is not a safe man to meddle with, and he might certainly do me more harm than I could do him."

The matter had dropped somewhat from his mind when, three months later, General Mathieson came into the office to have an interview with his principals.

After he had left the managing clerk was called in. On returning, he handed Dawkins a sheet of paper.

"You will prepare a fresh will for General Mathieson; it is to run exactly as at present, but this legacy is to be inserted after that to Miss Covington. It might just as well have been put in a codicil, but the General preferred to have it in the body of the will."

Dawkins looked at the instruction. It contained the words: "To John Simcoe, at present residing at 132 Jermyn Street, I bequeath the sum of ten thousand pounds, as a token of my gratitude for his heroic conduct in saving my life at the cost of great personal injury to himself from the grip of a tiger, in the year 1831."

"By Jove, he has done well for himself!" Dawkins muttered, as he sat down to his desk after the managing clerk had handed him the General's will from the iron box containing papers and documents relating to his affairs. "Ten thousand pounds! I wish I could light upon a general in a fix of some sort, though I don't know that I should care about a tiger. It is wonderful what luck some men have. I ought to get something out of this, if I could but see my way to it. Fancy the keeper of a billiard room and gaming house coming in for such a haul as this! It is disgusting!"

He set about preparing a draft of the will, but he found it difficult to keep his attention fixed upon his work, and when the chief clerk ran his eye over it he looked up in indignant surprise.

"What on earth is the matter with you, Mr. Dawkins? The thing is full of the most disgraceful blunders. In several cases it is not even sense. During all the time that I have been in this office I have never had such a disgraceful piece of work come into my hands before. Why, if the office boy had been told to make a copy of the will, he would have done it vastly better. What does it mean?"

"I am very sorry, sir," Dawkins said, "but I don't feel very well to-day, and I have got such a headache that I can scarcely see what I am writing."

"Well, well," his superior said, somewhat mollified, "that will account for it. I thought at first that you must have been drinking. You had better take your hat and be off. Go to the nearest chemist and take a dose, and then go home and lie down. You are worse than of no use in the state that you are. I hope that you will be all right in the morning, for we are, as you know, very busy at present, and cannot spare a hand. Tear up that draft and hand the will and instructions to Mr. Macleod. The General will be down here at ten o'clock to-morrow to see it; he is like most military men, sharp and prompt, and when he wants a thing done he expects to have it done at once."

"You are feeling better, I hope, this morning?" he said, when Dawkins came into the office at the usual hour next day, "though I must say that you look far from well. Do you think that you are capable of work?"

"I think so, sir; at any rate my head is better."

It was true that the clerk did not look well, for he had had no sleep all night, but had tossed restlessly in bed, endeavoring, but in vain, to hit on some manner of extracting a portion of the legacy from the ex-proprietor of the gambling house. The more he thought, the more hopeless seemed the prospect. John Simcoe was eminently a man whom it would be unsafe to anger. The promptness and decision of his methods had gained him at least the respect of all the frequenters of his establishment, and just as he had sternly kept order there, so he would deal with any individual who crossed his path. He held the best cards, too; and while a disclosure of the past could hardly injure him seriously, he had the means of causing the ruin and disgrace of Dawkins himself, if he ventured to attack him.

The clerk was himself shrewd in his own way, but he had the sense to feel that he was no match for John Simcoe, and the conclusion that he finally came to was that he must wait and watch events, and that, so far as he could see, his only chance of obtaining a penny of the legacy was to follow implicitly the instructions Simcoe had given him, in which case possibly he might receive a present when the money was paid.

About a fortnight after he knew the will had been signed by General Mathieson, Simcoe went down to a small house on Pentonville Hill, where one of the ablest criminals in London resided, passing unsuspected under the eyes of the police in the character of a man engaged in business in the City. A peculiar knock brought him to the door.

"Ah, is it you, Simcoe?" he said; "why, I have not seen you for months. I did not know you for the moment, for you have taken all the hair off your face."

"I have made a change, Harrison. I have given up the billiard rooms, and am now a swell with lodgings in Jermyn Street."

"That is a change! I thought you said the billiards and cards paid well; but I suppose you have got something better in view?"

"They did pay well, but I have a very big thing in hand."

"That is the right line to take up," the other said. "You were sure to get into trouble with the police about the card-playing before long, and then the place would have been shut up, and you might have got three months; and when you got out the peelers would have kept their eyes upon you, and your chances would have been at an end. No, I have never had anything to do with small affairs; I go in, as you know, for big things. They take time to work out, it is true; and after all one's trouble, something may go wrong at the last moment, and the thing has to be given up. Some girl who has been got at makes a fool of herself, and gets discharged a week before it comes off; or a lady takes it into her head to send her jewels to a banker's, and go on to the Continent a week earlier than she intended to do. Then there is a great loss in getting rid of the stuff. Those sharps at Amsterdam don't give more than a fifth of the value for diamonds. It is a heart-rending game, on the whole; but there is such excitement about the life that when one has once taken it up it is seldom indeed that one changes it, though one knows that, sooner or later, one is sure to make a slip and get caught. Now, what will you take? Champagne or brandy?"

"I know that your brandy is first-rate, Harrison, and I will sample it again."

"I have often thought," went on the other, after the glasses had been filled and cigars lighted, "what a rum thing it was that you should come across my brother Bill out among the islands. He had not written to me for a long time, and I had never expected to hear of him again. I thought that he had gone down somehow, and had either been eaten by sharks or killed by the natives, or shot in some row with his mates. He was two years older than I was, and, as I have told you, we were sons of a well-to-do auctioneer in the country; but he was a hard man, and we could not stand it after a time, so we made a bolt for it. We were decently dressed when we got to London. As we had been at a good school at home, and were both pretty sharp, we thought that we should have no difficulty in getting work of some sort.

"We had a hard time of it. No one would take us without a character, so we got lower and lower, till we got to know some boys who took us to what was called a thieves' kitchen—a place where boys were trained as pick-pockets. The old fellow who kept it saw that we were fit for higher game than was usual, and instead of being sent out to pick up what we could get in the streets we were dressed as we had been before, and sent to picture-galleries and museums and cricket matches, and we soon became first-rate hands, and did well. In a short time we didn't see why we should work for another man, and we left him without saying good-by.

"It was not long before he paid us out. He knew that we should go on at the same work, and dressed up two or three of his boys and sent them to these places, and one day when Bill was just pocketing a watch at Lord's one of these boys shouted out, 'Thief! thief! That boy has stolen your watch, sir,' and Bill got three months, though the boy could not appear against him, for I followed him after they had nabbed Bill, and pretty nearly killedhim.

"Then I went on my travels, and was away two or three years from London. Bill had been out and in again twice; he was too rash altogether. I took him away with me, but I soon found that it would not do, and that it would soon end in our both being shut up. So I put it fairly to him.

"'We are good friends, you know, Bill,' I said, 'but it is plain to me that we can't work together with advantage. You are twenty and I am eighteen, but, as you have often said yourself, I have got the best head of the two. I am tired of this sort of work. When we get a gold ticker, worth perhaps twenty pounds, we can't get above two for it, and it is the same with everything else. It is not good enough. We have been away from London so long that old Isaacs must have forgotten all about us. I have not been copped yet, and as I have got about twenty pounds in my pocket I can take lodgings as a young chap who has come up to walk the hospitals, or something of that sort. If you like to live with me, quiet, we will work together; if not, it is best that we should each go our own way—always being friends, you know.'

"Bill said that was fair enough, but that he liked a little life and to spend his money freely when he got it. So we separated. Bill got two more convictions, and the last time it was a case of transportation. We had agreed between ourselves that if either of us got into trouble the other should call once a month at the house of a woman we knew to ask for letters, and I did that regularly after he was sent out. I got a few letters from him. The first was written after he had made his escape. He told me that he intended to stay out there—it was a jolly life, and a free one, I expect. Pens and paper were not common where he was; anyhow he only wrote once a year or so, and it was two years since I had heard from him when you wrote and said you had brought me a message from Bill.

"Ever since we parted I have gone on the same line, only I have worked carefully. I was not a bad-looking chap, and hadn't much difficulty in getting over servant girls and finding out where things were to be had, so I gradually got on. For years now I have only carried on big affairs, working the thing up and always employing other hands to carry the job out. None of them know me here. I meet them at quiet pubs and arrange things there, and I need hardly say that I am so disguised that none of the fellows who follow my orders would know me again if they met me in the street. I could retire if I liked, and live in a villa and keep my carriage. Why, I made five thousand pounds as my share of that bullion robbery between London and Brussels. But I know that I should be miserable without anything to do; as it is, I unite amusement with business. I sometimes take a stall at the Opera, and occasionally I find a diamond necklace in my pocket when I get home. I know well enough that it is foolish, but when I see a thing that I need only put out my hand to have, my old habit is too strong for me. Then I often walk into swell entertainments. You have only to be well got up, and to go rather late, so that the hostess has given up expecting arrivals and is occupied with her guests, and the flunky takes your hat without question, and you go upstairs and mix with the people. In that way you get to know as to the women who have the finest jewels, and have no difficulty in finding out their names. I have got hold of some very good things that way, but though there would have been no difficulty in taking some of them at the time, I never yielded to that temptation. In a crowded room one never can say whose eyes may happen to be looking in your direction.

"I wonder that you never turned your thoughts that way. From what you have told me of your doings abroad, I know that you are not squeamish in your ideas, and with your appearance you ought to be able to go anywhere without suspicion."

"I am certainly not squeamish," Simcoe said, "but I have not had the training. One wants a little practice and to begin young, as you did, to try that game on. However, just at present I have a matter in hand that will set me up for life if it turns out well, but I shall want a little assistance. In the first place I want to get hold of a man who could make one up well, and who, if I gave him a portrait, could turn me out so like the original that anyone who had only seen him casually would take me for him."

"There is a man down in Whitechapel who is the best hand in London at that sort of thing. He is a downright artist. Several times when I have had particular jobs in hand, inquiries I could not trust anyone else to make, I have been to him, and when he has done with me and I have looked in the glass there was not the slightest resemblance to my own face in it. I suppose the man you want to represent is somewhere about your own height?"

"Yes, I should say that he is as nearly as may be the same. He is an older man than I am."

"Oh, that is nothing! He could make you look eighty if you wanted it. Here is the man's address; his usual fee is a guinea, but, as you want to be got up to resemble someone else, he might charge you double."

"The fee is nothing," Simcoe said. "Then again, I may want to get hold of a man who is a good hand at imitating handwriting."

"That is easy enough. Here is the address of a man who does little jobs for me sometimes, and is, I think, the best hand at it in England. You see, sometimes there is in a house where you intend to operate some confoundedly active and officious fellow—a butler or a footman—who might interrupt proceedings. His master is in London, and he receives a note from him ordering him to come up to town with a dressing case, portmanteau, guns, or something of that kind, as may be suitable to the case. I got a countess out of the way once by a messenger arriving on horseback with a line from her husband, saying that he had met with an accident in the hunting-field, and begging her to come to him. Of course I have always previously managed to get specimens of handwriting, and my man imitates them so well that they have never once failed in their action. I will give you a line to him, saying that you are a friend of mine. He knows me under the name of Sinclair. As a stranger you would hardly get him to act."

"Of course, he is thoroughly trustworthy?" Simcoe asked.

"I should not employ him if he were not," the other said. "He was a writing-master at one time, but took to drink, and went altogether to the bad. He is always more or less drunk now, and you had better go to him before ten o'clock in the morning. I don't say that he will be quite sober, but he will be less drunk than he will be later. As soon as he begins to write he pulls himself together. He puts a watchmaker's glass in his eye and closely examines the writing that he has to imitate, writes a few lines to accustom himself to it, and then writes what he is told to do as quickly and as easily as if it were his own handwriting. He hands it over, takes his fee, which is two guineas, and then goes out to a public-house, and I don't believe that the next day he has the slightest remembrance of what he has written."

"Thank you very much, Harrison; I think that, with the assistance of these two men, I shall be able to work the matter I have in hand without fear of a hitch."

"Anything else I can do for you? You know that you can rely upon me, Simcoe. You were with poor Bill for six years, and you stood by him to the last, when the natives rose and massacred the whites, and you got Bill off, and if he did die afterwards of his wounds, anyhow you did your best to save him. So if I can help you I will do it, whatever it is, short of murder, and there is my hand on it. You know in any case I could not round on you."

"I will tell you the whole business, Harrison. I have thought the matter pretty well out, but I shall be very glad to have your opinion on it, and with your head you are like to see the thing in a clearer light than I can, and may suggest a way out of some difficulties."

He then unfolded the details of his scheme.

"Very good!" the other said admiringly, when he had finished. "It does credit to you, Simcoe. You risked your life, and, as you say, very nearly lost it to save the General's, and have some sort of a right to have his money when he has done with it. Your plan of impersonating the General and getting another lawyer to draw out a fresh will is a capital one; and as you have a list of the bequests he made in his old one, you will not only be able to strengthen the last will, but will disarm the opposition of those who would have benefited by the first, as no one will suffer by the change. But how about the boy?"

"The boy must be got out of the way somehow."

"Not by foul play, I hope, Simcoe. I could not go with you there."

"Certainly not. That idea never entered my mind; but surely there can be no difficulty in carrying off a child of that age. It only wants two to do that: one to engage the nurse in talk, the other to entice the child away, pop him into a cab waiting hard by, and drive off with him."

"I doubt whether the courts would hand over the property unless they had some absolute proof that the child was dead."

"They would not do so for some time, no doubt, but evidence might be manufactured. At any rate I could wait. They would probably carry out all the other provisions of the will, and with the ten thousand pounds and the three or four thousand I have saved I could hold on for a good many years."

"How about the signature to the will?"

"I can manage that much," Simcoe said. "I had some work in that way years ago, and I have been for the last three months practicing the General's, and I think now that I can defy any expert to detect the difference. Of course, it is a very different thing learning to imitate a signature and writing a long letter."

The other agreed, and added, "I should be careful to employ a firm oflawyers of long standing. If you were to go to shady people it would in itself cause suspicion."

"Yes, I quite feel that, and I want, if possible, to get hold of people who just know the General by sight, so as to have a fairly good idea of his face without knowing him too well. I think I know of one. At the club the other day Colonel Bulstrode, a friend of the General's, said to him, 'I wish you would drive round with me to my lawyers'; their place is in the Temple. I want someone to sign as a witness to a deed, and as it is rather important, I would rather have it witnessed by a friend than by one of the clerks. It won't take you a minute.'"

"I should think that would do very well; they would not be likely to notice him very particularly, and probably the General would not have spoken at all. He would just have seen his friend sign the deed, and then have affixed his own signature as a witness. Well, everything seems in your favor, and should you need any help you can rely upon me."

CHAPTER VIII.

GENERAL MATHIESON'S SEIZURE.

Three months later John Simcoe called for a letter directed to "Mr. Jackson, care of William Scriven, Tobacconist, Fetter Lane." The address was in his own handwriting. He carried it home before opening it. The writing was rough and the spelling villainous.

"Samoa.

"My Dear Jack: I was mitely glad when the old brig came in and Captain Jephson handed me a letter from you, and as you may guess still more pleased to find with it an order for fifty pounds. It was good and harty of you, but you allus was the right sort. I have dun as you asked me; I went to the wich man and for twelve bottles of rum he gave me the packet inclosed of the stuff he uses. There aint much of it, but it is mitely strong. About as much as will lie on the end of a knife will make a man foam at the mouth and fall into convulsions, three times as much as that will kill him outrite. He says there aint no taste in it. I hope this will suit your purpus. You will be sorry to hear that Long Peter has been wiped out; he was spered by a native, who thort Pete wanted to run away with his wife, wich I don't believe he did for she wernt no way a beuty. Vigors is in a bad way; he has had the shakes bad twice and I don't think that he can last much longer. Trade is bad here, but now I have got the rino I shall buy another cocoanut plantation and two or three more wives to work it, and shall be comfortible. I am a pore hand with the pen, so no more from your friend,

"Ben Stokes."

A week later Hilda wrote to her friend:

"My Dear Netta: I am writing in great distress. Three days ago uncle had a terrible fit. He was seized with it at the club, and I hear that his struggles were dreadful. It was a sort of convulsion. He was sensible when he was brought home, but very weak; he does not remember anything about it. Fortunately, Dr. Pearson, who always attends us, was one of the party, and he sent off cabs for two others. Dr. Pearson came home with him. Of course I asked him what it was, and he said that it was a very unusual case, and that he and the other doctors had not yet come to any decision upon it, as none of them had ever seen one precisely like it. He said that some of the symptoms were those of an epileptic fit, but the convulsions were so violent that they rather resembled tetanus than an ordinary fit. Altogether he seemed greatly puzzled, and he would give no opinion as to whether it was likely to recur. Uncle is better to-day; he told me that he, Mr. Simcoe, and four others had been dining together. He had just drunk his coffee when the room seemed to swim round, and he remembered nothing more until he found himself in bed at home. Mr. Simcoe came home with him, and the doctor said, I must acknowledge, that no one could have been kinder than he was. He looked quite ill from the shock that he had had. But still I don't like him, Netta; in fact, I think I dislike him more and more every day. I often tell myself that I have not a shadow of reason for doing so, but I can't help it. You may call it prejudice: I call it instinct.

"You can well imagine how all this has shocked me. Uncle seemed so strong and well that I have always thought he would live to a great age. He is sixty-eight, but I am sure he looks ten years younger—at least he did so; at present he might be ninety. But I can only hope that the change is temporary, and that he will soon be his dear self again. The three doctors are going to have a meeting here to-morrow. I shall be anxious, indeed, to hear the result. I hope that they will order him a change, and that we can go down together, either to his place or mine; then I can always be with him, whereas here he goes his way and I go mine, and except at meal-times we scarcely meet. If he does go I shall try and persuade him to engage a medical man to go with us. Of course, I do not know whether a doctor could be of any actual use in case of another attack, but it would be a great comfort to have one always at hand."

The letter stopped here, and was continued on the following evening.

"The consultation is over; Dr. Pearson had a long talk with me afterwards. He said that it was without doubt an epileptic fit, but that it differed in many respects from the general type of that malady, and that all of them were to some extent puzzled. They had brought with them a fourth doctor, Sir Henry Havercourt, who is the greatest authority on such maladies. He had seen uncle, and asked him a few questions, and had a talk with Dr. Pearson, and had from him a minute account of the seizure. He pronounced it a most interesting and, as far as he knew, a unique case, and expressed a wish to come as a friend to see how the General was getting on. Of course he inquired about his habits, asked what he had had for dinner, and so on.

"'The great point, Dr. Pearson,' I said, after the consultation was over, 'is, of course, whether there is likely to be any recurrence of the attack.' 'That is more than I can say,' he answered gravely; 'at present he can hardly be said to have recovered altogether from the effects of this one, which is in itself an unusual feature in the case. As a rule, when a person recovers from an epileptic fit he recovers altogether—that is to say, he is able to walk and talk as before, and his face shows little or no sign of the struggle that he has undergone. In this case the recovery is not altogether complete. You may have noticed that his voice is not only weak, but there is a certain hesitation in it. His face has not altogether recovered its natural expression, and is slightly, very slightly, drawn on one side, which would seem to point to paralysis; while in other respects the attack was as unlike a paralytic stroke as it could well have been. Thus, you see, it is difficult in the extreme for us to give any positive opinion concerning a case which is so entirely an exceptional one. We can only hope for the best, and trust to the strength of his constitution. At any rate, we all agree that he needs absolute quiet and very simple and plain diet. You see, he has been a great diner-out; and though an abstemious man in the way of drinking, he thoroughly appreciates a good dinner. All this must be given up, at any rate for a time. I should say that as soon as he is a little stronger, you had better take him down into the country. Let him see as few visitors as possible, and only very intimate friends. I do not mean that he should be lonely or left to himself; on the contrary, quiet companionship and talk are desirable.'

"I said that though the country might be best for him, there was no medical man within three miles of his place, and it would be terrible were we to have an attack, and not know what to do for it. He said that he doubted if anything could be done when he was in such a state as he was the other night, beyond sprinkling his face with water, and that he himself felt powerless in the case of an attack that was altogether beyond his experience. Of course he said it was out of the question that I should be down there alone with him, but that I must take down an experienced nurse. He strongly recommended that she should not wear hospital uniform, as this would be a constant reminder of his illness.

"I said that I should very much like to have a medical man in the house. Money was no object, and it seemed to me from what he said that it would also be desirable that, besides being a skillful doctor, he should be also a pleasant and agreeable man, who would be a cheerful companion to him as well as a medical attendant.

"He agreed that this would certainly be very desirable, and that he and the others were all anxious that the case should be watched very carefully. He said that he would think the matter over, and that if he could not find just the man that would suit, he would ask Sir Henry Havercourt to recommend us one.

"He said there were many clever young men to whom such an engagement for a few months would be a godsend. He intended to run down himself once a fortnight, from Saturday until Monday, which he could do, as his practice was to a large extent a consulting one. I could see plainly enough that though he evidently put as good a face upon it as he could, he and the other doctors took by no means a hopeful view of the case.

"It is all most dreadful, Netta, and I can hardly realize that only three days ago everything was bright and happy, while now it seems that everything is uncertain and dark. There was one thing the doctor said that pleased me, and that was, 'Don't let any of his town friends in to see him; and I think that it would be as well that none of them should go down to visit him in the country. Let him be kept altogether free from anything that would in the smallest degree excite him or set his brain working.' I told him that no one had seen him yet, and that I would take good care that no one should see him; and I need hardly tell you that Mr. Simcoe will be the first person to be informed of the doctor's orders."

A week later General Mathieson came downstairs for the first time. The change in him was even greater than it had seemed to be when he was lying on the sofa in his room; and Tom Roberts, who had been the General's soldier-servant years before, and had been in his service since he left the army, had difficulty in restraining his tears as he entered, with his master leaning heavily on his arm.

"I am shaky, my dear Hilda, very shaky," the General said. "I feel just as I did when I was laid up with a bad attack of jungle fever in India. However, no doubt I shall pick up soon, just I did then. Pearson tells me that he and the others agree that I must go down into the country, and I suppose I must obey orders. Where is it we are to go?"

"To your own place, uncle."

"My own place?" he repeated doubtfully, and then after a pause, "Oh, yes, of course! Oh, yes!"

There was a troubled look in his face, as if he was trying to recall memories that had somehow escaped him, and Hilda, resolutely repressing the impulse to burst into a flood of tears, said cheerfully:

"Yes, I shall be very glad to be back at Holmwood. We won't go down by train, uncle. Dr. Pearson does not think that you are strong enough for that yet. He is going to arrange for a comfortable carriage in which you can lie down and rest. We shall make an early start. He will arrange for horses to be sent down so that we can change every ten or twelve miles, and arrive there early in the afternoon. It is only seventy miles, you know."

"Yes, I have driven up from there by the coach many a time when I was a boy, and sometimes since; have I not, Tom?"

"Yes, General. The railway was not made till six or seven years ago."

"No, the railway wasn't made, Hilda; at least, not all the way."

Hilda made signs to Tom not to leave the room, and he stood by his master's shoulder, prompting him occasionally when his memory failed him.

"You must get strong very fast, uncle, for Dr. Pearson said that you cannot go until you are more fit to bear the fatigue."

"I shall soon get strong, my dear. What is to-day?"

"To-day is Friday, uncle."

"Somehow I have lost count of days," he said. "Well, I should think that I shall be fit to go early next week; it is not as if we were going to ride down. I was always fond of riding, and I hope I shall soon be after the hounds again. Let me see, what month is this?"

"It is early in June, uncle; and the country will be looking its best."

"Yes, yes; I shall have plenty of time to get strong before cub-hunting begins."

So the conversation dragged on for another half hour, the General's words coming slower and slower, and at the end of that time he dropped asleep. Hilda made a sign to Roberts to stay with him, and then ran up to her own room, closed the door behind her, and burst into a passion of tears. Presently there was a tap at the door, and her maid came in.

"Tom has just slipped out from the dining room, miss, and told me to tell you that the General was sleeping as peacefully as a child, and he thought it was like enough that he would not wake for hours. He said that when he woke he and William would get him up to his own room."

"Thank you, Lucy." The door closed again. Hilda got up from the bed on which she had lain down, and buried herself in the depths of a large cushioned chair. There she sat thinking. For the first time she realized how immense was the change in her uncle. She had seen him several times each day, but he had spoken but a few words, and it only seemed to her that he was drowsy and disinclined to talk. Now she saw how great was the mental as well as the physical weakness.

"It is terrible!" she repeated over and over again to herself. "What a wreck—oh, what a dreadful wreck! Will he ever get over it?"

She seemed absolutely unable to think. Sometimes she burst into sobs, sometimes she sat with her eyes fixed before her, but seeing nothing, and her fingers twining restlessly round each other. Presently the door opened very gently, and a voice said, "May I come in?" She sprang to her feet as if electrified, while a glad cry of "Netta!" broke from her lips. A moment later the two girls were clasped in a close embrace.

"Oh, Netta, how good of you!" Hilda said, after she had sobbed for some time on her friend's shoulder. "Oh, what a relief it is to me!"

"Of course I have come, you foolish girl. You did not suppose I was going to remain away after your letter? Aunt is with me; she is downstairs, tidying herself up. We shut up the house and left the gardener in charge, and here we are, as long as you want us."

"But your pupils, Netta?"

"I handed them all over to another of the Professor's assistants, so we need not bother about them. I told aunt that I should not be down for an hour. Mrs. Brown is looking after her, and getting her a cup of tea, and I asked her to bring two cups up here. I thought that you would prefer for us to have a chat by ourselves. Now tell me all about it, dear; that is, if there is anything fresh since you wrote."

Hilda told her the doctor's opinion and the plans that had been formed.

"Dr. Pearson brought a Dr. Leeds here with him this morning. He says he is very clever. His term as house surgeon at Guy's or St. Bartholomew's, I forget which, has just expired, and as he had not made any definite plans he was glad to accept the doctor's offer to take charge of my uncle. He seemed, from what little I saw of him, a pleasant man, and spoke in a cheerful voice, which will be a great thing for uncle. I should think that he is six or seven and twenty. Dr. Pearson said he was likely to become a very distinguished man in his profession some day. He is going to begin at once. He will not sleep here, but will spend most of his time here, partly because he wants to study the case, and partly because he wants uncle to get accustomed to him. He will travel down with us, which will be a great comfort to me, for there is no saying how uncle may stand the journey. I suggested that we should have another carriage, as the invalid carriage has room for only one inside besides the patient, but he laughed, and said that he would ride on the box with Tom Roberts; there will be room for two there, as we are going to post down. Of course, you and your aunt will go down by train, and be there to meet us; it will make it so much brighter and more cheerful having you to receive us than if we had to arrive all alone, with no one to say welcome."

"And is your uncle so very weak?"

"Terribly weak—weak both mentally and physically," and she gave an account of the interview that afternoon.

"That is bad indeed, Hilda; worse than I had expected. But with country air, and you and me to amuse him, to say nothing of the doctor, we may hope that he will soon be a very different man."

"Well, I will not stay talking here any longer, Netta; we have left your aunt half an hour alone, and if she were not the kindest soul in the world, she would feel hurt at being so neglected, after coming all this way for my sake. You don't know what good your coming has effected. Before you opened the door I was in the depth of despair; everything seemed shaken, everything looked hopeless. There seemed to have been a sort of moral earthquake that had turned everything in my life topsy-turvy, but now I feel hopeful again. With you by my side I think that I can bear even the worst."

They went down to the drawing room, where they found Mrs. Brown, the housekeeper, having a long gossip over what had taken place with Miss Purcell, whom, although a stranger, she was unaffectedly glad to see, as it seemed to take some of her responsibilities off her shoulders, and she knew that Netta's society would be invaluable to Hilda.

It was not until a week later that, after another consultation, the doctors agreed that it was as well that the General should be moved down to his country place. Dr. Pearson was opinion that there was some improvement, but that it was very slight; the others could see no change since they had seen him ten days before. However, they agreed with their colleague that although there might be a certain amount of danger in moving him to the country, it was best to risk that, as the change might possibly benefit him materially.

"Have you formed any opinion of the case, Dr. Leeds?" Sir Henry asked.

"I can scarcely be said to have any distinct opinion, Sir Henry. The symptoms do not tally with those one would expect to find after any ordinary sort of seizure, although certainly they would point to paralysis rather than epilepsy. I should, had the case come before me in the ordinary way in the ward of a hospital, have come to the conclusion that the seizure itself and the after-effects pointed rather to the administration of some drug than to any other cause. I admit that I am not acquainted with any drug whose administration would lead to any such results; but then I know of no other manner in which they could be brought about save by some lesion of a blood vessel in the brain of so unusual a character that no such case has hitherto been reported in any work with which I am acquainted. This, I say, would be my first theory in the case of a patient of whose previous history I was entirely unaware, and who came under my charge in a hospital ward; but I admit that in the present case it cannot be entertained for a moment, and I must, during my attendance upon General Mathieson, watch closely for symptoms that would aid me in localizing brain lesion or other cause."

He spoke modestly and quietly in the presence, as he was, of some of the leading men of his profession. The theory he had enunciated had not occurred to any of them, but, as he spoke, they all recognized that the symptoms might under other circumstances have led them to a similar conclusion. They were silent for a minute when he ceased speaking, then Sir Henry said gravely:

"I admit, Dr. Leeds, that some of the symptoms, indeed the fit itself, might in the case of a patient of whose history we were ignorant seem to point to some obscure form of poisoning, since they do not accord with what one would expect in ordinary forms of brain seizures of this kind. However, there is no doubt that we are all somewhat prone, when we meet with a case possessing unusual or altogether exceptional features, to fall back upon the theory of poisoning. In this case, fortunately, the circumstances are such as to preclude the possibility of entertaining the idea for a moment; and, as you say, you must endeavor to find, watching him as you will do, some other cause of what I admit is a mysterious and obscure case; and knowing you as I do, I am sure that you will mention this theory, even as a theory, to no one.

"We are all aware that there are many cases which come before us where we may entertain suspicions, and strong suspicions, that the patient has been poisoned, and yet we dare not take any steps because, in the first place, we have no clew as to how or by whom he or she has been poisoned, and because, if after death an autopsy should prove that we were mistaken, it would be nothing short of professional ruin. Here, as you said, the theory is happily irreconcilable with the circumstances of the case, and no drug known to European science would produce so strange a seizure or the after-effects. Of course, as we all know, on the west coast of Africa, and it is believed in India, the natives are acquainted with poisons which are wholly unknown, and will probably remain unknown, since medical men who have endeavored to investigate the matter have almost always fallen victims themselves to poisons administered by the people whose secrets they were endeavoring to discover.

"However, we can happily put that altogether aside. Dr. Pearson tells us that he intends to go down once a fortnight, and has promised to furnish us with the results of his own observations, and his own reports of this very interesting case. If General Mathieson had, in the course of his military career, ever been struck in the head by a bullet, I should say unhesitatingly that some splinter, possibly very minute, had obtruded into the brain matter; but this has, I learn, not been the case. The only serious injury that he has ever received was when he was terribly torn and nearly killed by a tiger some twenty years ago in India. It may be useful to you, Dr. Leeds, to keep this in your mind. There can be no doubt that scratches and bites, even of the domestic cat, occasionally give rise to violent inflammations, and probably, indeed I believe it to be the case, those of the great cats of India are still more poisonous. As is the case with the bite of a mad dog, the poison may in some cases remain latent for a considerable time, until some circumstance may arouse it into activity. I would suggest that should any scars caused at that time remain, you should examine them carefully, and ascertain whether there is any sign of inflammatory action there. I grant the improbability of any consequences arising so many years after the event, but at the same time in a case of this kind, where we are perfectly at a loss to explain what we see, it is as well to look for the cause in every direction, however improbable it may appear."

"Thank you, Sir Henry; I will certainly do so. I was not aware before of the General having suffered such an injury, and I will go this afternoon and spend a few hours in looking through the medical works at the library of the India Office to see if there are any records of serious disturbance caused in the system by wounds inflicted by tigers a considerable time after they have apparently healed."

The meeting then broke up, and two days later General Mathieson was taken down to his seat in Warwickshire. Post horses were in readiness all along the road, and the journey was accomplished quickly and without fatigue to the patient, who slept the greater part of the distance. At each change Dr. Leeds got down and had two or three minutes' talk with Hilda, and when the General was awake gave him a spoonful of restorative medicine. His presence close at hand was a great comfort to Hilda, upon whom the strain of watching her uncle was very great, and she was thankful indeed when they arrived at the end of the journey, and found Netta and her aunt, who had gone down by that morning's train together with the housekeeper and her own maid, waiting on the steps to receive them.

CHAPTER IX.

A STRANGE ILLNESS.

For three months General Mathieson remained in the country. His improvement was very gradual—so gradual, indeed, that from week to week it was scarce noticeable, and it was only by looking back that it was perceptible. At the end of that time he could walk unaided, there was less hesitation in his speech, and his memory was distinctly clearer. He passed much of his time on a sofa placed in the shade in the garden, with Hilda and Netta sitting by him, working and talking.

Netta had always been a favorite of his from the time that he first met her in Hanover; and he had, when she was staying with his niece the year before, offered her a very handsome salary if she would remain with her as her companion. The girl, however, was reluctant to give up her occupation, of which she was very fond, still less would she leave her aunt; and although the General would willingly have engaged the latter also as an inmate of the house, to act as a sort of chaperon to Hilda when she drove out alone shopping, Netta refused in both their names.

"You would not have left the army, General, whatever temptations might have been held out to you. I am happy in thinking that I am doing good and useful work, and I don't think that any offer, even one so kind and liberal as yours, would induce me to relinquish it."

Her presence now was not only an inestimable comfort to Hilda, but of great advantage to the General himself. Alone Hilda would have found it next to impossible to keep the invalid interested and amused. He liked to talk and be talked to, but it was like the work of entertaining a child. Netta, however, had an inexhaustible fund of good spirits. After her long intercourse with children who needed entertainment with instruction, and whose attention it was absolutely necessary to keep fixed, she had no difficulty in keeping the conversation going, and her anecdotes, connected with her life in Germany and the children she had taught, were just suited to the General's mental condition.

Little Walter was of great assistance to her. He had come down with his nurse as soon as they were fairly settled at Holmwood, and his prattle and play were a great amusement to his grandfather. Whenever the conversation flagged Netta offered to tell him a story, which not only kept him quiet, but was listened to with as much interest by the General as by the child. Dr. Leeds was often a member of the party, and his cheery talk always had its effect in soothing the General when, as was sometimes the case, he was inclined to be petulant and irritable.

They had been a fortnight at Holmwood before the doctor discovered Netta's infirmity. She happened to be standing at a window with her back to him when he asked her a question. Receiving no reply, he repeated it in a louder tone, but he was still unanswered. Somewhat surprised, he went up to her and touched her; she faced round immediately.

"Were you speaking to me, Dr. Leeds?"

"Yes, I spoke to you twice, Miss Purcell, but you did not hear me."

"I have been perfectly deaf from childhood," she said; "I cannot hear any sound whatever. I never talk about it; people ask questions and wonder, and then, forgetting that I do not hear, they persist in addressing me in loud tones."

"Is it possible that you are deaf?"

"It is a melancholy fact," she said with a smile, and then added more seriously, "It came on after measles. When I was eight years old my good aunt, who had taken me to some of the best aurists in London, happened to hear that a Professor Menzel had opened an establishment in Hanover for teaching deaf mutes to speak by a new system of watching people's lips. She took me over there, and, as you see, the result was an undoubted success, and I now earn my living by acting as one of the professor's assistants, and by teaching two or three little girls who board at my aunt's."

"The system must be an admirable one indeed," the doctor said. "I have, of course, heard of it, but could not have believed that the results were so excellent. It never entered my mind for a moment that you were in any way deficient in hearing, still less that you were perfectly deaf. I have noticed that, more than is common, you always kept your eyes fixed on my face when I was speaking to you."

"You would have noticed it earlier had we been often alone together," she said, "for unless I had kept my eyes always upon you I should not have known when you were speaking; but when, as here, there are always several of us together, my eyes are at once directed to your face when you speak, by seeing the others look at you."

"Is it necessary to be quite close to you when one speaks?"

"Oh, not at all! Of course I must be near enough to be able to see distinctly the motion of the lips, say at twenty yards. It is a great amusement to me as I walk about, for I can see what is being said by people on the other side of the road, or passing by in a vehicle. Of course one only gets scraps of conversations, but sometimes they are very funny."

"You must be quite a dangerous person, Miss Purcell."

"I am," she laughed; "and you must be careful not to say things that you don't want to be overheard when you are within reach of my eyes. Yesterday, for instance, you said to Hilda that my aunt seemed a wonderfully kind and intelligent old lady; and you were good enough to add some complimentary remarks about myself."

Dr. Leeds flushed.

"Well, I should not have said them in your hearing, Miss Purcell; but, as they were complimentary, no harm was done. I think I said that you were invaluable here, which is certainly the case, for I really do not know how we should be able to amuse our patient if it were not for yourassistance."

"Hilda and I had a laugh about it," Netta said; "and she said, too, that it was not fair your being kept in the dark as to our accomplishment."

"'Our accomplishment!'" he repeated in surprise. "Do you mean to say that Miss Covington is deaf also? But no, that is impossible; for I called to her yesterday, when her back was turned, and the General wanted her, and she answered immediately."

"My tongue has run too fast," the girl said, "but I don't suppose she would mind your knowing what she never speaks of herself. She was, as you know, living with us in Hanover for more than four years. She temporarily lost her hearing after an attack of scarlet fever, and the doctors who were consulted here feared that it might be permanent. Her father and mother, hearing of Dr. Hartwig as having the reputation of being the first aurist in Europe, took her out to him. He held out hopes that she could be cured, and recommended that she should be placed in Professor Menzel's institution as soon as she could understand German, so that, in case a cure was not effected, she might be able to hear with her eyes. By great good fortune he recommended that she should live with my aunt, partly because she spoke English, and partly because, as I was already able to talk, I could act as her companion and instructor both in the system and in German.

"In three years she could get on as well as I could, but the need for it happily passed away, as her hearing was gradually restored. Still, she continued to live with us while her education went on at the best school in the town, but of course she always talked with me as I talked with her, and so she kept up the accomplishment and has done so ever since. But her mother advised her very strongly to keep the knowledge of her ability to read people's words from their lips a profound secret, as it might tend to her disadvantage; for people might be afraid of a girl possessed of the faculty of overhearing their conversation at a distance."

"That explains what rather puzzled me the other day," the doctor said. "When I came out into the garden you were sitting together and were laughing and talking. You did not notice me, and it struck me as strange that, while I heard the laughing, I did not hear the sound of your voices until I was within a few paces of you. When Miss Covington noticed me I at once heard your voices."

"Yes, you gave us both quite a start, and Hilda said we must either give up talking silently or let you into our secret; so I don't think that she will be vexed when I tell her that I have let it out."

"I am glad to have the matter explained," he said, "for really I asked myself whether I must not have been temporarily deaf, and should have thought it was so had I not heard the laughing as distinctly as usual. I came to the conclusion that you must, for some reason or other, have dropped your voices to a whisper, and that one or the other was telling some important secret that you did not wish even the winds to hear."

"I think that this is the only secret that we have," Netta laughed.

"Seriously, this is most interesting to me as a doctor, and it is a thousand pities that a system that acts so admirably should not be introduced into this country. You should set up a similar institution here, Miss Purcell."

"I have been thinking of doing so some day. Hilda is always urging me to it, but I feel that I am too young yet to take the head of an establishment, but in another four or five years' time I shall think seriously about it."

"I can introduce you to all the aurists in London, Miss Purcell, and I am sure that you will soon get as many inmates as you may choose to take. In cases where their own skill fails altogether, they would be delighted to comfort parents by telling them how their children may learn to dispense altogether with the sense of hearing."

"Not quite altogether," she said. "It has happened very often, as it did just now, that I have been addressed by someone at whom I did not happen to be looking, and then I have to explain my apparent rudeness by owning myself to be entirely deaf. Unfortunately, I have not always been able to make people believe it, and I have several times been soundly rated by strangers for endeavoring to excuse my rudeness by a palpable falsehood."

"Really, I am hardly surprised," Dr. Leeds said, "for I should myself have found it difficult to believe that one altogether deaf could have been taught to join in conversation as you do. Well, I must be very careful what I say in future while in the society of two young ladies possessed of such dangerous and exceptional powers."

"You need not be afraid, doctor; I feel sure that there is no one here to whom you would venture to give us a bad character."

"I think," he went on more seriously, "that Miss Covington's mother was very wise in warning her against her letting anyone know that she could read conversations at a distance. People would certainly be afraid of her, for gossipmongers would be convinced that she was overhearing, if I may use the word, what was said, if she happened to look at them only casually."

At the end of three months the General became restless, and was constantly expressing a wish to be brought back to London.

"What do you think yourself, Dr. Leeds?" Dr. Pearson said, when he paid one of his usual visits.

"He is, of course, a great deal better than he was when he first came down," the former replied, "but there is still that curious hesitation in his speech, as if he was suffering from partial paralysis. I am not surprised at his wanting to get up to town again. As he improves in health he naturally feels more and more the loss of his usual course of life. I should certainly have advised his remaining here until he had made a good deal further advancement, but as he has set his mind upon it, I believe that more harm would be done by refusing than by his going. In fact, I think that he has, if anything, gone back in the last fortnight, and above all things it is necessary to avoid any course that might cause irritation, and so set up fresh brain disturbances."

"I am quite of your opinion, Leeds. I have noticed myself that he hesitates more than he did a short time since, and sometimes, instead of joining in the conversation, he sits moody and silent; and he is beginning to resent being looked after and checked."

"Yes; he said to me the other day quite angrily, 'I don't want to be treated as a child or a helpless invalid, doctor. I took a mile walk yesterday. I am beginning to feel quite myself again; it will do me a world of good to be back in London, and to drive down to the club and to have a chat with my old friends again.'"

"Well, I think it best that he should not be thwarted. You have looked at the scars from time to time, I suppose?"

"Yes; there has been no change in them, they are very red, but he tells me—and what is more to the point, his man tells me—that they have always been so."

"What do you think, Leeds? Will he ever be himself again? Watching the case from day to day as you have done, your opinion is worth a good deal more than mine."

"I have not the slightest hope of it," the young doctor replied quietly. "I have seen as complete wrecks as he is gradually pull themselves round again, but they have been cases where they have been the victims of drink or of some malady from which they had been restored by a successful operation. In his case we have failed altogether to determine the cause of his attack, or the nature of it. We have been feeling in the dark, and hitherto have failed to discover a clew that we could follow up. So far there has been no recurrence of his first seizure, but, with returning strength and returning brain work, it is in my opinion more than likely that we shall have another recurrence of it. The shock has been a tremendous one to the system. Were he a younger man he might have rallied from it, but I doubt whether at his age he will ever get over it. Actually he is, I believe, under seventy; physically and mentally, he is ninety."

"That is so, and between ourselves I cannot but think that a long continuance of his life is not to be desired. I believe with you that he will be a confirmed invalid, requiring nursing and humoring like a child, and for the sake of Miss Covington and all around him one cannot wish that his life should be prolonged."

"I trust that, when the end comes, Dr. Pearson, it will be gradual and painless, and that there will be no recurrence of that dreadful seizure."

"I hope so indeed. I have seen many men in bad fits, but I never saw anything to equal that. I can assure you that several of the men who were present—men who had gone through a dozen battles—were completely prostrated by it. At least half a dozen of them, men whom I had never attended before, knowing that I had been present, called upon me within the next two or three days for advice, and were so evidently completely unstrung that I ordered them an entire change of scene at once, and recommended them to go to Homburg, take the waters, and play at the tables; to do anything, in fact, that would distract their minds from dwelling upon the painful scene that they had witnessed. Had it not been for that, one would have had no hesitation in assigning his illness to some obscure form of paralysis; as it is, it is unaccountable. Except," he added, with a smile, "by your theory of poison."

The younger doctor did not smile in return. "It is the only cause that I can assign for it," he said gravely. "The more I study the case, the more I investigate the writings of medical men in India and on the East and West Coast of Africa, the more it seems to me that the attack was the work of a drug altogether unknown to European science, but known to Obi women, fetich men, and others of that class in Africa. In some of the accounts of people accused of crime by fetich men, and given liquor to drink, which they are told will not affect them if innocent, but will kill them if guilty, I find reports of their being seized with instant and violent convulsions similar to those that you witnessed. These convulsions often end in death; sometimes, where, I suppose, the dose was larger than usual, the man drops dead in his tracks while drinking it. Sometimes he dies in convulsions; at other times he recovers partially and lingers on, a mere wreck, for some months. In other cases, where, I suppose, the dose was a light one, and the man's relatives were ready to pay the fetich man handsomely, the recovery was speedy and complete; that is to say, if, as is usually the case, the man was not put to death at once upon the supposed proof of his guilt. By what possible means such poison could have found its way to England, for there is no instance of its nature being divulged to Europeans, I know not, nor how it could have been administered; but I own that it is still the only theory by which I can account for the General's state. I need not say that I should never think of giving the slightest hint to anyone but yourself as to my opinion in the matter, and trust most sincerely that I am mistaken; but although I have tried my utmost I cannot overcome the conviction that the theory is a correct one, and I think, Dr. Pearson, that if you were to look into the accounts of the various ways in which the poisons are sold by old negro women to those anxious to get rid of enemies or persons whose existence is inconvenient to them, and by the fetich men in these ordeals, you will admit at least that had you been practicing on the West Coast, and any white man there had such an attack as that through which the General has passed, you would without hesitation have put it down to poison by some negro who had a grudge against him."

"No doubt, no doubt," the other doctor admitted; "but, you see, we are not on the West Coast. These poisons are, as you admit, absolutely unobtainable by white men from the men and women who prepare them. If obtainable, when would they have been brought here, and by whom? And lastly, by whom administered, and from what motive? I admit all that you say about the African poisons. I lately had a long talk about them with a medical man who had been on the coast for four or five years, but until these other questions can be answered I must refuse to believe that this similarity is more than accidental, and in any possible way due to the same cause."

"That is what I have told myself scores of times, and it would be a relief to me indeed could I find some other explanation of the matter. Then, you think that he had better come up to London?"

"I leave the matter in your hands, Dr. Leeds. I would give him a few days longer and try the effect of a slight sedative; possibly his desire to get up to town may die out. If so, he is without doubt better here. If, however, you see that his irritation increases, and he becomes more and more set upon it, by all means take him up. How would you do so? By rail or road?"

"Certainly by rail. I have been trying to make him feel that he is a free agent, and encouraged him in the belief that he is stronger and better. If then I say to him, 'My dear General, you are, of course, free to do as you like, and it may be that the change will be beneficial to you; if the ladies can be ready to-morrow, let us start without further delay,' I consider it quite possible that this ready and cheerful acquiescence may result in his no longer desiring it. One knows that in this respect sick people are very like fractious children. They set their minds on some special article of food, as a child does on a toy, and when it comes they will refuse to touch it, as the child will throw the coveted toy down."

It turned out so in this case. The moment the General found that the doctor was willing that he should go up to town, and the ladies quite ready to accompany him at once, he himself began to raise objections.

"Perhaps it would be as well that we should wait another month," he replied. A little pretended opposition strengthened this view, and the return was postponed. At the end of the month he had made so much progress that, when the longing for London was again expressed, Dr. Leeds offered no opposition, and two days later the whole party went up.

CHAPTER X.

TWO HEAVY BLOWS.

During the four months that General Mathieson had remained at Holmwood no one had been more constant in his inquiries as to his health than Mr. Simcoe. He had seen Hilda before she started, and had begged her to let him have a line once a week, saying how her uncle was going on.

"I will get Dr. Leeds to write," she said. "My own opinion will be worth nothing, but his will be valuable. I am afraid that he will find time hang heavily on his hands, and he will not mind writing. I do not like writing letters at the best of times, but in the trouble we are in now I am sure that I shall not be equal to it."

Dr. Leeds willingly undertook the duty of sending a short weekly bulletin, not only to Mr. Simcoe, but to a dozen other intimate friends.

"It is not half an hour's work," he said, when Netta offered to relieve him by addressing the envelopes or copying out his report; "very few words will be sufficient. 'The General has made some slight progress this week,' or 'The General remains in very much the same state,' or 'I am glad to be able to record some slight improvement.' That, with my signature, will be quite sufficient, and when I said that half an hour would be enough I exaggerated: I fancy that it will be all done in five minutes."

Mr. Simcoe occasionally wrote a few lines of thanks, but scarcely a day passed that he did not send some little present for the invalid—a bunch of the finest grapes, a few choice peaches, and other fruit from abroad. Of flowers they had plenty in their own conservatories at Holmwood, while game was abundant, for both from neighbors and from club friends they received so large a quantity that a considerable proportion was sent back in hampers to the London hospitals.

Some of Mr. Simcoe's presents were of a different description. Among them was a machine that would hold a book at any angle desired, while at the same time there was a shelf upon which a cup or tumbler, a spare book or newspaper, could be placed.

"At any rate, Hilda, this Mr. Simcoe of yours is very thoughtful and kind towards your uncle," Netta said.

"Yes," Hilda admitted reluctantly, "he certainly is very thoughtful, but I would much rather he did not send things. We can get anything we want from

Warwick or Leamington, or indeed from London, merely by sending a line or a telegram. One hates being under obligations to a man one does not like."

"It seems to me at present that you are unjust, Hilda; and I certainly look forward to seeing him in London and drawing my own conclusions."

"Yes, no doubt you will see him, and often enough too," Hilda said pettishly. "Of course, if uncle means to go to his club, it will be impossible to say that he is unfit to see his friends at home."

Netta, however, did not see Mr. Simcoe on their return, for Dr. Leeds, on the suggestion of Hilda, stated in his last report that the General would be going up to town in a day or two, but that he strongly deprecated any visits until he could see how the invalid stood the journey.

There was no doubt that he stood it badly. Just at first the excitement seemed to inspire him with strength, but this soon died away, and he had to be helped from the railway carriage to the brougham, and lifted out when he arrived at home. Dr. Leeds saw to his being carried upstairs, undressed, and put to bed.

"He is weaker than I thought," he said in reply to Hilda's anxious look when he joined the party downstairs. "I cannot say that it is want of physical strength, for he has walked over a mile several times without apparent fatigue. It seems to me that it is rather failure of will power, or brain power, if you like. I noticed that he very frequently sat looking out of the window, and it is possible that the succession of objects passing rapidly before the eye has had the same effect of inducing giddiness that waltzing has to one unaccustomed to it. I trust that to-morrow the effect will have passed off. I had, as you know, intended to sleep at a friend's chambers to-night; but I should not think of doing so now, but will sit up with him. I will get Roberts to take watch and watch with me. I can lie down on the sofa, and he can wake me should there be any change. I sent him off in a cab, as soon as we got your uncle into bed, to fetch Dr. Pearson; if he is at home, he will be here in a few minutes."

It was, however, half an hour before Dr. Pearson came, as he was out when the cab arrived. He had on the way learned from Tom Roberts the state in which the General had arrived, and he hurried upstairs at once to his room.

"So he has broken down badly, Leeds?"

"Very badly."

"I did not expect it. When I saw him last Sunday he seemed to have made so much progress that I thought there could be no harm in his being brought up to London, though, as I said to you, I thought it would be better to dissuade him from going to his club. He might see a few of his friends and have a quiet chat with them here. His pulse is still much fuller than I should have expected from the account his man gave of him. There is a good deal of irregularity, but that has been the case ever since the attack."

"I think that it is mental rather than bodily collapse," the younger man said. "A sudden failure of brain power. He was absolutely unable to make any effort to walk, or indeed to move his limbs at all. It was a sort of mental paralysis."

"And to some slight extent bodily also," Dr. Pearson said, leaning over the bed and examining the patient closely. "Do you see there is a slight, but distinct, contortion of the face, just as there was after that fit?"

"I see there is. He has not spoken since we lifted him from the railway carriage, and I am afraid that to-morrow we shall find that he has lost, partially or entirely, the power of speech. I fear that this is the beginning of the end."

Dr. Pearson nodded.

"There can be little doubt of it, nor could we wish it to be otherwise. Still, he may linger for weeks or even months."

Hilda read the doctor's opinion in his face when he went downstairs.

"Oh, doctor, don't say he is going to die!" she cried.

"I do not say that he is going to die at once, my dear. He may live for some time yet, but it is of no use concealing from you that neither Dr. Leeds nor myself have the slightest hope of his ultimate recovery. There can be no doubt that paralysis is creeping over him, and that it is most unlikely that he will ever leave his bed again.

"Yes, I know it is hard, dear," he said soothingly, as she burst into tears, "but much as you will regret his loss you cannot but feel that it is best so. He could never have been himself again, never have enjoyed his life. There would have been an ever-present anxiety and a dread of a recurrence of that fit. You will see in time that it is better for him and for you that it should be as it is, although, of course, you can hardly see that just at present. And now I must leave you to your kind friends here."

Miss Purcell knew well enough that just at present words of consolation would be thrown away, and that it was a time only for silent sympathy, and her gentle words and the warm pressure of Netta's hand did more to restore Hilda's composure than any repetition of the doctor's well-meant assurance that all was for the best could do.

"Would you like me to write a line in your name to Colonel Bulstrode?" she asked.

“No, no!” Hilda cried; “it would look as if we had made up your minds that uncle was going to die. If he were conscious it would be different; for I know that Colonel Bulstrode is his greatest friend and is named one of his trustees, and uncle might want to talk to him. Oh, how one wishes at a time like this that one had a brother, or that he had a son alive, or that there was someone who would naturally step in and take everything into his hands!”

“There are his lawyers,” Miss Purcell suggested.

“Yes, I did not think of them. Mr. Pettigrew is the other trustee, and is, I know, joint guardian with me of Walter. I am sorry now that we did not leave the dear little fellow down at Holmwood, it will be so sad and dull for him here, and he would have been very happy in the country. But perhaps it is best as it is; if my uncle recovers consciousness he is sure to ask for him. He had come to be very fond of him, and Walter has been so much with him lately.”

“Yes, his eyes always used to follow the child about in his play,” Miss Purcell said. “I think it is best that he should be here, and as the nursery is at the top of the house he will not be in anyone’s way.”

There was but little change in General Mathieson’s condition next morning, although a slight movement, when Hilda spoke to him, showed that he was dimly conscious of her presence, and when she brought the child down and he laid his hand on that of the General, and said “Good-morning, grandfather,” according to his custom, he opened his eyes for a moment, and there was a slight movement of the lips, as if he were trying to speak.

“Thank you, Miss Covington,” Dr. Leeds said; “the experiment was worth making, and it proves that his state of unconsciousness is not complete.”

Walter always took his dinner with the others when they lunched.

“Where is the child?” Hilda asked the footman; “have you sent him up to tell nurse that lunch is ready?”

“I have not sent up, miss, because nurse has not come back with him from his walk.”

“No doubt she will be back in a few minutes,” Hilda said. “She is very punctual; I never knew her late before.”

THE NURSE WAS SITTING ON A CHAIR, SOBBING BITTERLY.

Lunch was half over when Tom Roberts came in with a scared expression on his usually somewhat stolid face.

"If you please, miss, nurse wishes to speak to you."

"What is the matter, Roberts?" Hilda exclaimed, starting up. "Has Walter met with an accident?"

"Well, no, miss, not as I know of, but nurse has come home, and she is just like a wild thing; somehow or other Master Walter has got lost."

Hilda, followed by Netta and Miss Purcell, ran out into the hall. The nurse, a woman of two or three and thirty, the daughter of one of the General's tenants, and who had been in charge of the child since he arrived a baby from India, was sitting on a chair, sobbing bitterly. Her bonnet hung down at the back of her head, her hair was unloosed, and she had evidently been running wildly to and fro. Her appearance at once disarmed Hilda, who said soothingly:

"How has it happened, nurse? Stop crying and tell us. I am sure that it could not have been your fault, for you are always so careful with him. There is no occasion to be so terribly upset. Of course he will soon be found. The first policeman who sees him will be sure to take him to the station. Now how did it happen?"

"I was walking along Queen's Road, miss," the woman said between her sobs, "and Master Walter was close beside me. I know that special, because we had just passed a crossing, and I took hold of his hand as we went over—when a man—he looked like a respectable working-man—came up to me and said, 'I see you are a mother, ma'am.' 'Not at all,' said I; 'how dare you say such a thing? I am a nurse; I am in charge of this young gentleman.' 'Well,' said he, 'I can see that you have a kind heart, anyhow; that is what made me speak to you. I am a carpenter, I am, and I have been out of work for months, and I have a child at home just about this one's age. He is starving, and I haven't a bit to put in his mouth. The parish buried my wife three weeks ago, and I am well-nigh mad. Would you give me the money to buy him a loaf of bread?' The man was in such distress, miss, that I took out my purse and gave him a shilling, and thankful he was; he was all but crying, and could not say enough to thank me. Then I turned to take hold of Walter's hand, and found that the child had gone. I could not have been more than two or three minutes talking; though it always does take me a long time to take my purse out of my pocket, still I know that it could not have been three minutes altogether.

"First of all, I went back to the crossing, and looked up and down the street, but he wasn't there; then I thought that perhaps he had walked on, and was hiding for fun in a shop doorway. When I could not see him up or down I got regular frighted, and ran up and down like a mad thing. Once I came back as far as the house, but there were no signs of him, and I knew that he could not have got as far as this, even if he had run all the way. Then I thought of the mews, and I ran back there. Master Walter was very fond of horses, and he generally stopped when we got to the entrance of the mews, and stood looking for a minute or two at the grooms cleaning the horses, and I thought that he might have gone in there. There were two or three men about, but none had seen the child. Still I ran on, and looked into several stables, a-calling for him all the time. When he wasn't there, I went well-nigh stark mad, and I ran up and down the streets asking everyone I met had they seen a child. Then I came back here to tell you."

"We shall soon hear of him, nurse. Roberts, do you and William start out at once. Go first to the police station and give notice that the child is missing—he cannot have wandered far—and then do you and James go all round the neighborhood and tell every policeman that you meet what has happened. You can ask in all the shops in Queen's Road and the streets near; he may have wandered into one of them, and as he was alone, they may have kept him until someone came to inquire after him. Now, Netta, will you put on your bonnet and come out with me?"

"Shall I come with you too, Hilda?"

"No, thank you, Miss Purcell. In the first place we shall walk too fast for you, and in the second it would be as well for you to be here to comfort him if he is brought back while we are out. We will come every half-hour to hear if there is news of him. You had better go upstairs and make yourself tidy, nurse, and then you can come out and join in the hunt. But you look so utterly worn out and exhausted that I think perhaps you had better sit quiet for a time; you may be sure that it will not be long before some of us bring him back.

"I could not sit still, Miss Covington," the woman said. "I will just run upstairs and put myself straight, and then go out again."

"Try and calm yourself, nurse, or you will be taken for a madwoman; you certainly looked like one when you came in."

Two minutes later Hilda and her friend started.

"Let us go first into Kensington Gardens, Netta; he often went there to play, and if he came down into the main road, he would very likely wander in. It is probable that nurse may have been longer speaking to that man than she thinks, and that he had time to get a good way before she missed him."

The gardens were thoroughly searched, and the park-keepers questioned, but there were no signs of Walter. Then they called at the house to see whether there was any news of him. Finding that there was not, they again went out. They had no real hopes of finding him now, for Hilda was convinced that he was not in any of the streets near. Had he been, either the nurse or the men would have found him.

"He has, no doubt, been either taken by some kind-hearted person who has found him lost," she said, "and who has either given notice to the police, or he has been taken by them to the police station. Still, it relieves one to walk about; it would be impossible to sit quiet, doing nothing. The others will have searched all the streets near, and we had better go up the Edgware Road, search in that direction, and give notice to any policemen we find."

But the afternoon went on and no news was received of the missing child. It was a relief to them when Dr. Leeds, who had gone off watch for a few hours at twelve o'clock, returned. He looked grave for a moment when he heard the news, but said cheerfully, "It is very annoying, Miss Covington, but you need not alarm yourself; Walter is bound to turn up."

"But he ought to have been sent to the police station long before this," Hilda said tearfully.

"Of course he ought, if all people possessed common-sense; unfortunately, they don't. I expect that at the present moment he is eating bread and jam, or something of that sort in the house of some kind-hearted old lady who has taken him in, and the idea of informing the police has never occurred to her for a moment, and, unfortunately, may not occur for some little time. However, if you will give me the details of his dress, I will go at once with it to the printer's and get two or three hundred notices struck off and sent round, to be placed in tradesmen's windows and stuck up on walls, saying that whoever will bring the child here will be handsomely rewarded. This is sure to fetch him before long."

There was but little sleep that night at General Mathieson's. The master of the house still lay unconscious, and from time to time Dr. Leeds came down to say a few cheering words to the anxious girls. Tom Roberts walked the streets all night with the faint idea of finding the child asleep on a doorstep, and went three times to the police station to ask if there was any news. The first thing in the morning Hilda went with Dr. Leeds to Scotland Yard, and the description of the child was at once sent to every station in London; then she drove by herself to the office of Messrs. Farmer & Pettigrew, and waited there until the latter gentleman arrived. Mr. Pettigrew, who was a very old friend of the family, looked very grave over the news.

"I will not conceal from you, Miss Covington," he said, when she had finished her story, "that the affair looks to me somewhat serious; and I am afraid that you will have to make up your mind that you may not see the little fellow as soon as you expect. Had he been merely lost, you should certainly have heard of him in a few hours after the various and, I may say, judicious steps that you have taken. A child who loses himself in the streets of London is morally certain to come into the hands of the police in a very few hours."

"Then what can have become of him, Mr. Pettigrew?"

"It may be that, as not unfrequently happens, the child has been stolen for the sake of his clothes. In that case he will probably be heard of before very long. Or it may be a case of blackmail. Someone, possibly an acquaintance of one of the servants, may have known that the child, as the grandson and heir of General Mathieson, would be a valuable prize, and that, if he could be carried off, his friends might finally be forced to pay a considerable sum to recover him. I must say that it looks to me like a planned thing. One of the confederates engages the silly woman, his nurse, in a long rambling talk; the other picks the child quietly up or entices him away to the next corner, where he has a cab in waiting, and drives off with him at once. However, in neither case need you fear that the child will come to serious harm. If he has been stolen for the sake of his clothes the woman will very speedily turn him adrift, and he will be brought home to you by the police in rags. If, on the other hand, he has been taken for the purpose of blackmail, you may be sure that he will be well cared for, for he will, in the eyes of those who have taken him, be a most valuable possession. In that case you may not hear from the abductors for some little time. They will know that, as the search continues and no news is obtained, his friends will grow more and more anxious, and more ready to pay handsomely for his return. Of course it is a most annoying and unfortunate business, but I really do not think that you have any occasion to feel anxious about his safety, and it is morally certain that in time you will have him back, safe and sound. Now how is your uncle? I hope that he shows signs of rallying?"

"I am sorry to say there was no sign whatever of his doing so up to eight o'clock this morning, and, indeed, Dr. Pearson told me that he has but little hope of his doing so. He thinks that there has been a slight shock of paralysis. Dr. Leeds speaks a little more hopefully than Dr. Pearson, but that is his way, and I think that he too considers that the end is not far off."

"Your friends, Miss Purcell and her niece, are still with you, I hope?"

"Yes; they will not leave me as long as I am in trouble. I don't know what I should do without them, especially now this new blow has fallen upon me."

"Well, my dear, if you receive any communication respecting this boy send it straight to me. I do not know whether you are aware that you and I have been appointed his guardians?"

"Yes; uncle told me so months ago. But I never thought then that he would not live till Walter came of age, and I thought that it was a mere form."

"Doubtless it seemed so at the time," Mr. Pettigrew agreed; "your uncle's was apparently an excellent life, and he was as likely as anyone I know to have attained a great age."

"There is nothing you can advise me to do at present?"

"Nothing whatever, besides what you have done. The police all over London will be on the lookout for a lost child; they will probably assume at once that he has been stolen for his clothes, and will expect to see the child they are in search of in rags. They will know, too, the quarter in which he is most likely to be found. If it is for this purpose that he has been stolen you can confidently expect to have him back by to-morrow at latest; the woman would be anxious to get rid of him without loss of time. If the other hypothesis is correct you may not hear for a fortnight or three weeks; the fellows in that case will be content to bide their time."

Hilda drove back with a heavy heart. Netta herself opened the door, and her swollen eyes at once told the truth.

"Uncle is dead?" Hildaexclaimed.

"Yes, dear; he passed away half an hour ago, a few minutes after Dr. Leeds returned. The doctor ran down himself for a moment, almost directly he had gone up, and said that the General was sinking fast, and that the end might come at any moment. Ten minutes later he came down and told us that all was over."

CHAPTER XI.

A STARTLING WILL.

Mr. Pettigrew at once took the management of affairs at the house in Hyde Park Gardens into his hands, as one of the trustees, as joint guardian of the heir, and as family solicitor. Hilda was completely prostrated by the two blows that had so suddenly fallen, and was glad indeed that all necessity for attending to business was taken off her hands.

"We need not talk about the future at present," Mr. Pettigrew said to her; "that is a matter that can be considered afterwards. You are most fortunate in having the lady with whom you so long lived here with you, and I trust that some permanent arrangement may be made. In any case you could not, of course, well remain here alone."

"I have not thought anything about it yet," she said wearily. "Oh, I wish I were a man, Mr. Pettigrew; then I could do something myself towards searching for Walter, instead of being obliged to sit here uselessly."

"If you were a man, Miss Covington, you could do nothing more at present than is being done. The police are keeping up a most vigilant search. I have offered a reward of five hundred pounds for any news that may lead to the child's discovery, and notices have even been sent to the constabularies of all the home counties, requesting them to make inquiries if any tramp or tramps, accompanied by a child of about the age of our young ward, have been seen passing along the roads. But, as I told you when you called upon me, I have little doubt but that it is a case of blackmail, and that it will not be long before we hear of him. It is probable that the General's death has somewhat disconcerted them, and it is likely that they may wait to see how matters go and who is the person with whom they had best open negotiations. I have no doubt that they are in some way or other keeping themselves well informed of what is taking place here."

The funeral was over, the General being followed to the grave by a number of his military friends and comrades, and the blinds at the house in Hyde Park Gardens were drawn up again. On the following morning Mr. Pettigrew came to the house early. He was a man who was methodical in all his doings, and very rarely ruffled. As soon as he entered, however, Hilda saw that something unusual had happened.

"Have you heard of Walter?" she exclaimed.

"No, my dear, but I have some strange and unpleasant news to give you. Yesterday afternoon I received an intimation from Messrs. Halstead & James, saying that they had in their possession the will of the late General Mathieson bearing date the 16th of May of the present year. I need not say that I was almost stupefied at the news. The firm is one of high standing, and it is impossible to suppose that any mistake has arisen; at the same time it seemed incredible that the General should thus have gone behind our backs, especially as it was only three months before that we had at his request drawn out a fresh will for him. Still, I am bound to say that such cases are by no means rare. A man wants to make a fresh disposition of his property, in a direction of which he feels that his own solicitors, especially when they are old family solicitors, will not approve, and, therefore, he gets it done by some other firm, with the result that, at his death, it comes like a bombshell to all concerned. I can hardly doubt that it is so in this case, although what dispositions the General may have made of his property, other than those contained in the last will we drew up, I am unable to say. At any rate one of the firm will come round to our office at twelve o'clock with this precious document, and I think that it is right that you should be present when it is opened. You will be punctual, will you not?"

"You can rely upon my being there a few minutes before twelve, Mr. Pettigrew. It all seems very strange. I knew what was the general purport of my uncle's last will, for he spoke of it to me. It was, he said, the same as the one before it, with the exception that he had left a handsome legacy to the man who had saved his life from a tiger. I was not surprised at this at all. He had taken a very great fancy to this Mr. Simcoe, who was constantly here, and it seemed to me only natural that he should leave some of his money to a man who had done him so great a service, and who, as he told me, had nearly lost his own life in doing it."

"Quite so," the lawyer agreed; "it seemed natural to us all. His property was large enough to permit of his doing so without making any material difference to his grandchild, who will come into a fine estate with large accumulations during his long minority. Now I must be off."

There was a little council held after the lawyer had left.

"They say troubles never comes singly," Hilda remarked, "and certainly the adage is verified in my case."

"But we must hope that this will not be so, my dear," Miss Purcell said.

"It cannot be any personal trouble, aunt," for Hilda had fallen back into her old habit of so addressing her, "because uncle told me that, as I was so well off, he had only put me down for a small sum in his will, just to show that he had not forgotten me. I feel sure that he will have made no change in that respect, and that whatever alteration he may have made cannot affect me in the least; except, of course, he may have come to the conclusion that it would be better to appoint two men as guardians to Walter, but I hardly think that he would have done that. However, there must be something strange about it, or he would not have gone to another firm of solicitors. No, I feel convinced that there is some fresh trouble at hand."

The carriage drew up at the office in Lincoln's Inn at five minutes to twelve. Mr. Pettigrew had not included Miss Purcell and Netta in the invitation, but Hilda insisted upon their coming with her. They were shown at once into his private room, where some extra chairs had been placed. Colonel Bulstrode was already there, and Mr. Farmer joined his partner as soon as they were seated.

"This is a most singular affair, Miss Covington," he said, "and I need hardly say that it is a matter of great annoyance as well as surprise to Pettigrew and myself. Of course General Mathieson was perfectly free to go to any other firm of solicitors, but as we have made the wills for his family and yours for the last hundred years, as well as conducted all their legal business, it is an unpleasant shock to find that he has gone elsewhere, and I must say that I am awaiting the reading of this will with great curiosity, as its contents will doubtless furnish us with the reason why he had it thus prepared."

Just at the stroke of twelve Mr. Halstead and Mr. James were announced.

"We thought it as well," the former said, "for us both to come, Mr. Farmer, for we can understand your surprise at finding that a later will than that which is doubtless in your possession is in existence, and we are ready to explain the whole circumstances under which it was drawn out by us. General Mathieson came one day to our office. He brought with him the card of Colonel Bulstrode; but this was unnecessary, for some months ago the General was at our office with the Colonel. He was only there for the purpose of fixing his name as a witness to the colonel's signature, as our client, like many others, preferred having a personal friend to witness his signature instead of this being done by one of our clerks."

"That was so," the Colonel interjected.

"General Mathieson," Mr. Halstead went on, "was only in our office a minute or two on that occasion, but of course that was sufficient for us to recognize him when he called again. He told us that he desired us to draw out a will, and that as he had determined to appoint Mr. Pettigrew one of his trustees and guardian to his heir, he thought it as well to employ another firm to draw up the will.

"We pointed out that such a precaution was altogether needless when dealing with a firm like yours, and he then said, 'I have another reason. I am making a change in one of the provisions of the will, and I fancy that Farmer & Pettigrew might raise an argument upon it. Here are the instructions,' I said, 'You will permit me to read them through, General, before giving you a decided answer.' Had the will contained any provision that we considered unjust we should have declined to have had anything to do with the matter; but as it in no way diverted the property from the natural heir, and was, as far as we could see, a just and reasonable one, we saw no cause for refusing to carry out his instructions; for we have known, as doubtless you have known, many similar instances, in which men, for some reason or other, have chosen to go outside their family solicitors in matters which they desired should remain entirely a secret until after their death. Had General Mathieson come to us as an altogether unknown person we should have point-blank refused to have had anything to do with the business; but as an intimate friend of our client Colonel Bulstrode, and as being known to us to some extent personally, we decided to follow the instructions given us in writing. I will now, with your permission, read the will."

"First let me introduce Miss Covington to you," Mr. Farmer said. "She is the General's nearest relative, with the exception of his grandson. These ladies are here with her as her friends."

Mr. Halstead bowed, then broke the seals on a large envelope, drew out a parchment, and proceeded to read it. Messrs. Farmer & Pettigrew listened with increasing surprise as he went on. The legacies were absolutely identical with those in the will that they had last prepared. The same trustees and guardians for the child were appointed, and they were unable to understand what had induced General Mathieson to have what was almost a duplicate of his previous will prepared so secretly. The last paragraph, however, enlightened them. Instead of Hilda Covington, John Simcoe was named as heir to the bulk of the property in the event of the decease of Walter Rivington, his grandson, before coming of age.

Hilda gave an involuntary start as the change was announced, and the two lawyers looked at each other in dismay. Mr. Halstead, to whom the General had explained his reasons for gratitude to John Simcoe, saw nothing unusual in the provision, which indeed was heralded with the words, "as my only near relative, Hilda Covington, is well endowed, I hereby appoint my dear friend, John Simcoe, my sole heir in the event of the decease of my grandson, Walter

Rivington, before coming of age, in token of my appreciation of his heroic rescue of myself from the jaws of a tiger, in the course of which rescue he was most seriously wounded."

When he had finished he laid down the will and looked round.

"I hope," he said, "that this will be satisfactory to all parties."

"By gad, sir," Colonel Bulstrode said hotly, "I should call this last part as unsatisfactory as possible."

"The will is identical," Mr. Farmer said, without heeding the Colonel's interjection, "with the one that General Mathieson last executed. The persons benefited and the amounts left to them are in every case the same, but you will understand the dismay with which we have heard the concluding paragraph when I tell you that General Mathieson's heir, Walter Rivington, now a child of six or seven years old, disappeared—I think I may say was kidnaped—on the day preceding General Mathieson's death, and that all efforts to discover his whereabouts have so far been unsuccessful."

Mr. Halstead and his partner looked at each other with dismay, even greater than that exhibited by the other lawyers.

"God bless me!" Mr. Halstead exclaimed. "This is a bad business indeed—and a very strange one. Do you think that this Mr. Simcoe can have been aware of this provision in his favor?"

"It is likely enough that he was aware of it," Mr. Pettigrew said; "he was constantly in the company of General Mathieson, and the latter, who was one of the frankest of men, may very well have informed him; but whether he actually did do so or not of course I cannot say. Would you have any objection to my looking at the written instructions?"

"Certainly not. I brought them with me in order that they may be referred to as to any question that might arise."

"It is certainly in the General's own handwriting," Mr. Pettigrew said, after looking at the paper. "But, indeed, the identity of the legacies given to some twenty or thirty persons, and of all the other provisions of the will, including the appointment of trustees and guardians, with those of the will in our possession, would seem in itself to set the matter at rest. Were you present yourself when the General signed it?"

"Certainly. Both Mr. James and myself were present. I can now only express my deep regret that we acceded to the General's request to draw up the will."

"It is unfortunate, certainly," Mr. Farmer said. "I do not see that under the circumstances of his introduction by an old client, and the fact that you had seen him before, anyone could blame you for undertaking the matter. Such cases are, as you said, by no means unusual, and I am quite sure that you would not have undertaken it, had you considered for a moment that any injustice was being done by its provisions."

"May I ask to whom the property was to go to by the first will?"

"It was to go to Miss Covington. I am sure that I can say, in her name, that under other circumstances she would not feel in any way aggrieved at the loss of a property she can well dispense with, especially as the chances of that provision coming into effect were but small, as the child was a healthy little fellow, and in all respects likely to live to come of age."

"I do not care in the least for myself," Hilda said impetuously. "On the contrary, I would much rather that it had gone to someone else. I should not have at all liked the thought that I might benefit by Walter's death, but I would rather that it had been left to anyone but this man, whom I have always disliked, and whom Walter also disliked. I cannot give any reason why. I suppose it was an instinct, and now the instinct is justified, for I feel sure that he is at the bottom of Walter's disappearance."

"Hush! hush! my dear young lady," Mr. Farmer said, holding up his hand in dismay, "you must not say such things; they are libelous in the extreme. Whatever suspicions you may have—and I own that at present things look awkward—you must not mention those suspicions until you obtain some evidence in their support. The disappearance of the child at this moment may be a mere coincidence—a singular one, if you like—and we shall, of course, examine the matter to the utmost and sift it to the bottom, but nothing must be said until we have something to go on."

Hilda sat silent, with her lips pressed tightly together and an expression of determination upon her face. The other solicitors speedily left, after more expressions of regret.

"What are we going to do next, Mr. Pettigrew?" Hilda asked abruptly, as the door closed behind them.

"That is too difficult a matter to decide off-hand, but after going into the whole matter with my co-trustee, Colonel Bulstrode, with the assistance of my partner, we shall come to some agreement as to the best course to take. Of course we could oppose the probate of this new will, but it does not seem to me that we have a leg to stand upon in that respect. I have no doubt that Halstead & James will retire altogether from the matter, and refuse to act further. In that case it will be my duty, of course, to acquaint Simcoe with the provisions of the will, and to inform him that we, as trustees, shall not proceed to take any further steps in the matter until the fate of Walter

Rivington is ascertained, but shall until then administer the estate in his behalf. It will then be for him to take the next step, and he certainly will not move for some months. After a time he will, of course, apply to the court to have it declared that Walter Rivington, having disappeared for a long time, there is reasonable presumption of his death. I shall then, in your name and mine, as the child's guardians, be heard in opposition, and I feel sure that the court will refuse to grant the petition, especially under the serious and most suspicious circumstances of the case. In time Simcoe will repeat the application, and we shall of course oppose it. In fact, I think it likely that it will be a good many years before the court will take the step asked, and all that time we shall be quietly making inquiries about this man and his antecedents, and we shall, of course, keep up a search for the child. It may be that his disappearance is only a coincidence, and that he has, as we at first supposed, been stolen for the purpose of making a heavy claim for his return."

"You may be sure that I shall not rest until I find him, Mr. Pettigrew," Hilda said. "I shall devote my life to it. I love the child dearly; but even were he a perfect stranger to me I would do everything in my power, if only to prevent this man from obtaining the proceeds of his villainy."

Mr. Farmer again interposed.

"My dear Miss Covington," he said, "you really must not speak like this. Of course, with us it is perfectly safe. I admit that you have good reason for your indignation, but you must really moderate your expressions, which might cause infinite mischief were you to use them before other people. In the eye of the law a man is innocent until he is proved guilty, and we have not a shadow of proof that this man has anything to do with the child's abduction. Moreover, it might do harm in other ways. To begin with, it might render the discovery of the child more difficult; for if his abductors were aware or even suspected that you were searching in all directions for him, they would take all the greater pains to conceal his hiding-place."

"I will be careful, Mr. Farmer, but I shall proceed to have a search made at every workhouse and night refuge and place of that sort in London, and within twenty miles round, and issue more placards of your offer of a reward of five hundred pounds for information. There is no harm in that."

"Certainly not. Those are the measures that one would naturally take in any case. Indeed, I should already have pushed my inquiries in that direction, but I have hitherto felt sure that had he been merely taken for his clothes, the police would have traced him before now; but as they have not been able to do so, that it was a case of blackmail, and that we should hear very shortly from the people that had stolen him. I sincerely trust that this may the case, and that it will turn out that this man Simcoe has nothing whatever to do with it. I will come down and let you know what steps we are taking from time to time, and learn the directions in which you are pushing your inquiries."

Neither Miss Purcell nor Netta had spoken from the time they had entered the room, but as soon as they took their places in the carriage waiting for them, they burst out.

"What an extraordinary thing, Hilda! And yet," Miss Purcell added, "the search for Walter may do good in one way; it will prevent you from turning your thoughts constantly to the past and to the loss that you have suffered."

"If it had not been for Walter being missing, aunt, I should have thought nothing of uncle's appointing Mr. Simcoe as heir to his property if anything should happen to him. This man had obtained an extraordinary influence over him, and there can be no doubt from uncle's statement to me that he owed his life solely to him, and that Simcoe indeed was seriously injured in saving him. He knew that I had no occasion for the money, and have already more than is good for a girl to have at her absolute disposal; therefore I am in no way surprised that he should have left him his estate in the event of Walter's death. All that is quite right, and I have nothing to say against it, except that I have always disliked the man. It is only the extraordinary disappearance of Walter, just at this moment, that seems to me to render it certain that Simcoe is at the bottom of it. No one else could have had any motive for stealing Walter, more than any other rich man's child. His interest in his disappearance is immense. I have no doubt uncle had told him what he had done, and the man must have seen that his chance of getting the estate was very small unless the child could be put out of the way."

"You don't think," Netta began, "that any harm can have happened to him?"

"No, I don't think that. Whether this man would have shrunk from it if there were no other way, I need not ask myself; but there could have been no occasion for it. Walter is so young that he will very soon forget the past; he might be handed over to a gypsy and grow up a little vagrant, and as there is no mark on him by which he might be identified, he would be lost to us forever. You see the man can afford to wait. He has doubtless means of his own—how large I do not know, but I have heard my uncle say that he had handsome chambers, and certainly he lived in good style. Now he will have this legacy of ten thousand pounds, and if the court keeps him waiting ten or fifteen years before pronouncing Walter dead, he can afford to wait. Anyhow, I shall have plenty of time in which to act, and it will require a lot of thinking over before I decide what I had best do."

She lost no time, however, in beginning to work. Posters offering the reward of five hundred pounds for information of the missing boy were at once issued, and stuck up not only in London, but in every town and village within thirty miles. Then she obtained from Mr. Pettigrew the name of a firm of trustworthy private detectives and set them to make inquiries, in the first place at all the institutions where a lost child would be likely to be taken if found, or where it might have been left by a tramp. Two days after the reading of the will she received the following letter from John Simcoe:

"DEAR MISS COVINGTON: I have learned from Messrs. Farmer & Pettigrew the liberal and I may say extraordinary generosity shown towards myself by the late General Mathieson, whose loss I most deeply deplore. My feelings of gratitude are at the present moment overwhelmed by the very painful position in which I find myself. I had, of course, heard, upon calling at your door to make inquiries, that little Walter was missing, and was deeply grieved at the news, though not at the time dreaming that it could affect me personally. Now, however, the circumstances of the case are completely changed, for, by the provisions of the will, I should benefit pecuniarily by the poor child's death. I will not for a moment permit myself to believe that he is not alive and well, and do not doubt that you will speedily recover him; but, until this occurs, I feel that some sort of suspicion must attach to me, who am the only person having an interest in his disappearance. The thought that this may be so is distressing to me in the extreme. Since I heard of his disappearance I have spent the greater part of my time in traversing the slums of London in hopes of lighting upon him. I shall now undertake wider researches, and shall to-day insert advertisements in all the daily papers, offering one thousand pounds for his recovery. I feel sure that you at least will not for a moment entertain unjust suspicions concerning me, but those who do not know me well may do so, and although at present none of the facts have been made public, I feel as if I were already under a cloud, and that men in the club look askance at me, and unless the child is found my position will speedily become intolerable. My only support in this trial is my consciousness of innocence. You will excuse me for intruding upon your sorrow at the present moment, but I felt compelled to write as I have done, and to assure you that I will use every effort in my power to discover the child, not only for his own sake and yours, but because I feel that until he is discovered I must continue to rest under the terrible, if unspoken, suspicion of being concerned in his disappearance.

"Believe me, yours very truly,
"JOHN SIMCOE."

CHAPTER XII.

DR. LEEDS SPEAKS.

After reading John Simcoe's letter, Hilda threw it down with an exclamation of contempt.

"Read it!" she said to Netta, who was alone with her.

"The letter is good enough as it stands," Netta remarked, as she finished it.

"Good enough, if coming from anyone else," Hilda said scornfully, "perhaps better than most men would write, but I think that a rogue can generally express himself better than an honest man."

"Now you are getting cynical—a new and unpleasant phase in your character, Hilda. I have heard you say that you do not like this man, but you have never given me any particular reason for it, beyond, in one of your letters, saying that it was an instinct. Now do try to give me a more palpable reason than that. At present it seems to be only a case of Dr. Fell. You don't like him because you don't."

"I don't like him because from the first I distrusted him. Personally, I had no reason to complain; on the contrary, he has been extremely civil, and indeed willing to put himself out in any way to do me small services. Then, as I told you, Walter disliked him, too, although he was always bringing chocolates and toys for him; so that the child's dislike must have been also a sort of instinct. He felt, as I did, that the man was not true and honest. He always gave me the impression of acting a part, and I have never been able to understand how a man of his class could have performed so noble and heroic an act as rushing in almost unarmed to save another, who was almost a stranger to him, from the grip of a tiger. So absolutely did I feel this that I have at times even doubted whether he could be the John Simcoe who had performed this gallant action."

"My dear Hilda, you are getting fanciful! Do you think that your uncle was likely to be deceived in such a matter, and that he would not have a vivid remembrance of his preserver, even after twenty years?"

"That depends on how much he saw of him. My uncle told me that Mr. Simcoe brought some good introductions from a friend of his at Calcutta who came out in the same ship with him. No doubt he dined at my uncle's two or three times—he may even have stayed a few days in the house—possibly more; but as commanding the district my uncle must have been fully occupied during the day, and can have seen little of him until, I suppose, a week or so after his arrival, when he invited him to join in the hunt for a tiger. Although much hurt on that occasion, Simcoe was much less injured than my uncle, who lay between life and death for some time, and Simcoe had left before he was well enough to see him. If he had dined with my uncle a few times after this affair, undoubtedly his features would have been so impressed on him that he would have recognized him, even after twenty years; but, as it was, he could have no particular interest in this gentleman, and can have entertained but a hazy recollection of his features. In fact, the General did not recognize him when he first called upon him, until he had related certain details of the affair. It had always been a sore point with my uncle that he had never had an opportunity of thanking his preserver, who had, as he believed, lost his life at sea before he himself was off his sick bed, and when he heard the man's story he was naturally anxious to welcome him with open arms, and to do all in his power for him. I admit that this man must either have been in Benares then, or shortly afterwards, for he remembered various officers who were there and little incidents of cantonment life that could, one would think, be only known to one who had been there at the time."

"But you say he was only there a week, Hilda?"

"Only a week before this tiger business; but it was a month before he was able to travel. No doubt all the officers there would make a good deal of a man who had performed such a deed, and would go and sit with him and chat to while away the hours; so that he would, in that time, pick up a great deal of the gossip of the station."

"Well, then, what is your theory, Hilda? The real man, as you say, no doubt made a great many acquaintances there; this man seems to have been behind the scenes also."

"He unquestionably knew many of the officers, for uncle told me that he recognized several men who had been out there when he met them at the club, and went up and addressed them by name."

"Did they know him also?"

"No; at first none of them had any idea who he was. But that is not surprising, for they had seen him principally when he was greatly pulled down; and believing him to be drowned, it would have been strange indeed if they had recalled his face until he had mentioned who he was."

"Well, it seems to me that you are arguing against yourself, Hilda. Everything you say points to the fact that this man is the John Simcoe he claims to be. If he is not Simcoe, who can he be?"

"Ah! There you ask a question that I cannot answer."

"In fact, Hilda, you have nothing beyond the fact that you do not like the man, and believe that he is not the sort of man to perform an heroic and self-sacrificing action, on behalf of this curious theory of yours."

"That is all at present, but I mean to set myself to work to find out more about him. If I can find out that this man is an impostor we shall recover Walter; if not, I doubt whether we shall ever hear of him again."

Netta lifted her eyebrows.

"Well, at any rate, you have plenty of time before you, Hilda."

The next morning Dr. Leeds, who had not called for the last three or four days, came in to say that he was arranging a partnership with a doctor of considerable eminence, but who was beginning to find the pressure of work too much for him, and wanted the aid of a younger and more active man.

"It is a chance in a thousand," he said. "I owe it largely to the kind manner in which both Sir Henry Havercourt and Dr. Pearson spoke to him as to my ability. You will excuse me," he went on, after Hilda had warmly congratulated him, "for talking of myself before I have asked any questions, but I know that, had you obtained any news of Walter, you would have let me know at once."

"Certainly I should; but I have some news, and really important news, to give you." And she related the production of the new will and gave him the details of its provisions.

He looked very serious.

"It is certainly an ugly outlook," he said. "I have never seen this Simcoe, but I know from the tone in which you have spoken of him, at least two or three times, that he is by no means a favorite of yours. Can you tell me anything about him?"

"Not beyond the fact that he saved the General's life from a tiger a great many years ago. Shortly after that he was supposed to be lost at sea. Certainly the vessel in which he sailed went down in a hurricane with, as was reported, all hands. He says that he was picked up clinging to a spar. Of his life for the twenty years following he has never given a very connected account, at least as far as I know; but some of the stories that I have heard him tell show that he led a very wild sort of life. Sometimes he was working in a small trader among the islands of the Pacific, and I believe he had a share in some of these enterprises. Then he claims to have been in the service of a native prince somewhere up beyond Burmah, and according to his account took quite an active part in many sanguinary wars and adventures of all sorts."

The doctor's face grew more and more serious as she proceeded.

"Do I gather, Miss Covington, that you do not believe that this man is what he claims to be?"

"Frankly that is my opinion, doctor. I own that I have no ground whatever for my disbelief, except that I have naturally studied the man closely. I have watched his lips as he spoke. When he has been talking about these adventures with savages he spoke without effort, and I have no doubt whatever that he did take part in such adventures; but when he was speaking of India, and especially when at some of the bachelor dinners uncle gave there were officers who had known him out there, it was clear to me that he did not speak with the same freedom. He weighed his words, as if afraid of making a mistake. I believe that the man was playing a part. His tone was genial and sometimes a little boisterous, as it might well be on the part of a man who had been years away from civilization; but I always thought from his manner that all this was false. I am convinced that he is a double-faced man. When he spoke I observed that he watched in a furtive sort of way the person to whom he was speaking, to see the effect of his words; but, above all, I formed my opinion upon the fact that I am absolutely convinced that this man could never have performed the splendid action of facing a wounded tiger unarmed for the sake of one who was, in fact, but a casual acquaintance."

"You will excuse me if I make no comment on what you have told me, Miss Covington. It is a matter far too serious for any man to form a hasty opinion upon. I myself have never seen this man, but I am content to take your estimate of his character. One trained, as you were for years, in the habit of closely watching faces cannot but be a far better judge of character than those who have not had such training. I will take two or three days to think the matter over; and now will you tell me what steps you are taking at present to discover Walter?"

She told him of what was being done.

"Can you suggest anything else, Dr. Leeds?"

"Nothing. It seems to me that the key to the mystery is in the hands of this man, and that it is there it must be sought, though at present I can see no way in which the matter can be set about. When one enters into a struggle with a man like this, one must be armed at all points, prepared to meet craft with craft, and above all to have a well-marked-out plan of campaign. Now I will say good-morning. I suppose Miss Purcell and her niece will stay on with you, at any rate for a time?"

"For a long time, I hope," she said.

"May I ask if you have stated the view that you have given me to Miss Netta Purcell?"

"Yes, I have told her. She is disposed to treat it as an absurd fancy on my part, but if I can get anything to go upon which will convince her that there is even a faint possibility of my being right, she will go through fire and water to assist me."

"I can well believe that," the doctor said. "I am sure that she has a strong character, although so lively and full of fun. Of course, having been thrown with her for four months, I am able to form a very fair opinion of her disposition."

After Dr. Leeds had left, Hilda began to build castles for her friend.

"It would be a splendid thing for her," she said. "He is certainly not a man to speak in the way he did unless he thoroughly meant it. I should think that they were just suited to each other; though it would be really a pity that the scheme I had set my mind upon for getting her over here as head of an institution for teaching deaf and dumb children on Professor Menzel's plan should come to nothing. Perhaps, though, he might be willing that she should act as the head of such an establishment, getting trained assistants from those she knows in Hanover and giving a few hours a day herself to the general supervision, if only for the sake of the good that such an institution would do among, perhaps the most unfortunate of all beings. I am quite sure that, so far, she has no thought of such a thing. However, perhaps I am running on too fast, and that he only means what he said, that he admired her character. I suppose there is no reason that because a man admires a girl's character he should fall in love with her, and yet Netta is so bright and cheerful, and at the same time so kind and thoughtful, I can hardly imagine that any man, thrown with her as he has been, could help falling in love with her."

Netta was surprised when Hilda told her that Dr. Leeds had been inclined to view her theory seriously.

"Really, Hilda? Certainly he is not the sort of man to be carried away by your enthusiasm, so please consider all that I have said upon the subject as unspoken, and I will stand neutral until I hear further what he says."

"He did not say very much, I admit, Netta; but he said that he would take the matter seriously into consideration and let me know what he thinks in two or three days."

"I am afraid that he wants to let you down gently," Netta said. "Well, well, don't looked vexed! I will say no more about it until this solemn judgment is delivered."

Netta was in the room when Dr. Leeds called, two days later.

"Netta is in all my counsels, Dr. Leeds," Hilda said, "and she is, as a rule, a capital hand at keeping a secret, though she did let mine slip out to you."

There was no smile on the doctor's face, and both girls felt at once that the interview was to be a serious one.

"I am well aware that I can speak before Miss Purcell," he said, "although there are very few people before whom I would repeat what I am going to say. I have two questions to ask you, Miss Covington. What is the date of this last will of your uncle's?"

"It is dated the 16th of May."

"About a fortnight before the General's alarming seizure?"

Hilda bowed her head in assent. The next question took her quite by surprise.

"Do you know whether this man Simcoe was one of the party when the seizure took place?"

"He was, doctor. My uncle told me that he was going to dine with him, and Dr. Pearson mentioned to me that he was next to the General and caught him as he fell from his chair."

Dr. Leeds got up and walked up and down the room two or three minutes.

"I think that now things have come to the present pass you ought to know what was the opinion that I originally formed of General Mathieson's illness. Dr. Pearson and Sir Henry Havercourt both differed from me and treated my theory as a fanciful one, and without foundation; and of course I yielded to such superior authority, and henceforth kept my ideas to myself. Nevertheless, during the time the General was under my charge I failed altogether to find any theory or explanation for his strange attack and subsequent state, except that which I had first formed. It was a theory that a medical man is always most reluctant to declare unless he is in a position to prove it, or at least to give some very strong reason in its favor, for a mistake would not only cost him his reputation, but might involve him in litigation and ruin his career altogether. But I think that I ought to tell you what my opinion is, Miss Covington. You must not take it for more than it is worth, namely as a theory; but it may possibly set you on a new track and aid you in your endeavor to discover the missing child."

The surprise of the two girls increased as he continued, after a pause:

"Ever since the day when I was first requested to act as the General's resident medical man I have devoted a considerable time to the study of books in which, here and there, could be found accounts of the action of the herbs in use among the Obi women, fetich men, and so-called wizards on the West Coast of Africa, also in India, and among the savage tribes of the Malay Archipelago and the Pacific Islands. What drugs they use has never been discovered, although many efforts have been made to obtain a knowledge of them, both in India and on the West Coast; but doctors have found it necessary to abandon the attempt, several of them having fallen victims of the jealousy of these people because of the researches they were making. But at the least the effects of the administration of these drugs have been frequently described, and in some respects these correspond so closely to those noticeable in the General's case that I say now, as I said at first, I believe the General's illness was caused by the administration of some drug absolutely unknown to European science."

"You think that my uncle was poisoned?" Hilda exclaimed in a tone of horror, while Netta started to her feet with clenched hands and flushed face.

"I have not used the word 'poisoned,' Miss Covington, though in fact it comes to that. It may not have been administered with the intention of killing; it may have been intended only to bring on a fit, which, in due time, might have been attended by others; but the dose may have been stronger than its administrator intended."

"And you think, Dr. Leeds—you think that it was administered by——"

"No, Miss Covington; I accuse no one. I have no shadow of proof against anyone; but taking this illness, with the abduction of the child, it cannot be denied that one's suspicions must, in the first case, fall upon the man who has profited by the crime, if crime it was. On May 16 this will was drawn up, bequeathing the property to a certain person. The circumstances of the will were curious, but from what I learned from you of the explanation given by the lawyers who drew it up, it seems fair and above-board enough. The General was certainly greatly under the influence of this man, who had rendered him the greatest service one man can render another, and that at the risk of his own life. Therefore I do not consider that this will, which was, so to speak, sprung upon you, is in itself an important link in the chain. But when we find that twelve or fourteen days afterwards the General was, when at table, seized with a terrible fit of an extraordinary and mysterious nature, and that the man who had an interest in his death was sitting next to him, the coincidence is at least a strange one. When, however, the General's heir is abducted, when the General is at the point of death, the matter for the first time assumes a position of the most extreme gravity.

"At first, like you, I thought that Walter had either been stolen by some woman for the sake of his clothes, or that he had been carried off by someone aware that he was the General's heir, with a view to obtaining a large sum of money as his ransom. Such things have been done before, and will, no doubt, be done again. The first hypothesis appears to have failed altogether; no woman who had robbed a child of his clothes would desire to detain him for an hour longer than was necessary. The inquiries of the police have failed altogether; the people you have employed have ascertained that neither at the workhouses of London nor in the adjacent counties has any child at all answering to Walter's description been left by a tramp or brought in by the police or by someone who had found him wandering about. It cannot be said that the second hypothesis is also proved to be a mistaken one; the men who took him away would be obliged to exercise the greatest caution when opening negotiations for his release, and it might be a month or more before you heard from them.

"Therefore, it would be unfair to this man Simcoe to assume that he is the author of the plot until so long a period has passed that it is morally certain that the boy was not stolen for the purpose of blackmail. However, we have the following suspicious circumstances: first, that, as I believe, the General was drugged by some poison of whose nature we are ignorant beyond that we read of very similar cases occurring among natives races in Africa and elsewhere. Then we have the point that no one would have had any interest in the General's death, with the exception of the man he had named as his heir in the event of the child's death. We know by the man's statement that he was for many years living among tribes where poisons of this kind are used by the wizards and fetich men to support their authority and to remove persons against whom they have a grudge. Lastly, we have the crowning fact of the abduction of the child, who stood between this man and the estates. All this is at best mere circumstantial evidence. We do not know for certain what caused the General's fit, we have no proof that Simcoe had any hand in the abduction, and whatever our opinion may be, it is absolutely necessary that we do not breathe a hint to anyone."

Hilda did not speak; the shock and the horror of the matter were too much for her. She sat with open lips and blanched face, looking at Dr. Leeds. Netta, however, leaped to her feet again.

"It must be so, Dr. Leeds. It does not seem to me that there can be a shadow of doubt in the matter, and anything that I can do to bring the truth to light I will do, however long a time it takes me."

"Thank you, Netta," Hilda said, holding out her hand to her friend; "as for me, I will devote my life to clearing up this mystery."

"I am afraid, Miss Covington, that my engagements henceforth will prevent my joining actively in your search, but my advice will always be at your service, and it may be that I shall be able to point out methods that have not occurred to you."

"But, oh, Dr. Leeds!" Hilda exclaimed suddenly; "if this villain poisoned my uncle, surely he will not hesitate to put Walter out of his path."

"I have been thinking of that," Dr. Leeds exclaimed, "but I have come to the conclusion that it is very unlikely that he will do so. In the first place, he must have had accomplices. The man who spoke to the nurse and the cabman who drove the child away must both have been employed by him, and I have no doubt whatever that the child has been placed with some persons who are probably altogether ignorant of his identity. Walter was a lovable child, and as soon as he got over his first grief he would no doubt become attached to the people he was with, and although these might be willing to take a child who, they were told, had lost its parents, and was homeless and friendless, without inquiring too closely into the circumstances, it is unlikely in the extreme that they would connive at any acts of violence. It is by no means easy to murder and then to dispose of the body of a child of seven, and I should doubt whether this man would attempt such a thing. He would be perfectly content that the boy would be out of his way, that all traces of him should be lost, and that it would be beyond the range of probability that he could ever be identified, and, lastly, even the most hardened villains do not like putting their necks in a noose. Moreover, if in the last extremity his confederates, believing that he had made away with the child, tried to blackmail him, or some unforeseen circumstance brought home to him the guilt of this abduction, he would be in a position to produce the child, and even to make good terms for himself for doing so. You yourself, whatever your feelings might be as to the man whom you believe to be the murderer of your uncle, would still be willing to pay a considerable sum and allow him to leave the country, on condition of his restoring Walter. Therefore I think that you may make your mind easy on that score, and believe that whatever has happened to him, or wherever he may be, there is no risk of actual harm befalling him."

"Thank you very much, doctor. That is indeed a relief. And now have you thought of any plan upon which we had best set to work?"

"Not at present, beyond the fact that I see that the power you both possess of reading what men say, when, as they believe, out of earshot, ought to be of material advantage to you. As Miss Purcell has promised to associate herself with you in the search, I should say that she would be of more use in this direction than you would. You have told me that he must be perfectly aware of your dislike for him, and would certainly be most careful, were you in his presence, although he might not dream of this power that you possess. But he has never seen your friend, and would not be on his guard with her. I have at present not thought over any plan by which she could watch him—that must be for after consideration—but it seems to me that this offers some chance of obtaining a clew."

"I am ready to do anything, Dr. Leeds," Netta said firmly. "You only have to find out a way, and I will follow out your instructions to the letter. First we must find out whether Hilda's theory about this man, which I scoffed at when she first spoke of it to me, is correct."

"You mean the theory that this man is not John Simcoe at all, but someone who, knowing the facts of the rescue from the tiger, and being also well acquainted with people and things in Benares, has personated him? I will not discuss that now. I have an appointment to meet a colleague for consultation in a difficult case, and have already run the time very close. You shall see me again shortly, when I have had time to think the whole matter over quietly."

CHAPTER XIII.

NETTA VISITS STOWMARKET.

"Well, Netta," Hilda said, after Dr. Leeds had left them, "I suppose you will not in future laugh at my instincts. I only wish that they had been stronger. I wish I had told my dear uncle that I disliked the man so thoroughly that I was sure there was something wrong with him, and implored him not to become very intimate with him. If I had told him how strongly I felt on the subject, although, of course, he could have left or given him any sum that he chose, I do think it would have had some influence with him. No doubt he would have laughed at what he would have called my suspicious nature, but I think he would not have become so friendly with the man; but, of course, I never thought of this. Oh, Netta! my heart seems broken at the thought that my dear uncle, the kindest of men, should have been murdered by a man towards whom his thoughts were so kindly that he appointed him his heir in the event of Walter's death. If he had left him double the sum he did, and had directed that in case of Walter's death the property should go to hospitals, the child might now have been safe in the house. It is heartbreaking to think of."

"Well, dear," Netta said, "we have our work before us. I say 'we' because, although he was no relation to me, I loved him from the first, when he came over with the news of your father's death. Had I been his niece as well as you, he could not have treated me more kindly than he did when I was staying with you last year, and during the last four months that I have been with you. One could see, even in the state he was in, how kind his nature was, and his very helplessness added to one's affection for him. I quite meant what I said, for until this matter is cleared up, and until this crime, if crime it really is, is brought to light, I will stay here, and be your helper, however the long the time may be. There are two of us, and I do not think that either of us are fools, and we ought to be a match for one man. There is one thing we have, that is a man on whom we can rely. I do not mean Dr. Leeds; I regard him as our director. I mean Tom Roberts; he would have given his life, I am sure, for his master, and I feel confident that he will carry out any instructions we may give him to the letter."

"I am sure he will, Netta. Do you think we ought to tell him our suspicions?"

"I should do so unhesitatingly, Hilda. I am sure he will be ready to go through fire and water to avenge his master's death. As aunt is out I think it will be as well to take him into our confidence at once."

Hilda said nothing, but got up and rang the bell. When the footman entered she said, "Tell Roberts that I want to speak to him." When the man came up she went on, "We are quite sure, Tom, that you were most thoroughly devoted to your master, and that you would do anything in your power to get to the bottom of the events that have brought about his death and the carrying off of his grandson."

"That I would, miss; there is not anything that I would not do if you would only set me about it."

"Well, Roberts, I am about to take you into our confidence, relying implicitly upon your silence and on your aid."

"You can do that, miss, safely enough. There is nothing now that I can do for my master; but as for Master Walter, I would walk to China if I thought that there was a chance of finding him there."

"In the first place you must remember, Roberts, that we are acting only upon suspicion; we have only that to go upon, and our object must be to find some proofs to justify those suspicions."

"I understand, miss; you have got an idea, and you want to see if it is right?"

"We ourselves have little doubt of it, Roberts. Now please sit down and listen to me, and don't interrupt me till I have finished."

Then she related the grounds that she had for suspicion that the General's death and Walter's abduction were both the work of John Simcoe, and also her own theory that this man was not the person who had saved the General's life. In spite of her warning not to interrupt, Tom Roberts' exclamations of fury were frequent and strongly worded.

"Well, miss!" he exclaimed, when she had finished and his tongue was untied, "I did not think that there was such a villain upon the face of the earth. Why, if I had suspected this I would have killed him, if I had been hung for it a week after. And to think that he regular took me in! He had always a cheerful word for me, if I happened to open the door for him. 'How are you, Tom?' he would say, 'hearty as usual?' and he would slip a crown into my hand to drink his health. I always keep an account of tips that I receive, and the first thing I do will be to add them up and see how much I have had from him, and I will hand it over to a charity. One don't like setting out to help to bring a man to the gallus when you have got his money in your pocket. I must have been a fool, miss, not to have kept a better watch, but I never thought ill of the man. It seemed to me that he had been a soldier. Sometimes when he was talking with me he would come out with barrack-room sayings, and though he never said that he had served, nor the General neither, I thought that he must have done so. He had a sort of way of carrying his shoulders which you don't often see among men who have not learned the goose-step. I will wait, miss, with your permission, until I have got rid of that money, and then if you say to me, 'Go to that man's rooms and take him by the throat and squeeze the truth out of him,' I am ready to do it."

"We shall not require such prompt measures as that, Tom; we must go about our work carefully and quietly, and I fear that it will be a very long time before we are able to collect facts that we can act upon. We have not decided yet how to begin. I may tell you that the only other person who shares our suspicions is Dr. Leeds. We think it best that even Miss Purcell should know nothing about them. It would only cause her great anxiety, and the matter will, therefore, be kept a close secret among our four selves. In a few days our plans will probably be complete, and I think that your share in the business will be to watch every movement of this man and to ascertain who are his associates; many of them, no doubt, are club men, who, of course, will be above suspicion, but it is certain that he must have had accomplices in the abduction of the child. Whether he visits them or they visit him, is a point to find out. There is little chance of their calling during daylight, and it is in the evening that you will have to keep a close eye on him and ascertain who his visitors are."

"All right, miss, I wish he did not know me by sight; but I expect that I can get some sort of a disguise so that he won't recognize me."

"I don't think that there will be any difficulty about that. Of course we are not going to rely only upon you; Miss Purcell and myself are both going to devote ourselves to the search."

"We will run him down between us, miss, never fear. It cannot be meant that such a fellow as this should not be found out in his villainy. I wish that there was something more for me to do. I know several old soldiers like myself, who would join me willingly enough, and we might between us carry him off and keep him shut up somewhere, just as he is doing Master Walter, until he makes a clean breast of it. It is wonderful what the cells and bread and water will do to take a fellow's spirit down. It is bad enough when one knows how long one has got to bear it; but to know that there is no end to it until you choose to speak would get the truth out of Old Nick, begging your pardon for naming him."

"Well, we shall see, Roberts. That would certainly be a last resource, and I fear that it would not be so effectual as you think. If he told us that if he did not pay his usual visit to the boy it would be absolutely certain we should never see him alive again, we should not dare retain him."

"Well, miss, whatever you decide on I will do. I have lost as a good master as ever a man had, and there is nothing that I would not do to bring that fellow to justice."

The girls waited impatiently for the next visit of Dr. Leeds. It was four days before he came.

"I hoped to have been here before," he said, "but I have been so busy that it has not been possible for me to manage it. Of course this business has always been in my mind, and it seems to me that the first step to be taken is to endeavor to ascertain whether this fellow is really, as you believe, Miss Covington, an impostor. Have you ever heard him say in what part of the country he formerly resided?"

"Yes; he lived at Stowmarket. I know that some months ago he introduced to uncle a gentleman who was manager at a bank there, and had known him from boyhood. He was up for a few days staying with him."

"That is certainly rather against your surmise, Miss Covington; however, it is as well to clear that matter up before we attempt anything else."

"I will go down and make inquiries, doctor," Netta said quietly. "I am half a head shorter than Hilda, and altogether different in face; therefore, if he learns that any inquiries have been made, he will be sure that whoever made them was not Hilda."

"We might send down a detective, Miss Purcell."

"No; I want to be useful," she said, "and I flatter myself that I shall be able to do quite as well as a detective. We could hardly take a detective into our confidence in a matter of this kind, and not knowing everything, he might miss points that would give us a clew to the truth. I will start to-morrow. I shall tell my aunt that I am going away for a day or two to follow up some clew we have obtained that may lead to Walter's discovery. In a week you shall know whether this man is really what he claims to be."

"Very well, Miss Purcell; then we will leave this matter in your hands."

"By the way, doctor," Hilda Covington said, "we have taken Roberts into our confidence. We know that we can rely upon his discretion implicitly, and it seemed to us that we must have somebody we can trust absolutely to watch this man."

"I don't think that you could have done better," he said. "I was going to suggest that it would be well to obtain his assistance. From what I have heard, very few of these private detectives can be absolutely relied upon. I do not mean that they are necessarily rogues, who would take money from both sides, but that, if after trying for some time they consider the matter hopeless, they will go on running up expenses and making charges when they have in reality given up the search. What do you propose that he shall do?"

"I should say that, in the first place, he should watch every evening the house where Simcoe lives, and follow up everyone who comes out and ascertain who they are. No doubt the great majority of them will be clubmen, but it is likely that he will be occasionally visited by some of his confederates."

"I think that is an excellent plan. He will, of course, also follow him when he goes out, for it is much more likely that he will visit these fellows than that they should come to him. In a case like this he would assuredly use every precaution, and would scarcely let them know who he is and where he resides."

"No doubt that is so, doctor, and it would make Roberts' work all the easier, for even if they came to the man's lodgings he might be away, following up the track of someone who had called before him."

Netta returned at the end of four days.

"I have not succeeded," she said, in answer to Hilda's inquiring look as she came in. "The man is certainly well known at Stowmarket as John Simcoe; but that does not prove that he is the man, and just as he deceived your uncle he may have deceived the people down there. Now I will go upstairs and take off my things, and then give you a full account of my proceedings.

"My first step," she began on her return, "was, of course, to find out what members of the Simcoe family lived there. After engaging a room at the hotel, which I can assure you was the most unpleasant part of the business, for they seemed to be altogether unaccustomed to the arrival of young ladies unattended, I went into the town. It is not much of a place, and after making some little purchases and inquiring at several places, I heard of a maiden lady of that name. The woman who told me of her was communicative. 'She has just had a great piece of luck,' she said. 'About ten months back a nephew, whom everyone had supposed to have been lost at sea, came home with a great fortune, and they say that he has behaved most handsomely to her. She has always bought her Berlin wool and such things here, and she has spent three or four times as much since he came home as she did before, and I know from a neighbor, of whom she is a customer, that the yards and yards of flannel that she buys for making up into petticoats for poor children is wonderful. Do you know her, miss?' I said that I did not know her personally, but that some friends of mine, knowing that I was going to Stowmarket, had asked me to inquire if Miss Simcoe was still alive. I said casually that I might call and see her, and so got her address.

"I then went to call upon her. She lives in a little place called Myrtle Cottage. I had been a good deal puzzled as to what story I should tell her. I thought at first of giving myself out as the sister of the young lady to whom her nephew was paying his addresses; and as we knew nothing of him except that he was wealthy, and as he had mentioned that he had an aunt at Stowmarket, and as I was coming down there, I had been asked to make inquiries about him. But I thought this might render her so indignant that I should get nothing from her. I thought, therefore, I had better get all she knew voluntarily; so I went to the house, knocked, and asked whether Miss Simcoe was in. I was shown by a little maid into the parlor, a funny, little, old-fashioned room. Presently Miss Simcoe herself came in. She was just the sort of woman I had pictured—a kindly-looking, little old maid.

"'I do not know whether I have done wrong, Miss Simcoe,' I said, 'but I am a stranger here, and having over-worked myself at a picture from which I hope great things, I have been recommended country air; and a friend told me that Stowmarket was a pretty, quiet, country town, just the place for an over-worked Londoner to gain health in, so I came down and made some inquiries for a single lady who would perhaps take me in and give me a comfortable home for two or three months. Your name has been mentioned to me as being just the lady I am seeking."

"'You have been misinformed,' she said, a little primly. 'I do not say that a few months back I might not have been willing to have entertained such an offer, but my circumstances have changed since then, and now I should not think for a moment of doing so.'

"Rising from my seat with a tired air, I said that I was much obliged to her, but I was very sorry she could not take me in, as I was sure that I should be very comfortable; however, as she could not, of course there was an end of it.

"'Sit down, my dear,' the old lady said. 'I see that you are tired and worn out; my servant shall get you a cup of tea. You see,' she went on, as I murmured my thanks and sat down, 'I cannot very well do what you ask. As I said, a few months ago I should certainly have been very glad to have had a young lady like yourself to stay with me for a time; I think that when a lady gets to my age a little youthful companionship does her good. Besides, I do not mind saying that my means were somewhat straitened, and that a little additional money would have been a great help to me; but everything was changed by the arrival of a nephew of mine. Perhaps you may have heard his name; he is a rich man, and I believe goes out a great deal, and belongs to clubs and so on.'

"I said that I had not heard of him, for I knew nothing about society, nor the sort of men who frequented clubs.

"'No, of course not, my dear,' she said. 'Well, he had been away for twenty years, and everyone thought he was dead. He sailed away in some ship that was never heard of again, and you may guess my surprise when he walked in here and called me aunt.'

"'You must have been indeed surprised, Miss Simcoe,' I said; 'it must have been quite a shock to you. And did you know him at once?'

"'Oh, dear, no! He had been traveling about the world, you see, for a very long time, and naturally in twenty years he was very much changed; but of course I soon knew him when he began to talk.'

"'You recognized his voice, I suppose?' I suggested.

"'No, my dear, no. Of course his voice had changed, just as his appearance had done. He had been what he called knocking about, among all sorts of horrible savages, eating and drinking all kinds of queer things; it made my blood run cold to listen to him. But I never asked any questions about these things; I was afraid he might say that when he was among the cannibals he used to eat human flesh, and I don't think that I could like a man who had done that, even though he was my nephew.'

"'Did he go out quite as a boy, Miss Simcoe?' I asked.

"'Oh, no! He was twenty-four, I think, when he went abroad. He had a situation in the bank here. I know that the manager thought very highly of him, and, indeed, he was everywhere well spoken of. My brother Joshua—his father, you know—died, and he came in for two or three thousand pounds. He had always had a great fancy for travel, and so, instead of looking out for some nice girl and settling down, he threw up his situation and started on his travels.'

"'Had his memory been affected by the hot suns and the hardships that he had gone through?' I asked.

"'Oh, dear! not at all. He recognized everyone almost whom he had known. Of course he was a good deal more changed than they were.'

"'They did not recognize him any more than you did?'

"'Not at first,' she said. 'When a man is believed to have been dead for twenty years, his face does not occur to old friends when they meet an apparent stranger.'

"'That is quite natural,' I agreed. 'What a pleasure it must have been to him to talk over old times and old friends!'

"'Indeed it was, my dear. He enjoyed it so much that for three days he would not move out of the house. Dear me! what pleasant talks we had.'

"'And you say, Miss Simcoe, that his coming has quite altered your position?'

"'Yes, indeed. The very first thing he said after coming into the house was that he had come home resolved to make me and my sister Maria thoroughly comfortable. Poor Maria died some years ago, but of course he did not know it. Then he said that he should allow me fifty pounds a year for life.'

"'That was very kind and nice indeed, Miss Simcoe,' I said.

"By this time, seeing that my sympathy was with her, her heart opened altogether to me, and she said that she felt sure that her nephew would not like it were she to take in a lodger, and might indeed consider it a hint that he might have been more liberal than he was. But she invited me to stay three days with her while I was looking about for suitable lodgings. I found that her house was a regular rendezvous for the tabbies of the neighborhood. Every afternoon there were some four or five of them there. Some brought work, others came in undisguisedly to gossip. Many of these had known John Simcoe in his younger days, and by careless questioning I elicited the fact that no one would have recognized him had it not been for Miss Simcoe having told them of his arrival.

"The manager of the bank I rather shrank from an encounter with, but I managed to obtain from Miss Simcoe a letter her nephew had written to her when he was away from home a short time before he left England, and also one written by him since his return. So far as I could see, there was not the slightest resemblance between them.

"I thought that I might possibly get at someone less likely to be on his guard than the bank manager, and she happened to mention as an interesting fact that one of the clerks who had entered the bank a lad of seventeen, only a month or two before her nephew left, was now married to the daughter of one of her gossips. I said that her story had so deeply interested me that I should be glad to make his acquaintance.

"He came with his wife the evening before I left. He was very chatty and pleasant, and while there was a general conversation going on among the others, I said to him that I was a great student of handwriting, and I flattered myself that I could tell a man's character from his handwriting; but I owned that I had been quite disconcerted by two letters which Miss Simcoe waskind enough to show me from her nephew, one written before he left the bank, the other dated three or four months ago.

"'I cannot see the slightest resemblance between the two,' I said, 'and do not remember any instance which has come under my knowledge of the handwriting of any man or woman changing so completely in the course of twenty years. The one is a methodical, business sort of writing, showing marks of steady purpose, regularity of habits, and a kindly disposition. I won't give you my opinion of the other, but the impression that was left upon my mind was far from favorable.'

"'Yes, there has been an extraordinary change,' he agreed. 'I can recollect the former one perfectly, for I saw him sign scores of letters and documents, and if he had had an account standing at the bank now I should without question honor a check so signed. No doubt the great difference is accounted for by the life that Mr. Simcoe has led. He told me himself that for years, at one time, he had never taken a pen in hand, and that he had almost forgotten how to write; and that his fingers had grown so clumsy pulling at ropes, rowing an oar, digging for gold, and opening oysters for pearls, that they had become all thumbs, and he wrote no better than a schoolboy.'

"'But that is not the case, Mr. Askill,' I said; 'the writing is still clerkly in character, and does not at all answer to his own description.'

"'I noticed that myself, and so did our chief. He showed me a letter that he had received from Simcoe, asking him to run up for a few days to stay with him in London. He showed it to me with the remark that in all his experience he had never seen so great and complete a change in the handwriting of any man as in that of Mr. Simcoe since he left the bank. He considered it striking proof how completely a man's handwriting depends upon his surroundings. He turned up an old ledger containing many entries in Simcoe's handwriting, and we both agreed that we could not see a single point of resemblance.'

"'Thank you,' I said; 'I am glad to find that my failure to recognize the two handwritings as being those of the same man has been shared by two gentlemen who are, like myself in a humble way, experts at handwriting.'

"The next morning I got your letter, written after I had sent you the address, and told Miss Simcoe that I was unexpectedly called back to town, but that it was quite probable that I should ere long be down again, when I would arrange with one or other of the people of whom she had kindly spoken to me. That is all I have been able to learn, Hilda."

"But it seems to me that you have learned an immense deal, Netta. You have managed it most admirably."

"At any rate, I have got as much as I expected, if not more; I have learned that no one recognized this man Simcoe on his first arrival in his native town, and it was only when this old lady had spread the news abroad, and had told the tale of his generosity to her, and so prepared the way for him, that he was more or less recognized; she having no shadow of doubt but that he was her long-lost nephew. In the three days that he stopped with her he had no doubt learned from the dear old gossip almost every fact connected with his boyhood, the men he was most intimate with, the positions they held, and I doubt not some of the escapades in which they might have taken part together; so that he was thoroughly well primed before he met them. Besides, no doubt they were more anxious to hear tales of adventure than to talk of the past, and his course must have been a very easy one.

"Miss Simcoe said that he spent money like a prince, and gave a dinner to all his old friends, at which every dainty appeared, and the champagne flowed like water. We may take it as certain that none of his guests ever entertained the slightest doubt that their host was the man he pretended to be. There could seem to them no conceivable reason why a stranger should come down, settle an income upon Miss Simcoe, and spend his money liberally among all his former acquaintances, if he were any other man than John Simcoe.

"Lastly, we have the handwriting. The man seems to have laid his plans marvelously well, and to have provided against every unforeseen contingency; yet undoubtedly he must have altogether overlooked the question of handwriting, although his declaration that he had almost forgotten how to use his pen was an ingenious one, and I might have accepted it myself if he had written in the rough, scrambling character you would expect under the circumstances. But his handwriting, although in some places he had evidently tried to write roughly, on the whole is certainly that of a man accustomed at one time of his life to clerkly work, and yet differing as widely as the poles from the handwriting of Simcoe, both in the bank ledger and in the letter to his aunt.

"I think, Hilda, that although the matter cannot be decided, it certainly points to your theory that this man is not the John Simcoe who left Stowmarket twenty years ago. He attempted, and I think very cleverly, to establish his identity by a visit to Stowmarket, and no doubt did so to everyone's perfect satisfaction; but when we come to go into the thing step by step, we see that everything he did might have been done by anyone who happened to have a close resemblance to John Simcoe in figure and some slight resemblance in face, after listening for three days to Miss Simcoe's gossip."

CHAPTER XIV.

AN ADVERTISEMENT.

"I cannot wait for Dr. Leeds to come round," Hilda said the next morning at breakfast. "You and I will pay him a visit in Harley Street. I am sure that he will not grudge a quarter of an hour to hear what you have done."

"What mystery are you two girls engaged in?" Miss Purcell asked, as she placidly poured out the tea.

"It is a little plot of our own, aunt," Netta said. "We are trying to get on Walter's track in our own way, and to be for a time amateur detectives. So far we have not found any decisive clew, but I think that we are searching in the right direction. Please trust us entirely, and we hope some day we shall have the triumph of bringing Walter back, safe and sound."

"I pray God that it may be so, my dear. I know that you are both sensible girls, and not likely to get yourselves into any silly scrape."

"I don't think we are, aunt; but I am afraid that neither of us would consider any scrape a foolish one that brought us even a little bit nearer to the object of our search. At any rate, aunt, it will reassure you to know that we are acting in concert with Dr. Leeds, of whom I know that you entertain the highest opinion."

"Certainly I do. Of course I am no judge whatever as to whether he is a good doctor, but I should think, from what Dr. Pearson says, that he must, in the opinion of other medical men, be considered an exceptionally clever man for his age; and having seen him for four months and lived in close contact with him, I would rather be attended by him than by anyone else I have ever met. His kindness to the General was unceasing. Had he been his son, he could not have been more patient and more attentive. He showed wonderful skill in managing him, and was at once sympathetic and cheerful. But, more than that, I admired his tact in filling the somewhat difficult position in which he was placed. Although he was completely one of the family, and any stranger would have supposed that he was a brother, or at least a cousin, there was always something in his manner that, even while laughing and chatting with us all, placed a little barrier between us and himself; and one felt that, although most essentially a friend, he was still there as the General's medical attendant.

"It was a difficult position for a man of his age to be placed in. Had he been like most of the doctors we knew in Germany, a man filled with the idea that he must always be a professor of medicine, and impressing people with his learning and gravity, it might have been easy enough. But there is nothing of that sort about him at all; he is just as high-spirited and is as bright and cheerful as other young men of about the same age, and it was only when he was with the General that his gentleness of manner recalled the fact that he was a doctor. As I say, it was a difficult position, with only an old woman like myself and two girls, who looked to him for comfort and hope, who treated him as if he had been an old friend, and were constantly appealing to him for his opinion on all sorts of subjects.

"I confess that, when he first came here with Dr. Pearson, I thought that it was a very rash experiment to introduce a young and evidently pleasant man to us under such circumstances, especially as you, Hilda, are a rich heiress and your own mistress; and feeling as I did that I was in the position of your chaperon, I must say that at first I felt very anxious about you, and it was a great relief to me when after a time I saw no signs, either on his part or yours, of any feeling stronger than friendship springing up."

Hilda laughed merrily.

"The idea never entered into my mind, aunt; it is funny to me that so many people should think that a young man and a young woman cannot be thrown together without falling in love with each other. At present, fortunately, I don't quite understand what falling in love means. I like Dr. Leeds better, I think, than any young man I ever met, but I don't think that it can be in the least like what people feel when they fall in love. Certainly it was always as uncle's doctor, rather than as a possible suitor for my hand—that is the proper expression, isn't it?—that I thought of him."

"So I was glad to perceive, Hilda; and I was very thankful that it was so. Against him personally I had nothing to say, quite the contrary; but I saw that he was greatly attached to a profession in which he seems likely to make himself a fine position, and nothing could be more uncomfortable than that such a man should marry a girl with a fine country estate. Either he would have to give up his profession or she would have to settle down in London as the wife of a physician, and practically forfeit all her advantages."

Hilda again laughed.

"It is wonderful that all these things should never have occurred to me, aunt. I see now how fortunate it was that I did not fall in love with him. And now, Netta, as we have finished breakfast, we will put on our things at once and go and consult our physician in ordinary. We have a fair chance of being the first to arrive if we start immediately. I told Roberts to have the carriage at the door at half-past nine, and he does not begin to see patients until ten."

"Bravo! Miss Purcell," Dr. Leeds exclaimed, when she had given him an account of her mission. "Of course there is nothing absolutely proved, but at least it shows that his identity is open to doubt, since none of the people he had known recognized him at first sight, and of course all his knowledge of them may have been picked up from the gossiping old lady, his aunt. Something has been gained, but the evidence is rather negative than positive. It is possible that he is not the man that he pretends to be; though at present, putting aside the question of handwriting, we must admit that the balance of probability is very much the other way. To begin with, how could this man, supposing him to be an impostor, know that John Simcoe was born in Stowmarket, and had relatives living there?"

"I forgot to mention that, Dr. Leeds. An advertisement was inserted in the county paper, saying that if any relatives of John Simcoe, who left England about 1830, would communicate with someone or other in town they would hear something to their advantage. I was told this by one of Miss Simcoe's friends, who saw it in the paper and brought it in to her. She was very proud of having made the discovery, and regarded herself quite in the light of a benefactor to Miss Simcoe. I remarked, when she told me, that it was curious he should have advertised instead of coming down himself to inquire. Miss Simcoe said that she had expressed surprise to him, and that he had said he did so because he should have shrunk from coming down, had he not learned there was someone to welcome him."

"Curious," Dr. Leeds said thoughtfully. "We may quite put it out of our minds that the reason he gave was the real one. A man of this kind would not have suffered any very severe shock had he found that Stowmarket and all it contained had been swallowed up by an earthquake. No, certainly that could not have been the reason; we must think of some other. And now, ladies, as this is the third card I have had brought in since you arrived, I must leave the matter as it stands. I think that we are getting on much better than we could have expected."

"That advertisement is very curious, Netta," Hilda said as they drove back. "Why should he have put it in? It would have been so much more natural that he should have gone straight down."

"I cannot think, Hilda. It did not strike me particularly when I heard of it, and I did not give it a thought afterwards. You see, I did not mention it, either to you or Dr. Leeds, until it flashed across my mind when we were talking. Of course I did not see the advertisement itself, but Miss Simcoe told me that there had been a good deal of discussion before she answered it, as some of them had thought that it might be a trick."

"When was it he went down?"

"It was in August last year; and it was in the first week in September that he came here."

"He went down to get or manufacture proof of his identity," Hilda said. "As it turned out, uncle accepted his statement at once, and never had the smallest doubt as to his being John Simcoe. The precaution, therefore, was unnecessary; but at the same time it certainly helps him now that a doubt has arisen. It would have been very strange if a man possessing sufficient means to travel in India should have had no friends or connections in England. I was present when he told my uncle that he had been down to see his aunt at Stowmarket, and in the spring he brought a gentleman who, he said, was manager of the Stowmarket Bank, in which he had himself been at one time a clerk. So you see he did strengthen his position by going down there."

"It strengthens it in one way, Hilda, but in the other it weakens it. As long as no close inquiries were made, it was doubtless an advantage to him to have an aunt of the same name in Stowmarket, and to be able to prove by means of a gentleman in the position of manager of the bank that he, John Simcoe, had worked under him three or four and twenty years ago. On the other hand, it was useful to us as a starting-point. If we had been utterly in the dark as to Simcoe's birthplace or past career, we should have had to start entirely in the dark. Now, at any rate, we have located the birthplace of the real man, and learned something of his position, his family, and how he became possessed of money that enabled him to start on a tour round the world. I adhere as firmly as before to the belief that this is not the real man, and the next step is to discover how he learned that John Simcoe had lived at Stowmarket. At any rate it would be as well that we should find the advertisement. It might tell us nothing, but at the least we should learn the place to which answers were to be sent. How should we set about that?"

"I can get a reader's ticket for the British Museum, because the chief librarian was a friend of uncle's and dined with him several times," Hilda replied. "If I write to him and say that I want to examine some files of newspapers, to determine a question of importance, I am sure that he will send me a ticket at once. I may as well ask for one for you also. We may want to go there again to decide some other point."

Hilda at once wrote a note and sent Tom Roberts with it to the Museum, and he returned two hours later with the tickets.

"There are three Suffolk papers," the chief assistant in the Newspaper Department said courteously, on their sending up the usual slip of paper. "Which do you want?"

"I do not know. I should like to see them all three, please; the numbers for the first two weeks in August last."

In a few minutes three great volumes were placed on the table. These contained a year's issue, and on turning to the first week in August they found that the advertisement had appeared in all of the papers. They carefully copied it out, and were about to leave the library when Netta said:

"Let us talk this over for a minute or two before we go. It seems to me that there is a curious omission in the advertisement."

"What is that?"

"Don't you see that he does not mention Stowmarket? He simply inquires for relations of John Simcoe, who was supposed to have been lost at sea. It would certainly seem to be more natural that he should put it only in the paper that was likely to be read in Stowmarket, and surely he would have said 'relatives of John Simcoe, who left Stowmarket in the year 1830.' It looks very much as if, while he knew that Simcoe was a Suffolk man, he had no idea in what part of the county he had lived."

"It is very curious, certainly, Netta; and, as you say, it does seem that if he had known that it had been Stowmarket he would have said so in the advertisement. Possibly!" Hilda exclaimed so sharply that a gentleman at an adjoining table murmured "Hush!" "he did did not know that it was in Suffolk. Let us look in the London papers. Let us ask for the files of the *Times* and *Standard*."

The papers were brought and the advertisement was found in both of them.

"There, you see," Netta said triumphantly, "he still says nothing about Suffolk."

She beckoned to the attendant.

"I am sorry to give you so much trouble, but will you please get us the files of three or four country papers of the same date. I should like them in different parts of the country—Yorkshire, for instance, and Hereford, and Devonshire."

"It is no trouble, miss," he replied; "that is what we are here for."

In a few minutes the three papers were brought, and Netta's triumph was great when she found the advertisement in each of them.

"That settles it conclusively," she said. "The man did not know what part of the country John Simcoe came from, and he advertised in the London papers, and in the provincial papers all over the country."

"That was a splendid idea of yours, Netta. I think that it settles the questionas to the fact that the theory you all laughed at was correct, and that this man is not the real John Simcoe."

When they got back, Hilda wrote a line to Dr. Leeds:

> "DEAR DOCTOR: I do think that we have discovered beyond doubt that the man is an impostor, and that whoever he may be, he is not John Simcoe. When you can spare time, please come round. It is too long to explain."

At nine o'clock that evening Dr. Leeds arrived, and heard of the steps that they had taken.

"Really, young ladies," he said, "I must retire at once from my post of director of searches. It was an excellent thought to ascertain the exact wording of the advertisement, and the fact that the word Stowmarket did not appear in it, and that it was inserted in other county papers, was very significant as to the advertiser's ignorance of John Simcoe's birthplace. But the quickness with which you saw how this could be proved up to the hilt shows that you are born detectives, and I shall be happy to sit at your feet in future."

"Then you think that it is quite conclusive?"

"Perfectly so. The real John Simcoe would, of course, have put the advertisement into the county paper published nearest to Stowmarket, and he would naturally have used the word Stowmarket. That omission might, however, have been accidental; but the appearance of the advertisement in the London papers, and as you have seen, in provincial papers all over England, appears to me ample evidence that he did not know from what county Simcoe came, and was ready to spend a pretty heavy amount to discover it. Now, I think that you should at once communicate with Mr. Pettigrew, and inform him of your suspicion and the discovery that you have made. It is for him to decide whether any steps should be taken in the matter, and, if so, what steps. As one of the trustees he is responsible for the proper division of the estates of General Mathieson, and the matter is of considerable importance to him.

"I think now, too, that our other suspicions should also be laid before him. Of course, these are greatly strengthened by his discovery. John Simcoe, who saved your uncle's life at the risk of his own, was scarcely the sort of man who would be guilty of murder and abduction; but an unknown adventurer, who had passed himself off as being Simcoe, with the object of obtaining a large legacy from the General, may fairly be assumed capable of taking any steps that would enable him to obtain it. If you'd like to write to Mr. Pettigrew and make an appointment to meet him at his office at three o'clock to-morrow afternoon, I will be here half an hour before and accompany you."

The lawyer was somewhat surprised when Dr. Leeds entered the office with the two ladies, but that astonishment became stupefaction when they told their story.

"In the whole of my professional career I have never heard a more astonishing story. I own that the abduction of the child at that critical moment did arouse suspicions in my mind that this Mr. Simcoe, the only person that could be benefited by his disappearance, might be at the bottom of it, and I was quite prepared to resist until the last any demand that might be made on his part for Walter to be declared to be dead, and the property handed over to him. But that the man could have had any connection whatever with the illness of the General, or that he was an impostor, never entered my mind. With regard to the first, it is still a matter of suspicion only, and we have not a shadow of proof to go upon. You say yourself, Dr. Leeds, that Dr. Pearson, the General's own medical attendant, and the other eminent physicians called in, refused absolutely to accept your suggestion, because, exceptional as the seizure and its effects were, there was nothing that absolutely pointed to poison. Unless we can obtain some distinct evidence on that point, the matter must not be touched upon; for even you would hardly be prepared to swear in court that the General was a victim to poison?"

"No. I could not take my oath to it, but I certainly could declare that the symptoms, to my mind, could be attributed to poison only."

"In the case of the abduction of the boy," the lawyer went on, "the only absolute ground for our suspicion is that this man and no one else would have benefited by it; and this theory certainly appears to be, after the discoveries you have made, a very tenable one. It all comes so suddenly on me that I cannot think of giving any opinion as to the best course to be adopted. I shall, in the first place, consult Mr. Farmer, and in the next place shall feel it my duty to take my co-trustee, Colonel Bulstrode, into my confidence, because any action that we may take must, of course, be in our joint names. He called here the other day and stated to me that he regarded the whole matter of Walter's abduction to be suspicious in the extreme. He said he was convinced that John Simcoe was at the bottom of it, his interest in getting the boy out of the way being unquestionable, and that we must move heaven and earth to find the child. He agreed that we can do nothing about carrying out the will until we have found him. I told him of the steps that we have been taking and their want of success. 'By gad, sir,' he said, 'he must be found, if we examine every child in the country.' I ventured to suggest that this would be a very difficult undertaking, to which he only made some remark about the cold-bloodedness of lawyers, and said that if there were no other way he would dress himself up as a costermonger and go into every slum of London.

Whether you would find him a judicious assistant in your searches I should scarcely be inclined to say, but you would certainly find him ready to give every assistance in his power."

The next day, at three o'clock, Colonel Bulstrode was announced. He was a short man, of full habit of body. At the present moment his face was even redder than usual.

"My dear Miss Covington," he burst out, as he came into the room, "I have just heard of all this rascality, and what you and your friend Miss Purcell have discovered. By gad, young ladies, I feel ashamed of myself. Here am I, Harry Bulstrode, a man of the world, and, as such, considered that this affair of the man Simcoe being made heir in case of the child's death and the simultaneous disappearance of the boy to have been suspicious in the extreme, and yet I have seen no way of doing anything, and have been so upset that my temper has, as that rascal Andrew, my old servant, had the impudence to tell this morning, become absolutely unbearable. And now I find that you two girls and a doctor fellow have been quietly working the whole thing out, and that not improbably my dear old friend was poisoned, and that the man who did it is not the man he pretended to be, but an infernal impostor, who had of course carried the child away, and may, for anything we know, have murdered him. It has made me feel that I ought to go to school again, for I must be getting into my second childhood. Still, young ladies, if, as is evident, I have no sense to plan, I can at least do all in my power to assist you in your search, and you have only to say to me, 'Colonel Bulstrode, we want an inquiry made in India,' and I am off by the first P. and O."

"Thank you very much, Colonel," Hilda said, trying to repress a smile. "I was quite sure that from your friendship for my dear uncle you would be ready to give us your assistance, but so far there has been no way in which you could have aided us in the inquiries that we have made. Indeed, as Dr. Leeds has impressed upon us, the fewer there are engaged in the matter the better; for if this man knew that we were making all sorts of inquiries about him, he might think it necessary for his safety either to put Walter out of the way altogether, or to send him to some place so distant that there would be practically no hope whatever of our ever discovering him. At present I think that we have fairly satisfied ourselves that this man is an impostor, and that the real John Simcoe was drowned, as supposed, in the ship in which he sailed from India. Who this man is, and how he became acquainted with the fact that John Simcoe saved my uncle's life in India, are mysteries that so far we have no clew to; but these matters are at present of minor importance to us. Before anything else we want to find where Walter is hidden, and to do this we are going to have this man watched. He cannot have carried off Walter by himself, and, no doubt, he meets occasionally the people who helped him, and who are now hiding Walter. It is scarcely probable that they come to his lodgings. He is not likely to put himself into anyone's power, and no doubt goes by night in some disguise to meet them. As, of course, he knows you perfectly well, it would be worse than useless for you to try to follow him. That is going to be done by Tom Roberts."

"Well, my man Andrew might help him," the Colonel said. "Simcoe has often dined with me at the club, but he never came to my chambers. One man cannot be always on the watch, and Andrew can take turns with Roberts. He is an impudent rascal, but he has got a fair share of sense; so, when you are ready, if you will drop me a line, he shall come here and take his instructions from you."

"Thank you very much, Colonel. That certainly would be of assistance. It is only of an evening that he would be wanted, for we are quite agreed that these meetings are sure to take place after dark."

CHAPTER XV.

VERY BAD NEWS.

A month passed. Tom Roberts and Andrew watched together in Jermyn Street, the former with a cap pulled well down over his face and very tattered clothes, the latter dressed as a groom, but making no attempt to disguise his face. During that time everyone who called at the house in Jermyn Street was followed, and their names and addresses ascertained, one always remaining in Jermyn Street while the other was away. The man they were watching had gone out every evening, but it was either to one or the other of the clubs to which he belonged, or to the theater or opera.

"You will trace him to the right place presently, Roberts," Hilda said cheerfully, when she saw that he was beginning to be disheartened at the non-success of his search. "You may be sure that he will not go to see these men oftener than he can help. Does he generally wear evening clothes?"

"Always, miss."

"I don't think there is any occasion to follow him in future when he goes out in that dress; I think it certain that when he goes to meet these men he will be in disguise. When you see him come out dressed altogether differently to usual, follow him closely. Even if we only find where he goes it will be a very important step."

On the seventh week after the disappearance of Walter, Mr. Pettigrew came in one morning at eleven o'clock. His air was very grave.

"Have you heard news, Mr. Pettigrew?" Hilda asked.

"I have very bad news. Mr. Comfrey, a lawyer of not the highest standing, who is, I have learnt, acting for this fellow, called upon me. He said, 'I am sorry to say that I have some painful news to give you, Mr. Pettigrew. Yesterday the body of a child, a boy some six or seven years old, was found in the canal at Paddington. It was taken to the lockhouse. The features were entirely unrecognizable, and the police surgeon who examined it said that it had been in the water over a month. Most of its clothing was gone, partly torn off by barges passing over the body; but there still remained a portion of its underclothing, and this bore the letters W. R. The police recognized them as those of the child who has been so largely advertised for, and, as my client, Mr. Simcoe, had offered a thousand pounds reward, and as all information was to be sent to me, a policeman came down, just as I was closing the office, to inform me of the fact.

"'I at once communicated with my client, who was greatly distressed. He went to Paddington the first thing this morning, and he tells me that he has no doubt whatever that the remains are those of Walter Rivington, although he could not swear to his identity, as the features are altogether unrecognizable. As I understand, sir, that you and Miss Covington were the guardians of this unfortunate child, I have driven here at once in order that you may go up and satisfy yourselves on the subject. I understand that an inquest will be held to-morrow.'"

Hilda had not spoken while Mr. Pettigrew was telling his story, but sat speechless with horror.

"It cannot be; surely it cannot be!" she murmured. "Oh, Mr. Pettigrew! say that you cannot believe it."

"I can hardly say that, my dear; the whole affair is such a terrible one that I can place no bounds whatever to the villainy of which this man may be capable. This may be the missing child, but, on the other hand, it may be only a part of the whole plot."

"But who else can it be if it has Walter's clothes on?"

"As to that I can say nothing; but you must remember that this man is an extraordinarily adroit plotter, and would hesitate at nothing to secure this inheritance. There would be no very great difficulty in obtaining from some rascally undertaker the body of a child of the right age, dressing him up in some of our ward's clothes, and dropping the body into the canal, which may have been done seven weeks ago, or may have been done but a month. Of course I do not mean to say that this was so. I only mean to say that it is possible. No. I expressed my opinion, when we talked it over before, that no sensible man would put his neck in a noose if he could carry out his object without doing so; and murder could hardly be perpetrated without running a very great risk, for the people with whom the child was placed would, upon missing it suddenly, be very likely to suspect that it had been made away with, and would either denounce the crime or extort money by holding a threat over his head for years."

"Yes, that may be so!" Hilda exclaimed, rising to her feet. "Let us go and see at once. I will take Netta with me; she knows him as well as I do."

She ran upstairs and in a few words told Netta the news, and in five minutes they came down, ready to start.

"I have told Walter's nurse to come with us," Hilda said. "If anyone can recognize the child she ought to be able to do so. Fortunately, she is still in the house."

"Now, young ladies," the lawyer said before they started, "let me caution you, unless you feel a moderate certainty that this child is Walter Rivington, make no admission whatever that you see any resemblance. If the matter comes to a trial, your evidence and mine cannot but weigh with the court as against that of this man who is interested in proving its identity with Walter. Of course, if there is any sign or mark on the body that you recognize, you will acknowledge it as the body of our ward. We shall then have to fight the case on other grounds. But unless you detect some unmistakable mark, and it is extremely unlikely that you will do so in the state the body must be in, confine yourself to simply stating that you fail to recognize it in any way."

"There never was any mark on the poor child's body," Hilda said. "I have regretted it so much, because, in the absence of any descriptive marks, the chance of his ever being found was, of course, much lessened."

The lawyer had come in a four-wheeled cab, and in this the party all took their places. Not a word was spoken on the way, except that Hilda repeated what Mr. Pettigrew had said to the nurse. It was with very white faces that they entered the lockhouse. The little body was lying on a board supported by two trestles. It was covered by a piece of sailcloth, and the tattered garments that it had had on were placed on a chair beside it. Prepared as she was for something dreadful, the room swam round, and had Hilda not been leaning on Mr. Pettigrew's arm she would have fallen. There was scarce a semblance of humanity in the little figure. The features of the face had been entirely obliterated, possibly by the passage of barges, possibly by the work of simple decay.

"Courage, my dear!" Mr. Pettigrew said. "It is a painful duty, but it must be performed."

The three women stood silent beside the little corpse. Netta was the first to speak.

"I cannot identify the body as that of Walter Rivington," she said. "I don't think that it would be possible for anyone to do so."

"Is the hair of the same color?" the policeman who was in charge of the room asked.

"The hair is rather darker than his," Netta said; "but being so long in the water, and in such dirty water, it might have darkened."

“That was never Master Walter’s hair!” the nurse exclaimed. “The darling had long, soft hair, and unless those who murdered him cut it short, it would not be like this. Besides, this hair is stiffer. It is more like the hair of a workhouse child than Master Walter’s.”

“That is so,” Hilda said. “I declare that I not only do not recognize the body as that of my ward, but that I am convinced it is not his.”

“Judging only by the hair,” Mr. Pettigrew said, “I am entirely of your opinion, Miss Covington. I have stroked the child’s head many times, and his hair was like silk. I have nothing else to go by, and am convinced that the body is not Walter Rivington’s.”

They then looked at the fragments of clothes. In two places they were marked “W. R.”

“That is my marking, miss,” the nurse said, after closely examining the initials. “I could not swear to the bits of clothes, but I can to the letters. You see, miss, I always work a line above the letters and another below them. I was taught to do it so when I was a girl in our village school, and I have always done it since. But I never saw anyone else mark them so. You see the letters are worked in red silk, and the two lines in white. The old woman who taught us said that it made a proper finish to the work. Yes, Miss Covington, I can swear to these things being Master Walter’s.”

“You could not swear to their being those in which he went out the morning he was lost, nurse?”

“I can, sir, because there is nothing missing except what he had on. I have all his things properly counted, and everything is there.”

At this moment there was a little stir outside, and Hilda glanced down and whispered to Netta:

“Let down your fall; I do not want this man to recognize you.”

Just as she did so John Simcoe entered. He bowed to Hilda.

“I am sorry, indeed, to meet you under such painful circumstances.”

“I beg you not to address me, sir,” she said haughtily. “I wish to have no communication with or from you. Your coming here reminds me of the thirty-seventh verse of the nineteenth chapter of St. John. You can look it out, sir, if you happen to have a Bible at home. Fortunately it is not wholly applicable, for we are all absolutely convinced that this poor little body is not that of General Mathieson’s grandson.”

So saying she stepped out of the little house, followed by the others; leaving John Simcoe white with passion.

"You should not have shown your hand so plainly, Miss Covington."

"I could not help it," the girl said. "He has called a dozen times at the house and has always received the message, 'Not at home,' and he must know that I suspect him of being Walter's abductor."

"What is the verse you referred him to, Hilda?" Netta said. "I confess that I do not know any verse in St. John that seems to be at all applicable to him."

"The quotation is, 'They shall look on Him whom they pierced.'"

Netta could not help smiling. Mr. Pettigrew shook his head.

"You are really too outspoken, Miss Covington, and you will get yourself into trouble. As it is, you have clearly laid yourself open to an action for libel for having practically called the man a murderer. We may think what we like, but we are in no position to prove it."

"I am not afraid of that," she said. "I wish that he would do it; then we should have all the facts brought out in court, and, even if we could not, as you say, prove everything, we could at least let the world know what we think. No, there is no chance of his doing that, Mr. Pettigrew."

"It is fortunate for us, Miss Covington, that our clients are for the most part men. Your sex are so impetuous and so headstrong that we should have a hard time of it indeed if we had to take our instructions from them."

"Mr. Pettigrew, you will please remember that there are three of my sex in this cab, and if you malign us in this way we will at once get out and walk."

The old lawyer smiled indulgently.

"It is quite true, my dear. Women are always passionately certain that they are right, and neither counsel nor entreaty can get them to believe that there can be any other side to a case than that which they take. Talk about men ruining themselves by litigation; the number that do so is as nothing to that of the women who would do so, were they to get as often involved in lawsuits! When Dickens drew the man who haunted the courts he would have been much nearer the mark had he drawn the woman who did so. You can persuade a man that when he has been beaten in every court his case is a lost one; but a woman simply regards a hostile decision as the effect either of great partiality or of incompetence on the part of the judge, and even after being beaten in the House of Lords will attend the courts and pester the judges with applications for the hearing of some new points. It becomes a perfect mania with some of them."

"Very well, Mr. Pettigrew. I would certainly carry my case up to the highest court, and if I were beaten I would not admit that I was in the wrong; still, I do not think that I should pester the poor old judges after that. I suppose we shall all have to come up again to-morrow to the inquest?"

"Certainly. Nurse has recognized the clothes, and I suppose you all recognize the marks, Miss Covington?"

"Yes; I have no doubt whatever that the clothes are Walter's."

"Of course we shall be represented by counsel," Mr. Pettigrew went on. "We must not let the jury find that this is Walter's body if we can possibly prevent it."

"You think that they will do so?"

"I am afraid of it. They will know nothing of the real circumstances of the case; they will only know that the child has been missing for nearly two months, and that, in spite of large rewards, no news has been obtained of him. They will see that this child is about the same age, that the clothes in which it was found are those worn by the missing boy. They will themselves have viewed the body and have seen that identification is almost impossible. This man will give his evidence to the effect that he believes it to be Walter Rivington's body. We shall give it as our opinion that it is not; that opinion being founded upon the fact that the few patches of hair left on the head are shorter and coarser than this was. To us this may appear decisive, but the counsel who will, no doubt, appear for Simcoe, will very legitimately say this fact has no weight, and will point out that no real judgment can be formed upon this. The child was missing—probably stolen for the sake of its clothes. Seeing the description in the handbills and placards, the first step would be to cut off its hair, which disposes of the question of length, and, as he will point out, hair which, when very long, seems soft and silky, will stand up and appear almost bristly when cropped close to the head. I am afraid that, in the face of all that we can say, the coroner's jury will find that the body is Walter's. As to the cause of death they will probably give an open verdict, for even if the surgeon has found any signs of violence upon the body, these may have been inflicted by passing barges long after death."

"Will you have it brought forward that Simcoe has an interest in proving the body to be Walter's?"

"I think not. There would be no use in beginning the fight in the coroner's court. It will all have to be gone into when he applies to the higher courts for an order on the trustees of the will to proceed to carry out its provisions. Then our case will be fully gone into. We shall plead that in the first place the will was made under undue influence. We shall point to the singularity of the General's mysterious attack, an attack which one of the doctors who attended him at once put down to poison, and that at the moment of the attack Simcoe was sitting next to him at dinner. We shall point to the extraordinary coincidence that the child who stood between Simcoe and the inheritance disappeared on the evening when the General was *in extremis*, and, lastly, we shall fire our last shot by declaring that the man is not the John Simcoe named in the will, but is an impostor who assumed his name and traded upon his brave action on the General's behalf.

"But I do not want the fight to begin until we are in a better position than at present to prove what we say. As yet, however satisfactory to us, we have not got beyond the point of conjecture and probabilities, and I trust that, before we have to fight the case, we shall obtain some absolute facts in support of our theory. The man would be able at present to put into court a number of highly respectable witnesses from Stowmarket, and of officers he has met here, who would all testify to his being John Simcoe, and as against their evidence our conjectures would literally go for nothing. No doubt you will all receive notices to attend this evening. The policeman took your names and addresses, and will have told the officer in charge of the case the nature ofthe evidence you will probably give. And please remember that, in giving evidence, you must carefully abstain from saying anything that would lead the jury to perceive that you have any personal feeling against Simcoe, for they would be likely to put down your declaration of inability to recognize the body as a result of a bias against him. Do not let it be seen that there is any personal feeling in the matter at all."

The summonses arrived that evening and the next morning they drove to the coroner's court, Miss Purcell accompanying them. They found Mr. Pettigrew awaiting them at the door.

"There is another case on before ours," he said, "and I should advise you to take a drive for half an hour, and, when you come back, to sit in the carriage until I come for you. The waiting room is a stuffy little place, and is at present full of witnesses in the case now on, and as that case is one of a man killed in a drunken row, they are not of a class whom it is pleasant to mix with."

When they returned, he again came out. "I have just spoken to the coroner and told him who you are, and he has kindly given permission for you to go up to his own room. The case he has now before him may last another half hour."

It was just about that time when Mr. Pettigrew came up and said that their case was about to commence, and that they must go down and take their places in court. This was now almost empty; a few minutes before it had been crowded by those interested in the proceedings, which had terminated in the finding of manslaughter against four of those concerned in the fray. The discovery of a child's body in the canal was far too common an event to afford any attraction, and with the exception of the witnesses, two counsel seated in the front line facing the coroner, and two or three officials, there was no one in court. As soon as the little stir caused by the return of the jury from viewing the body had ceased, the coroner addressed them.

"We shall now, gentlemen of the jury, proceed to the case of the body of the child said to be that of Walter Rivington, which was found under very strange and suspicious circumstances near this end of the canal. You will hear that the child was missing from his home in Hyde Park Gardens on the 23d of October, and for his discovery, as some of you are doubtless aware, large sums have been offered. The day before yesterday the drags were used for the purpose of discovering whether another child, who was lost, and who had been seen going near the bank, had been drowned. In the course of that search this body was brought up. You have already viewed it, gentlemen. Dr. MacIlvaine will tell you that it has certainly been a month in the water, perhaps two or three weeks longer. Unfortunately the state of the body is such that it is impossible now to ascertain the cause of death, or whether it was alive when it fell in, or was placed in, the water. Fortunately some of its clothes still remain on the body, and one of the witnesses, the nurse of the missing boy, will tell you that the marks upon them were worked by herself, and that she can swear to them. Whether any other matters will come before you in reference to the case, which, from the fact that the child was grandson of the late General Mathieson and heir to his property, has attracted much attention, I cannot say. The first witness you will hear is the lock-keeper, who was present at the finding of the body."

Before the witness was called, however, one of the counsel rose and said:

"I am instructed, sir, to appear to watch the proceedings on behalf of Mr. John Simcoe, who, by the death of Walter Rivington, inherits under the will of the late General Mathieson."

The coroner bowed. The other counsel then rose.

"And I, sir, have been instructed by Mr. Pettigrew and Colonel Bulstrode, the trustees under the will, the former gentleman being also joint guardian with Miss Hilda Covington of the missing child, to watch the case on their behalf."

There was again an exchange of bows, and the lock-keeper then entered the box. His evidence was given in few words. He simply deposed to assisting in dragging the canal, and to the finding of the body.

"Have you any questions to ask the witness?" the coroner said, turning to the barristers.

The counsel employed by Mr. Pettigrew rose.

"Yes, sir; I have a few questions to ask. Now, Mr. Cousins, you say that you took part in dragging the canal. You are in charge of the drags, are you not?"

"Yes, sir; they are always kept in readiness at the lockhouse."

"How came you to use the drags? I suppose you don't take them down and spend a day or two in dragging the canal unless you have reason for supposing that a body is there."

"No, sir. The afternoon before a woman came up crying and said that her child had fallen into the water. He had gone out in the morning to play, and when dinner-time came and he didn't return she searched everywhere for him, and two children had just told her that they were playing with him on the bank of the canal, and that he had fallen in. They tried to get him out, but he sank, and they were so frightened that they ran home without saying anything. But they thought now that they had better tell. I said that she had better go to the police station and repeat her statement, and they would send a constable to help me. She did that, and came back with the policeman. It was getting late then, but we took a boat and dragged the canal for two or three hours. The next morning she came again, and said that the boys had shown her just where her child fell in, and we dragged there and found this body. We brought it ashore, and after we had carried it to the lockhouse we set to work again, but could not find any other body."

"What became of the woman?"

"She was with us till we fetched up this body. When she saw it she ran away crying, and did not come back again."

"You have not seen her since, Mr. Cousins?"

"No, sir; I have not seen her since. I believe the constable made inquiries about her."

"Thank you, I have nothing more to ask."

The policeman then entered the box and gave his evidence shortly, as to assisting in the operation of dragging and to finding the body.

"About this woman who gave the alarm," the barrister asked. "Have you seen her, constable?"

"No, sir; not since the body was found. Thinking it strange that she did not come back, I reported it at the station. She had given the name of Mary Smith and an address in Old Park. I was told to go round there, but no such person was known, and no one had heard of a child being lost. On my reporting this, inquiries were made all round the neighborhood; but no one had heard of such a woman, nor of a missing child."

"This is a very strange circumstance, sir, and it looks as if the whole story of the drowning child was a fabrication. The fact that the body of the child whose death we are considering was found close to the spot would certainly seem to point to the fact that some person or persons who were cognizant of the fact that this body was there were for some reasons anxious that it should be found, and so employed this woman to get the drags used at that point in order that the body might be brought to light."

"It is certainly a very strange business," the coroner said, "and I hope that the police will spare no efforts to discover this woman. However, as she is not before us, we must proceed with the case."

Then the officer of the court called out the name of Mary Summerford, and the nurse went into the witness box.

"I understand, Mary Sommerford, that you were nurse to Walter Rivington?"

"I was, sir."

"Will you tell the jury when you last saw him, and how it was that he was lost?"

She told the story as she had told it to Hilda on the day that he was missing.

"You have seen the clothes found on the body. Do you recognize them as those that he was wearing when you last saw him?"

"Yes, sir."

"How do you recognize them?"

"Because his initials are worked in two places. I worked them myself, and can swear to them."

"You cannot recognize the body, nurse?"

"I do not believe it is the body of my young master," she said; "his hair was lovely—long and silky. What hair remains on the body is very short, and what I should call stubbly."

"But the hair might have been cut short by the people who stole him," the coroner said. "It is the first precaution they would take to evade the search that would at once be set on foot."

"Yes, sir, but I don't think that it would have grown up so stiff."

"My experience of workhouse children," the coroner remarked, "is that whatever the hair they may have had when they entered the house, it is stiff enough to stand upright when cut close to the head. There is nothing else, is there, which leads you to doubt the identity of the child?"

"No, sir, I cannot say that there is; but I don't believe that it is Master Walter's body."

Hilda, Netta, and Mr. Pettigrew all gave their evidence. The two former stated that they identified the clothes, but, upon the same ground as the nurse, they failed to recognize the body as that of Walter Rivington. All were asked if they could in any way account for the finding of the child's body there. The question had been foreseen, and they said that, although they had used every means of discovering the child, they had obtained no clew whatever as to his whereabouts from the time that he was stolen to the time they were summoned to identify the body.

"You quite assume that he was stolen, and not that he wandered away, as children will do when their nurses are gossiping?"

"We are convinced that he was stolen, sir, because the search was begun so momentarily after he was missed that he could hardly have got out of sight, had he merely wandered away on foot. Notice was given to the police an hour after he disappeared, and every street in this part of London was scoured immediately."

"Children of that age, Miss Covington, have often a fancy for hiding themselves; and this child may have hidden somewhere close until he saw his nurse pass by, and then made off in the opposite direction. The spot where the child's body was found is little more than a quarter of a mile from the corner where he was missed. He might have wandered up there, found himself on the canal bank, and childlike, have begun to play, and so slipped into the water."

John Simcoe was the last witness called. He gave his evidence to the effect that he had seen the body, and that personally he saw no reason to doubt that it was that of Walter Rivington.

His counsel then rose.

"You are, I believe, Mr. Simcoe, owing to the death of this poor child, the principal legatee under the will of General Mathieson?"

"I am sorry to say that I am. The whole business has caused me immense distress. I have felt that, being the only person that would benefit by the child's death, those who did not know me would have a suspicion that I might have had a hand in his mysterious disappearance."

"You have taken an active part in the search for him?"

"I offered a reward of one thousand pounds for any information that would lead to his discovery, and I believe that I have traveled up and down every obscure slum in London in hopes of lighting upon him."

"Even without the provision in the will which made you next heir you benefited by it, did you not?"

"I did, most munificently. General Mathieson had himself informed me that I should find, by his will, that he had not been ungrateful for a service that I rendered him many years ago; but I was not aware of the sum that he had left me. As to the distant contingency of inheriting in case of the child's death, I was altogether ignorant of it; but had I known it, it would in no way have affected me. The little fellow was a fine healthy child, and, therefore, the thought that he might not live to come of age would never have entered my mind."

As the other counsel had no question to ask, the evidence was now concluded.

"Well, gentlemen, you have heard the evidence," the coroner said. "Dr. MacIlvaine has told you, as indeed you might judge for yourselves on viewing the body, that it is impossible, in its advanced state of decomposition, to say whether the child was alive or dead at the time he fell, or was placed in the canal. As to who were the guilty persons who beguiled the child away, if he was beguiled, we have no shadow of evidence, and it may well be that he was stolen for the sake of his clothes. The cutting short of his hair certainly points to the truth of this theory, as does also the fact that no vestige has been found of his upper clothing. It is probable that some woman enticed him away, and kept him for some time with her, and then, when she became alarmed by the search made for him, carried him in his sleep from the house, and perhaps laid him down by the canal, thinking that he would be found there in the morning, and that the poor child awoke in the dark, wandered about, and fell into the canal.

"However, this is only theory; but it is at least supported by the mysterious incident of the unknown woman who, by means of a tale which appears beyond doubt to have been wholly fictitious, caused the water at that spot to be dragged. The fact that on the second day she pointed out almost the exact point where the body was found would seem to show that the child could scarcely have fallen in the water, as she suggested, for in that case she could not have known the precise spot. It would seem, then, more likely that either the child died a natural death, perhaps from confinement or bad treatment, or possibly that, terribly alarmed at the search that was being maintained, he was put out of the way and then thrown into the canal at this spot. In that case we may admit that it is certainly strange that she should risk discovery by the course she took, and I can only account for it on the ground that she had been, ever since his death, suffering from remorse, and possibly she may have thought that she might in some sort of way atone for her conduct were she to point out where the child was, and so secure for him Christian burial. That, however, is not before us at present, and I see no advantage in an adjournment for an indefinite time until this mystery is solved. The police have taken the matter in hand, and will spare no pains to discover the woman. If they do so, undoubtedly proceedings will be taken in another court. The point that we have to consider is who this child was, and how he came to his death. Unfortunately we are absolutely without any evidence of what became of him from the time he got lost up to the discovery of his body, and I think that you cannot do otherwise than find an open verdict.

"As to the question of identity, there can, I think, be no shadow of doubt. The clothes in which he was found prove him beyond question to have been Walter Rivington, although the body itself is absolutely beyond identification. I do not think that you need give any weight to the nurse's failure to recognize him, or to her opinion about the hair. She is naturally reluctant to acknowledge, even to herself, that the child which was lost by her inadvertence is dead, and the ladies would be equally reluctant to admit that all hope was over."

The jury put their heads together, and there was evidently no difference of opinion, for in two or three minutes they sat down again and the foreman stood up.

"You have decided on your verdict?" the coroner asked.

"We have, sir. We find that the body is that of Walter Rivington, and that he was found dead in the canal, but how he came there and by what means he came by his death, there is no evidence to show."

"Thank you, gentlemen; that is precisely the verdict that I should myself have given."

CHAPTER XVI.

A FRESH CLEW.

"Just the verdict that I expected," Mr. Pettigrew said, as he and the ladies issued from the courthouse.

"I suppose that it is for the best, Mr. Pettigrew, but it seems hard, when we could have said so much, to be obliged to hold our tongues altogether."

"No doubt you will have an opportunity later on, Miss Covington. Our tongues are tied until we can obtain some sort of proof to go upon. We cannot go into court with merely suspicions; we must get facts. All we have done at present is to obtain some sort of foundation on which to work; but facts we shall, I hope, get ere long from what we may discover of this fellow's movements. He is likely to be less careful now that it has been decided that Walter is dead. He is doubtless well aware of the fact that trustees have a year given them before proceeding to carry out the provisions of a will, and, therefore, for that time he will keep quiet. At the end of the year his solicitor will write us a courteous letter, asking when we shall be in a position to distribute the estate in accordance with the provisions of the will. We shall reply that we are not in a position to do so. Then, after a time, will come letters of a more and more peremptory character, and at last a notice that they are about to apply to the courts for an order for us to act upon the provisions of the will. About two years after the General's death the matter will probably come on. I may say that I have already sent checks to all the small legatees."

"Thank you, I was aware of that, because Tom Roberts came to me yesterday with his check for two hundred pounds," and said, "Look here, Miss Covington; you said you meant to keep me on just the same as in the General's time, so this won't be of any use to me, and I should like to spend it in any way that you think best to find out what has become of Master Walter.' Of course I told him that the money could not be spent in that way, and that the work that he was doing was of far greater use than ten times that sum would be."

"I will send you your check to-morrow, Miss Covington. The sum we have paid to the people who have been searching, and all other expenses that may be incurred, will, of course, come out of the estate. You have not as yet settled, I suppose, as to your future plans?"

"No, except that I shall certainly keep on the house in Hyde Park Gardens for the present. It is, of course, ridiculously large for me, but I don't want the trouble of making a move until I make one permanently, and shall therefore stay here until this matter is finally cleared up. Miss Purcell has most kindly consented to remain as my chaperon, and her plans and those of her niece will depend upon mine."

They had sent away their carriage when they entered the court, and they walked quietly home, Mr. Pettigrew returning at once to his office. The next morning Tom Roberts accosted Hilda as she entered the breakfast room, with a face that showed he had news.

"We have traced him down to one of his places at last, miss. I said to Andrew, 'We must keep a special sharp look out to-night, for like enough, now that the inquest is over, he will be going to talk over the matter with his pals.' Well, miss, last night, at half-past nine, out he comes. He wasn't in evening dress, for although, as usual, he had a topcoat on, he had light trousers and walking boots. He did not turn the usual way, but went up into Piccadilly. We followed him. I kept close behind him, and Andrew at a distance, so that he should not notice us together. At the Circus he hailed a cab, and as he got in I heard him say to the driver, 'King's Cross Station.' As soon as he had gone off Andrew and I jumped into another cab, and told the man to drive to the same place, and that we would give him a shilling extra if he drove sharp.

"He did drive sharp, and I felt sure that we had got there before our man. I stopped outside the entrance, Andrew went inside. In five minutes he arrived, paid the driver his fare, and went in. I had agreed to wait two or three minutes outside, while Andrew was to be at the ticket office to see where he booked for. I was just going in when, to my surprise, out the man came again and walked briskly away. I ran in and fetched Andrew, and off we went after him. He hadn't more than a minute's start, and we were nearly up to him by the time he had got down to the main road. We kept behind him until we saw him go up Pentonville Hill, then Andrew went on ahead of him and I followed. We agreed that if he looked back, suspicious, I should drop behind. Andrew, when he once got ahead, was to keep about the same distance in front of him, so as to be able to drop behind and take it up instead of me, while I was to cross over the road if I thought that he had discovered I was following him.

"However, it did not seem to strike him that anyone was watching him, and he walked on briskly until he came to a small house standing by itself, and as he turned in we were in time to see that the door was opened to him by a man. Andrew and I consulted. I went in at the gate, took my shoes off, and went round the house. There was only a light in one room, which looked as if there were no servants. The curtains were pulled together inside, and I could see nothing of what was going on. He stopped there for an hour and a half, then came out again, hailed a cab halfway down the hill, and drove off. Andrew and I had compared watches, and he had gone back to Jermyn Street, so that we should be able to know by the time the chap arrived whether he had gone anywhere else on his way back. When I joined him I found that the man must have driven straight to the Circus and then got out, for he walked in just twenty minutes after I had seen him start."

"That is good news indeed, Roberts. We will go and see Mr. Pettigrew directly after breakfast. Please order the carriage to be round at a quarter to ten."

Netta was as pleased as her friend when she heard that a step had been made at last.

"I am sick of this inaction," she said, "and want to be doing something towards getting to the bottom of the affair. I do hope that we shall find some way in which I can be useful."

"I have no doubt at all that you will be very useful when we get fairly on the track. I expect that this will lead to something."

After Tom Roberts had repeated his story to Mr. Pettigrew, Hilda said:

"I brought Roberts with me, Mr. Pettigrew, that he might tell the story in his own way. It seems to me that the best thing now would be to employ a private detective to find out who the man is who lives in Rose Cottage. This would be out of the line of Tom Roberts and Colonel Bulstrode's servant altogether. They would not know how to set about making inquiries, whereas a detective would be at home at such work."

"I quite agree with you," the lawyer said. "To make inquiries without exciting suspicion requires training and practice. An injudicious question might lead to this man being warned that inquiries were being made about him and might ruin the matter altogether. Of course your two men will still keep up their watch. It may be that we shall find it is of more use to follow the track of this man than the other. But you must not be too sanguine; the man at Rose Cottage may be an old acquaintance of Simcoe. Well, my dear," he went on, in answer to a decided shake of the head on Hilda's part, "you must call the man by the only name that he is known by, although it may not belong to him. I grant that the manner in which he drove into King's Cross station and then walked out on foot would seem to show that he was anxious to throw anyone who might be watching him off the scent, and that the visit was, so to speak, a clandestine one. But it may relate to an entirely different matter; for this man may be, for aught we know, an adept in crime, and may be in league with many other doubtful characters."

"It may be so, Mr. Pettigrew, but we will hope not."

"Very well, my dear," the lawyer said. "I will send for a trustworthy man at once, and set him to work collecting information regarding the occupant of the cottage. And now I have a point upon which I wish to ask your opinion. I have this morning received a letter from this man's solicitor, asking if we intend to undertake the funeral of the body which the coroner's jury have found to be that of Walter Rivington; and announcing that, if we do not, his client will himself have it carried out."

"What do you think, Mr. Pettigrew?" Hilda said hesitatingly. "We may be wrong, you know, and it may be Walter's body."

"I have been thinking it over," the lawyer replied, "and I must say it is my opinion that, as we have all stated our conviction that it is not, we should only stultify ourselves if we now undertook the funeral and put a stone, with his name on, over the grave. If we should at any time become convinced that we have been wrong, we can apply for a faculty to remove the coffin to the family vault down in Warwickshire."

"If we could do that I should not mind," Hilda said; "but even the possibility of Walter being buried by the man who we firmly believe was the cause of his death is terrible."

"Yes, I can quite understand your feelings, but I think that it is necessary that the family should make a protest against its being supposed that they recognize the child, by declining to undertake the funeral. No protest could well be stronger."

"If you think that, Mr. Pettigrew, we certainly had best stand aside and let that poor child be buried by this man."

Two days later they were driving in the Row. It was Hilda's first appearance there since the General's death, and, after talking it over with Netta, she now appeared there in order to show that she was perfectly convinced that the child which had been found in the canal was not her little cousin. The details of the proceedings of the coroner's court had, of course, been read by all her friends, and her appearance in the park would be the best proof that she could give that the family were absolutely convinced that the body was not that of Walter.

Miss Purcell and Netta were with her. The latter had on, as usual, a thick veil. This she always wore when driving through any locality where she might meet John Simcoe.

"That is the man," Hilda said to her in a sharp tone; "the farther of those two leaning on the rail the other side of the road."

As Hilda fixed her eyes on the man she saw him give a sudden movement.

Then he said to the man next to him:

"Do you see that girl in deep mourning? It is that little vixen, Hilda Covington. Confound her, she is at the bottom of all this trouble, and I believe she would give ten thousand out of her own pocket to checkmate me."

The carriage was opposite to them now. Hilda looked straight in front of her, while Netta, who was sitting with her back to the horses, took up the watch.

"She would have to be sharp indeed to do that," the other man said. "So far everything has gone without a hitch, and I don't see a single weak point in your case. The most troublesome part has been got over."

And now some carriages going the other way cut off the view, and Netta could read no further. She drew a long breath as Hilda's eyes turned towards her.

"What did you read?" the latter asked.

Netta repeated what she had caught, and then Hilda took up the conversation.

"It is quite evident that this man, whoever he is, is an accomplice. He is a gentlemanly-looking man, and I fancy that he sat in the stalls near to us one evening this spring. However, it is quite clear that he is a confederate of Simcoe. Just repeat his words over again. They were in answer to his remark that I would give ten thousand pounds to be able to checkmate him."

Netta repeated the answer of Simcoe's companion.

"You see, Netta, there is something to find out that would checkmate him; that is quite evident. He thinks that I cannot find it out. It must be, I should think, that Walter is kept in hiding somewhere. It could not mean that he had killed my uncle, for he would hardly tell that to anyone, and so put himself in their power."

"It may mean that you cannot find out that he is not John Simcoe," Netta suggested.

"Possibly; but he cannot know we suspect that."

"It might be about the last will, Hilda."

The latter shook her head.

"We have never thought that there could be anything wrong about it. The will was drawn up by Colonel Bulstrode's lawyers, and they knew my uncle by sight; besides, all the legacies were exactly the same as in the other will, the signature and the written instructions were in his handwriting, and he signed it in the solicitor's office in the presence of two of their clerks. No, I don't think he can possibly mean that. It must be either Walter's abduction or that he is not John Simcoe, and I should say that the former is much the more likely. You see, he had no need of an accomplice in the matter of getting evidence as to identity, whereas he did need an accomplice in the carrying off of Walter. I should say that he is far too clever a man to let anyone into any of his secrets, unless he needed his assistance. I wonder who the man with him can be. He is dressed in good style, and I have certainly met him somewhere. I believe, as I said, it was at the opera. I should have thought that a man of that class is the last Simcoe would choose as a confederate."

Miss Purcell looked from one to the other as they talked. She had by this time been taken completely into their confidence, but had refused absolutely to believe that a man could be guilty of such wickedness as that which they suspected. On their return home they found a letter awaiting them from Mr. Pettigrew:

"My Dear Miss Covington [it ran]: My detective has not yet finished his inquiries, but has at least discovered that the proprietor of Rose Cottage, for they say that the place belongs to him, is somewhat of a mystery to his neighbors. He lives there entirely alone. He goes out regularly in a morning, it is supposed to some occupation in the City. No tradesmen ever call at the door; it is supposed that he brings home something for his breakfast and cooks it for himself, and that he dines in the City and makes himself a cup of tea in the evening, or else that he goes out after dark. Sometimes, of summer evenings, he has been seen to go out just at twilight, dressed in full evening costume—that is to say, it is supposed so, for he wore a light overcoat—but certainly a white necktie, black trousers, and patent leather boots. Of course, in all this there is nothing in itself absolutely suspicious. A man engaged in the City would naturally enough take his meals there, and may prefer to do everything for himself to having the bother of servants. Also, if his means permit it, he may like to go to theaters or places of amusement, or may go out to visit business friends. I have, of course, directed the detective to follow him to town and find out what is his business, and where employed. I will let you know result to-morrow."

The next day brought the letter.

"The man's name is William Barens. He has a small office on the third floor of a house of business in Great St. Helens, and on the doorway below his name is the word 'accountant,' The housekeeper knows nothing about him, except that he has occupied the room for the last twelve years, and that he is a gentleman who gives no trouble. He always puts his papers away at night in his safe, so that his table can be properly dusted. She knows that he has clients, as several times, when he has been away for his dinner hour, she has been asked when he would return. He is a well-spoken gentleman, though not as particular about his dress as some; but liberal with his money, and gives her as handsome a tip at Christmas as some people who have three or four rooms, and, no doubt, think themselves much finer people. This certainly does not amount to much. By the way, the old woman said that she knew he was employed by several tradesmen in the neighborhood to keep their books for them."

Two days later there was another communication:

"My Dear Miss Covington: My man has taken a step which I should certainly have forbidden, had he told me beforehand of his intention. He watched the man go out, and then, having previously provided himself with instruments for picking locks, he opened the door and went in. On the table were several heavy ledgers and account books, all bearing the names of tradesmen in the neighborhood, with several files of accounts, bills, and invoices. These fully bore out what the woman had told him. Besides the chairs, table, and safe, the only other articles of furniture in the room were an office washing stand and a large closet. In the latter were a dress suit and boots, and a suit of fashionable walking clothes, so that it is evident that he often changed there instead of going home. I am sorry to say that all this throws no further light upon the man's pursuits, and had it not been for Simcoe's visit to him, it would be safe to say that he is a hard-working accountant, in a somewhat humble, but perhaps well-paying line; that he is a trifle eccentric in his habits, and prefers living a cheap, solitary life at home, while spending his money freely in the character of a man about town in the evening. I cannot say that the prospect in this direction seems hopeful. I have told my man that for the present we shall not require his services further."

"It does not seem very satisfactory, certainly," Hilda said with a sigh; "I am afraid that we shall have to keep on watching Simcoe. I wish I could peep into his room as this detective did into that of the Pentonville man."

"I don't suppose that you would find anything there, Hilda; he is not the sort of man to keep a memorandum book, jotting down all his own doings."

"No," Hilda said with a laugh; "still, one always thinks that one can find something."

Had Hilda Covington had her wish and looked into John Simcoe's room that morning, she would certainly have derived some satisfaction from the sight. He had finished his breakfast before opening a letter that lay beside him.

"What a plague the old woman is with her letters! I told her that I hated correspondence, but she persists in writing every month or so, though she never gets any reply except, 'My dear Aunt: Thanks for your letter. I am glad to hear that you are well.—Your affectionate nephew.' Well, I suppose I must read it through."

He glanced over the first page, but on turning to the second his eye became arrested, and he read carefully, frowning deeply as he did so. Then he turned back and read it again. The passage was as follows:

> "I had quite an interesting little episode a day or two after I last wrote. A young lady—she said her name was Barcum, and that she was an artist—came in and asked if I would take her in as a lodger. She was a total stranger to the place, and had come down for her health, and said that some tradesman had recommended her to come here, saying that, as a single lady, I might be glad to accommodate her. Of course I told her that I did not take lodgers. She got up to go, when she nearly fainted, and I could not do less than offer her a cup of tea. Then we got very chatty, and as I saw that she was really too weak to go about town looking for lodgings, I invited her to stay a day or two with me, she being quite a lady and a very pleasant-spoken one. She accepted, and a pleasanter companion I never had. Naturally I mentioned your name, and told her what adventures you had gone through, and how kind you were. She was greatly interested, and often asked questions about you, and I do think that she almost fell in love with you from my description. She left suddenly on receipt of a letter that called her up to town, saying that she would return; but I have not heard from her since, and I am greatly afraid that the poor child must be seriously ill. She was a pretty and intelligent-looking girl, with dark eyes and hair, and I should say that when in good health she must be very bright. Of course, she may have changed her mind about coming down. I am sure she would have written if she had been well."

"Confound the old gossip!" John Simcoe said angrily, as he threw the letter down. "I wonder what this means, and who this girl can be? It is clear enough that, whoever she is, she was sent down there to make inquiries about me. It is that girl Covington's doing, I have no doubt, though it was not the minx herself, for the description does not tally at all. She has light brown hair and grayish sort of eyes. There is one comfort, she would learn nothing to my disadvantage from the old woman, nor, I believe, from anyone at Stowmarket. In fact, she would only get more and more confirmation of my story. I have no fear upon that score, but the thing shows how that girl is working on my track. As for the lawyer, he is an old fool; and if it hadn't been for her I would bet a hundred to one that he would never have entertained any suspicion that all was not right. It is her doing all through, and this is a piece of it. Of course she could have no suspicion that I was not John Simcoe, but I suppose she wanted to learn if there was any dark spot in my history—whether I had ever been suspected of robbing a bank, or had been expelled from school for thieving, or something of that sort. I begin to be downright afraid of her. She had a way of looking through me, when I was telling my best stories to the General, that always put me out. She disliked me from the first, though I am sure I tried in every way to be pleasant to her. I felt from the day I first saw her that she was an enemy, and that if any trouble ever did come it would be through her. I have no doubt she is moving heaven and earth to find Walter; but that she will never do, for Harrison is as true as steel, and he is the only man who could put them on the right track. Moreover, I have as much pull over him as he has over me. He has never had a doubt about my being John Simcoe; he doesn't know about the other affair, but only that Walter stood between me and the estate, and he was quite ready to lend me a hand to manage to get him out of the way. So in that business he is in it as deep as I am, while I know of a score of schemes he has been engaged in, any one of which would send him abroad for life. I expect those inquiries were made at Stowmarket to endeavor to find out whether any child had been sent down there. If so, Miss Covington is not so sharp as I took her to be. Stowmarket would be the very last place where a man, having relations and friends there, would send a child whom he wished to keep concealed. Still it is annoying, confoundedly annoying; and it shows that these people, that is to say Hilda Covington, are pushing their inquiries in every direction, likely or unlikely.

"The only comfort is, the more closely they search the sooner they will come to the conclusion that the boy is not to be found. I believe that, though they declared they did not recognize the body, they had no real doubt about it, and they only said so because if they had admitted it, the trustees would have had no excuse for not carrying out the provisions of the will. That text the girl had the impudence to quote to me looked as if she believed the body was Walter's, and that I had killed him, though it may be that she only said it to drive me to bringing the whole business into court, by bringing an action against her for libel; but I am not such a fool as to do that. Just at present there is a lot of public feeling excited by the circumstances of the child's loss and the finding of the body, and even if I got a verdict I fancy that the jury would be all on the girl's side, and give me such trifling damages that the verdict would do me more harm than good. No, our game clearly is to let the matter rest until it has died out of the public mind. Then we shall apply formally for the trustees to be called upon to act. No doubt they will give us a great deal of trouble, but Comfrey says that he thinks that the order must be granted at last, though possibly it may be withheld, as far as the estate is concerned, for some years. At any rate I ought to get the ten thousand at once, as the question whether the boy is alive or dead cannot affect that in the slightest."

CHAPTER XVII.

NETTA ACTS INDEPENDENTLY.

"It seems to me, Hilda, that somehow or other we are wasting our time," Netta said one morning suddenly, as they were sitting together.

"How do you mean, Netta?"

"Well, you see, we relied a great deal on being able to overhear conversation from a distance; and, except those few words we gathered in the Park, we have absolutely done nothing that way."

"But how can we do more than we are doing?"

"I don't know; that is what is troubling me. You know, dear, that I am quite content to give up my own work to help you. At first, of course, aunt and I would have stayed here, at any rate for a time, to keep you company; but your uncle has been dead now for more than eight months, and time is going on. If I were really helping you I would stop, if it were five years; but in fact I am not helping you in the way we intended."

"You are helping me, Netta!" Hilda exclaimed with tears in her eyes. "How should I have got on through all this sad time if you had not been here to comfort and cheer me?"

"Yes, but the necessity for that is over. You have your friends, and though you don't go out yet, you often go to Lady Moulton's and some of your other friends', and they come to see you."

"Yes, and you will never go with me, Netta, nor see them when they come."

"No, dear; I have nothing in common with them. I do not know the people of whom you talk, and should simply sit there uncomfortably, so I prefer to be out of it altogether. Then I really miss my work. Ever since you came to us some eight years ago I have been teaching eight or ten hours a day. I like the work; it is immensely interesting, and I am happy in seeing my pupils improve."

"And all this means," Hilda said sorrowfully, "you are going to say that it is time for you to go back."

"No, it does not necessarily mean that—there is an alternative; I must either be doing something or go back."

"But, as I said before, Netta, what can we do, more than we have done?"

"That is what I have been thinking, Hilda. Anyhow, I mean to try to do something before I give it up and go to Germany again."

"I warn you, Netta, that I shall be furious if you do that. I am my own mistress now, for Mr. Pettigrew will let me do as I like now I am nineteen, and am quite determined that our old plan shall be carried out, and that you shall start an institution like that of Professor Menzel somewhere near London. You have been twelve months away, your pupils have already taken to other teachers, and there cannot be the least occasion for your assistance in an institution that is now well stocked with teachers, while here you could do enormous good. Anyhow, whether you stay or not, I shall, as soon as all this is settled, take a large house standing in its own grounds, in some healthy place near London, and obtain teachers."

"Well, we need not talk of that just yet," Netta said quietly; "it will be time enough when I have failed in carrying out my plans."

"But what are your plans?"

"I have not quite settled myself; and when I do I mean to work entirely in my own way, and shall say nothing about it until I come to you and say I have succeeded, or I have failed."

Hilda opened her eyes in surprise.

"But why should I be kept in the dark?"

"Because, dear, you might not approve of my plans," Netta replied coolly.

"You are not thinking of doing anything foolish, I hope?" Hilda exclaimed.

"If it were foolish it would be excusable where the counsels of wisdom have failed," Netta laughed; and then more seriously, "Nothing would be foolish if it could possibly lead to the discovery of Walter's hiding place."

That afternoon, when Hilda drove out with Miss Purcell to make some calls, Netta rang the bell, and when Tom Roberts came in she said:

"I want to have a long talk with you, Roberts. But mind, what I say is to be kept a perfect secret between ourselves."

"Yes, miss," he said in surprise.

"Now, sit down," she went on; "we can talk more comfortably so. Now, Roberts, there is no doubt that we are not making much headway with our search."

"That we are not, Miss Netta," he agreed. "I did think that we had gained something when we traced him to that house on Pentonville Hill, but it does not seem that anything has come of it, after all."

"Then it is quite time that we took some other steps," she said decisively.

"I am ready, miss," he replied eagerly. "You tell me what to do, and I am game to do it."

"Well, there are two or three things I have in my mind. First of all, I want to be able to watch John Simcoe and this Pentonville man when they are talking together."

"Yes, I understand," he said; "but how is it to be done?"

"That is what I want to find out. Now, in the first place, about this house. Which way did the window look of the room where there was a light?"

"That window was at the side of the house, miss; a little way round the corner. We noticed the light there, but there was another window looking out on the front. We did not see any light there, as the shutters were closed."

"And you say that the curtains of the other window were pulled very close?"

"Yes, they crossed each other most of the way down."

"Now, the question in my mind, Roberts, is which would be easier—to cut a slit in the curtain, or to bore a hole in the shutter, or to take a brick out carefully from the side wall and then to deepen the hole until we got to the wall-paper, and then make a slight hole there?"

Roberts looked at her with astonishment. "Do you really mean it, miss?"

"Certainly I mean it; it seems to me that our only chance of ever finding Walter is to overhear those men's talk."

"Then, miss, I should say that the simplest way would be to cut a window pane out."

"Yes; but, you see, it is pretty certain that that curtain will not be drawn until they come in, and they would notice it at once. If we took out a pane in the front window the shutter would prevent our seeing or hearing, and the man would be sure to notice the pane was missing as he walked up from the gate to the house."

"I should say, miss, that the best plan would be for me to manage to get into the house some time during the day and to hide in that room, under the table or sofa or somewhere, and listen to them."

She shook her head.

"In the first place, Roberts, you would certainly be murdered if they found you there."

"I would take my chance of that, miss; and you may be sure that I would take a brace of the General's pistols with me, and they would not find it such easy work to get rid of me."

"That may be so," Netta said, "but if in the struggle you shot them both, our last chance of ever hearing of Walter would be gone. You yourself might be tried for murder, and it would be assumed, of course, that you were a burglar; for the explanation that you had broken into the house only to hear a conversation would scarcely be believed. Moreover, you must remember that we don't know how often these men meet. Simcoe has not been there since you tracked him there six months ago, and the only thing we have since found out is that the man I saw him with in the park is the man who lives in that house. It would never do for you to make an entrance into the house night after night and week after week, to run the risk of being detected there, or seized as you entered, or caught by the police as a burglar. No, as far as I can see, the only safe plan is to get out a brick very carefully in the side wall and to make a hole behind it through the paper. It might be necessary to make an entry into the house before this was done, so as to decide which was the best spot for an opening. A great deal would depend upon the paper in the room. If it is a light paper, with only a small amount of pattern upon it, any hole large enough to see through might be noticed. If it is a dark paper, well covered, a hole might be made without any fear of its catching the eye. You see, it must be a rather large hole, for, supposing the wall is only nine inches thick, a person standing outside could not see what was passing inside unless the hole were a good size."

"But I doubt much if you would be able to hear them, Miss Netta."

"No, I don't think that I should; especially as people talking of things of that sort, even if they had no great fear of being overheard, would speak in a low voice. But that would not matter if I could see their faces. I should know what they were saying."

Roberts did not think it right to offer any remark on what appeared to him to be impossible, and he confined himself to saying in a respectful voice, "Indeed, Miss Netta."

"I am stone-deaf," she said, "but have learned to read what people are saying from the movement of their lips."

Although the "Indeed, miss," was as respectful as before, Netta saw that he did not in the slightest degree believe her.

"Just go to the other end of the room, Roberts, and make some remark to yourself. Move your lips in the same way as if you were talking, but do not make any sound."

Roberts, with military obedience, marched to the other end of the room, placed himself in a corner, and turned round, facing her. His lips moved, and, confident that she could not know what he was saying, he expressed his natural sentiments.

The girl at once repeated the words: “Well, I’m jiggered! This is a rum start; Miss Netta has gone clean off her head.”

Roberts’ jaw dropped, and he flushed up to the hair.

“I am sure,” he began; but he was stopped by the girl’s merry laugh.

“Do not apologize, Roberts; it was natural enough that you should be surprised. Well, you see I can do as I say. We will now go on with our talk.”

Greatly abashed, Tom Roberts returned to the chair, murmuring to himself as he sat down, “Well, I’m blowed!” when he was roughly recalled to the necessity of keeping his mouth shut by her quiet remark, “Never mind about being blowed at present, Roberts; let us talk over another plan. Who are the keepers of the house in Jermyn Street?”

“It is kept by a man and his wife, miss. He has been a butler, I believe, and his wife was a cook. He waits upon the gentlemen who lodge there, and she cooks. They have a girl who sweeps and does the bedrooms and the scrubbing and that sort of thing.”

“What sort of a girl is she, Roberts?”

“She seems a nice sort of young woman, miss. Andrew has spoken to her more than I have, because, you see, my get-up aint likely to take much with a young girl.”

“I suppose she is not very much attached to her place?”

“Lor’, no, miss; she told Andrew that she was only six months up from the country, and they don’t pay her but eight pounds a year, and pretty hard work she has to do for it.”

“Well, Roberts, I want to take her place.”

“You want——” and Roberts’ voice failed him in his astonishment.

“Yes, I want to take her place, Roberts. I should think that if you or Andrew were to tell her that you have a friend up from the country who wants just such a place, and is ready to pay five pounds to get one, she might be ready to take the offer; especially as you might say that you knew of a lady who is in want of an under-housemaid and you thought that you could get her the place.”

“As to that, miss, I have no doubt that she would leave to-morrow, if she could get five pounds. She told Andrew that she hated London, and should go down home and take a country place as soon as she had saved up money to do so."

"All the better, Roberts; then all she would have to do would be to say that she had heard of a place near home, and wanted to leave at once. She did not wish to inconvenience them, but that she had a cousin who was just coming up to London and wanted a place, and that she would jump at it. She could say that her cousin had not been in service before, but that she was a thorough good cleaner and hard worker."

"And do you mean that you would go as a servant, Miss Netta? Why, it would not be right for you to do so."

"Anything would be right that led to the discovery of Walter's hiding place, Roberts. I have been accustomed to teaching, and I have helped my aunt to look after the house for years, and I do not in the slightest degree mind playing the part of a servant for a short time, in order to try and get at the bottom of this matter. You think that it can be managed?"

"I am sure it can be managed right enough, miss; but what Miss Covington would say, if she knew that I had a hand in bringing it about, I can't say."

"Well, you won't be drawn into the matter. I shall say enough to my aunt to satisfy her that I am acting for the best, and shall simply, when I go, leave a note for your mistress, telling her that I have gone to work out an idea that I have had in my mind, and that it would be no use for her to inquire into the matter until she hears of me again."

"What am I to tell Andrew, miss?"

"Simply tell him that a young woman has been engaged to watch Simcoe in his lodgings. Then tell him the story he has to tell the girl. I shall want three or four days to get my things ready. I shall have to go to a dressmaker's and tell her that I want three or four print gowns for a young servant about my own figure, and as soon as they are ready I shall be ready, too."

"Well, miss, I will do as you tell me, but I would say, quite respectful, I hope that you will bear in mind, if things goes wrong, that I was dead against it, and that it was only because you said that it was our only chance of finding Master Walter that I agreed to lend a hand."

"I will certainly bear that in mind," Netta said with a smile. "Talk it over with Andrew to-night; but remember he is only to know that a young woman has been engaged to keep a watch on Simcoe."

"He will be glad enough to hear, miss, that someone else is going to do something. He says the Colonel is so irritable because he has found out so little that there is no bearing with him."

"The Colonel is trying," Netta laughed. "As you know, he comes here two or three times a week and puts himself into such rages that, as he stamps up and down the room, I expect to hear a crash and to find that the dining-room ceiling has fallen down. He is a thoroughly kind-hearted man, but is a dreadful specimen of what an English gentleman may come to after he has had the command of an Indian regimentfor some years, and been accustomed to have his will obeyed in everything. It is very bad for a man."

"It is a good deal worse for his servant, miss," Tom Roberts said, in a tone of deep sympathy for his comrade. "I doubt whether I could have stood it myself; but though Andrew expresses his feelings strong sometimes, I know that if you offered him a good place, even in Buckingham Palace, he would not leave the Colonel."

Two days later Netta heard that the girl in Jermyn Street had joyfully accepted the offer, and had that morning told her master that she had heard that she was wanted badly at home, and that a cousin of hers would be up in a day or two, and would, she was sure, be very glad to take her place. The master agreed to give her a trial, if she looked a clean and tidy girl.

"I shall be clean and tidy, Roberts; and I am sure I shall do no injustice to her recommendation."

Roberts shook his head. The matter was, to his mind, far too serious to be joked about, and he almost felt as if he were acting in a treasonable sort of way in aiding to carry out such a project.

On the following Monday Hilda, on coming down to breakfast, found a note on the table. She opened it in haste, seeing that it was in Netta's handwriting, and her eyes opened in surprise and almost dismay as she read:

> "My Darling Hilda: I told you that I had a plan. Well, I am off to carry it out. It is of no use your asking what it is, or where I am going. You will hear nothing of me until I return to tell you whether I have failed or succeeded. Aunt knows what I am going to do."

Hilda at once ran upstairs to Miss Purcell's room.

"Where has Netta gone?" she exclaimed. "Her letter has given me quite a turn. She says that you know; but I feel sure that it is something very foolish and rash."

"I thought that you had a better opinion of Netta's common sense," Miss Purcell said placidly, smiling a little at Hilda's excitement. "It is her arrangement, dear, and not mine, and I am certainly not at liberty to give you any information about it. I do not say that I should not have opposed it in the first instance, had I known of it, but I certainly cannot say that there is anything foolish in it, and I admit that it seems to me to offer a better chance of success than any plan that has yet been tried. I don't think there is any occasion for anxiety about her. Netta has thought over her plans very carefully, and has gone to work in a methodical way; she may fail, but if so I don't think that it will be her fault."

"But why could she not tell me as well as you?" Hilda asked rather indignantly.

"Possibly because she did not wish to raise hopes that might not be fulfilled; but principally, I own, because she thought you would raise objections to it, and she was bent upon having her own way. She has seconded you well, my dear, all through this business."

"Yes, I know, aunt; she has been most kind in every respect."

"Well, my dear, then don't grudge her having a little plan of her own."

"I don't grudge her a bit," Hilda said impetuously, "and, as you are quite satisfied, I will try to be quite satisfied too. But, you see, it took me by surprise; and I was so afraid that she might do something rash and get into trouble somehow. You know really I am quite afraid of this man, and would certainly far rather run a risk myself than let her do so."

"Of that I have no doubt, Hilda; but I am quite sure that, if the case had been reversed, you would have undertaken this little plan that she has hit upon, to endeavor to relieve her of a terrible anxiety, just as she is doing for you."

"Well, I will be patient, aunt. How long do you think that she will be away?"

"That is more than I can tell you; but at any rate she has promised to write me a line at least twice a week, and, should I think it right, I can recall her."

"That is something, aunt. You cannot guess whether it is likely to be a week or a month?"

Miss Purcell shook her head.

"It will all depend upon whether she succeeds in hitting upon a clew as to where Walter is. If she finds that she has no chance of so doing she will return; if, on the other hand, she thinks that there is a probability that with patience she will succeed, she will continue to watch and wait."

"Miss Netta is not ill, I hope, miss?" Roberts said, when he came in to clear the breakfast things away.

“No she has gone away on a short visit,” Hilda replied. Had she been watching the old soldier’s face, she might have caught a slight contortion that would have enlightened her as to the fact that he knew more than she did about the matter; but she had avoided looking at him, lest he should read in her face that she was in ignorance as to Netta’s whereabouts. She would have liked to have asked when she went; whether she took a box with her, and whether she had gone early that morning or late the evening before; but she felt that any questions of the sort would show that she was totally in the dark as to her friend’s movements. In fact Netta had walked out early that morning, having sent off a box by the carrier on the previous Saturday when Hilda was out; Roberts having himself carried it to the receiving house.

It was four or five days before Dr. Leeds called again.

“Is Miss Purcell out?” he asked carelessly, when some little time had elapsed without her making her appearance.

“Is that asked innocently, Dr. Leeds?” Hilda said quickly.

The doctor looked at her in genuine surprise.

“Innocently, Miss Covington? I don’t think that I quite understand you.”

“I see, doctor, that I have been in error. I suspected you of being an accomplice of Netta’s in a little scheme in which she is engaged on her own account.” And she then told him about her disappearance, of the letter that she had received, and of the conversation with her aunt. Dr. Leeds was seriously disturbed.

“I need hardly say that this comes as a perfect surprise to me, Miss Covington, and I say frankly a very unpleasant one. But the only satisfactory feature is that the young lady’s aunt does not absolutely disapprove of the scheme, whatever it is, although it is evident that her approval is by no means a warm one. This is a very serious matter. I have the highest opinion of your friend’s judgment and sense, but I own that I feel extremely uneasy at the thought that she has, so to speak, pitted herself against one of the most unscrupulous villains I have ever met, whose past conduct shows that he would stop at nothing, and who is playing for a very big stake. It would be as dangerous to interfere between a tiger and his prey as to endeavor to discover the secret on which so much depends.”

“I feel that myself, doctor, and I own that I’m exceedingly anxious. Aunt has had two short letters from her. Both are written in pencil, but the envelope is in ink, and in her usual handwriting. I should think it probable that she took with her several directed envelopes. The letters are very short. The first was: ‘I am getting on all right, aunt, and am comfortable. Too early to say whether

I am likely to discover anything. Pray do not fidget about me, nor let Hilda do so. There is nothing to be uneasy about.' The second was as nearly as possible in the same words, except that she said, 'You and Hilda must be patient. Rome was not built in a day, and after so many clever people have failed you cannot expect that I can succeed all at once.'"

"That is good as far as it goes," the doctor said, "but you see it does not go very far. It is not until success is nearly reached that the danger will really begin. I do not mind saying to you that Miss Purcell is very dear to me. I have not spoken to her on the subject, as I wished to see how my present partnership was likely to turn out. I am wholly dependent upon my profession, and until I felt my ground thoroughly I determined to remain silent. You can imagine, therefore, how troubled I am at your news. Were it not that I have such implicit confidence in her judgment I should feel it still more; but even as it is, when I think how unscrupulous and how desperate is the man against whom she has, single-handed, entered the lists, I cannot but be alarmed."

"I am very glad at what you have told me, doctor. I had a little hope that it might be so. It seemed to me impossible that you could be living for four months with such a dear girl without being greatly attracted by her. Of course I know nothing of her feelings. The subject is one that has never been alluded to between us, but I am sure that no girl living is more fitted than she is to be the wife of a medical man. I would give much to have Netta back again, but Miss Purcell is obdurate. She says that, knowing as she does what Netta is doing, she does not think that she is running any risk—at any rate, none proportionate to the importance of finding a clew to Walter's hiding place."

"Will you ask her if she will write to her niece and urge her to return, saying how anxious you are about her? Or, if she will not do that, whether she will release her from her promise of secrecy, so that she may let us know what she is doing?"

"I will go and ask her now; I will bring her down so that you can add your entreaties to mine, doctor."

But Miss Purcell refused to interfere.

"I consider Netta's scheme to be a possible one," she said, "though I am certainly doubtful of its success. But she has set her heart upon it, and I will do nothing to balk her. I do not say that I am free from anxiety myself, but my confidence in Netta's cleverness, and I may say prudence, is such that I believe that the risk she is running is very slight. It would be cruel, and I think wrong at the present moment, when above all things it is necessary that her brain should be clear, to distress and trouble her by interfering with her actions."

"Perhaps you are right, Miss Purcell," the doctor said thoughtfully. "Being totally in the dark in the matter, I am not justified in giving a decisive opinion, but I will admit that it would not conduce either to her comfort or to the success of her undertaking were we to harass her by interfering in any way with her plan, which, I have no doubt, has been thoroughly thought out before she undertook it. No one but a madman would shout instructions or warnings to a person performing a dangerous feat requiring coolness and presence of mind. Such, I take it, is the scheme, whatever it is, in which she is engaged; and as you are the only one who knows what that scheme is, I must, however reluctantly, abide by your decision. When Miss Covington tells you the conversation that we have had together you will recognize how deeply I am interested in the matter."

CHAPTER XVIII.

DOWN IN THE MARSHES.

Comparatively few of those who nowadays run down to Southend for a breath of fresh air give a thought to the fact that the wide stretch of low country lying between the railroad and the Thames, from Pitsea to Leigh, was at one time, and that not so many centuries back, a mud flat, a continuation of the great line of sand that still, with but a short break here and there, stretches down beyond Yarmouth; still less that, were it not for the watchfulness of those who dwell upon it, it would in a short time revert to its original condition, the country lying below the level of higher water.

Along the whole face of the river run banks—the work, doubtless, of engineers brought over by Dutch William—strong, massive, and stone-faced, as they need be to withstand the rush and fret of the tide and the action of the waves when, as is often the case, the east wind knocks up ridges of short, angry water in Sea Reach. Similarly, the winding creeks are all embanked, but here dams of earth are sufficient to retain within its bounds the sluggish water as it rises and falls. Standing on any of these, the farmhouses and little homesteads lie below, their eaves for the most part level with the top of the bank, though there are a few knolls which rise above the level of the tidal water.

The most conspicuous objects are the brown sails of the barges, which seem to stand up in the midst of the brownish-green fields, the hulls being invisible. This cannot be called marsh land, for the ground is intersected by ditches, having sluices through which they discharge their water at low tide. Very fertile is the land in some spots, notably in Canvey Island, where there are great stretches of wheat and broad meadows deep with rich waving grass; but there are other places where the grass is brown and coarse, showing that, though the surface may be hard and dry, water lies not far below. Here a few cattle gather a scanty living, and the little homesteads are few and far between. Most of the houses are placed near the banks of the creeks. The barges serve as their wagons, and carry their hay up to London and bring down manure and other things required, or carry coal and lime to the wharves of Pitsea.

A rare place was this in the old smuggling days, and indeed until quite lately the trade was carried on, though upon a reduced scale. Vessels drifting slowly up the river would show a light as they passed a barge at anchor or a bawley hanging to its trawl, a light would be shown in answer, and a moment later a boat would row off to the ship, and a score of tubs or a dozen bales of tobacco be quickly transferred, and before morning the contents would be stowed in underground cellars in some of the little farmhouses on the creeks, or be hidden away in the Leigh marshes.

"Will Bill be in to-night with the barge?" a child asked a woman, as he came down from the bank to a not uncomfortable-looking homestead ten yards from its foot.

"I told you that you are to call him uncle," the woman said sharply, but not unkindly. "I have told you so over and over again, child."

"I generally do now, but one forgets sometimes."

"There is never any saying"—the woman went on in reply to his question —"there is never any saying; it all depends on tide and wind. Sometimes they have to anchor and lose a tide, or maybe two. Sometimes they get a cargo directly they get into the Pool or at Rochester; sometimes they wait two or three days. They have been away four days now; they might have been here yesterday, but may not come till to-morrow. One thing is certain, whenever he do come he will want something to eat, and I hope that they will bring it with them, for there is nothing here but bread and bacon."

"And do you think that I shall soon go home again, aunt?"

"There is no saying," the woman said evasively. "You are very comfortable here, aint you?"

"Oh, yes! There are the dogs and the ducks and the chickens, and uncle says that he will take me sometimes for a sail with him in the barge."

"Yes, I expect it won't be long first. You know, I used to go with him regular till, as I have told you, my little Billy fell overboard one night, and we knew nothing of it until he was gone, and I have never liked the barge since. Besides, I have plenty to do here. But I am going across to Rochester very soon. It's a good place for shopping, and I want groceries and little things for myself and more things for you. I will take you with me, but you will have to promise to be very good and careful."

"I will be careful," the child said confidently, "and you know that uncle said that when spring comes he will teach me to swim; and I shall like that, and if I tumble overboard it won't matter. He says that when I get a few years older I shall go with him regularly, and learn to steer and to manage the sails. I shall like that; but I should like to go back sometimes to see Hilda and Netta and my grandpapa."

"Well, well, my dear, we will see about it; they can't take you at present. I think that they have gone away traveling, and may not be back for a long time. And mind, you know you are not to talk about them. Just when you are here with me I don't care; but you know uncle does not like it, and if anyone asks, you must say just what he told you, that your father and mother are dead, and that Uncle Bill has took you."

"I shan't forget," the boy said. "I never do talk about it before him; it makes him angry. I don't know why, but it does."

"But he is always kind to you, Jack?"

"Oh, yes, he is very kind, and he often brings me things when he comes back; he brought me my dear little kitten. Pussy, where have you hidden yourself? Puss! puss!" And in answer a little ball of white fur bounded out from behind a chair, and the child was soon engaged in a game of romps with it.

"It is a shame!" the woman said, as she watched them; "I don't mind the other things, but I never liked this. I wonder who the poor little chap is. By the way he talked when he first came, about his home and his nurse and horses and carriages, his friends must be rich people. Bill has never understood why they wanted to get rid of him; but I suppose that he was in somebody's way, and, as he never speaks of his father and mother, but only of those two girls and his grandfather, who seems to have been an invalid, I expect that he must have lost his father and mother before he can remember. Well, he will be right enough here; I should miss him dreadful if he were to go away; he seems to have taken the place of my little Billy. And Bill takes to him, too, wonderfully. He said the other day that when the boy grew up he would buy a barge, a new one of the best kind, and that some day it should be the boy's own. So he won't do so bad, after all."

A stranger would have wondered at the comfort in the interior of the little farmhouse. The land round it was very poor. Three horses—which seemed as if they had nothing to do but to nibble the coarse grass—and a couple of cows wandered about on a few acres of land, inclosed by deep water ditches; a score or two of ducks and geese paddled in the mud in the bottom of the creek at low tide, or swam about in the water when it was up; and a patch of garden ground, attended to chiefly by the woman, surrounded the cottage. But all this would have afforded a scanty living indeed, were it not that the master, Bill Nibson, was the owner of the *Mary Ann* barge, an old craft with a somewhat dilapidated sail, which journeyed up and down the river with more or less regularity, laden, for the most part, with manure, hay, lime, bricks, or coal. This he navigated with the aid of a lad of fourteen, a waif, whose mother, a tramp, had died by the roadside one bitter cold night four years before. Bill had been summoned on the coroner's jury and had offered to take the boy.

"I can do with him on board the barge," he said; "he is only a little nipper now, but in a year or two he will be useful. The boy I have got wants to go to sea, and I shan't be sorry to get rid of him; he is getting too knowing for me altogether."

As no one else wanted the boy he was handed over to Bill, and was now a sharp lad, who, never having been instructed in the niceties of right and wrong, and being especially ignorant that there was any harm in cheating Her Majesty's Customs, was in all things a useful assistant to his master. He had, indeed, very soon imbibed the spirit, not uncommon among the dwellers on the marshes, that if managed without detection, the smuggling of tobacco and spirits was a meritorious action, advantageous to the community at large, and hurting no one except that mysterious and unknown entity, the queen's revenue. He was greatly attached to Bill, and took an occasional thrashing as a matter of course; regarding him as having saved him from the workhouse and having put him in a fair way of making a man of himself.

The next day at twelve o'clock the child, playing on the bank, ran in and reported that Joshua was coming along the bank, and in a few minutes the boy appeared.

"Morning, missis," he said. "Master sent me on to say that the barge got into the haven this morning, and that she will come on with the evening tide. He sent me on with this lump of meat, and these rokers he got from a bawley which came in just as we were getting up sail off Grain Spit. He says he has got a barrel of beer on board, that he will land as he passes. He will be along about nine o'clock. Well, Jack, how are you?"

"I am all right," the child said, "and so is Kitty. I am glad that you are back. How long are you going to stay?"

"I suppose that it will take us a couple of days to unload. Master is going as usual to hire a couple of men to get the line out, so I shall be over here by breakfast. He says that I may as well do a job of digging in the garden, as he wants to get some things in before we get frosty nights. Have you any message for him, missis?"

"You can tell him he may as well get a dish of eels from one of the Dutchmen there. I suppose there is one in the haven?"

"Two of them, missis; he will be able to get them, for one of them is the *Marden*, and the skipper has always let master have some, though he won't sell an eel to anyone else."

"Is there any business to be done?" the woman asked significantly.

The boy nodded.

"All right; tell him that I will get the horses in."

The child was put to bed upstairs at seven o'clock, although he in vain petitioned to be allowed to stop up until the barge came along. He already knew, however, by experience, that his request was not likely to be granted, as when the barge came along after dark he was always put to bed, the woman telling him that Bill didn't like him to be up when he came in, as he wanted to have a talk with her in quiet, and to eat his supper in peace.

An hour after dark the woman went out onto the bank and listened. In a quarter of an hour she heard the rattle of a block in the distance. She went down, stirred up the fire, and put on the kettle, and in twenty minutes the barge came along. The boat, instead of towing behind as usual, was alongside.

"You take her on, Joshua," its owner said, as he quietly got into the boat; "run in where the water is deep alongside, a quarter of a mile this side Pitsea. I will come along and get on board there as soon as I have finished this job. Keep a sharp lookout on the banks; some of the coastguardsmen may be about. If they hail you and ask if I am on board, say I landed as we passed here, to have a cup of tea, and that I shall not be five minutes."

Then he pushed the boat to shore. "Well, Betsy, how are you? I have got twenty kegs here, and five or six hundredweight of tobacco. I will get it up the bank, and you had better stow it away at once; I will lend you a hand as soon as it is all up."

As fast as he could carry the kegs up the banks she slipped slings round them, two at a time, hooked them to a milkmaid's yoke, and went off with them to a shed which served as a stable and cowhouse in the winter. Against this was a rick of hay. Putting the kegs down she returned for more, and by the time that they were all in the stable her husband had finished his share of the work and had carried the heavy bales of tobacco to the shed. The three horses were already there.

"Are you going to take them out at once?"

"No, not until I come back. I must get on board the barge as soon as possible. We will bundle them all in, in case any of those fellows should come along."

Three planks were removed from the side of the shed next to the stack, and an opening was seen. Some turf was taken up and a trapdoor exposed. The kegs and tobacco were speedily carried down into a large cellar, the trapdoor was closed, and the boards placed securely in position and fastened by six long screws. Then they returned to the house. The teapot and cups were on the table, the kettle was boiling, and in two or three minutes they were taking tea. Scarcely had they begun their meal when there was a knock at the door. Bill got up and opened it, and two coastguards entered.

"We saw there was a light burning, and thought that you might be here, Bill. The wind is bitter cold."

"Come in and have a cup of tea or a glass of rum, whichever you like best. As you say, the wind is bitter cold, and I thought that I would land and have a cup of tea. I shall catch the barge up before she gets to Pitsea."

The coastguardsmen accepted the offer of a cup of tea, glancing furtively round the room as they drank it.

"It is good tea."

"'Tis that," Bill said, "and it has never paid duty. I got it from an Indiaman that was on the Nore three weeks ago. She transshipped part of her cargo on my barge and floated next tide. It was one of the best jobs I've had for some time, and stood me in fifty pounds and a pound or two of tea."

"Perhaps a chest of it!" one of the men said with a laugh.

"Well, well, I am not sure that it was not a chest. I like my cup of tea, and so does Betsy; and there is no getting tea like this at Stanford."

They chatted for about ten minutes, when Bill remarked, "I must be going," and they went out together, and taking his place in his boat he rowed up the creek, while the coastguards continued their walk along the bank.

"He is not a bad 'un, Tom," one of them said. "I guess he is like a good many of the others, runs a keg occasionally. However, his place has been searched half a dozen times, and nothing has been found. We have drunk many a glass of ale with him at the 'Lobster Smack' at Hole Haven, and I am sure I don't want to catch him unless there is some information to go on. The barge passed us half an hour ago, and I knew that it was no use looking in her, but of course when the boatswain said this afternoon, 'Just follow that barge when she gets under way, and see if she goes on to Pitsea,' we had to do it; but the boat was late for us where the creek branches off round the island, and before we were across he must have got more than half an hour's start of us. And I am not sorry, Tom. We have got to do our duty, but we don't want to be at war with every good fellow on the marshes."

"Right you are, Dick; besides, they are as slippery as eels. Who can tell what they have got under their lime or manure? Short of unloading it to the bottom there would be no finding it, if they had anything; and it is a job that I should not care for. Besides, there aint no place to empty it on; and we could not go and chuck a cargo overboard unless we were quite certain that we should find something underneath. As you say, I dare say Bill runs a keg or two now and then, but I don't suppose that he is worse than his neighbors; I have always suspected that it was he who left a keg of whisky at our door last Christmas."

In the meantime Bill had overtaken his barge, and they soon had her alongside of the little wharf at Pitsea.

"Tide is just turning. She will be aground in half an hour," he said. "As soon as you have got these mooring ropes fastened, you had better fry that steak and have your supper. I shall be over by seven o'clock in the morning. If Harvey and Wilson come alongside before that, tell them they can have the job at the usual price, and can set to work without waiting for me. It will be pretty late before I am in bed to-night."

It was over a mile walk back to his cottage. As soon as he arrived he sat down to a hearty supper which his wife had prepared for him. He then got three pack-saddles out of the cellar, put them on the horses, and fastened four kegs on each horse. Tying one behind the other, he started, and in an hour the kegs were stowed in the cellars of four farmers near Stanford. It was midnight before he returned home. At half-past six he was down to breakfast.

"Well, uncle, how are you?" he asked the child, who was already up.

"I am not your uncle," the boy replied; "you are my uncle."

"Ah, well, it's a way of speaking down here. It does not mean that anyone is one's uncle; it is just a way of speaking."

The child nodded. He was learning many things.

"Then it is a way of speaking when I call you uncle?"

"No, no! That is different. A child like you would not call anyone uncle unless he was uncle; while a man my age calls anyone uncle."

"That is funny, isn't it?"

"Well, I suppose, when you think of it, it is; but, as I said, it is a way we have in this part of the country. Well, mother, have you got that fish nearly fried?"

"It will be ready in five minutes. This roker is a very thick one. I put it on as soon as I heard you stirring, and it is not quite ready yet. That was a pretty near escape last night, Bill."

"Yes; but, you see, they can hardly catch us unless they send men down in the afternoon. They cannot get along from the station without passing two or three creeks; and coming along with the tide, especially when there is a breath of wind to help her, we can do it in half the time. You see, I always get the things out from under the cargo and into the boat as we come along, so that the barge shall not be stopped."

"But they might send down a boat from the Thames Haven station, Bill."

"Yes; but then they don't know when the barge is in, or when it is going to start. So we get the best of them in that way. Besides, they have a good bit to go along the river face, and they have to cross a dozen deep cuts to get there. No, I have no fear of them, nor of the others either, as far as that goes. I have more than once had a word dropped, meant to put me on my guard, and instead of landing the things here have dropped them in a deep hole in the creek, where I could pick them up the next night I came in. Things have changed with us for the better, lass. Five years ago we had pretty hard work, with the farm and the old boat, to live at all comfortable; but since I have got into the swim things have changed with us, and I can tell you that I am making money hand over fist. I allow that there is a certain risk in it, but, after all, one likes it all the better for that. If the worst came to the worst they could but confiscate the old barge; if they gave me a heavy fine I could pay it, and if they gave me six months I could work it out, and buy a new barge and half a dozen farms like this on the day I came out."

"But the other would be more serious, Bill?"

"Well, yes; but I don't see any chance of that being found out. A gent comes to me at a spot we have settled on, say on the road halfway between Pitsea and Stanford; he hands me a box, sometimes two; I puts them on one of the horses, and rides over here with them; then I stows them away in that secret place off the store, where there aint a shadow of a chance of the sharpest-eyed coastguardsman ever finding them. They would be too delighted to light on the spirits and bacca to think of digging up the floor underneath. There they lie, till I take them down to the *Marden*. They put them into the eel tank, and next morning off she sails."

"But you have had heavy cases brought once or twice?"

"Only once—heavy enough to be troublesome. Ten cases there was then, each as heavy as a man could lift. It took me three journeys with three horses, and I had to dig a big hole in the garden to bury them till the *Marden* had got rid of her eels, and was ready to sail again. Yes, that was a heavy job, and I got a couple of hundred pounds for my share of the business. I should not mind having such a job twice a week. A few months of that, and I could buy the biggest farm on this side of Essex—that is to say, if I could make up my mind to cut it and settle down as a farmer."

"You will never do that, Bill; but you might settle down in Rochester, and buy half a dozen barges, with a tip-top one you would sail yourself. You might have a couple of men and a cabin forward, and a nice roomy place for yourself and me aft; and you could just steer when you liked, or sit down and smoke your pipe and watch her going through the fleet as we worked through the swatchway. That would be more your sort, Bill, and mine too. I know you have money enough laid by to get such a barge."

"That is so, Betsy. I allow that I could do that. I have been thinking of it for some time, but somehow or other one never works one's self up to the right point to give it all up of a sudden and cut the old place. Well, I suppose one of these days I shall do it, if it is only to please you."

"It would please me, you know, Bill. I don't see no harm in running the kegs or the bacca—it's what the people about here have been doing for hundreds of years—but I don't like this other business. You don't know what is in the cases, and you don't ask, but there aint much difficulty in guessing. And I don't much like this business of the child. I did not like it at all at first; but when I found that he had no father nor mother as he knew of, and so it was certain that no one was breaking their heart about him, I did not mind it; and I have taken to him, and he has pretty nearly forgotten about his home, and is as contented as if he had been here all his life. I have nothing more to say about him, though it is as certain as eggs is eggs that it has been a bad business. The boy has been cheated out of his money, and if his friends ever find him it is a nice row that we shall get into."

"You need not bother yourself about that," the man said; "he aint more likely to be found here than if he was across the seas in Ameriky. We have had him near nine months now, and in another three months, if you were to put him down in front of his own house, he would not know it. Everyone about here believes as he is my nevvy, the son of a brother of yours who died down in the Midlands, and left him motherless. No one asks any questions about him now, no more than they does about Joshua. No, no; we are all right there, missis; and the hundred pounds that we had down with him, and fifty pounds a year till he gets big enough to earn his own grub on the barge, all helps. Anyhow, if something should happen to me before I have made up my mind to quit this, you know where the pot of money is hidden. You can settle in Rochester, and get him some schooling, and then apprentice him to a barge-owner and start him with a barge of his own as soon as he is out of his time. You bear it in mind that is what I should like done."

"I will mind," she said quietly; "but I am as likely to be carried to the churchyard as you are, and you remember what I should like, and try, Bill, if you give up the water yourself, to see that he is with a man as doesn't drink. Most of the things we hears of—of barges being run down, and of men falling overboard on a dark night—are just drink, and nothing else. You are not a man as drinks yourself; you take your glass when the barge is in the creek, but I have never seen you the worse for liquor since you courted me fifteen years ago, and I tell you there is not a night when you are out on the barge as I don't thank God that it is so. I says to myself, when the wind is blowing on a dark night, 'He is anchored somewheres under a weather shore, and he is snug asleep in his cabin. There is no fear of his driving along through it and carrying on sail; there is no fear of his stumbling as he goes forward and pitching over'; and no one but myself knows what a comfort it is to me. You bring him up in the same way, Bill. You teach him as it is always a good thing to keep from liquor, though a pint with an old mate aint neither here nor there, but that he might almost as well take poison as to drink down in the cabin."

"I will mind, missis; I like the child, and have got it in my mind to bring him up straight, so let us have no more words about it."

CHAPTER XIX.

A PARTIAL SUCCESS.

Netta had been away three weeks when one morning, just as they were sitting down to breakfast, she suddenly came into the room. With a cry of joy Hilda ran into her arms.

"You wicked, wicked girl!" she exclaimed. "I know that I ought not to speak to you. You don't deserve that I should even look at you, but I cannot help it."

Miss Purcell embraced her niece more soberly, but Hilda saw by the expression of her face that her niece's return relieved her of a burden of anxiety which at times she had had difficulty in concealing.

"In the first place, Netta, before I even give you a cup of tea, tell me if this is a final return, or whether you are going to disappear again."

"That we will decide after you have heard my story," Netta said quietly.

"And have you got any news of Walter?"

"I am not sure; I think so. So you have kept my secret, aunt?"

"I promised that I would, dear, and of course I have kept my word, though it was very difficult to resist Hilda's pleading. Dr. Leeds, too, has been terribly anxious about you, and not a day has passed that he has not run in for a few minutes to learn if there was any news."

"I don't see why he should have known that I have been away."

"Why, my dear," Hilda said, "coming here as often as he does, he naturally inquired where you were, and as I was uncertain how long you would be away, and as he had always been in our counsels, I could hardly keep him in the dark, even had I wished to do so. Now, my dear, let us know all about it; there can be no possible reason for keeping silent any longer."

"Well, Hilda, the whole affair has been very simple, and there was not the least occasion for being anxious. I simply wanted to keep it quiet because I felt that you would raise all sorts of objections to the plan. We had, as you know, thought over a great many methods by which we might overhear a conversation between John Simcoe and the man on Pentonville Hill. But it seemed next to be impossible that it could be managed there. Suddenly the idea came into my brain that, as a servant at Simcoe's lodgings in Jermyn Street, I might have an excellent chance."

Hilda gave an exclamation of horror.

"My dear Netta, you never can really have thought of carrying this out?"

"I not only thought of it, but did it. With a little management the girl there was got hold of, and as it fortunately happened that she did not like London and wanted to take a country situation, there was very little difficulty, and she agreed to introduce me as a friend who was willing to take her place. Of course, it took a few days to make all the arrangements and to get suitable clothes for the place, and these I sent by parcel delivery, and on the morning of the day that the girl was to leave presented myself at the house. The man and his wife were good enough to approve of my appearance. They had, it seemed, three sets of lodgers, one on each floor; the man himself waited upon them, and my work was to do their rooms and keep the house tidy generally."

Again Hilda gave a gasp.

"There was nothing much in that," Netta went on, without heeding her. "I used to do most of the house work when we were in Germany, and I think that I gave every satisfaction. Of course the chief difficulty was about my deafness. I was obliged to explain to them that I was very hard of hearing unless I was directly spoken to. Mr. Johnstone always answered the bells himself when he was at home. Of course, when he was out it was my duty to do so. When I was downstairs it was simple enough, for I only had to go to the door of the room of which I saw the bell in motion. At first they seemed to think that the difficulty was insuperable; but I believe that in other respects I suited them so well that they decided to make the best of it, and when her husband was out and I was upstairs Mrs. Johnstone took to answering the door bells, or if a lodger rang, which was not very often, for her husband seldom went out unless they were all three away, she would come upstairs and tell me. Johnstone himself said to me one day that I was the best girl he had ever had, and that instead of having to go most carefully over the sitting rooms before the gentlemen came in for breakfast, he found that everything was so perfectly dusted and tidied up that there was really nothing for him to do.

"But oh, Hilda, I never had the slightest idea before how untidy men are! The way they spill their tobacco ash all over the room, and put the ends of their cigars upon mantelpieces, tables, and everywhere else, you would hardly believe it. The ground floor and the second floor were the worst, for they very often had men in of an evening, and the state of the rooms in the morning was something awful. Our man was on the first floor, and did not give anything like so much trouble, for he almost always went out in the evening and never had more than one or two friends in with him. One of these friends was the man we saw with him in the Row, and who, we had no doubt, was an accomplice of his. He came oftener than anyone else, very often coming in to fetch him. As he was always in evening dress I suppose they went to some club or to the theater together. I am bound to say that his appearance is distinctly that of a gentleman.

"I had taken with me two or three things that I foresaw I should want. Among them was an auger, and some corks of a size that would exactly fit the hole that it would make. Simcoe's bedroom communicated with the sitting room, and he always used this door in going from one room to the other; and it was evident that it was only through that that I could get a view of what was going on. I did not see how I could possibly make a hole through the door itself. It was on one side, next to that where the fireplace was, and there was a window directly opposite, and of course a hole would have been noticed immediately. The only place that I could see to make it was through the door frame. Its position was a matter of much calculation, I can assure you. The auger was half an inch bore. I dared not get it larger, and it would have been hopeless to try and see anything with a smaller one, especially as the hole would have to be four or five inches long. As I sometimes went into the room when they were together, either with hot water or grilled bones, or something of that sort, I was able to notice exactly where the chairs were generally placed. Simcoe sat with his back to the bedroom door, and the other man on the other side of the hearthrug, facing him. I, therefore, decided to make the hole on the side nearest to the wall, so that I could see the other man past Simcoe. Of course I wanted the hole to be as low as possible, as it would not be so likely to be noticed as it would were it higher up. I chose a point, therefore, that would come level with my eye when I was kneeling down.

"At about four o'clock in the afternoon they always went out, and from then till six Johnstone also took his airing, and I went upstairs to turn down the beds and tidy up generally. It was very seldom that any of them dined at home; I, therefore, had that two hours to myself. I got the line the hole should go by leaving the door open, fastening a stick to the back of a chair till it was, as nearly as I could judge, the height of the man's face, tying a piece of string to it and bringing it tight to the point where I settled the hole should start, and then marking the line the string made across the frame. Then there was a good deal more calculation as to the side-slant; but ten days ago I boldly set to work and bored the hole. Everything was perfectly right; I could see the head of the stick, and the circle was large enough for me to get all the man's face in view. Of course I had put a duster on the ground to prevent any chips falling onto the carpet.

"I was a little nervous when I set to work to drill that hole; it was the only time that I felt nervous at all. I had beforehand drilled several holes in the shelves of cupboards, so as to accustom myself to use the auger, and it did not take me many minutes before it came through on the other side. The corks were of two sizes; one fitted tightly into the hole, the other could be drawn in or out with very little difficulty. I had gone out one day and bought some tubes of paint of the colors that I thought would match the graining of the door frame. I also bought a corkscrew that was about an inch and a half shorter than the depth of the hole. It was meant to be used by a cross-piece that went through a hole at the top. I had got this cross-piece out with some trouble, and tied a short loop of string through the hole it had gone through. I put the corkscrew into one of the smaller corks and pushed it through until it was level with the frame on the sitting-room side, and found that by aid of the loop of string I could draw it out easily. Then I put one of the larger corks in at the bedroom side of the hole and pushed it in until it was level with that side. Then I painted the ends of the corks to resemble the graining, and when it was done they could hardly be noticed a couple of feet away.

"I had now nothing to do but to wait until the right moment came. It came last night. The man arrived about seven o'clock. Johnstone was out, and I showed him upstairs. Simcoe was already dressed, and was in the sitting room. I lost no time, but went into the bedroom, where the gas was burning, turned down the bed on the side nearest to the door, and then went round, and with another corkscrew I had ready in my pocket took out the inner cork, got hold of the loop, and pulled the other one out also. Even had I had my hearing, I could have heard nothing of what was said inside, for the doors were of mahogany, and very well fitted, and Johnstone had said one day that even if a man shouted in one room he would hardly be heard in the next, or on the landing. I pushed a wedge under the door so as to prevent its being opened suddenly. That was the thing that I was most afraid of. I thought that Simcoe could hardly move without coming within my line of sight, and that I should have time to jump up and be busy at the bed before he could open the door. But I was not sure of this, so I used the wedge. If he tried the door and could not open it, he would only suppose that the door had stuck and I could snatch out the wedge and kick it under the bed by the time he made a second effort.

"Kneeling down, I saw to my delight that my calculations had been perfectly right. I could see the man's face well, for the light of the candles fell full upon it. They talked for a time about the club and the men they were going to dine with, and I began to be afraid that there was going to be nothing more, when the man said, 'By the way, Simcoe, I went down to Tilbury yesterday.' What Simcoe said, of course, I could not hear; but the other answered, 'Oh, yes, he is all right, getting quite at home, the man said; and has almost ceased to talk about his friends.' Then I saw him rise, and at once jumped up and went on turning down the bed, lest Simcoe should have forgotten something and come in for it. However, he did not, and two or three minutes later I peeped in again. The room was all dark, and I knew that they had gone. Then I put my corks in again, saw that the paint was all right, and went downstairs. I told Mrs. Johnstone that, if I could be spared, I should like to go out for two or three hours this morning to see a friend in service. It was the time that I could best be spared. I should have finished the sitting rooms by eight o'clock, and as none of the men have breakfast until about eleven, there was plenty of time for me to make the beds after I got back."

Hilda was crying now. Her relief that hearing that Walter was alive and well was unbounded. She had absolutely refused to recognize the body found in the canal, but she could not but admit that the probabilities were all against her. It was certain that the clothes were his, the child's age was about the same, the body must have been in the water the right length of time, the only shadow of evidence to support her was the hair. She had taken the trouble to go to two or three workhouses, and found that the coroner's assertion that soft hair when cut quite close will, in a very short time, stand upright, was a correct one. She kept on hoping against hope, but her faith had been yielding, especially since Netta's absence had deprived her of the support that she obtained from her when inclined to look at matters from a dark point of view.

"Oh, Netta," she cried, "how can I thank you enough! How happy the news has made me! And to think that I have been blaming you, while you have been doing all this. You cannot tell what a relief it is to me. I have thought so much of that poor little body, and the dread that it was Walter's after all has been growing upon me. I have scarcely slept for a long time."

"I know, dear. It was because I saw that though you still kept up an appearance of hope, you were really in despair, and could tell from your heavy eyes when you came down of a morning that you had hardly slept, that I made up my mind something must be done. There was no hardship whatever in my acting as a servant for a month or two. I can assure you that I regarded it rather as fun, and was quite proud of the credit that my master gave me. Now, the question is, shall I go back again?"

"Certainly not, Netta. You might be months there without having such a piece of luck again. At any moment you might be caught listening, or they might notice the hole that you made so cleverly. Besides, we have gained a clew now to Walter's hiding place. But even that is as nothing to me in comparison with having learned that he is alive and well, and that he has ceased to fret and is becoming contented in his new home. We can afford to wait now. Sooner or later we are sure to find him. Before, I pictured him, if still alive, as shut up in some horrible cellar. Now I can be patient. I think that we are sure to find him before long."

"Well, I think, dear," Miss Purcell said quietly, "that we had better ring the bell and have some fresh tea made. Everything is perfectly cold, for it is three-quarters of an hour since it came up."

Hilda rang the bell and gave the necessary orders.

"Let Janet bring the things up, Roberts, and come back yourself when you have given the order. I want to send a line to Dr. Leeds. You will be delighted to hear that Miss Purcell has learned, at least, that Walter is alive and well; but mind," she went on, as the old soldier was about to burst out into exclamations of delight, "you must keep this altogether to yourself. It is quite possible that we have been watched as closely as we have been watching this man, and that he may in some way learn everything that passes here; therefore it must not be whispered outside this room that we have obtained any news."

"I understand, miss. I won't say a word about it downstairs."

Hilda scribbled a line in pencil to the doctor, saying that Netta was back and that she had obtained some news of a favorable description, and that, as she knew that at this hour he could not get away, she would come over with Netta at once to tell him what they had learned, and would be in Harley Street within half an hour of his getting the message.

As soon as they had finished breakfast they drove to the doctor's. They were shown up into the drawing room, where Dr. Leeds joined them almost immediately.

"We are not going to detain you more than two or three minutes," Hilda said, while he shook hands warmly with Netta. "You must come over this evening, and then you shall hear the whole story; but I thought that it was only fair that Netta should have the satisfaction of telling you herself what she had learned."

"It is very little, but so far as it goes it is quite satisfactory, Dr. Leeds. I heard, or rather I saw, the man we suspected of being Simcoe's accomplice say, 'By the way, I ran down to Tilbury yesterday.' Simcoe then said something, but what I could not tell, as his face was hidden from me, and the man in reply said, 'Oh, yes, he is all right, and has almost ceased to talk about his friends.' Now you must be content with that until this evening."

"I will be content with it," the doctor said, "if you will assure me that you are not going away again. If you will not, I will stop here and hear the whole story, even at the risk of a riot down in my waiting room."

"No, she is not going away, doctor; she had not quite settled about it when she got back this morning, but I settled it for her. I will take care that she does not slip out of my sight till after you have seen her and talked it all over."

“Then the matter is finally settled,” Netta said, “for unless I go in half an hour’s time I cannot go at all.”

“Then I will be patient until this evening.”

“Will you come to dinner, doctor?” Hilda said. “I have sent notes off to Mr. Pettigrew and Colonel Bulstrode to ask them to come, as I have news of importance to give them.”

“What will they do, Netta, when they find that you do not come back?” Hilda asked as they drove away.

“That has puzzled me a good deal. I quite saw that if I disappeared suddenly they might take it into their heads that something had happened to me, and might go to the police office and say I was missing. But that would not be the worst. Simcoe might guess, when he heard that I had gone without notice and left my things behind me, that I had been put there to watch him. He certainly would not suspect that he could have been overheard, for he must know that it would be quite impossible for any words to be heard through the doors; still, he would be uneasy, and might even have the child moved to some other locality. So I have written a note, which we can talk over when we get in. Of course they may think that I have behaved very badly in throwing them over like this, but it is better that they should do that than they should think there was anything suspicious about it. My wages are due to-morrow; like the girl I succeeded, I was to have eight pounds a year. I have left my box open, so that the mistress can see for herself that there is none of the lodgers’ property in it. There are two or three print dresses—I put on my Sunday gown when I came out—and the underclothes are all duly marked Jane Clotworthy.”

"What a name to take, Netta!"

"Yes, I do not know how I came to choose it. I was thinking what name I would take when Clotworthy flashed across my mind. I don't think that I ever heard the name before, and how I came to think of it I cannot imagine; it seemed to me a sort of inspiration, so I settled on it at once."

"Now, let me see the letter," Hilda asked, as soon as they returned home.

"I hardly liked to write it," Netta said, "it is such a wicked story; but I don't see how a person can act as detective without telling stories, and, at any rate, it is perfectly harmless."

"Oh, yes; it is quite certain, Netta, that you could not write and tell her that you have been in her house in disguise, and that, having found out what you wanted, you have now left her. Of course you must make up a story of some sort, or, as you say, Simcoe would at once suspect that you had been sent there to watch him. He might feel perfectly sure that no conversation could have been heard outside the room, but he could not be sure that you might not have been hidden under the table or sofa, or behind a curtain. When so much depends upon his thinking that he is absolutely safe, one must use what weapons one can. If you have any scruples about it, I will write the letter for you."

"No, I do not think the scruples will trouble me," Netta laughed. "Of course, I have had to tell stories, and one more or less will not weigh on my mind. Here is the letter. If you can think of any better reason for running away so suddenly, by all means let me have it."

The letter was written in a sprawling hand, and with many of the words misspelt. It began:

> "Dear Mrs. Johnstone: I am afraid you will think very badly of me for leaving you so sudding, after you and Mr. Johnstone have been so kind to me, but who should I meet at my friend's but my young man. We were ingaged to be married, but we had a quarrel, and that is why I came up to town so sudding. We has made it up. He only come up yesterday, and is going down this morning, and nothing would do but that I must go down with him and that we should get married directly. He says that as the banns has been published there aint any occasion to wait, and we might be married at the end of the week, as he has got everything ready and is in good employment. So the long and the short of it is, mam, that I am going down with him home this afternoon. As to the wages that was due to-morrow, of course I forfeit them, and sorry I am to give you troubil, by leaving you without a girl. My box is not locked, plese look in it and

you will see that there aint nothing there that isn't my own. In one corner you will find half a crown wrapped up in paper, plese take that to pay for the carriage of the box, the key is in the lock, and I send a labil to tie on."

"What do you think of that, Hilda?"

"I think it will do capitally. I don't think any better excuse could be made. But where will you have the box sent?"

"That is what we must settle together. It would not do to send it down to some little village, for if the address was unknown it might be sent back again."

"Yes; and if John Simcoe had any suspicions that the story was a false one he might go down there to make inquiries about Jane Clotworthy, and, finding no such name known there, and the box still lying at the station, his suspicion that he had been watched would become almost a certainty."

"I should think that Reading would be a good place to send to it. 'Jane Clotworthy, Luggage Office, Reading.' Then I could go down myself and ask for it, and could bring it up by the next train."

"Tom Roberts could do that, Netta; there is no reason why you should trouble about it."

"I think that I had better go myself. It is most unlikely that Simcoe would send down anyone to watch who took the box away, but if he should be very uneasy he might do so. He would be sure to describe me to anyone that he sent, so that it would be better that I should go myself."

"I think that your story is so plausible, Netta, that there is no risk whatever of his having any doubts about it, but still one cannot be too careful."

"Then I will wind up the letter.

"'Begging your pardon for having left you in the lurch so sudding. I remain, your obedient servant,

"'JANE CLOTWORTHY.

"'P.S.—I am very sorry.
"'P.S.—Plese give my respects to Mr. Johnstone, and excuse blots.'"

Hilda burst into a fit of laughter as she glanced at the postscript.

"That will do admirably, Netta," she said. "Now how had we better send it?"

"I should think that your maid had better take it. You might tell her to ring at the bell, hand it to the woman, and come away at once, without talking, except saying 'I was told to give you this.' Then she would be well away before Mrs. Johnstone had mastered the contents of the note. It had better be sent off at once, for by this time they will be getting in a way."

"I think that I had better send Roberts. No doubt Johnstone himself will be in, and will answer the door; and he might ask Lucy where she came from, and I don't want to tell her anything. Roberts could say that a young woman of his acquaintance, down Chelsea way, asked him to get on a 'bus and leave it for her. He can be trusted, if the man does detain him and ask him questions, to give sensible answers."

The letter was sealed and Roberts called up.

"Take a cab and go down with this to Jermyn Street," Hilda said. "I want it left at that house. If the man who opens the door asks you who you have brought it from, say from a young woman, a friend of yours, in a place down Chelsea way. I don't suppose that he will ask any other questions, and you had best say 'Good-morning,' and saunter off carelessly, as if, having done your errand, you had nothing else on hand. Of course you won't drive up to the door. Leave the cab round the corner, and come straight back here in it."

"All right, miss," he answered.

There was a little look of amusement in the man's face as he glanced at Netta that did not this time pass unnoticed by his mistress. She waited until the door had closed behind him, and then turned sharply on her friend.

"I believe, Netta, you have had Roberts in your confidence all the time, and while we have all been working ourselves into a fever as to where you could be, he has known it all along."

"One cannot work without accomplices," Netta laughed. "It was necessary that someone should make arrangements with the servant there for me to take her place, and who could I trust better than Roberts? I think Colonel Bulstrode's servant helped in the matter; at any rate, they managed it capitally between them. Of course it was Roberts who carried my box out that morning. You must not be angry with him, Hilda, for keeping it from you. I made him promise most faithfully that nothing should induce him to confess."

"I shan't be angry with him, Netta, but you may be sure that I shall give him a little lecture and say that I will have no more meddling on his part, except by my express orders. It is really annoying, you know, to think that all this time we were fretting about you there was Roberts going about laughing in his sleeve."

"Well, you know, Hilda, he has the discovery of Walter as much at heart as we have, and he has certainly not spared himself in the search for him."

“No, that he has not. He is a faithful fellow, and I promise you that I won’t be too hard on him.”

CHAPTER XX.

A DINNER PARTY.

It was the first time that anyone had dined at the house in Hyde Park Gardens since General Mathieson's death, and it seemed strange to Hilda when Mr. Pettigrew, at her request, faced her at the table. The gentlemen had all arrived within a minute or two of each other, and no word had been said by Hilda as to the subject about which she had specially asked them there. The table was well lighted and bright with flowers, and the lawyer and Colonel Bulstrode were both somewhat surprised at the cheerful tone in which Hilda began to talk as soon as they sat down. It was, however, eight months since the house was first shut up, and though all had sincerely regretted the General's death, it was an old story now, and they were relieved to find that it was evidently not Hilda's intention to recall the past.

During dinner the talk went on as usual, and it was not until the servants had left the room that Hilda said:

"Now, Mr. Pettigrew, I have no doubt that both you and Colonel Bulstrode are wondering what the matter of importance about which I asked you to come here can be. It is rather a long story, so instead of going upstairs we will stop here. My news is great news. We have discovered—at least my friend Miss Purcell has discovered—that without doubt Walter is alive and well."

An exclamation of surprise broke from Mr. Pettigrew and the Colonel.

"By gad, that is great news indeed!" the latter exclaimed; "and I congratulate you most heartily. I had quite given up all hope myself, and although I would have fought that fellow to the last, I never had any real doubt in my mind that the child they fished out of the canal was General's Mathieson's grandson."

"You astonish me indeed," Mr. Pettigrew said. "I own that, while I was able to swear that I did not recognize him, yet as a reasonable man I felt that the evidence was overpowering the other way. Though I would not dash your hopes by saying so, it appeared to me certain that, sooner or later, the courts would decide that the provisions of the will must be carried out. And so you discovered this, Miss Netta? May we ask how you did it?"

"Netta wanted her share in the matter to remain a secret, Mr. Pettigrew; but I told her that was out of the question, and that it was quite necessary that you and Colonel Bulstrode should know the precise facts, for that, as a lawyer, you could not take any action or decide upon any course to be pursued unless you knew the exact circumstances of the case. However, she asked me, as she has given me the whole particulars, to tell the story for her. When I have done she will answer any questions you may like to ask."

Hilda then repeated, almost word for word, the story Netta had told her. Mr. Pettigrew and the Colonel several times broke in with exclamations of surprise as she went on. Dr. Leeds sat grave and thoughtful.

"Splendidly done!" Colonel Bulstrode exclaimed when she brought her story to an end. "It was a magnificent idea, and it must have needed no end of pluck to carry it out as you did. But how, by looking at a fellow's mouth through a hole, you knew what he said beats me altogether."

"That part was very simple, Colonel Bulstrode," Netta said quietly. "I learned it by a new system that they have in Germany, and was myself a teacher in the institution. You may not know, perhaps, that I am stone-deaf."

"You are not joking, Miss Purcell; are you?" the Colonel said, looking at her earnestly. "Why, I have talked to you a dozen times and it never struck me that you were in the slightest degree deaf."

"I am absolutely so, as Miss Covington will tell you, and Mr. Pettigrew knows it also. Fortunately I did not lose my hearing until I was six years old, and I had not altogether lost the habit of speaking when I went out to Germany, three years later. Had I been born deaf and dumb I could have learned to understand what was said perfectly, but should never have spoken in a natural voice."

"Well, it is wonderful altogether, and I should not have believed it if a stranger had told me. However, the great thing at present is that you have found out that the child is alive. We ought not to be long in laying hands on him now, Pettigrew, eh?"

"I hope not, Colonel; but you must not be too sanguine about that; we have evidently very crafty scoundrels to deal with. Still, now that we feel sure that the child is alive and well, the matter is a comparatively straightforward one, and we can afford to work and wait patiently. Tilbury is only a bit of a village, but beyond that stretch great marshes—in fact, all South Essex as far as the mouths of the rivers Crouch, Blackwater, and Coln. He would say, 'I went down to Tilbury,' because Tilbury is the terminus of the railway. Possibly he may have crossed to Gravesend; possibly he may have gone inland to Upminster or some other village lying in that district; or he may have driven down as far as Foulness, which, so far as anybody knows anything about it, might be the end of the world. Therefore, there is a wide area to be searched."

"But he can be followed when he goes down again, Mr. Pettigrew?"

"Of course, my dear, that is what must be done, though there is no reason why we should not set about inquiries at once. But, you see, it is not so easy to follow a man about country roads as it is in the streets of London. No doubt he must drive or ride, unless, indeed, Walter is within two or three miles of the station, and you may be sure that if he sees a trap coming after him he will not go near the place where the child is. Possibly, again, he may not go near the place at all, but may meet someone who takes the money for the child's keep. It may be a bargeman who sails round to Harwich or somewhere along the south coast. It may be the steward of a steamer that goes regularly backwards and forwards to France.

"I don't want to dishearten you, my dear," he broke off, as he saw how Hilda's face fell as he went on, "but, you see, we have not common rogues to deal with; their whole proceedings have shown an exceptional amount of coolness and determination. Although I own that I can see nothing absolutely suspicious in the way that last will was drawn up and signed, still I have never been able to divest my mind of an idea that there is something radically wrong about it. But putting aside the strange death of your uncle, we have the cunning way in which the boy was stolen, the complete success with which our search was baffled, the daring attempt to prove his death by what we now know must have been the substitution of the body of some other child of the same age dressed in his clothes. All this shows how carefully every detail must have been thought out, and we must assume that equal care will be shown to prevent our recovering the boy. Were they to suspect that they had been traced to Tilbury, and were watched there, or that any inquiries were being made in the neighborhood, you may be sure that Walter would be at once removed some distance away, or possibly sent abroad, perhaps to Australia or the States. There could be no difficulty about that. There are hundreds of emigrants going out every week with their families, who would jump at the offer of a hundred pounds for adopting a child, and once away it would be next to impossible ever to come upon his traces. So, you see, we shall need to exercise the most extreme caution in our searches."

"I see, Mr. Pettigrew," Hilda said quietly, "that the difficulties are far greater than I ever dreamt of. It seemed to me that when we had found out that Walter was alive and well, and that Tilbury was, so to speak, the starting place of our search, it would be an easy matter to find him. Now I see that, except for the knowledge that he is alive, we are nearly as far off as ever."

"I think Mr. Pettigrew is rather making the worst of things, Miss Covington," Dr. Leeds said, speaking for the first time. "No doubt the difficulties are considerable, but I think we have good heads on our side too, as Miss Purcell has proved, and I feel confident that, now that we have learned as much as we have done, we shall be successful in the end."

"My opinion," Colonel Bulstrode said, "is that we ought to give these two fellows in custody as rogues, vagabonds, and kidnapers. Then the police will set to work to find out their antecedents, and at least while they are shut up they can do no harm. Gad, sir, we should make short work of them in India."

"I am afraid that that would hardly do, Colonel Bulstrode," Mr. Pettigrew said mildly. "We have practically nothing to go upon; we have no evidence that a magistrate would entertain for a moment. The men would be discharged at once, and we should no doubt be served the next morning with a writ for at least ten thousand pounds' damages, and, what is more, they would get them; and you may be very sure that you would never find the child."

"Then it is shameful that it should be so," the Colonel said warmly; "why, I served three years as a police officer in India, and when I got news that a dacoit, for instance, was hiding in a jungle near a village, down I would go, with a couple of dozen of men, surround the place, and make every man and woman a prisoner. Then the police would examine them, and let me tell you that they have pretty rough ways of finding out a secret. Of course I knew nothing about it, and asked no questions, but you may be sure that it was not long before they made someone open his mouth. Hanging up a man by his thumbs, for instance, freshens his memory wonderfully. You may say that this thorough way of getting at things is not according to modern ideas. I don't care a fig for modern ideas, and, as far as that goes, neither do the natives of India. My object is to find out the author of certain crimes; the villagers' object is to shield him. If they are obstinate, they bring it on themselves; the criminal is caught, and justice is satisfied. What is the use of police if they are not to catch criminals? I have no patience with the maudlin nonsense that prevails in this country, that a criminal should have every chance of escape. He is warned not to say anything that would incriminate himself, material evidence is not admitted, his wife mayn't be questioned. Why, it is downright sickening, sir. The so-called spirit of fairness is all on the side of the criminal, and it seems to me that our whole procedure, instead of being directed to punish criminals, is calculated to enable them to escape from punishment. The whole thing is wrong, sir—radically wrong." And Colonel Bulstrode wiped his heated forehead with a huge Indian silk handkerchief. Hilda laughed, Netta smiled, and Mr. Pettigrew's eyes twinkled.

"There is a good deal in what you say, Colonel Bulstrode, though I cannot go with you in the matter of hanging men up by their thumbs."

"Why, sir," broke in Colonel, "what is it? Their own native princes would have stretched them over a charcoal fire until they got the truth out of them."

"So, possibly, would our own forefathers, Colonel."

"Humph! They had a lot more common sense in those days than they have now, Mr. Pettigrew. There was no sentimentality about them; they were short and sharp in their measures. They were men, sir—men. They drank like men, and they fought like men; there was sterling stuff in them; they didn't weaken their bodies by drinking slops, or their minds by reading newspapers."

"Well, Colonel Bulstrode," Hilda said, smiling, "if it is not contrary to your convictions, we will go upstairs and have a cup of tea. No doubt there is something to be said for the old days, but there is a good deal to be said on the other side of the question, too."

When they went upstairs Dr. Leeds sat down by Netta.

"I am afraid that you blame me for what I did, Dr. Leeds," she said timidly.

"No, I do not blame you at all for doing it, but I do think that you ought to have consulted us all before undertaking it. Your intention was a noble one, but the risk that you ran was so great that certainly I should not have felt justified in allowing you to undertake it, had I had any voice in the matter."

"But I cannot see that it was dangerous," the girl said. "He could not have knocked me down and beaten me, even if he had caught me with my eye at the peep-hole. He could only have called up Johnstone and denounced me as an eavesdropper, and at the worst I should only have been turned straight out of the house."

"I do not think that that would have been at all his course of action. I believe, on the contrary, that although he would have spoken angrily to you, he would have said nothing to the lodging-house keeper. He would have at once guessed that you had not taken all this trouble merely to gratify a silly curiosity, but would have been sure that you had been employed as a spy. What he would have done I do not know, but he would certainly have had you watched as you watched him, and he would, in his conversation with his confederates, have dropped clews that would have sent us all off on wild-goose chases. I don't think that he would have ventured on getting you removed, for he would have known that he would have been suspected of foul play at once by those who had employed you. I hope you will give me a promise that you will never undertake any plan without consulting Miss Covington and myself. You can hardly realize what anxiety I have suffered while you have been away."

"I will promise willingly, Dr. Leeds. I did not think anything of the danger, and do not believe even now there was any; but I do think that Hilda would not have heard of my going as a servant, and that you would not have approved of it. Still, as I saw no harm in it myself, I thought that for once I would act upon my own ideas."

"There are circumstances under which no one need disapprove of a lady acting as a servant," he said quietly. "If a family misfortune has happened, and she has to earn her own living, I think that there are many who would be far happier in the position of a servant in a good family, than as an ill-paid and over-worked governess. The one is at least her own mistress, to a large extent, as long as she does her work properly; the other can never call her time her own. In your case, certainly, the kind object with which you undertook the task was a full justification of it, had you not been matching yourself against an unscrupulous villain, who, had he detected your disguise, would have practically hesitated at nothing to rid himself of you. It happened, too, in this case you were one of the few persons who could have succeeded; for, as you say, it would have been next to impossible for anyone unpossessed of your peculiar faculty to have overheard a conversation, doubtless conducted in a somewhat low voice, through such a hole as you made."

"Then you don't think any worse of me for it?"

"You need not be afraid of that," he said quietly. "My opinion is already so fixed on that subject that I doubt if anything you could do would shake it."

Then he got up and walked across to where the others were chatting together.

"Now, are we to have another council?" Hilda asked.

"I think not," Dr. Leeds said; "it seems to me that the matter requires a great deal of thinking over before we decide, and fortunately, as the man went down to Tilbury only two days ago, he is not likely to repeat his visit for another month at least, possibly for another three months. Men like that do not give away chances, and he would probably pay for three months' board for the child at a time, so as to avoid having to make the journey oftener, however confident he might be that he was not watched."

"I agree with you, Dr. Leeds," Mr. Pettigrew said. "It would never do to make a false step."

"Still," Hilda urged, "surely there cannot be any need to wait for his going down again. A sharp detective might find out a good deal. He could inquire whether there was anyone at Tilbury who let out traps. Probably nothing beyond a gig or a pony-cart could be obtained there. He would, of course, hire it for a drive to some place within three or four miles, and while it was got ready would casually ask if it was often let; he might possibly hear of someone who came down from town—a bagman, perhaps, who hired it occasionally for calling upon his customers in the villages round."

"I think that that is a capital suggestion," Mr. Pettigrew said. "I don't see why, while we are thinking over the best way to proceed, we should not get these inquiries made. They might be of some assistance to us. I will send a man down to-morrow or next day. As you say, it may give us something to go upon."

Netta went down two days later to Reading. She had the box labeled to Oxford, and took a third-class ticket for herself. She had a suspicion that a man who was lolling on a seat on the platform looked closely at her, and she saw him afterwards saunter away towards the luggage office. When the train came in her box was put into the van, and she got out at the next station and returned by the first train to London, feeling satisfied that she would never hear anything more of the box.

The next day a detective called who had been engaged earlier in the search for Walter and had frequently seen Hilda.

"Mr. Pettigrew said, Miss Covington, that I had better come to you and tell you exactly what I have done. I went down to Tilbury yesterday. I took with me one or two cases made up like a traveler's samples, and I presently found that the man at the public house by the water had a pony-trap which he let. I went over to him and said that I wanted it for the day.

"'How far are you going?' he asked.

"'I am going to Stanford,' I said; 'then by a crossroad by Laindon to Hornchurch and back.'

"'It is rather a long round for one day,' he said.

"''Tis a long round,' I said. 'Well, maybe I might sleep at Hornchurch, and go on to Upminster.'

"'You will have to pay a deposit of a couple of pounds,' he said, 'unless you like to take a boy.'

"I said I preferred driving myself, and that it was less weight for the pony. 'I suppose you often let it out?' I remarked.

"'Pretty often,' he said; 'you see, there is no way of getting about beyond this. It would pay me to keep a better trap if it wasn't that commercials generally work this country in their own vehicles, and take the road from Barking through Dagenham, or else from Brentwood or Chelmsford or one of the other Great Eastern stations. There is one in your line comes occasionally; he goes by the same route you are taking, and always has the trap to himself. He travels for some spirit firm, I think; he always brings down a couple of cases of bottles.'

"'That is my line too,' I said. 'He hasn't been here lately, I hope?'

"'Well, yes, he was here three or four days ago; he is a pretty liberal chap with his samples, I should say, for he always comes back with his cases empty.' Of course I hired the pony and trap. I drove through New Tilbury, Low Street, and Stanford. I put up there for three or four hours. At each place I went to all the public houses, and as I marked the liquors cheap I got several orders. I asked at every place had anyone in my line been round lately, and they all said no, and nobody had noticed the pony cart; but of course that did not prove that he might not have driven through there."

"You did not make any inquiries about a missing child?"

"No, Miss Covington. Mr. Pettigrew particularly told me that I was not to make any inquiries whatever."

"Yes, that is what we agreed upon, Bassett; we don't want to run the slightest risk of their suspecting that we are inquiring in that direction. My own idea is that you could do no harm if you went round several times, just as you did yesterday; and perhaps it would be better for you not to start from the same place, but to hire a vehicle and drive round the country, stopping at all the villages, and apparently trying to get orders for spirits or tobacco. That idea of yours is an excellent one, because your inquiry whether another man had been along in the same trade would seem natural. You might say everywhere that you had heard of his going round there, but that it did not look much like business driving a rickety little trap with a pony not worth fifty shillings. At any village public houses at which he stopped they could hardly help noticing it, and if you heard that he had put up there for an hour or two, it would certainly be something to go upon, and a search round there might lead to a result. However, do not go until you hear again from me. I will talk it over with Mr. Pettigrew, and see what he thinks of it."

"It certainly seems to me that we might light upon a clew that way, Miss Covington, and if he were to happen to hear that another man in the same line had been there asking questions about him, it would seem natural enough, because of course a commercial would like to know what line another in the same branch was following, and how he was doing. Then I will wait your further orders. There would be sure to be traps to be hired at Barking or Rainham, and if there are not, I could get one at Bromley. Indeed, as I should want it for a day or two, it would be just as well to get it there as farther east, and I should be likely to get a better-looking turnout. In little places a man with a good turnout is more likely to do business than one who looks second-rate altogether. It seems a sort of credit to the place; and they would give him orders where they would not to a man who made no sort of show. I should say, miss, that as I shall be going over the ground more than once, it would be best to send on the goods I get orders for; they don't amount to very much, and I should get about the same price that I gave for them. I know a clerk in the firm whose liquors I took down. I told him that I was going down in that part of Essex, and asked if they would give me a commission on anything that I could sell. They said 'yes' willingly enough, and the clerk said I was a respectable man who could be trusted; and so it will cost nothing, and will open the way for my making another call. Of course when I am known there I can ask questions more freely, sit in the bar-parlor, smoke a cigar with the landlord, and so on."

"I think that is an excellent idea. Well, at any rate you shall hear in the course of a day or two."

Miss Purcell had gone on quietly with her knitting and uttered no remarks while the man was present. Immediately he had left, she said, "I think, Netta, that we shall gradually get at it."

"Yes, I think so; that man seems really a sharp fellow. I had quite lost all faith in detectives, but I see that when they have really got something to go upon, they know how to follow it up."

Hilda wrote a long letter to Mr. Pettigrew, and received three words in answer: "By all means." So Bassett was written to and told to continue his career as a commercial traveler, but to abstain altogether, for the present, from any questions about the boy.

Ten days later Mr. Pettigrew forwarded a letter that he had received from Bassett, which was as follows:

> "Sir: I have to report that I have for the last fortnight been engaged in driving about the country in accordance with Miss Covington's instructions. The only place where I can ascertain that the pony and cart from Tilbury was noticed about that time was at Stanford. My inquiries there before had failed, but after dining at the inn, I went out into the yard behind, and asked the helper whether the same trap that I drove over in from Tilbury had been there since.
>
> "'Not since you were here last,' he said; 'at least if it was you as drove the pony over somewhere about three weeks ago. I did not see you then, I was doing a job over at the cowhouse. That pony aint been here since then, though he was here two days before. The man put him up for three or four hours, and hired a horse from the landlord to ride over to Billericay. He must have gone cross country, I should say, by the mud on its legs. However, he tipped me a bob, so I cleaned it up and said nothing to master; but the horse was all in a lather and must have been taken

along at a hunting pace all the way.' Waiting further orders,

"I remain,
"Yours respectfully,
"H. BASSETT."

Mr. Pettigrew came down himself in theevening.

"Well, Miss Covington, I think that the scent is getting warm. Now is the time that you must be very cautious. I think we may take it that the child is somewhere within ten or twelve miles of Stanford, north or east of it. The man was away for over three hours, and he rode fast. It's not likely that the horse was anything out of the way. However, allowing for half an hour's stay somewhere, I think we may take twelve miles as the limit. Still, a circle of twelve miles' radius covers a very large area. I have been looking up the map since that man set about inquiring down there. Twelve miles would include the whole of the marshes as far as Leigh. It goes up to Brentwood, Billericay, Downham, and touches Rayleigh; and in that semicircle would be some sixty or seventy villages, large and small."

"I have been looking at the map too, Mr. Pettigrew, and it does not seem to me at all likely that he would go near the places that you first mentioned; they are quite close to the Great Eastern Railway, by which he would have traveled, instead of going round such an enormous detour by Tilbury and Stanford."

"One would think so, my dear, certainly; but, you see, a man having the least idea that he was watched, which I admit we have no reason for believing that this fellow has, would naturally choose a very circuitous route. However, I think that we need hardly try so far to the north, to begin with; I should say that the area of our search need go no farther north than Downham, and that between a line running west from that place and the river the child is most likely to be hidden."

"I should say, Mr. Pettigrew, that the detective might engage four or five fellows who could act separately in villages on each of the roads running from Stanford east or northeast. The villages should be at least two miles away from Stanford, because he might start by one road and then turn off by another. But in two miles he would probably settle down on the road he was going to follow and we should, therefore, get the general direction of Walter's hiding place. Then, as soon as he passed, the watcher should follow him on foot till he met him coming back. If he did meet him, he would know that at any rate he had been farther; if he did not meet him, he would know that he had turned off somewhere between him and the village that he had passed. Netta and I have been talking the matter over, and it seems to us that this would be the best plan, and that it would be as well, also, to have a man to watch at Tilbury Station; because he may possibly choose some entirely different route the next time he comes, and the men in the villages, not knowing that he had come down at all, might be kept there for a month waiting for his next visit."

"You and your friend have certainly put your heads together to good purpose," the old lawyer said, "and I do not see any better plan than you suggest. You had better have Bassett down here, and give him your instructions yourself."

"Yes, Mr. Pettigrew; and I shall be glad if you will write a line to him to-night, for in three days it will be a month since this man last went down, or at any rate since we know that he went down. Of course, it may be three months before he goes again, and if he does not come in four or five days the men must be recalled; for although each of them could stop in a village for a day or two under the pretense of finding work in the neighborhood, they certainly could not stop for a month."

"Very well, I leave you a free hand in the matter, altogether, Miss Covington; for frankly I acknowledge that you are vastly more likely to ferret the thing out than I am."

CHAPTER XXI.

A BOX AT THE OPERA.

"I tell you what it is, Simcoe," Harrison said two months later, "this affair of yours is getting to be a good deal more troublesome than I bargained for. It all looked simple enough; one only had to pick up a child, drive him in a cab across London, then down in a trap to Pitsea, hand him over to a man I knew would take good care of him, and take the payments for him when they became due, which would be no trouble, as I had to see the man occasionally on my own business. Of course I expected that there would be a big hue and cry for him, but I had no fear whatever of his being found. Then I managed through another man to get that body from the workhouse undertaker, and you managed the rest easily enough; but I tell you that the matter is getting a good deal hotter than I ever thought it would.

"I told you that I had been followed several times after leaving your place, and one morning when I went out early I saw footmarks, showing that someone had been walking round my house and trying to look in at the windows. I have a strong suspicion that I have been followed to my office, and I know that someone got in there one day at my dinner hour. I know, because I always fasten a piece of thread, so that if the door is opened it breaks it. There is nothing there that anyone could make anything of, but it is just as well to know if anyone has been prying about. The woman of the house was sure that she had not been in there, nor had she let anyone in; so the lock must have been picked. Of course anyone is liable to have his office robbed when he is out and it is empty; but nothing was taken, and if a common thief had found nothing else he would probably have made off with my dress suit, which would have brought him a sov. in a second-hand clothes shop.

"You know I have an excessive objection to being watched. I have had nothing on hand lately, at any rate nothing that has come off, but I might have had, you know. Well, yesterday I was going down to see my man in the marshes, and to tell him that likely enough I should bring something down to him next week. I got out of the train at Tilbury, and, as you know, there are not a dozen houses anywhere near the station. Now, I have a habit of keeping my eyes open, and I saw a man sitting on an old boat. What called my attention particularly to him was that he was turned half round watching the entrance to the station as I came out. You can always tell whether a man is watching for someone, or whether he is merely looking generally in that direction, and this man was certainly watching for someone. The instant his eye fell upon me he turned round and stared at the river. The path to the public house lay just behind him. Now, it would be natural that hearing a footstep a man doing nothing would look round and perhaps say a word—ask the time, or something of that sort. Well, he didn't turn round. Now, it is my habit, and a very useful one, always to carry a glass of about the size of a folded letter in my pocket. Instead of going on to the public house I turned off from the path and walked away from the river. When I had got some little distance I took out my glass, and still walking along, I held it up so that I could see in it what was going on behind. The man was standing up, watching me. I put the glass in my pocket and dropped my handkerchief. I stooped down to pick it up, of course partly turning as I did so, and saw that he had instantly dropped into a sitting position again, with his back to me.

"That was good enough. I turned, cut across the fields, went straight back to the station and took the next ferry-boat to Gravesend, and came back that way. It is quite clear to me that not only is this girl on the track still, but the chase is getting to be a very hot one, and that not only are they watching you, but they are watching me, and have in some way or other, though how, I cannot guess, found out that I go down to Tilbury, and have accordingly sent a man down to follow me. Now, I tell you frankly, I will have no more to do with the matter—that is to say, as far as going down on your business. As I have told you, I have always managed my own affairs so well that the police and I have no acquaintance whatever; and I am not going to be spied upon and followed and have the 'tecs upon my track about an affair in which I have no interest at all, except that, you having stood by my brother, I was glad to do you any service I could. But this is getting serious. I don't like it. I have told you I have business with the man, and get things off abroad through him that I should have great trouble in getting rid of in any other way; but unless in quite exceptional cases, these things are so small that they could be hidden away for months without much risk of their being found, however sharp the hunt after them might be. As I am in no way pressed for money I can afford to wait, though I own that I like to get the things off my hands as soon as I can, and as I considered that I ran practically no risk in going down with them into Essex, I never kept them at my house. However, for a time I must do so. I must tell you that when I am going down I always write beforehand and make an appointment for him to have his barge at the wharf at Pitsea, and I send my letter addressed to him: 'Mr. William Nibson, barge *Mary Ann*, care of Mr. Scholey, Spotted Horse, Pitsea.' You had better write to him in future. You need not put anything inside the envelope except notes for twenty-five pounds, and the words, 'For the child's keep for six months.' I need not say that you had better disguise your writing, both on the envelope and on the inside, and it is best that you should get your notes from some bookmaker on a race-course. You tell me you often go to races now and do a little betting. They are not the sort of men who take the numbers of the notes they pay out, and it would be next to impossible for them to be traced to you."

"Thank you, Harrison; you have behaved like a true pal to me, and I am ever so much obliged to you. I quite see what you mean, and indeed it is as much for my interest as yours that you should not go down there any more. Confound that girl Covington! I am sure she is the moving spirit of it all. I always felt uneasy about her from the first, and was sure that if there was any trouble it would come from her. I wonder how the deuce she ever found out that you went down to Tilbury."

"That beats me too, Simcoe. As you may guess, I am always most cautious about it, and always take a very roundabout way of going to the station."

"I have been uneasy ever since that girl at our place left so suddenly. A fortnight afterwards we found that there was a hole bored through the doorpost. Of course it might have been bored before I went there; but in that case it is curious that it was never noticed before. I cannot help thinking that she did it."

"Yes, you told me; but you said that you tried the experiment, and found that when your man and his wife were talking there in a loud voice, and you had your ear at the hole, you could not catch a single word."

"Yes, that was certainly so. I could hear them talking, but I could not make out a word of their conversation. Still it is evident that somebody has been trying to hear. I cannot help thinking that it was that girl, though both Johnstone and his wife spoke very highly of her. Certainly the story she told them was true to a certain extent, for when they sent the box down to Reading I sent a man down there to watch, and she called to fetch it, and my man found out that she labeled it 'Oxford,' and took it away with her on the down train. As he had no directions to follow her farther he came back. After we found the hole I sent him down again; but he never came upon her traces, though he inquired at every village near Oxford."

"She may have been put there as a spy," the other said; "but as it is evident that she couldn't hear through that hole, it is clear that she could not have done them any good. That is, I suppose, why they called her off; so the puzzle still remains how they got on my track at Tilbury. I should like to have a good look at this Covington girl. I can admire a clever wench, even when she is working against me."

"There is 'The Huguenots' at Her Majesty's to-night, the first time this season. She very often goes in Lady Moulton's box, and it is likely enough that she will go to-night. It's the third box from the stage, on the first tier; I will go down to Bond Street and see if I can get hold of a box opposite, on the second or third tier. The money will be well laid out, for I should very much like you to study her face, and I won enough at pool at the club this afternoon to pay for it."

"Very well, then I will come round to your place. I really am curious to see the girl. I only caught a passing glimpse of her in the park that day."

Simcoe was not wrong in his conjecture, for Hilda dined at Lady Moulton's, and they took their places in the latter's box just as the first bar of the overture sounded. She was in half mourning now, and in black lace, with white camellias in her hair and breast, was, as Netta had told her before starting, looking her best.

"That is the girl," Simcoe exclaimed, as she went forward to the front of the box.

"Well, there is no denying that she is good-looking," the other said, as he turned his glasses upon her; "there is not a better-looking woman in the house. Plenty of self-possession too," he added, as Hilda took her seat and at once, in apparent ignorance that any glasses were upon her, took her own lorgnettes from their case and proceeded calmly to scan the stalls and boxes, to see who among her numerous acquaintances were there. As her eyes fell upon the two men sitting nearly opposite to her, her glasses steadied, then after a minute she lowered them.

"Lady Moulton, I regard it as a providence that you brought me here this evening. Do you see those two men there in the box nearly opposite, in the second tier? Well, one of the men is Simcoe, to whom my uncle left all his property if Walter should not live to come of age, and who I am absolutely convinced carried the child away."

"I see them, my dear; they are staring at you. I suppose they are as much interested in you as you in them."

Hilda again put her glasses to her eyes.

"She has just told Lady Moulton who I am," Simcoe said.

"She has a clever face, Simcoe—broad across the chin—any amount of determination, I should say. Ah! there, she is getting up to make room for somebody else."

"Stay where you are, my dear," Lady Moulton said, putting her hand on Hilda's arm; "there is plenty of room for three."

"Plenty," she replied; "but I want to watch those two men, and I cannot keep my glasses fixed on them while I am sitting in the front row."

"Hardly, my dear," Lady Moulton said with a smile. "Well, have your own way."

A fourth lady came in almost immediately. She took the third chair in the front, and Hilda, sitting half in the shade, was able to devote herself to her purpose free from general observation. She had already heard that Simcoe's companion had apparently suspected that he was watched, and had returned to town at once without speaking to anyone at Tilbury. She felt that he would probably henceforth choose some other route, and the chances of following him would be greatly diminished. The opportunity was a fortunate one indeed. For months she had been hoping that some day or other she could watch these men talking, and now, as it seemed by accident, just at the moment when her hopes had fallen, the chance had come to her.

"She has changed her place in order to have a better look at us," John Simcoe said, as she moved. "She has got her glasses on us."

"We came to stare at her. It seems to me that she is staring at us," Harrison said.

"Well, I should think that she knows my face pretty well by this time," Simcoe laughed. "I told you she has a way of looking through one that has often made me uncomfortable."

"I can quite understand that. I noticed myself that when she looked at us, without her glasses, there was a curious intentness in her expression, as if she was taking stock of every point about us. She cannot be the girl who has been to your lodging."

"Certainly not," the other said; "I know her a great deal too well for her to try that on. Besides, beyond the fact that the other was a good-looking girl too—and, by the way, that she had the same trick of looking full in your face when you spoke—there was no resemblance whatever between them."

The curtain now drew up, and silence fell upon the house, and the men did not speak again until the end of the first act. They then continued their conversation where they had left it off.

"She has moved, and has been attending to the opera," Simcoe said; "but she has gone into the shade again, and is taking another look at us."

"I am not given to nervousness, but upon my word those glasses fixed upon me make me quite fidgety."

"Pooh, man! she is not looking at you; she is looking at me. I don't know whether she thinks that she can read my thoughts, and find out where the child is hidden. By the way, I know nothing about this place Pitsea. Where is it, and which is the best way to get there?"

"You can drive straight down by road through Upminster and Laindon. The place lies about three miles this side of Benfleet. There are only about half a dozen houses, at the end of a creek that comes up from Hole Haven. But I should not think of going near the house. The latter, directed as I told you, is sure to find the man."

"Oh, I am not thinking of going! but I shall get a man to watch the fellows they sent down to watch you, and if I find that they seem to be getting on the right track, I shall run down at all hazards and take him away."

"Your best plan by far will be to go with him, on board Nibson's barge, up to Rochester. No doubt he can find some bargeman there who will take the boy in. Or, what would perhaps be better, hire a trap there, and drive him down to Margate or Ramsgate. There are plenty of schools there, and you might get up a yarn about his being a nephew of yours, and leave him there for a term or two. That would give you time to decide. By this time he will have but a very faint remembrance of his life in town, and anything that he may say about it will certainly meet with no attention."

"Would it be as well to do it at once, do you think?" Simcoe asked.

"No; we have no idea how many people they may have on the watch, and it would be only running unnecessary risks. Stick to the plan that we have already agreed on, of communicating only by writing. But I think your idea of sending two or three sharp fellows down there to find out what the party are doing is really a good one."

Hilda lowered her glasses as the curtain rose again. "Oh, Lady Moulton!" she whispered, "I have found out all that I have been so long wanting to know. I believe now that in three days I shall have the child home again."

Lady Moulton turned half round.

"How on earth have you found that out, Hilda? Are you a wizard indeed, who can read men's thoughts in their faces? I always thought that there was something uncanny about you, ever since that day of my fête."

To Harrison's relief, Miss Covington did not turn her glass towards him again during the evening. When the curtain fell on the next act a gentleman, to whom Lady Moulton had nodded in the stalls, came in. After shaking hands with her and her friends, he seated himself by the side of Hilda.

"Miss Covington," he said, "I have never had an opportunity of speaking to you since that fête at Lady Moulton's. I have understood that the gypsy on that occasion was engaged by you, and that there was, if you will excuse me saying so, some little mystery about it. I don't wish to pry into that, but if you should ever see the woman again you will oblige me very greatly by telling her that I consider I owe her a deep debt of gratitude. She said something to me then that made a tremendous impression upon me, and I do not mind telling you it brought me up with a round turn. I had been going ahead a great deal too fast, and I see now that, had I continued on the same course, I should have brought absolute ruin upon myself, and blighted my life in every way. The shock she gave me by warning me what would come if I did not give up cards and racing showed me my utter folly, and on that day I swore never to touch a card or lay a penny upon a horse for the rest of my life. When I tell you that I have completely pulled myself round, and that, by the aid of an old uncle, to whom I went and made a clean breast of all, I am now straight in every way, and, as you may have heard, am going to be married to Miss Fortescue in a fortnight, you may guess what deep reason I have to be grateful to this gypsy woman of yours, and how I hope that, should you come across her again, you will tell her so, and should there be any possible way in which I can prove my gratitude, by money or otherwise, I shall be delighted to do so."

"I will tell her, Captain Desmond," the girl said in a low voice. "I am sure that it will make her happy to know that she did some good that evening. I do not think that she is in need of money or assistance of any kind, but should she be so I will let you know."

"And do you really mean that you have discovered where General Mathieson's grandson is living?" Lady Moulton asked, as they rose to leave their seats when the curtain fell.

"I think so; I am almost sure of it."

Lady Moulton had heard a good deal from Hilda as to the situation. Mr. Pettigrew had strongly impressed upon both Hilda and Colonel Bulstrode that it was very important that the contents of the will should not be talked about. "We don't want our private affairs discussed in the press and made the subject of general talk," he had said, and it was only to Lady Moulton that Hilda had spoken freely of the matter, so far as the discovery of the new will, the change that had been made, and the singularity of Walter being missing. She had also mentioned her belief that Simcoe was at the bottom of this, but had breathed no words of her suspicion that the General had come to his death by foulplay, or of her own conviction that Simcoe was an impostor, although there had been some talk in the clubs over the matter, for Colonel Bulstrode was by no means so discreet as Hilda, and among his intimate friends spoke his mind with great vehemence and strength of language as to General Mathieson having made so singular a disposition of his property, and he made no secret of his suspicion that Simcoe was at the bottom of Walter's disappearance. Thus the matter had gradually gone the round of the clubs; but it was not until Simcoe's own counsel had drawn from him the fact that Walter's death would put him into possession of the estate that the public in general learned the facts.

"It was a clever move," Mr. Pettigrew had said, talking it over with his partner. "No doubt he was afraid that the question would be asked by our counsel, and he thought that it was better that the fact should come voluntarily from himself. His best plan by far was to brazen it out. No doubt nine men out of ten will consider that the affair is a very suspicious one, and some of them will give him the cold shoulder; but whatever their opinions, they dare not express them without laying themselves open to an action for libel, while, on the other hand, the fact that a man is heir to a good estate will always cause a good many to rally round him. Not the best of men, you know, but enough to prevent his being a lonely figure in a club.

"Yes, I think he was certainly well advised to declare his heirship voluntarily, instead of having it drawn from him. He must have known, of course, that sooner or later the matter would be made public, and it is better for him to get the talk and gossip over now instead of the matter being known for the first time when he begins to take legal steps to compel us to put him into possession of the estate."

"What on earth did you mean, Hilda," Lady Moulton said, as the door of the carriage was closed and they drove off from Her Majesty's, "by saying that you had discovered a clew by which you might in a few days find your little cousin?"

"I cannot tell you exactly how I discovered it. At present it is a secret that both my mother and uncle charged me to keep, but when these troubles are over I will explain it all to you, though I should certainly do so to no one else."

"Well, I suppose I must be content with that, Hilda. But it certainly does seem extraordinary to me that by merely seeing two men in a box on the other side of the house you should have obtained a clew to what you have for a year now been trying to get at."

"It does seem extraordinary, Lady Moulton, but it really is not so, and I hope to convince you that I am right by producing Walter in a week from the present time."

"I hope you will, Hilda. I sincerely hope so, both for the child's sake, yours, and my own. Of course, when he is found there will be no possible reason for your keeping yourself shut up as you have done. I have missed you very much, and shall be very glad to have you under my wing again."

"Thank you for saying so, Lady Moulton; but so far as I have formed my plans, they are that Walter's trustees shall either let or sell the house in Hyde Park Gardens, and that I shall go down for a time with him into the country. I have had a great deal of anxiety this last year, and I shall be very glad of complete rest for a time."

"That is reasonable enough, my dear, but I do hope that you are not thinking of burying yourself in the country for good. There, I am at home. Good-night, Hilda; thanks for the lift. It is not often my horses or my coachmen have a night off during the season."

CHAPTER XXII.

NEARING THE GOAL.

"I suppose Miss Netta is in bed?" Hilda asked, as she entered the house.

"Yes, miss; she and Miss Purcell went to their rooms soon after ten o'clock."

Hilda ran upstairs to Netta's room.

"Are you awake, Netta?" she asked, as she opened the door.

"Well, I think I was asleep, Hilda; I didn't intend to go off, for I made sure that you would come in for a chat, as usual, when you got back; but I think I must have dozed off."

"Well, if you had been so sound asleep that I had had to violently wake you up, I should have done so. I have had my chance, Netta. Simcoe and his friend were in a box opposite to ours, and I have learned where Walteris."

"That is news indeed," Netta exclaimed, leaping up; "that is worth being awakened a hundred times for. Please hand me my dressing-gown. Now let us sit down and talk it over comfortably."

Hilda then repeated the whole conversation that she had overheard.

"Splendid!" Netta exclaimed, clapping her hands; "and that man was right, dear, in feeling uncomfortable when your glasses were fixed on his face, though he little guessed what reason he had for the feeling. Well, it is worth all the four years you spent with us to have learned to read people's words from their lips. I always said that you were my best pupil, and you have proved it so now. What is to be done next?"

"We shall need a general council for that!" Hilda laughed. "We must do nothing rash now that success seems so close; a false move might spoil everything."

"Yes, we shall have to be very careful. This bargeman may not live near there at all; though no doubt he goes there pretty often, as letters are sent there for him. Besides, Simcoe may have someone stationed there to find out whether any inquiries have been made for a missing child."

"Yes, I see that we shall have to be very careful, Netta, and we must not spoil our chances by being over hasty."

They talked for upwards of an hour, and then went to their beds. The next morning Roberts took a note to Dr. Leeds. It contained only a few lines from

Hilda:

> "My Dear Dr. Leeds: We have found a most important clew, and are going to have a consultation, at which, of course, we want you to be present. Could you manage to be at Mr. Pettigrew's office at three o'clock? If so, on hearing from you, I will send to him to make an appointment."

The answer came back:

> "I congratulate you heartily, and will meet you at three o'clock at Pettigrew's office."

A note was at once sent off to the lawyer's to make the appointment, and the girls arrived with Miss Purcell two or three minutes before the hour, and were at once shown into Mr. Pettigrew's room, where Mr. Farmer immediately joined them.

"I will wait a minute or two before I begin," Hilda said. "I have asked Dr. Leeds to join us here. He has been so very kind throughout the whole matter that we thought it was only fair that he should be here."

"Certainly, I thoroughly agree with you. I never thought that terrible suspicion of his well founded, but he certainly took immense pains in collecting information of all sorts about these native poisons, and since then has shown the greatest desire to assist in any way."

A minute later Dr. Leeds was shown in.

"Now, Miss Covington," Mr. Farmer said, "we are ready to hear your communication."

Hilda then related what she had learned at the opera.

"Really, Miss Covington," Mr. Farmer continued, "it is a thousand pities that you and your friend cannot utilize your singular accomplishment in the detective line. You ought to make a fortune by it. I have, of course, heard from my partner of the education that you had in Germany, and of your having acquired some new system by which you can understand what people are saying by watching their lips, but I certainly had no conception that it could be carried to such an extent as you have just proved it can. It is like gaining a new sense. Now I suppose you have come to us for advice as to what had best be done next."

"That is it, Mr. Farmer. It is quite evident to us that we must be extremely careful, for if these people suspect that we are so far on their track, they might remove Walter at once, and we might never be able to light upon a clew again."

"Yes, I see that. Of course, if we were absolutely in a position to prove that this child has been kept down near Pitsea with their cognizance we could arrest them at once; but, unfortunately, in the words you heard there was no mention of the child, and at present we have nothing but a series of small circumstantial facts to adduce. You believe, Mr. Pettigrew tells me, that the man who calls himself John Simcoe is an impostor who has no right to the name, and that General Mathieson was under a complete delusion when he made that extraordinary will. You believe that, or at any rate you have a suspicion that, having got the General to make the will, he administered some unknown drug that finally caused his death. You believe that, as this child alone stood between him and the inheritance, he had him carried off with the assistance of the other man. You believe that the body the coroner's jury decided to be that of Walter Rivington was not his, and that the child himself is being kept out of the way somewhere in Essex, and you believe that the conversation that you most singularly overheard related to him.

"But, unfortunately, all these beliefs are unsupported by a single legal fact, and I doubt very much whether any magistrate would issue a warrant for these men's arrest upon your story being laid before him. Even if they were arrested, some confederate might hasten down to Pitsea and carry the child off; and, indeed, Pitsea may only be the meeting-place of these conspirators, and the child may be at Limehouse or at Chatham, or at any other place frequented by barges. Therefore we must for the present give up all idea of seizing these men. Any researches at Pitsea itself are clearly attended by danger, and yet I see no other way of proceeding."

"It seems," Dr. Leeds said, "that this other man, who appears to have acted as Simcoe's agent throughout the affair, took the alarm the other day, and instead of taking a trap as usual from Tilbury, returned to the station, took the ferry across to Gravesend, and then, as we suppose, came up to town again, told Simcoe that he found he was watched, and that Simcoe must himself take the matter up. Evidently, by what Miss Covington overheard, he had instructed him where and how to communicate with this bargeman, or in case of necessity to find him. I should think that the first step would be to withdraw the men now on watch, for it is possible that they may also send down men to places in the locality of Pitsea. In point of fact, your men have been instructed to make no such inquiries, but only to endeavor to trace where Simcoe's agent drives to. Still, I think it would be as well to withdraw them at once, as they can do no further good."

Mr. Pettigrew nodded.

"I know nothing of Pitsea," the doctor went on, "but I do know Hole Haven. When I was walking the hospital, three or four of us had a little sailing-boat, and used to go out from Saturday until Monday morning. Hole Haven was generally the limit of our excursions. It is a snug little harbor for small boats, and there is a comfortable old-fashioned little inn there, where we used to sleep. The coastguards were all sociable fellows, ready to chat with strangers and not averse to a small tip. Of course the same men will not be there now, nor would it be very safe to ask questions of them; for no doubt they are on friendly terms with the men on the barges which go up and down the creek. I might, however, learn something from them of the ways of these men, and I should think that, on giving my card to the petty officer in charge, I could safely question him. I don't suppose that he would know where this man Nibson has his headquarters. If he lives at Rochester, or Chatham, or at Limehouse, or Shadwell, he certainly would not know him; but if he lives at Pitsea he might know him. I fancy they keep a pretty sharp lookout on the barges. I know that the coastguard told me that there was still a good deal of smuggling carried on in the marshes between Leigh and Thames Haven. I fancy, from what he said, that the Leigh fishermen think it no harm to run a few pounds of tobacco or a keg of spirit from a passing ship, and, indeed, as there are so many vessels that go ashore on the sands below, and as they are generally engaged in unloading them or helping them to get off, they have considerable facilities that way. At any rate, as an old frequenter of the place and as knowing the landlord—that is to say if there has been no change there —no suspicion could fall upon me of going down there in reference to your affair. To-day is Friday. On Sunday morning, early, I will run down to Gravesend, hire a boat there, and will sail down to Hole Haven. It will be an outing for me, and a pleasant one; and at least I can be doing no harm."

"Thank you very much indeed, Dr. Leeds," Hilda said warmly; "that is a splendid idea."

On Sunday evening Dr. Leeds called at Hyde Park Gardens to report his day's work.

"I think that my news is eminently satisfactory. I saw the petty officer in command of the coastguard station, and he willingly gave me all the information in his power. He knew the bargee, Bill Nibson. He is up and down the creek, he says, once and sometimes twice a week. He has got a little bit of a farm and a house on the bank of the creek a mile and a half on this side of Pitsea. They watch him pretty closely, as they do all the men who use the creek; there is not one of them who does not carry on a bit of smuggling if he gets the chance.

"'I thought that was almost given up,' I said. 'Oh, no; it is carried on,' he replied, 'on a much smaller scale than it used to be, but there is plenty of it, and I should say that there is more done that way on the Thames than anywhere else. In the first place, Dutch, German, and French craft coming up the channels after dark can have no difficulty whatever in transferring tobacco and spirits into barges or fishing-boats. I need hardly say it is not ships of any size that carry on this sort of business, but small vessels, such as billy-boys and craft of that sort. They carry their regular cargoes, and probably never bring more than a few hundredweight of tobacco and a dozen or so kegs of spirits. It is doubtful whether their owners know anything of what is being done, and I should say that it is generally a sort of speculation on the part of the skipper and men. On this side the trade is no doubt in the hands of men who either work a single barge or fishing-boat of their own, or who certainly work it without the least suspicion on the part of the owners.

"'The thing is so easily arranged. A man before he starts from Ostend or Hamburg, or the mouth of the Seine, sends a line to his friends here, at Rochester or Limehouse or Leigh, "Shall sail to-night. Expect to come up the south channel on Monday evening." The bargeman or fisherman runs down at the time arranged, and five or six miles below the Nore brings up and shows a light. He knows that the craft he expects will not be up before that time, for if the wind was extremely favorable, and they made the run quicker than they expected, they would bring up in Margate Roads till the time appointed. If they didn't arrive that night, they would do so the next, and the barge would lay there and wait for them, or the fishermen would go into Sheerness or Leigh and come out again the next night.

"'You might wonder how a barge could waste twenty-four or forty-eight hours without being called to account by its owners, but there are barges which will anchor up for two or three days under the pretense that the weather is bad, but really from sheer laziness.

"'That is one way the stuff comes into the country, and, so far as I can see, there is no way whatever of stopping it. The difficulty, of course, is with the landing, and even that is not great. When the tide turns to run out there are scores, I may say hundreds, of barges anchored between Chatham and Gravesend. They generally anchor close in shore, and it would require twenty times the number of coastguards there are between Chatham and Gravesend on one side, and Foulness and Tilbury on the other, to watch the whole of them and to see that boats do not come ashore.

"'A few strokes and they are there. One man will wait in the boat while the other goes up onto the bank to see that all is clear. If it is, the things are carried up at once. Probably the barge has put up some flag that is understood by friends ashore; they are there to meet it, and in half an hour the kegs are either stowed away in lonely farmhouses or sunk in some of the deep ditches, and there they will remain until they can be fished up and sent off in a cart loaded with hay or something of that sort. You may take it that among the marshes on the banks of the Medway and Thames there is a pretty good deal done in the way of smuggling still. We keep a very close eye upon all the barges that come up here, but it is very seldom that we make any catch. One cannot seize a barge like the *Mary Ann*, that is the boat belonging to Nibson, with perhaps sixty tons of manure or cement or bricks, and unload it without some specific information that would justify our doing so. Indeed, we hardly could unload it unless we took it out into the Thames and threw the contents overboard. We could not carry it up this steep, stone-faced bank, and higher up there are very few places where a barge could lie alongside the bank to be unloaded. We suspect Nibson of doing something that way, but we have never been able to catch him at it. We have searched his place suddenly three or four times, but never found anything suspicious.'

"'May I ask what family the man has?' I said.

"He shook his head. 'There is his wife—I have seen her once or twice on board the barge as it has come in and out—and there is a boy, who helps him on the barge—I don't know whether he is his son or not. I have no idea whether he has any family, but I have never seen a child on the barge.'

"All this seemed to be fairly satisfactory. I told him that we suspected that a stolen child was kept in Nibson's house, and asked him whether one of his men off duty would, at any time, go with me in a boat and point out the house. He said that there would be no difficulty about that. My idea, Miss Covington, was that it would be by far the best plan for us to go down with a pretty strong party—that is to say, two or three men—and to go from Gravesend in a boat, arriving at Hole Haven at eleven or twelve o'clock at night. I should write beforehand to the coastguard officer, asking him to have a man in readiness to guide us, and then row up to the house. In that way we should avoid all chance of a warning being sent on ahead from Pitsea, or from any other place where they might have men on watch.

"I mentioned this to the officer, and he said, 'Well, I don't see how you could break into the man's house. If the child is not there you might find yourself in a very awkward position, and if Nibson himself happened to be at home he would be perfectly justified in using firearms.' I said of course that was a point I must consider. It is indeed a point on which we must take Mr. Pettigrew's opinion. But probably we shall have to lay an information before the nearest magistrate, though I think myself that if we were to take the officer into our confidence—and he seemed to me a bluff, hearty fellow—he would take a lot of interest in the matter, and might stretch a point, and send three or four men down after dark to search the place again for smuggled goods. You see, he has strong suspicions of the man, and has searched his place more than once. Then, when they were about it, we could enter and seize Walter. Should there be a mistake altogether, and the child not be found there, we could give the officer a written undertaking to hold him free in the very unlikely event of the fellow making a fuss about his house being entered."

The next morning Hilda again drove up with Netta to see Mr. Pettigrew.

"We must be careful, my dear; we must be very careful," he said. "If we obtain a search warrant, it can only be executed during the day, and even if the coastguards were to make a raid upon the place, we, as civilians, would not have any right to enter the house. I don't like the idea of this night business—indeed, I do not see why it should not be managed by day. Apparently, from what Dr. Leeds said, this Hole Haven is a place where little sailing-boats often go in. I don't know much of these matters, but probably in some cases gentlemen are accompanied by ladies, and no doubt sometimes these boats go up the creeks. Now, there must be good-sized boats that could be hired at Gravesend, with men accustomed to sailing them, and I can see no reason why we should not go down in a party. I should certainly wish to be there myself, and think Colonel Bulstrode should be there. You might bring your two men, and get an information laid before an Essex magistrate and obtain a warrant to search this man's place for a child supposed to be hidden there. By the way, I have a client who is an Essex magistrate; he lives near Billericay. I will have an information drawn out, and will go myself with it and see him; it is only about five miles to drive from Brentwood Station. If I sent a clerk down, there might be some difficulty, whereas, when I personally explain the circumstances to him, he will, I am sure, grant it. At the same time I will arrange with him that two of the county constabulary shall be at this place, Hole Haven, at the time we arrive there, and shall accompany us to execute the warrant. Let me see," and he turned to his engagement book, "there is no very special matter on for to-morrow, and I am sure that Mr. Farmer will see to the little matters that there are in my department. By the way, it was a year yesterday since the General's death, and we have this morning been served with a notice to show cause why we should not proceed at once to distribute the various legacies under his will. I don't think that refers to the bequest of the estates, though, of course, it may do so, but to the ten thousand pounds to which Simcoe is clearly entitled. Of course, we should appear by counsel in any case; but with Walter in our hands we can bring him to his knees at once, and he will have to wait some time before he touches the money. We cannot prevent his having that. He may get five years for abducting the child, but that does not affect his claim to the money."

"Unless, Mr. Pettigrew, we could prove that he is not John Simcoe."

"Certainly, my dear," the lawyer said, with an indulgent smile. "Your other theories have turned out very successful, I am bound to admit; but for this you have not a shadow of evidence, while he could produce a dozen respectable witnesses in his favor. However, we need not trouble ourselves about that now. As to the abduction of the child, while our evidence is pretty clear against the other man, we have only the fact against Simcoe that he was a constant associate of his, and had an immense interest in the child being lost. The other man seems to have acted as his intermediary all through, and so far as we actually know, Simcoe has never seen the child since he was taken away. Of course, if Walter can prove to the contrary, the case is clear against him; but without this it is only circumstantial, though I fancy that the jury would be pretty sure to convict. And now, how about the boat? Who will undertake that? We are rather busy at present, and could scarcely spare a clerk to go down."

"We will look after that, Mr. Pettigrew; it is only an hour's run to Gravesend, and it will be an amusement for us. We will take Roberts down with us. What day shall we fix it for?"

"Well, my dear, the sooner the better. I shall get the warrant to-morrow, and there is no reason why the constable should not be at Hole Haven the next day, at, say, two in the afternoon. So if you go down to-morrow and arrange for a boat, the matter may as well be carried out at once, especially as I know that you are burning with anxiety to get the child back. Of course this rascal of a bargeman must be arrested."

"I should think that would depend partly on how he has treated Walter," Hilda said. "I don't suppose he knows who he is, or anything of the circumstances of the case; he is simply paid so much to take charge of him. If he has behaved cruelly to him it is of course right that he should be punished; but if he has been kind to him I don't see why he should not be let off. Besides, we may want him as a witness against the others."

"Well, there is something in that. Of course we might, if he were arrested, allow him to turn Queen's evidence, but there is always a certain feeling against this class of witness. However, we needn't discuss that now. I suppose that we ought to allow an hour and a half or two hours to get to this place from Gravesend, but you can find that out when you hire the boat. Of course, it will depend a good deal on which way the tide is. By the way, you had better look to that at once; for if it is not somewhere near high tide when we get to Hole Haven there may not be water enough to row up the creek."

He called in one of the clerks, and told him to go out to get him an almanac with a tide-table.

"I want to know when it will be high water the day after to-morrow at Gravesend," he said.

"I can tell you that at once, sir. When I came across Waterloo Bridge this morning at a quarter to nine the tide was running in. I should say that it was about half-flood, and would be high about twelve o'clock. So that it will be high about half-past one o'clock on Wednesday. It is about three-quarters of an hour earlier at Gravesend. I don't know whether that is near enough for you, sir?"

"Yes, that is near enough, thank you. So, you see," he went on after the clerk had left the room, "the tide will be just about high when you get to Gravesend, and you will get there in about an hour, I should say. I don't know exactly how far this place is, but I should say seven or eight miles; and with a sail, or, if the wind is contrary, a couple of oars, you will not be much above an hour, and I should think that there will be still plenty of water in the creek. You had better see Colonel Bulstrode. As joint trustee he should certainly be there."

They drove at once to the Colonel's and found him in. He had not heard of the discovery Hilda had made, and was greatly excited at the prospect of so soon recovering Walter, and bringing, as he said, "the rascals to book."

The next morning they went down with Roberts to Gravesend, to engage a large and roomy boat with two watermen for their trip. Just as they were entering Hyde Park Gardens, on their return, a man passed them. Roberts looked hard at him, and then said, "If you don't want me any more now, miss, I should like to speak to that man; he is an old fellow-soldier."

"Certainly, Roberts. I shall not want you again for some time."

Roberts hurried after the man. "Sergeant Nichol," he said, as he came up to him, "it is years since I saw you last."

"I remember your face, if I do not remember your name," the man said.

"I am Tom Roberts. I was in your company, you know, before you went onto the staff."

"I remember you now, Roberts," and the two shook hands heartily. "What are you doing now? If I remember right, you went as servant to General Mathieson when you got your discharge."

"Yes; you see, I had been his orderly for two or three years before, and when I got my discharge with my pension, I told him that I should like to stop with him if he would take me. I was with him out there for five years after; then I came home, and was with him until his death, and am still in the service of his niece, Miss Covington, one of the young ladies I was with just now. And what are you doing?"

"I am collector for a firm in the City. It is an easy berth, and with my pension I am as comfortable as a man can wish to be."

So they chatted for half an hour, and when they parted Roberts received a hearty invitation to look in at the other's place at Kilburn.

"Both my boys are in the army," he said, "and likely to get on well. My eldest girl is married, my youngest is at home with her mother and myself; they will be pleased to see you too. The missus enjoys a gossip about India, and is always glad to welcome any old comrade of mine."

CHAPTER XXIII.

WALTER.

The wind was westerly, and the boat ran fast down the river from Gravesend; Roberts and Andrew, both in civilian clothes, were sitting in the bows, where there were stowed a large hamper and a small traveling-bag with some clothes. One waterman sat by the mast, in case it should be necessary to lower sail; the other was aft at the tiller. The men must have thought that they had never had so silent and grave a pleasure party before: two elderly gentlemen and two girls, none of whom seemed inclined to make merry in any way. Colonel Bulstrode, indeed, tried hard to keep up a conversation about the ships, barges, and other craft that they met, or which lay at anchor in the stream, and recalling reminiscences of trips on Indian rivers.

Netta was the only one of his hearers who apparently took any interest in the talk. To her the scene was so new that she regarded everything with attention and pleasure, and looked with wonder at the great ships which were dragged along by tiny tugs, wondered at the rate at which the clumsy-looking barges made their way through the water, and enjoyed the rapid and easy motion with which their own boat glided along. Mr. Pettigrew was revolving in his mind the problem of what should next be done; while Hilda's thoughts were centered upon Walter, and the joy that it would be to have him with her again.

"This is Hole Haven," the boatman in the stern said, as a wide sheet of water opened on their left.

"Why don't you turn in, then?" Colonel Bulstrode asked.

"There is scarce water enough for us, sir; they are neap tides at present, and in half an hour the sands will begin to show all over there. We have to go inonto the farther side—that is, where the channel is. You see those craft at anchor; there is the landing, just in front of the low roof you see over the bank. That is the 'Lobster Smack,' and a very comfortable house it is; and you can get as good a glass of beer there as anywhere on the river."

As they turned into the creek they saw two constables on the top of the bank, and at the head of the steps stood a gentleman talking with a coastguard officer.

"That is my friend, Mr. Bostock," Mr. Pettigrew said. "He told me that, if he could manage it, he would drive over himself with the two constables. I am glad that he has been able to do so; his presence will strengthen our hands."

A coast guard boat, with four sailors in it, was lying close to the steps, and the officer came down with Mr. Bostock, followed by the two constables. The magistrate greeted Mr. Pettigrew and took his place in the boat beside him, after being introduced to the two ladies and the Colonel. The officer with the two constables stepped into the coastguard boat, which rowed on ahead of the other.

"I could not resist the temptation of coming over to see the end of this singular affair, of which I heard from Mr. Pettigrew," Mr. Bostock said to Hilda. "The officer of the coastguard is going on, partly to show us the way to the house, and partly because it will be a good opportunity for him to search the place thoroughly for smuggled goods. He tells me that the barge is up the creek now; it went up yesterday evening. So we may find the fellow at home."

"Now, my men," Colonel Bulstrode said to the boatmen, "we have got to follow that boat. You will have plenty of time for beer when you get there, and a good lunch besides. So pull your hardest; we have not got very far to go. Can either of you men row?"

"I AM A MAGISTRATE OF THE COUNTY OF ESSEX."

"I can pull a bit," Roberts said, and, aided by the sail and the three oars, the boat went along at a fair rate through the water, the coastguard boat keeping a short distance ahead of them. After a quarter of an hour's rowing the bargeman's house came in view. The revenue officer pointed to it.

"Now, row your hardest, men," Colonel Bulstrode said; "we have but a hundred yards further to go."

The two boats rowed up to the bank together; Mr. Bostock sprang out, as did the constables and sailors, and ran up the bank, the others following at once. As they appeared on the bank a boy working in the garden gave a shrill whistle; a man immediately appeared at the door and looked surprised at the appearance of the party. He stepped back a foot, and then, as if changing his mind, came out and closed the door after him.

"I am a magistrate of the County of Essex," Mr. Bostock said, "and I have come to see a warrant executed for the search of your house for a child named Walter Rivington, who is believed to be concealed here, and who has been stolen from the care of his guardians."

"I know nothing of any child of that name," the man replied, "but I have a child here that I am taking care of for a gentleman in London; I have had him here for just a year, and no one has made any inquiries about him. You are welcome to enter and see if he is the one you are in search of. If he is, all that I can say is that I know nothing about his being stolen, and shall be very sorry to lose him."

He stood aside, and the two constables entered, followed closely by Hilda. The latter gave a cry of joy, for seated on the ground, playing with a box of soldiers, was Walter. She would hardly have known him anywhere else. His curls had been cut short, his face was brown and tanned, and his clothes, although scrupulously clean, were such as would be worn by any bargeman's boy at that age. The child looked up as they entered. Hilda ran to him, and caught him up in her arms.

"Don't you know me, Walter? Don't you remember Cousin Hilda?"

"Yes, I remember you," the child said, now returning her embrace. "You used to tell me stories and take me out in a carriage for drives. Where have you been so long? And where is grandpapa? Oh, here is Netta!" and as Hilda put him down he ran to her, for during the four months spent in the country she had been his chief playmate.

"I have learned to swim, Netta. Uncle Bill has taught me himself; and he is going to take me out in his barge some day."

The woman, who had come in with her arms covered with lather, from the little washhouse adjoining the house, now came forward.

"I hope, miss, that there is nothing wrong," she said to Hilda. "We have done our best for the little boy, and I have come to care for him just as if he had been my own; and if you are going to take him away I shall miss him dreadful, for he is a dear little fellow," and she burst into tears.

Walter struggled from Netta's arms, and ran to the woman, and, pulling her by the apron, said:

"Don't cry, Aunt Betsy; Jack is not going away from you. Jack will stay here; he likes going in a barge better than riding in a carriage."

"Well, Miss Covington," Mr. Bostock said, "the recognition appears to be complete on both sides; now what is the next step? Do you give this man into custody for unlawfully concealing this child and aiding and abetting in his abduction?"

"Will you wait a minute while I speak to Mr. Pettigrew?" she said; and they went out of the house together.

"Well, what do you think, Mr. Pettigrew?"

"I have been thinking it over all the way as we came down," the lawyer said. "Of course, we have no shadow of proof that this man was aware who the child was, and, in fact, if he had seen the placards offering altogether fifteen hundred pounds for his recovery, we must certainly assume that he would have given him up; for however well he may have been paid for taking charge of him, the offer would have been too tempting for a man of that kind to have resisted. No doubt he had strong suspicions, but you can hardly say that it amounted to guilty knowledge that the child had been abducted. If Walter had been ill-treated I should have said at once, 'Give him into custody'; but this does not seem to have been the case."

"No; they have evidently been very kind to him. I am so grateful for that that I should be sorry to do the man any harm."

"That is not the only point," the lawyer went on. "It is evident that the other people very seldom come down here, and from what you heard, in future Simcoe is going to write. If we arrest this man the others will know at once that the game is up. Now, if you will take the child away quietly, we can tell the man that he shall not be prosecuted, providing that he takes no steps whatever to inform his employers that the child is gone; even if one of them came down here to see the child, the wife must say that he is away on the barge. Anyhow, we shall have ample time to decide upon what steps to take against Simcoe, and can lay hands upon him whenever we choose; whereas, if he got an inkling that we had discovered the child, he and his associate would probably disappear at once, and we might have lots of trouble to find them."

"Yes, I think that would be a very good plan, Mr. Pettigrew. I will ask him and his wife to come out."

"That will be the best way, my dear. We could hardly discuss the matter before Bostock."

Hilda went in. As soon as she spoke to the man and his wife Mr. Bostock said, "If you want a conference, Miss Covington, I will go out and leave you to talk matters over."

He and the two constables withdrew, and Mr. Pettigrew came in.

"Now, my man," he began, "you must see that you have placed yourself in a very awkward position. You are found taking care of a child that has been stolen, and for whose recovery large rewards have been offered all over the country. It is like the case of a man found hiding stolen goods. He would be called upon to account for their being in his possession. Now, it is hardly possible that you can have been ignorant that this child was stolen. You may not have been told so in words, but you cannot have helped having suspicions. From what the child no doubt said when he first came here, you must have been sure that he had been brought up in luxury. No doubt he spoke of rides in a carriage, of servants, his nurse, and so on. However, Miss Covington is one of the child's guardians, and I am the other, and we are most reluctant to give you in charge. It is evident, from the behavior of the child, and from the affection that he shows to yourself and your wife, that you have treated him very kindly since he has been here, and these toys I see about show that you have done your best to make him happy."

"That we have, sir," the man said. "Betsy and I took to him from the first. We have no children of our own, none living at least, and we have made as much of him as if he had been one of our own—perhaps more. We have often talked it over, and both thought that we were not doing the fair thing by him, and were, perhaps, keeping him out of his own. I did not like having anything to do with it at first, but I had had some business with the man who gave him to me, and when he asked me to undertake the job it did not seem to me so serious an affair as it has done since. I am heartily sorry that we have had any hand in it; not only because we have done the child harm, but because it seems that we are going to lose him now that we have come to care for him as if he was our own."

"Of course you played only a minor part in the business, Nibson. We quite understand that, and it is the men who have carried out this abduction that we want to catch. Do you know the name of the man who brought the child to you?"

"I don't, sir. He knows where to find me, but I have no more idea than a child unborn who he is or where he lives. When he writes to me, which he generally does before he comes down, which may be two or three times a month, or may be once in six months, he signs himself Smith. I don't suppose that is his right name, but I say fairly that if I knew it, and where he lived, I would not peach upon him. He has always been straight with me in the business I have done with him, and I would rather take six months for this affair than say anything against him."

"We are not asking you at present to say anything against him, and he is not the principal man in this business. I believe he is only acting as agent for another more dangerous rascal than himself. We are not prepared at the present moment to arrest the chief scoundrel. Before we do that we must obtain evidence that will render his conviction a certainty. We have reason to believe that this man that you know will not come down for some time, and that you will receive the money for the child's keep by post; but if we abstain altogether from prosecuting you in this matter, you must give us your word that you will not take any steps whatever to let them know that the child is no longer with you. He says that you promised to take him out in your barge. Well, if by any chance this man—not your man, but the other—comes down here, and wants to see the child, you or your wife will lead him to believe that he is on board your barge. It will also be necessary that, if we do arrest them, you should enter as a witness to prove that the man handed the child over to you. You could let it be seen that you are an unwilling witness, but the evidence of the handing over of the child will be an absolute necessity."

"All right, sir, I will undertake that. There is no fear of my letting him know that the child has gone, for I don't know where to write him; and if he or the other should come down, if I am here I shall have no difficulty in keeping it from him that the child has gone, for my man has never set foot in this house. He just meets me on the road near Pitsea, says what he has to say, and gives me what he has to give me, and then drives off again. Of course, if I am summoned as a witness, I know that the law can make me go. I remember now that when he gave me the child he said he was doing it to oblige a friend of his, and he may be able to prove that he had nothing to do with carrying it off."

"That is as it may be," the lawyer said dryly. "However, we are quite content with your promise."

"And I thank you most heartily, you and your wife," Hilda Covington said warmly, "for your kindness to the child. It would have made me very happy all this time if I could have known that he was in such good hands, but I pictured him shut up in some vile den in London, ill treated, and half starved. He has grown very much since he has been with you, and looks a great deal more boyish than he did."

"Yes, he plays a good deal with my barge boy, who has taken to him just as we have."

"Well, your kindness will not be forgotten nor unrewarded, Mr. Nibson."

"I'm sure we don't want any reward, miss; we have been well paid. But even if we hadn't been paid at all after the first month, we should have gone on keeping him just the same."

"Now, Walter," Hilda said, "we want you to come home with us; we have all been wanting you very badly. Nurse and Tom Roberts have been in a terrible way, and so has Dr. Leeds. You remember him, don't you? He was very kind to you all the time that you were down in the country."

The child nodded. "I should like to see Tom Roberts and nurse, but I don't want to go away. I am going out in the barge soon."

"Well, dear, I dare say that we shall be able to arrange for you to come down sometimes, and to go out in it, especially as you have learned to swim. We are going away now in a boat."

"I often go out in the boat," Walter pouted. "I go with Joshua; he is a nice boy, Joshua is, and I like him."

"Well, dear, we will see what we can do for Joshua."

"You are sure that I shall come back and go out in the barge?"

"Quite sure, dear; and perhaps I will go out with you, too."

"Yes, you must go, like a good boy," Mrs. Nibson said. "You know, dear, that I shall always love you, and shall be very, very glad if the ladies can spare you to come down to see me sometimes. You won't forget me, will you?"

"No, Aunt Betsy, I shall never forget you; I promise you that," the child said. "And I don't want to go away from you at all, only Cousin Hilda says I must."

Mr. Pettigrew went out to tell Mr. Bostock that they should not give Nibson into custody.

"The principal scoundrels would take the alarm instantly," he said, "and, above all things, we want to keep them in the dark until we are ready to arrest them. It will be much better that we should have this man to call as a witness than that he should appear in the dock as an accomplice."

"I think that you are right there," the magistrate agreed; "and really, he and his wife seem to have been very kind to the child. I have been talking to this young barge boy. It seems he is no relation of these people. His mother was a tramp, who died one winter's night on the road to Pitsea. He was about ten or eleven years old then, and they would have sent him to the workhouse; but Nibson, who was on the coroner's jury, volunteered to take him, and I dare say he finds him very useful on board the barge. At any rate, he has been well treated, and says that Nibson is the best master on the river. So the fellow must have some good in him, though, from what the coastguard officer said, there are very strong suspicions that he is mixed up in the smuggling business, which, it seems, is still carried on in these marshes. Well, no doubt you have decided wisely; and now, I suppose, we shall be off."

At this moment they were joined by the coastguard officer.

"He has done us again," he said. "We have been investigating these outhouses thoroughly, and there is no question that he has had smuggled goods here. We found a clever hiding-place in that cattle-shed. It struck me that it was a curious thing that there should be a stack of hay built up right against the side of it. So we took down a plank or two, and I was not surprised to find that there was a hollow in the stack. One of the men stamped his foot, and the sound showed that there was another hollow underneath. We dug up the ground, and found, six inches below it, a trapdoor, and on lifting it discovered a hole five or six feet deep and six feet square. It was lined with bricks, roughly cemented together. It is lucky for him that the place is empty, and I should think that after this he will go out of the business for a time. Of course we cannot arrest a man merely for having a hidden cellar; I fancy that there are not many houses on the marshes that have not some places of the sort. Indeed, I am rather glad that we did not catch him, for in other respects Nibson is a decent, hard-working fellow. Sometimes he has a glass or two at the 'Lobster Smack,' but never takes too much, and is always very quiet and decent in his talk. I doubt whether the men would have found that hiding-place if I had not been there; they all know him well, and would not get him into a scrape if they could help it, though there are some fellows on the marshes they would give a month's pay to catch with kegs or tobacco."

The door of the house opened, and the three women and Nibson came out with Walter, who was now dressed in the clothes that they had brought down for him.

While the others were getting ready to enter the boat the officer took Nibson aside.

"You have had a close squeak of it, Nibson; we found your hiding-place under the stack, and it is lucky for you that it was empty. So we have nothing to say to you. I should advise you to give it up, my man; sooner or later you are bound to be caught."

The man's brow had darkened as the officer began, but it cleared up again.

"All right," he said; "I have been thinking for the last half hour that I shall drop the business altogether, but when a man once gets into it, it is not so easy to get out. Now that you have found that cellar, it is a good excuse to cut it. I can well say that I dare not risk it again, for that, after so nearly catching me, you would be sure to keep an extra sharp eye on me in the future."

"You give me your word for that, Nibson?"

"Yes, sir; I swear off it altogether from the present day."

"Good. I will take your word for it, and you can go in and come out as you like without being watched, and you need not fear that we shall pay you another visit."

Walter went off in fair spirits. The promise that he should come down again and see his friends and have a sail in the barge lessened the pang of leaving, and as Hilda's and Netta's faces came more strongly back to him, as they talked to him and recalled pleasant things that had almost faded from his memory, he went away contentedly, while Betsy Nibson went back to the house and had what she called "a good cry." She too, however, cheered up when her husband told her how narrow an escape he had had, and how he had given his word that he would drop smuggling altogether.

"That makes my mind easier than it has been for years, Bill. And will you give up the other thing, too? There may not be much harm in running kegs and bacca, but there is no doubt about its being wrong to have anything to do with stolen goods and to mix yourself up with men who steal them."

"Yes, I will give that up, too, Betsy; and, as soon as I have time to look round, I will give an order for a new barge to be built for me. I have been ashamed of the old thing for a long time past with her patched sails. Of course, she suited my purpose, for when the other barges kept on their course it gave me a good excuse for anchoring; but it aint pleasant to have every barge passing you. There is old Joe Hargett; he said the other day that, if I ever thought of getting a new barge, he would give a hundred for her. He has got a set of decent sails, and he is a pretty handy carpenter, and no doubt he will make her look decent again. A hundred pounds aint much, but it will help. I can get a new one complete, sails and all, for fourteen or fifteen hundred, and have a hundred or two left in the bag afterwards. I tell you what, Betsy, I will get an extra comfortable cabin made, and a place forward for Joshua. It will be dull for you here now the child is gone, and it would be a sight more comfortable for us both to be always together."

"That it will, Bill," she said joyfully. "I was always very happy on board till we lost our Billy. I took a dislike to it then, and was glad enough to come here; but I have got over it now, and this place is very lonely during the long winter nights when you are away."

Then they talked over the barge, and how the cabin should be fitted up, and, in spite of having lost Walter, the evening was a pleasant one to them.

That was not the only conversation that took place that day with reference to a new barge for Bill Nibson. As they rowed up against the tide, Hilda said:

"We must do something for that bargeman, Colonel Bulstrode. I am sure we cannot be too grateful to him and his wife for their treatment of Walter. Think how different it might have been had he fallen into bad hands. Now he looks the picture of health; the change in the life and the open air has done wonders. You know, Dr. Leeds said that the officer of the coastguard had told him that Nibson's barge was one of the oldest and rottenest crafts on the river. Now, I propose that we buy him a new one. What would it cost, Colonel Bulstrode?"

"I have not the slightest idea," the Colonel replied; "it might cost five hundred pounds, or it might cost five thousand, for all I know."

"I will ask the waterman," Hilda said, and raising her voice she said, "How much do barges cost when they are new?"

"From ten or eleven hundred up to fifteen," the man said.

"Does that include sails and all?"

"Yes, miss; down to the boat."

"Who is considered the best barge-builder?"

"Well, there are a good many of them, miss; but I should say that Gill, of Rochester, is considered as good as any."

"What do you think, Mr. Pettigrew?" Hilda said. "Should we, as Walter's guardians, be justified in spending this money? Mind, I don't care a bit whether we are or not, because I would buy it myself if it would not be right for us to use his money."

"I am afraid that it would not be right," Mr. Pettigrew said. "As a trustee of the property, I should certainly not feel myself justified in sanctioning such a sum being drawn, though I quite admit that this good couple should be rewarded. I cannot regard a barge as a necessary; anything in reason that the child could require we should be justified in agreeing to. Of course, whatever may be his expenses at a public school, we should pay them without hesitation; but for a child of that age to give a present of fifteen hundred pounds would be altogether beyond our power to sanction."

"Very well," Hilda said decidedly, "then I shall take the matter into my own hands, and I shall go down to Rochester to-morrow and see if these people have a barge ready built. I don't know whether they are the sort of things people keep in stock."

"That I can't say, my dear. I should think it probable that in slack times they may build a barge or two on speculation, for the purpose of keeping their hands employed, but whether that is the case now or not I don't know. If these people at Rochester have not got one you may hear of one somewhere else. I want you all to come up to the office one day next week to talk over this matter of the order Simcoe is applying for—for us to carry out the provisions of the will—at any rate, as far as his legacy is concerned."

"Very well, Mr. Pettigrew, I will come up any time that you write to me, but you know that I have very strong opinions about it."

"I know your opinions are strong, as ladies' opinions generally are," Mr. Pettigrew said with a smile; "but, unfortunately, they are much more influenced by their own view of matters than by the legal bearing of them. However, we will talk that over when we meet again."

The arrival of Walter occasioned the most lively joy in Hyde Park Gardens. Hilda had written to his nurse, who had gone home to live with her mother when all hope of finding Walter had seemed to be at an end, to tell her that he would probably be at home on Wednesday evening, and that she was to be there to meet him. Her greeting of him was rapturous. It had been a source of bitter grief to her that he had been lost through a momentary act of carelessness on her part, and the relief that Hilda's letter had caused was great indeed. The child was scarcely less pleased to see her, for he retained a much more vivid recollection of her than he did of the others. He had already been told of his grandfather's death, but a year had so effaced his memory of him that he was not greatly affected at the news. In the course of a few hours he was almost as much at home in the house as if he had never left it.

CHAPTER XXIV.

A NEW BARGE.

The next morning Hilda went down to Rochester with Netta, Tom Roberts accompanying them. They had no difficulty in discovering the barge-builder's. It seemed to the girls a dirty-looking place, thickly littered as it was with shavings; men were at work on two or three barges which seemed, thus seen out of the water, an enormous size.

"Which is Mr. Gill?" Hilda asked a man passing.

"That is him, miss," and he pointed to a man who was in the act of giving directions to some workmen. They waited until he had finished, and then went up to him.

"I want to buy a barge, Mr. Gill," Hilda said.

"To buy a barge!" he repeated in surprise, for never before had he had a young lady as a customer.

Hilda nodded. "I want to give it to a bargeman who has rendered me a great service," as if it were an everyday occurrence for a young lady to buy a barge as a present. "I want it at once, please; and it is to be a first-class barge. How much would it cost?"

The builder rubbed his chin. "Well, miss, it is a little unusual to sell a barge right off in this way; as a rule people want barges built for them. Some want them for speed, some want them for their carrying capacity."

"I want a first-class barge," Hilda replied. "I suppose it will be for traffic on the Thames, and that he will like it to be fast."

"Well, miss," the builder said slowly, for he could not yet quite persuade himself that this young lady was really prepared to pay such a sum as a new barge would cost, "I have got such a barge. She was launched last week, but I had a dispute with the man for whom I built her, and I said that I would not hold him to his bargain, and that he could get a barge elsewhere. He went off in a huff, but I expect he will come back before long and ask me to let him have her, and I should not be altogether sorry to say that she is gone. She is a first-class barge, and I expect that she will be as fast as anything on the river. Of course, I have got everything ready for her—masts, sails, and gear, even down to her dingey—and in twenty-four hours she would be ready to sail. The price is fifteen hundred pounds," and he looked sharply at Hilda to see what effect that communication would have. To his great surprise she replied quietly:

"That is about the sum I expected, Mr. Gill. Can we look at her?"

"Certainly, miss; she is lying alongside, and it is nearly high tide."

He led the way over piles of balks of timber, across sloppy pieces of ground, over which at high tide water extended, to the edge of the wharf, where the barge floated. She was indeed all ready for her mast; her sides shone with fresh paint, her upper works were painted an emerald green, a color greatly in favor among bargemen, and there was a patch of the same on her bow, ready for the name, surrounded by gilt scrollwork.

"There she is, miss; as handsome a barge as there is afloat."

"I want to see the cabin. What a little place!" she went on, as she and Netta went down through a narrow hatchway, "and how low!"

"It is the usual height in barges, miss, and the same size, unless especially ordered otherwise."

"I should like the cabin to be made very comfortable, for I think the boatman will have his wife on board. Could it not be made a little larger?"

"There would be no great difficulty about that. You see, this is a water-tight compartment, but of course it could be carried six feet farther forward and a permanent hatchway be fixed over it, and the lining made good in the new part. As to height, one might put in a good-sized skylight; it would not be usual, but of course it could be done."

"And you could put the bed-place across there, could you not, and put a curtain to draw across it?"

"Yes, that could be managed easy enough, miss; and it would make a very tidy cabin."

"Then how much would that costextra?"

"Forty or fifty pounds, at the outside."

"And when could you get it all finished, and everything painted a nice color?"

"I could get it done in a week or ten days, if you made a point ofit."

"I do make a point of it," Hilda said.

"What do you say to our leaving this bulkhead up as it is, miss, and making a door through it, and putting a small skylight, say three feet square, over the new part? You see, it will be fifteen feet wide by six feet, so that it will make a tidy little place. It would not cost more than the other way, not so much perhaps; for it would be a lot of trouble to get this bulkhead down, and then, you see, the second hand could have his bunk in here, on the lockers, and be quite separate."

"Isn't there a cabin at the other end?"

"Well, there is one, miss; you can come and look at it. That is where the second hand always sleeps when the bargeman has got his wife on board."

"I think that it would be better to have the second hand sleep there," Hilda said. "This is very rough," she went on, when she inspected the little cabin forward; "there are all the beams sticking out. Surely it can be made more comfortable than this."

"We could matchboard the timbers over if you like, but it is not usual."

"Never mind, please do it; and put some lockers up for his clothes, and make it very comfortable. Has the barge got a name yet?"

"Well, miss, we have always called her the *Medway*; but there is no reason that you should stick to that name. She has not been registered yet, so we can call her any name you like."

"Then we will call her the *Walter*," Hilda said, for the girls had already settled this point between them.

"And now, Mr. Gill, I suppose there is nothing to do but to give you a check for fifteen hundred pounds, and I can pay for the alterations when I come down next Monday week. Can you get me a couple of men who understand the work—bargees, don't you call them? I want them to take her as far as Hole Haven and a short way up the creek."

"I can do that easily enough," the builder said; "and I promise you that everything shall be ready for sailing, though I don't guarantee that the paint in the new part of the cabin will be dry. All the rest I can promise. I will set a strong gang of men on at once."

A few days later Hilda wrote a line to William Nibson, saying that she intended to come down with the child on the following Monday, and hoped that he would be able to make it convenient to be at home on thatday.

"She is not long in coming down again, Betsy," he said, when on the Friday the barge went up to Pitsea again, and he received the letter, which was carried home and read by his wife, he himself being, like most of his class at the time, unable to read or write. "I suppose the child pined in his new home, and she had to pacify him by saying that he should come down and see us next week. That will suit me very well. I have a load of manure waiting for me at Rotherhithe; it is for Farmer Gilston, near Pitsea, so that I shall just manage it comfortably. Next week I will go over to Rochester and see if I can hear of a good barge for sale."

On the following Monday morning the girls again went down to Rochester, this time taking Walter with them; having the previous week sent off three or four great parcels by luggage train. Roberts went to look for a cart to bring them to the barge-builder's, and the girls went on alone.

"There she lies, miss," Mr. Gill said, pointing to a barge with new tanned sails lying out in the stream; "she is a boat any man might be proud of."

"She looks very nice indeed," Hilda said, "though, of course, I am no judge of such things."

"You may be sure that she is all right, Miss Covington."

"Is the paint dry, down below?"

"Yes. I saw that you were anxious about it, so put plenty of drier in. So that, though she was only painted on Saturday morning, she is perfectly dry now. But you are rather earlier than I had expected."

"Yes; we have sent a lot of things down by rail. Our man is getting a cart, and I dare say they will be here in a quarter of an hour."

The things were brought on a large hand-cart, and as soon as these were carried down to the boat they went off with Mr. Gill to the barge.

"There, miss," he said, as he led the way down into the cabin; "there is not a barge afloat with such a comfortable cabin as this. I put up two or three more cupboards, for as they will sleep in the next room there is plenty of space for them."

Except in point of height, the cabin was as comfortable a little room as could be desired. It was painted a light slate color, with the panels of the closets of a lighter shade of the same. The inner cabin was of the same color. A broad wooden bedstead extended across one end, and at the other were two long cupboards extending from the ceiling to the floor. The skylight afforded plenty of light to this room, while the large one in the main cabin gave standing height six feet square in the middle.

"It could not have been better," Hilda said, greatly pleased.

"Well, miss, I took upon myself to do several things in the way of cupboards, and so on, that you had not ordered, but seeing that you wanted to have things comfortable I took upon myself to do them."

"You did quite right, Mr. Gill. This big skylight makes all the difference in height. I see that you have painted the name, and that you have got a flag flying from the masthead."

"Yes; bargemen generally like a bit of a flag, that is to say if they take any pride in their boat. You cannot trade in the barge until you have had it registered; shall I get that done for you?"

"Yes, I should be very much obliged if you would."

"And in whose name shall I register it? In yours?"

"No; in the name of William Nibson. If you want his address it is Creek Farm, Pitsea."

"Well, miss, he is a lucky fellow. I will get it done, and he can call here for the register the first time he comes up the Medway."

Roberts was sent ashore again for a number of hooks, screws, and a few tools.

"Now, Mr. Gill, we are quite ready to start. We shall get things straight on the voyage."

"You will have plenty of time, miss; she will anchor off Grain Spit till the tide begins to run up hard. You won't be able to get up the creek till an hour before high tide."

"That won't matter," Hilda said; "it will not be dark till nine."

"You can get up the anchor now," the builder said to two men who had been sitting smoking in the bow.

The barge's boat was lying bottom upwards on the hatches and another boat lay behind her.

"This boat does not belong to her, Mr. Gill; does she?" Hilda asked.

"No, miss; that is the men's boat. When they have got the barge to where she is to be moored, they will row down to Hole Haven, and get a tow up with the first barge that comes down after the tide has turned. How will you be coming back, Miss Covington?"

"We have arranged for a gig to be at Hole Haven at eight o'clock to drive us to Brentwood, where we shall take train to town. We shall not be up before half-past eleven, but as we have our man with us that does not matter; besides, the carriage is to be at the station to meet the train."

The girls and Walter watched the operation of getting up the anchor and of setting the foresail and jib. They remained on deck while the barge beat down the long reach pastthe dockyards, and then with slackened sheets rounded the wooded curve down into Gillingham Reach, then, accompanied by Roberts, they went below. Here they were soon hard at work. The great packages were opened, and mattresses and bedclothes brought out.

"This reminds one of our work when you first came to us," Netta laughed, as they made the bed.

"Yes, it is like old times, certainly. We used to like to work then, because we were doing it together; we like it still more to-day, because not only are we together, but we are looking forward to the delight that we are going to give."

Carpets were laid down, curtains hung to the bed, and a wash-hand stand fixed in its place. A hamper of crockery was unpacked and the contents placed on the shelves that had been made for them, and cooking utensils arranged on the stove, which had been obtained for them by the builder. By this time Roberts had screwed up the hooks in the long cupboards, and in every spot round both cabins where they could be made available. Then numerous japanned tin boxes, filled with tea, sugar, and other groceries, were stowed away, and a large one with a label, "Tobacco," placed on a shelf for Bill Nibson's special delectation. Curtains that could be drawn were fixed to the skylights, looking-glasses fastened against the walls, and by the time that the barge neared Sheerness their labors were finished. Then the forward cabin was similarly made comfortable. Walter had assisted to the best of his power in all the arrangements, and when he became tired was allowed to go up on deck, on his promise to remain quiet by the side of the helmsman.

"Now I think that everything is in its place," Hilda said at last, "and really they make two very pretty little rooms. I can't say that the one in the bow is pretty, but at any rate it is thoroughly comfortable, and I have no doubt that Joshua will be as pleased with it as the Nibsons are with theirs. Oh, dear, how dusty one gets! and we never thought of getting water on board for the jugs."

On going up on deck, however, they observed two barrels lashed together.

"Are those water?" Hilda asked the man at the tiller.

"Yes, ma'am."

"How do you get it out? I don't see a tap."

"You put that little pump lying by the side into the bunghole. I will do it for you, miss."

"Now we will go downstairs and tidy up, and then come and sit up here and enjoy ourselves," said Hilda.

When they were below they heard a rattle of the chain, and, on going up, found that the barge had come to anchor in the midst of some thirty or forty others. The foresail had been run down and the jib lowered, but the great mainsail, with its huge, brightly painted sprit, was still standing. Roberts now opened a hamper that had been left on deck, and produced luncheon. Cold meat and beer were handed to the two watermen, who went up into the bow to eat it. An hour later the tide began to slacken, and many of the barges got up sail.

"Shall we get up the anchor, ma'am?" one of the watermen asked.

"There's plenty of time, is there not?" Hilda asked.

"Yes, ma'am, but we thought that you would like to see how she goes with the others."

"Yes, I should like that," Hilda said, and in a few minutes the barge was under sail again.

"She is a clipper, and no mistake," the man at the tiller said, as one by one they passed the barges that had started ahead of them, and Walter clapped his hands in delight.

"We may as well go down to the lower end of the Hope, miss. We shall have plenty of time to get back again before there is water enough for us in the creek."

For three hours they sailed about, the girls enjoying it as much as Walter.

"I do think, Netta, that I shall have to buy a barge on my own account. It is splendid, and, after all, the cabins are large enough for anything."

"You had better have a yacht," Netta laughed. "You would soon get tired of always going up and down the river."

"One might do worse," Hilda said. "Of course, now we shall give up that big house in Hyde Park Gardens, which is ridiculous for me and the boy. We have each got a country house, and when we want a thorough change I would infinitely rather have a yacht than a small house in town. I don't suppose that it would cost very much more. Besides, you know, it is arranged that I am always to have rooms at your house at the institute. That is to be the next thing seen after; you know that is quite agreed upon."

"I shall be glad to be at work again," Netta said. "Now that Walter is found, there is certainly nothing to keep us any longer in town."

"I know that it must have been horribly dull for you, Netta, but you see that you are partly to blame yourself for refusing to go out with me."

"That would have been duller still," Netta laughed. "I should have been a long time before I got to know people, and there is no good in knowing people when you are going right away from them in a short time, and may never meet them again."

At last the men said that there would be water enough to get up the creek.

"We shan't be able to sail up, miss; you see, the wind will be right in our teeth. But that don't matter; we can pole her up. The tide will take us along, and we shall only have to keep her straight and get her round the corners."

"Are you sure that there will be water enough?"

"Yes, miss. You see, she is empty, and doesn't draw much more than a foot of water."

As they entered the haven the head sails were dropped and the mainsail brailed up. The tide was running in strong, and, as the men had said, they had nothing to do but to keep the barge in the deepest part of thechannel.

"How do you think they will be coming, Bill?" Betsy Nibson said, as she joined her husband, who was standing on the bank dressed in his Sunday clothes.

"I cannot say, Betsy; if I had known I should have gone to meet them. They cannot drive here from Pitsea, but must walk; and, of course, I would have been there if I had been sure of their coming that way. But I should think most likely that they will drive to the haven and come up by boat."

"There is a new barge coming up the creek," Joshua said. "You can see that she is new by her spars and sails."

"That's so, boy," Bill agreed. "She has got a flag I haven't seen before at her masthead. It is white, and I think there are some red letters on it—her name, I suppose. 'Tis not often that a new barge comes up to Pitsea. She is a fine-looking craft," he went on, as a turning in the creek brought her wholly into view. "A first-class barge, I should say. Yes, there is no doubt about her being new. I should say, from the look of her spars, she cannot have made many trips up and down the river."

"She has got a party on board," Mrs. Nibson said presently. "There are two women and a child. Perhaps it's them, Bill. They may have some friend in the barge line, and he has offered to bring them down, seeing that this is a difficult place to get at."

"I believe you are right, Betsy. They are too far off to see their faces, but they are certainly not barge people."

"They are waving their handkerchiefs!" Betsy exclaimed; "it is them, sure enough. Well, we have wondered how they would come down, but we never thought of a barge."

The three hurried along the bank to meet the barge. Walter danced and waved his hat and shouted loudly to them as they approached.

"You did not expect to see us arrive in a barge, Mrs. Nibson," Hilda called out as they came abreast of them.

"No, indeed, miss; we talked it over together as to how you would come, but we never thought of a barge."

"It belongs to a friend of ours, and we thought that it would be a pleasant way of coming. She is a new boat. You must come on board and have a look at her before we land."

In a few minutes the barge was alongside the bank, opposite the house. A plank was run across and Walter scampered over it to his friends.

"Bless his little face!" Mrs. Nibson said, as she lifted him up to kiss her. "What a darling he looks, Bill! And he has not forgotten us a bit."

"He could not well forget in a week," Bill said, rather gruffly, for he, too, was moved by the warmth of the child's welcome. "Well, let us go on board and pay our respects. She is a fine barge, surely; and she has got the same name as the child."

"Why, it is not 'Jack,'" his wife said, looking up.

"Jack!" her husband repeated scornfully. "Didn't they call him Walter the other day? Go on, wife; the lady is waiting at the end of the plank for you."

Mrs. Nibson put the child down and followed him across the plank, smoothing her apron as she went.

"My best respects, miss," she said, as Hilda shook hands with her warmly.

"We are glad to see you again, Mrs. Nibson, and hope that you have not missed Walter very much."

"I cannot say that I have not missed him a good deal, miss, but, luckily, we have had other things to think about. We are giving up the farm; it is lonesome here in the winter, and I am going to take to barge life again."

"Well, what do you think of this barge, Mr. Nibson?" Hilda asked.

"I allow she is a handsome craft, and she ought to be fast."

"She is fast. We have been sailing about until there was enough water in the creek, and we have passed every barge that we have come near. She is comfortable, too. Come below and look at her cabin."

"Well, I never!" Mrs. Nibson said, pausing in astonishment at the foot of the ladder. "I have been in many barge cabins, but never saw one like this." Her surprise increased when the door of the bulkhead was opened and she saw the sleeping cabin beyond. "Did you ever, Bill?"

"No, I never saw two cabins in a barge before," her husband said. "I suppose, miss, the owner must have had the cabin specially done up for his own use sometimes, and the crew lived forward."

"There is a place forward for the second hand," she replied, "and I suppose the owner will sleep here."

"Of course it is a loss of space, but she will carry a big load, too. Who is the owner, miss, if I may make so bold as to ask?"

"The registered owner is William Nibson," Hilda said quietly.

The bargeman and his wife gazed at each other in astonishment.

"But," he said hesitatingly, "I have never heard of any owner of that name."

"Except yourself, Nibson."

"Yes, except myself; but I am not an owner, as I have sold the *Mary Ann*."

"There is no other owner now," she said, "that I know of, of that name. The barge is yours. It is bought as testimony of our gratitude for the kindness that you have shown Walter, and you see it is named after him."

"It is too much, miss," said Bill huskily, while his wife burst into tears. "It is too much altogether. We only did our duty to the child, and we were well paid for it."

"You did more than your duty," Hilda said. "The money might pay for food and shelter and clothes, but money cannot buy love, and that is what you gave, both of you; and it is for that that we now pay as well as we can."

"Miss Covington should say 'I,'" Netta broke in, "for it is her present entirely. Walter's trustees could not touch his money for the purpose, and so she has done it herself."

"Hush, Netta! You should have said nothing about it," Hilda said; and then, turning to Nibson, went on, "I am his nearest relative—his only relative, in fact—besides being his guardian, and, therefore, naturally I am the most interested in his happiness; and as, fortunately, I am myself very well off, I can well afford the pleasure of helping those who have been so good to him. Please do not say anything more about it. Now we will go on deck for a few minutes, and leave you and your wife to look round. We will show Joshua his cabin."

So saying, she and Netta went on deck. Joshua, led by Walter, was just crossing the plank. He had not received a special invitation, and he felt too shy to go on board with these ladies present. Walter, however, had run across to him, and at last persuaded him to come.

"Well, Joshua," Hilda said, as she reached him, "what do you think of the barge?"

"She is as good a one as ever I seed," the boy said.

"Well, Joshua, she belongs to Mr. Nibson."

"To Bill?" Joshua exclaimed. "You don't mean it, miss."

"I do mean it," she said; "this is his barge."

"Well, I shouldn't have thought that Bill was that artful!" Joshua exclaimed almost indignantly. "Fancy his keeping it from the missis and me that he had been and bought a new barge! But she is a fine one, there aint no doubt about that."

"Come forward and look at your cabin, Joshua. I think you will say that it is more comfortable than usual."

"Well, I am blowed!" the boy ejaculated, as he followed her down the ladder and looked round. "Why, it is a palace, that is wot it is; it is more comfortable than the master's cabin aft in most barges. And what a bed! Why, it is soft enough for a hemperor."

"There are no sheets, Joshua. They told me that the men never use sheets in barges."

"Lor' bless you! no, ma'am. We mostly stretch ourselves on the locker and roll ourselves up in a blanket, if we are lucky enough to have one. Why, I don't know as I shan't be afraid of getting into that bed, though I does take a header in the water every morning. There are lockers on both sides, too, and a basin. Who ever heard of such a thing as a basin? Why, miss, we allus washes in the pail on deck."

"Well, I should think that it would be a good deal more comfortable to wash down here in a basin on a cold morning."

"Well, I suppose it might, miss; it be sharp sometimes outside. Why, there is oilcloth all over the floor, and a mat to wipe one's feet at the bottom of the ladder, and a rug by the side of the bed! I never did see such things. Bill must have gone clean off his chump. Well, I am blessed!"

"It is Miss Covington who has given Bill the barge and seen to its being fitted up," Netta said, "and she has done her best to make your cabin as comfortable as possible, because you have been so kind to Walter."

"And I hope to do some more for you, Joshua, when I can see my way to do it. You will find two or three suits of clothes for your work in those lockers. I do not know that they will quite fit, but I dare say if they don't Mrs. Nibson can alter them for you, and you will find shirts and warm underclothing, and so on, in that cupboard."

Joshua sat down suddenly on a locker, completely overpowered with what seemed to him the immensity of his possessions.

There the girls left him, and they went up on deck again.

Going aft, they sat down and talked for a few minutes, and were then joined by Nibson and his wife. The latter still bore traces of tears on her cheeks, and there was a suspicious redness about Bill's eyes.

"We won't try to say what we would like to say," the man began, "'cause we could not say it, but we feels it just the same. Here we are with everything man or woman could wish for, ready to hand."

"As I have said before, Nibson, please do not say anything more about it. It has made me quite as happy to get this barge for you, and to make it comfortable, as it can do you both to receive it. And now we will go ashore."

In the house they found that tea was ready, save pouring the water into the pot. A ham and a couple of cold chickens were on the table, and jam and honey were specially provided for Walter. Joshua did not make one of the party. After recovering from the contemplation of his own cabin he had gone aft and remained in almost awe-struck admiration at the comfort and conveniences there, until summoned by Bill to take his place and help to get the new boat into the water, and to row the ladies down to Hole Haven.

CHAPTER XXV.

A CRUSHING EXPOSURE.

The case of the application by John Simcoe for an order for the trustees of the will of the late General Mathieson to carry its provisions into effect was on the list of cases for the day. Tom Roberts was walking up and down in Westminster Hall, waiting for it to come on, when he saw a face he knew.

"Hullo, Sergeant Nichol, what brings you here?"

"Just curiosity, Roberts. I happened to see in the list of cases one of Simcoe against the trustees of General Mathieson. 'What,' I said to himself, 'Simcoe? That is the name of the chap who saved General Mathieson's life.' I remember their being both brought into cantonment, as well as if it were yesterday. I was with Paymaster-Sergeant Sanderson, the fellow who bolted a short time afterwards with three hundred pounds from the pay-chest and never was heard of afterwards. We heard that Simcoe was drowned at sea; and sorry we all were, for a braver fellow never stepped in shoe leather, and there was not a man there who did not feel that he owed him a debt of gratitude for saving the brigadier's life. So when I saw the paper I said to myself, 'Either the man was not drowned at all, or he must be some relation of his. I will go into court and have a look at him.'"

"It is the same man, but I am sorry to say that, though he may be as brave as a lion, he is a rogue. But you can see him without going into court. That is him, talking with the man in a wig and gown and that little man in black, who is, I suppose, his lawyer. He knows me, so I won't go near him; but you can walk as close as you like to him, and take a good look at him."

Not content with looking once, Sergeant Nichol passed him backwards and forwards three times. When he rejoined Roberts the latter saw that he looked flushed and excited.

"What is it, sergeant?"

"I don't believe it is Simcoe at all," the sergeant said. "It is that man Sanderson I was speaking about just now. Several of us noticed how like he was to Simcoe, but the expression of their faces was different. Simcoe was five or six years younger, and had a pleasant expression; Sanderson had a hard face. None of us liked him, he was a man one could never get friendly with; you might be in the same mess for years and not know more about him at the end than you did at the beginning. Of course, they would both be changed a good deal by this time, but I don't believe that Simcoe would have grown so as to be like this man; and I am sure that Sanderson would. He had a mark on him that I should know him by. One day when he was a recruit his musket went off, and the ball went through his left forearm. It was only a flesh wound, but it left a blackened scar, and I will bet all that I am worth that if you turned up that fellow's sleeve you would find it there."

"That is very important, sergeant. I will go and tell my young lady; she is talking with her lawyers and Colonel Bulstrode at the other end of the hall."

Hilda clapped her hands.

"What do you say now, Mr. Pettigrew? I was right, after all. Bring your friend up, Roberts, and let us hear his story ourselves."

Sergeant Nichol was fetched, and repeated the story that he had told to Roberts.

"Thank you very much, sergeant," the barrister said. "Please remain here while we talk it over. What do you think of this, Mr. Pettigrew?"

"It would seem to explain the whole matter that has puzzled us so. I did not tell you, because it was not in my opinion at all necessary to the case, that Miss Covington has always maintained that the man was not Simcoe, and so positive was she that her friend, Miss Purcell, went down to Stowmarket to make inquiries. It was certainly believed by his friends there that he was Simcoe, and this to my mind was quite conclusive. But I am bound to say that it did not satisfy Miss Covington."

"May I ask, Miss Covington, why you took up that opinion in the first place?"

"Because I was convinced that he was not the sort of man who would have risked his life for another. After Miss Purcell came back from Stowmarket we found out that just before he called on my uncle he advertised for relatives of the late John Simcoe, and that the advertisement appeared not in the Suffolk papers only, but in the London and provincial papers all over the country; and it was evident, if this man was John Simcoe, he would not advertise all over England, instead of going down to Stowmarket, where his family lived, and where he himself had lived for years. He received a reply from an old lady, an aunt of John Simcoe's, living there, went down and saluted her as his aunt, at once offered to settle a pension of fifty pounds a year on her, and after remaining for three days in her house, no doubt listening to her gossip about all John Simcoe's friends, went and introduced himself to them. There was probably some resemblance in height and figure, and an absence of twenty years would have effected a change in his face, so that, when it was found that his aunt unhesitatingly accepted him, the people there had no doubt whatever that it was their old acquaintance. Therefore, this in no way shook my belief that he was not the man.

"It turns out now, you see, that there was another man at Benares at the time who was remarkably like him, and that this man was a scoundrel and a thief. When he deserted no doubt he would take another name, and having doubtless heard that John Simcoe was dead, and remembering the remarks made as to his likeness to him, he was as likely to take that name as any other, though probably not with any idea of making any special use of it. When in England he may have heard General Mathieson's name mentioned, and remembering that Simcoe had saved the life of the General, may have thought that the name and the likeness might enable him to personate the man. He first set about establishing his identity by going down to Stowmarket, and after that it was easy. I have thought it all over so many times that although it never struck me that there might have been at Benares some man bearing a striking resemblance to John Simcoe, all the rest is exactly as I had figured it out to my mind. Now I will leave you, gentlemen, to decide what use you will make of the discovery, while I go and tell my friends of it."

The seats allotted to the general public were empty, as a case of this sort offered but slight attraction even to the loungers in the hall, but a large number of barristers were present. It had been whispered about that there were likely to be some unexpected developments in the case. The counsel engaged on both sides were the leaders of the profession, who could hardly have been expected to be retained in a mere case of a formal application for an order for trustees to act upon a will.

"The facts of the case, my lord," the counsel who led for John Simcoe commenced, "are simple, and we are at a loss to understand how the trustees of the late General Mathieson can offer any opposition to our obtaining the order asked for. Nothing can be more straightforward than the facts. The late General Mathieson, early in March, 1852, made a will, which was duly signed and witnessed, bequeathing, among other legacies, the amount of ten thousand pounds to Mr. John Simcoe, as a mark of his gratitude for his having saved him from a tiger some twenty years before in India. The act was one of heroic bravery, and Mr. Simcoe nearly lost his own life in saving that of the General."

He then related with dramatic power the incidents of the struggle.

"There is, then, no matter of surprise that this large legacy should have been left to Mr. Simcoe by the General, who was a man of considerable wealth. The bulk of the property was left to his grandson, and in the event of his dying before coming of age it was to go to a niece, a Miss Covington, to whom only a small legacy was left; she being herself mistress of an estate and well provided for. Two months afterwards the General, upon reflection, decided to enlarge his gift to Mr. Simcoe, and he, therefore, in another will named him, in place of Miss Covington, who was amply provided for, his heir in the event of his grandson's death. I may say that the second will was not drawn up by the solicitors who had framed the first will. Probably, as often happens, the General preferred that the change he had effected should not be known until after his death, even to his family solicitors. He, therefore, went to a firm of equal respectability and standing, Messrs. Halstead & James, who have made an affidavit that he interviewed them personally on the matter, and gave them written instructions for drawing up his will, and signed it in their presence.

"I may say that in all other respects, including the legacy of ten thousand pounds, the wills were absolutely identical. The trustees, after waiting until the last day permitted by law, have, to our client's surprise, proved the first of these two wills, ignoring the second; on what ground I am at a loss to understand. As my client is entitled to ten thousand pounds under either will it might be thought that the change would make little difference to him; but unhappily the circumstances have entirely changed by the fact that the General's grandson was lost or stolen on the day before his death, and in spite of the most active efforts of the police, and the offer of large rewards—my client, who was deeply affected by the loss of the child, himself offering a thousand pounds for news of his whereabouts—nothing was heard of him until two months after his disappearance, when his body was found in the canal at Paddington, and after hearing evidence of identification, and examining the clothes, which all parties agreed to be those of the missing child, the jury returned a verdict that the body was that of Walter Rivington, and that there was no proof of how he came by his end.

"As the residence of General Mathieson was in Hyde Park Gardens, no doubt the poor child strolled away from the care of a careless nurse, came to the canal, and, walking near the bank, fell in and was drowned. No one could have been more grieved than my client at this, and although it practically put him into possession of a large property, he would, I am sure, gladly forfeit a large portion of it rather than come into possession of it in so melancholy a manner. I have not heard of the slightest reason why the last will of General Mathieson should be put aside. I believe that no question could arise as to his state of mind at the time that it was made. It may be that a plea of undue influence may be raised, but this, to those who knew the General, would appear absurd. He was a man of active habits, and vigorous both in mind and body. Here was no case of a man living in the house and influencing an old gentleman approaching his dotage. They met only at clubs and at dinners; and although the General was rightly and naturally attached to Simcoe, he was certainly not a man to be influenced against his will. I beg, therefore, to ask, my lord, that you will pronounce in favor of this second will, and issue an order to the trustees to carry out its provisions forthwith."

"But upon the face of your appeal to the court, Sir Henry, there is no question as to the validity of the will you propound set up by the trustees?"

"None, my lord. In fact, at the time the case was put down we were ignorant that there would be any attempt on the part of the trustees to dispute the second will, and that they should do so came upon us as a surprise. However, at a consultation between my learned friend and myself just before we came into court, it was agreed that, if your lordship would permit it, we would take the two matters at once. One of the trustees is a member of the firm who are and have been the family lawyers of General Mathieson, and of his father before him, for a long period of years. They are gentlemen of well-known honor, who are, I am sure, as anxious as we are to obtain from your lordship a judicial decision on which they can act."

"It is irregular," the judge said, "but as both parties seemed agreed upon it, it will doubtless save much expense to the estate if the whole matter can be settled at once. I will permit the whole matter to be taken. Now, brother Herbert, we will hear you on the other side."

"I am sorry to say, my lord, that it will be impossible for me to imitate my learned brother in the brevity with which he opened the case. So far from the facts being extremely simple, they are, I may say, of a very complicated nature. We own that we have no explanation to offer with regard to the second will. It was strange, very strange, that General Mathieson, a man of methodical habits, having just drawn up his will, should go to another firm of solicitors and draw up a fresh one, but the fact that the whole of the minor bequests are the same in the two wills is certainly a very strong proof, as also is the fact that the instructions for drafting the will were written by the General himself, or, at any rate, by someone intimately acquainted with the contents of that will, which we admit was difficult to believe could be the case, as the will, from the time it was signed by the General, has not been out of Messrs. Farmer & Pettigrew's hands until it was taken for probate the other day.

"Now, my lord, I trust that you will allow me a certain amount of license while I go into this somewhat singular story. Twenty-three years ago, General Mathieson's life was saved in India by Mr. John Simcoe. Mr. Simcoe himself was seriously wounded, and when he recovered somewhat he was recommended by the surgeon who attended him to go down to Calcutta at once and take a sea voyage. He did so, and embarked upon the ship *Nepaul*, which was lost in a terrible gale in the Bay of Bengal a few days later, with, as was supposed, all hands. Twenty years passed, and then to the surprise, and I may say to the delight of the General, who had much grieved over the loss of his preserver, Mr. Simcoe presented himself. For a moment the General did not recognize him; but it was not long before he became convinced of his identity, for he knew the officers who had been at the station at the time, and was well up in the gossip of the place, and the General at once hailed him as the man who had saved his life, introduced him to many friends, got him put up at a good club, and became, I may say, very fond of him. Mr. Simcoe brought up a friend or two who had known him at Stowmarket, where he had an aunt still living, and the result of all this was that the General requested Messrs. Farmer & Pettigrew to draw up a new will bequeathing to John Simcoe the sum of ten thousand pounds.

"Then came the singular episode of the second will. A fortnight later, when at dinner at his club, the General was smitten with a strange kind of fit, from which he recovered, but only lived for a few months, a half-paralyzed invalid. He was attended during that time by Dr. Leeds—a gentleman with a very high reputation, and now practicing in Harley Street as a consulting physician. The General was brought up to town, but broke down during the journey and died two days later.

"Now we come to the second strange fact in this strange case. A day before his death his grandson, Walter Rivington, was missing. The efforts of the police, aided by a number of private detectives, failed to obtain any clew to the child until a body was found in the canal at Paddington. That the body was dressed in some of the clothes worn by the child when carried off was unquestionable; but the three persons who knew Walter Rivington best, namely, Miss Covington, a friend of hers named Miss Purcell, who had been all the summer assisting her to nurse General Mathieson, and the child's own nurse, all declared that the body was not that of the General's grandson. They were unable to adduce anything in support of this belief beyond the fact that the hair of the child found was short and to some extent bristly, whereas that of Walter Rivington was long and silky. The jury, however, adopted the view of the coroner that hair, however soft, when cut close to the skull will appear more or less bristly, and gave a verdict to the effect that the body was that of Walter Rivington. Miss Covington and her friends refused to accept the verdict, and continued their search for the child.

"Without occupying your attention by going into details, my lord, I may briefly say that a close watch was set on Mr. Simcoe, and it was found that he was exceedingly intimate with a man of whom no one seemed to know anything; and before I go further I will ask, my lord, that you will give orders that Mr. Simcoe shall not leave the court until I have finished."

"You are not asking without strong reason, I trust, brother Herbert?"

"Certainly not, my lord."

The order was, therefore, given. Simcoe grew very white in the face, but otherwise maintained an air of stolid indifference.

"I will now go back for a moment, my lord. General Mathieson was attended by three of the leading physicians in London at the time of his seizure. The symptoms were so peculiar that in all their experience they had not met a similar case. Dr. Leeds, however, differed from them, but being their junior could not press his opinion; but he told them that his opinion was that the fit was due to the administration of some drug unknown to the British Pharmacopœia, as the effects were precisely similar to those in cases that he had read of in Africa and among other savage people, where a poison of this kind was used by the native fetich men or wizards. That opinion was confirmed rather than diminished by the subsequent progress of the malady and the final death of his patient. The one man who could benefit by the General's death was sitting next to him at dinner at the time of his seizure, and that man, according to his own statement, had been for many years knocking about among the savages of the South Sea Islands and the islands of the Malay Archipelago.

"I do not accuse John Simcoe of this crime, but I need hardly say that the mere possibility of such a thing heightened the strong feeling entertained by Miss Covington that Simcoe was the author of the abduction of Walter Rivington. She and her devoted friend, Miss Purcell, pursued their investigations with unflagging energy. They suspected that the man who was very intimate with Simcoe had acted as his agent in the matter, and a casual remark which was overheard in a singular manner, which will be explained when the case goes into another court, that this man was going to Tilbury, gave them a clew. Then, in a manner which many persons might find it very hard to believe, Miss Covington learned from a conversation between the two men, when together in a box at Her Majesty's Theater, that the lad was in charge of a bargeman living near the little village of Pitsea, in Essex. From that place, my lord, he was brought last week, and Miss Covington will produce him in court, if your lordship wishes to see him. Thus, then, it is immaterial to us whether your lordship pronounces for the first or second will.

"But, my lord, I have not finished my story. Under neither of the wills does that man take a farthing. The money was left to John Simcoe; and John Simcoe was drowned over twenty years ago. The man standing over there is one William Sanderson, a sergeant on the paymaster's staff at Benares when the real John Simcoe was there. There happened to be a resemblance between this man and him, so strong that it was generally remarked upon by his comrades. This man Sanderson deserted soon after Simcoe was drowned, taking with him three hundred pounds of the paymaster's money. There was a sharp hue and cry after him, but he managed to make his escape. All this is a certainty, but we may assume without much difficulty that the man changed his name as soon as he got to Calcutta, and nothing was more likely than that he should take the name of John Simcoe, whom he had been told that he so strongly resembled.

"For twenty years we hear nothing further of William Sanderson, nor do we hear when he returned to London. Probably he, in some way or other, came across the name of General Mathieson, and remembering what John Simcoe had done for the General, he, on the strength of his personal likeness, and the fact that he had, for twenty years, gone by that name, determined to introduce himself to him, with the result you know. He was clever enough to know that he must answer questions as to his history before he left England, and it was desirable to obtain witnesses who would, if necessary, certify to him. But he knew nothing of Simcoe's birthplace or history; so he inserted advertisements in a great number of London and provincial newspapers, saying that the relations of the John Simcoe who was supposed to have been drowned in the Bay of Bengal in the year 1832 would hear of something to their advantage at the address given. A maiden aunt, living at Stowmarket, did reply. He went down there at once, rushed into her arms and called her aunt, and told her that it was his intention to make her comfortable for life by allowing her fifty pounds per annum. He stayed with her for three days, and during that time obtained from her gossip full details of his boyhood and youth, his friends and their occupation, and he then went out and called upon John Simcoe's old companions, all of whom took him on his own word and his knowledge of the past and his recognition by his aunt.

"So things might have remained. This man, after undergoing what punishment might be awarded to him for his abduction of Walter Rivington, could have claimed the ten thousand pounds left him by General Mathieson, had it not been that, by what I cannot but consider a dispensation of Providence, an old comrade of his, Staff-Sergeant Nichol, was attracted to the hall this morning by seeing the name of Simcoe and that of General Mathieson coupled in the cause list. This man was in the hall talking to his professional advisers, and Nichol, walking close to him, to see if he could recognize the man whom he had last seen carried wounded into Benares, at once recognized in the supposed John Simcoe the deserter and thief, Sergeant Sanderson. He passed him two or three times, to assure himself that he was not mistaken. Happily the deserter had a mark that was ineffaceable; he had, as a recruit, let off his rifle, and the ball had passed through the fleshy part of the forearm, leaving there, as Sergeant Nichol has informed me, an ineffaceable scar, blackened by powder. If this man is not Sergeant Sanderson, and is the long-lost John Simcoe, he has but to pull up the sleeve of his left arm and show that it is without scar."

The man did not move; he was half stunned by the sudden and terrible exposure of the whole of his plans. As he did not rise the counsel said:

"My lord, I must ask that you give an order for the arrest of this man, William Sanderson, as a deserter and a thief; also upon the charge of conspiring, with others, the abduction of Walter Rivington."

"Certainly, brother Herbert," the judge said, as he saw that the accused made no motion to answer the challenge of the counsel. "Tipstaff, take that man into custody on the charge of aiding in the abduction of Walter Rivington. As to the other charge, I shall communicate with the authorities of the India Office, and leave it to them to prosecute if they choose to do so. After this lapse of years they may not think it worth while to do so, especially as the man is in custody on a still graver charge."

The tipstaff moved toward the man, who roused himself with a great effort, snatched a small glass ball from a pocket inside his waistcoat, thrust it between his teeth, and bit it into fragments, and, as the officer laid his hand upon him, fell down in a fit. Dr. Leeds, who had come in just as the trial began, rose to his feet.

"I am a doctor, my lord. My name is Leeds, and the opinion I held of the cause of General Mathieson's death is now proved to be correct. The symptoms of this fit are precisely similar to those of General Mathieson's seizure, and this man has taken some of the very poison with which he murdered the General."

For a minute Sanderson struggled in violent convulsions, then, as Dr. Leeds bent over him, his head fell back suddenly. Dr. Leeds felt his pulse and then rose to his feet.

"My lord," he said, "the case is finally closed. He has gone to a higher judgment seat."

CHAPTER XXVI.

A LETTER FROM ABROAD.

Three days later, when Hilda returned from a drive, she found that Dr. Leeds was in the drawing room with Miss Purcell and Netta, whose face at once told what had happened.

"I have asked the question at last, Miss Covington," Dr. Leeds said, coming forward to shake hands, "and Netta has consented to be my wife."

"I am heartily glad. That you would ask her I knew from what you told me; and although I knew nothing of her thoughts in the matter, I felt sure that she would hardly say no. Netta, darling, I am glad. Long ago I thought and hoped that this would come about. It seemed to me that it would be such a happy thing."

"Auntie said just the same thing," Netta said, smiling through her tears, as Hilda embraced her. "As you both knew, you ought to have given me some little hint; then I should not have been taken quite by surprise. I might have pretended that I did not quite know my own mind, and ask for time to think it over, instead of surrendering at once."

"But you did make a condition, Netta," Dr. Leeds laughed.

"Not a condition—a request, if you like, but certainly not a condition."

"Netta said that her heart was greatly set on the work she had always looked forward to, and she hoped that I should let her do something in that way still. Of course I have heard you both talk over that institute a score of times, and I was as much impressed as yourselves with the enormous boon that it would be. I should be sorry indeed that the plan should be given up. I need hardly say that in the half hour we have had together we did not go deeply into it, but we will have a general council about it, as soon as we can get down to plain matter of fact. Netta can talk it over with you, and I can talk it over with her; and then we can hold a meeting, with Miss Purcell as president of the committee."

But matters were not finally settled until the ladies were established at Holmwood with Walter, and Dr. Leeds came down for a short holiday of two or three days. Then the arrangements were made to the satisfaction of all parties. A large house, standing in grounds of considerable extent, was to be taken in the suburbs of London, Netta was to be lady superintendent, her aunt assisting in the domestic arrangements. Miss Purcell insisted that her savings should be used for furnishing the house. Hilda was to put in as a loan, for the others would receive it in no other way, five thousand pounds for working capital. She determined to take a house near the institute, so that she could run in and out and assist Netta in teaching. Dr. Leeds was to drive up every morning to Harley Street, where his work was over by two o'clock, except when he had to attend consultations. No arrangements would be necessary about the house, as this was the residence of his partner, and he only had his own set of rooms there. He was steadily making his way, and to his surprise already found that the report in the papers of his successful diagnosis of the cause of General Mathieson's death had resulted in a considerable addition to his practice, as a number of people consulted him on obscure, and in many cases fanciful, maladies, in which they had come to entertain the idea that they were suffering from the effects of poison.

Now that she was going to assist at the institution and had no intention of entering society again in London, Hilda had no longer any objection to the power she had acquired being known, and, when questioned on the subject of the trial, made no secret of the manner in which she had made the discovery at the opera, and mentioned that she was going to assist in an institution that was about to be established for teaching the system by which she had benefited to deaf children.

The matter excited considerable interest in medical circles, and by the time that the institution was ready the number of applicants was greater than could be entertained. By this time Dr. Leeds and Netta were married. The engagement was a short one, and the wedding took place within two months of their going down into the country with Hilda. Being anxious that as many as possible should participate in the benefits of the system, the doors of the institute were at once opened to outdoor pupils, who were boarded in the neighborhood. Six of Netta's pupils in Hanover were brought over as teachers, and a few weeks from its being opened the institution was in full swing. As Dr. Leeds wished that no profit whatever be made by the undertaking, in which desire he was cordially joined by his wife and Hilda, the charges were extremely low, except in the case of children of wealthy parents, the surplus in their case being devoted to taking in, free of payment, children of the poor.

Before Netta's marriage the interest in the Mathieson case was revived by the appearance of a letter in the principal London papers. All search for the man who had assisted Sanderson in the abduction of the child had been fruitless. He had probably taken steps to receive information of how matters were going on in court, and long before an officer arrived at Rose Cottage with a warrant for his arrest he had left, and the police had failed to find any trace of his subsequent movements. The letter bore the simple heading, "United States," and ran as follows:

"To the Editor.

"Sir: I scarcely know why I write this letter, but I suppose even an habitual criminal does not care to remain under an unjust suspicion. I acknowledge that I come under that category, and that my life has been spent in crime, although never once has suspicion attached to me, until I became mixed up in the Simcoe-Mathieson affair. I wish to state solemnly that I was absolutely ignorant that the name John Simcoe was an assumed one. That was the name he gave me when I first knew him, and I believed that he was, as he represented, the man who had saved General Mathieson's life from a tiger. That he had subsequently lived a rough life in the South Seas I was aware, for he came to me with a message sent by a brother of mine when at the point of death. The man had been a chum of his out there and had gallantly carried him off when he had received the wound from which he subsequently died, in a fight with a large body of natives. I have absolute assurance that this was true, for my brother would never have sent anyone to me except under altogether extraordinary circumstances. The man called on me when he first returned to England, but I saw little of him for the first two years, and then he came to me and said that he had looked up General Mathieson, and that the General had taken to him, and put him down in his will for ten thousand pounds. He said that General Mathieson was worth a hundred thousand, and that he had planned to get the whole. Not being in any way squeamish, I agreed at once to help him in any way in my power.

"His plan briefly was that he should obtain a fresh will, appointing him sole heir to the General's estate in the event of a boy of six or seven years old dying before he came of age. He had somehow obtained a copy of the General's will, and had notes in the General's handwriting. There were two things to be done, first that he should get instructions for the draft of the will drawn up in precise imitation of the General's handwriting, containing all the provisions of the former will, except that he was made heir in place of Miss Covington in the event of his grandson's death. There are a dozen men in London who can imitate handwriting so as to defy detection, and I introduced him to one of them, who drew up the instructions. Then I introduced him to a man who is the cleverest I know—and I know most of them—at getting up disguises.

"He had already ascertained that the General had on one occasion been for a minute or two in the offices of Messrs. Halstead & James. They would, therefore, have a vague, and only a vague, remembrance of him. He had obtained a photograph of the General, who was about his own height and figure, and although there was no facial resemblance, the man, by the aid of this photograph, converted him into a likeness of the General that would pass with anyone who had seen him but once casually. So disguised, he went to the offices of these solicitors, told a plausible story, and gave them the written instructions. In the meantime he had been practicing the General's signature, and being a good penman had got to imitate it so accurately that I doubt if any expert would have suspected the forgery. The lawyers were completely deceived, and he had only to go there again three days later, in the same disguise, and sign the will.

"So much for that. Then came the General's seizure. I most solemnly declare that I had no shadow of suspicion that it was not a natural fit, and that if I had had such a suspicion I should have chucked the whole thing over at once, for though, as I have said, an habitual criminal, that is to say, one who plans and directs what may be called sensational robberies, I have always insisted that the men who have worked under me should go unprovided with arms of any kind, and in no case in which I have been concerned has a drop of blood been shed. As to the carrying off of the boy, it was entirely managed by me. I had agents, men on whom I could rely, as a word of mine would have sent them to penal servitude for life. We knew that suspicion would fall upon Simcoe, and that it was important that he should be able to account for every hour of his time. Therefore, on the day the child was carried away he went down to Stowmarket, while I managed the affair and took the child down to the place where he was hidden in the Essex marshes. It was I also who made the arrangements by which the body of the child about the same age, who had died in the workhouse, was placed in the canal in some of the clothes the missing heir had worn when taken away. I owe it to myself to say that in all this there was no question of payment between this man and myself. I am well off, and I acted simply to oblige a man who had stood by the side of my brother to death. Whether his name was Simcoe or Sanderson mattered nothing to me; I should have aided him just the same. But I did believe that it was Simcoe, and that, having risked his life to save that of General Mathieson, he had as good a right as another to his inheritance. He never hinted to me that it would be a good thing if the child was got rid of altogether. He knew well enough that if he had done so I would not only have had nothing to do with it, but that I would have taken steps to have put a stop to his game altogether. Now I have only to add that, having fairly stated the part that I bore in this affair, I have nothing more to say, except that I have now retired from business altogether, and that this is the last that the world will hear of William Sanderson's accomplice."

For four or five years Hilda Covington devoted much of her time to assisting Netta Leeds in her work, but at the end of that time she married. Her husband was a widower, whose wife had died in her first confinement. His name was Desmond. He sold out of the army, and Hilda never had reason to regret that she had played the part of a gypsy woman at Lady Moulton's fête.

Walter grew up strong and healthy, and is one of the most popular men of his county. His early love for the water developed, and he served his time as a midshipman in one of Her Majesty's ships, and passed as a lieutenant. He then retired from the service and bought a fine yacht, which he himself commanded. His friends were never able to understand why he allowed his nominal skipper, William Nibson, to take his wife on board, and gave up two cabins for their accommodation. The barge *Walter* passed into the hands of Joshua, who, for many years, sailed her most successfully. He is now an elderly man, and his four sons are skippers of as many fine barges, all his own property.

THE END.

Lightning Source UK Ltd.
Milton Keynes UK
UKHW010630240622
404913UK00001B/279